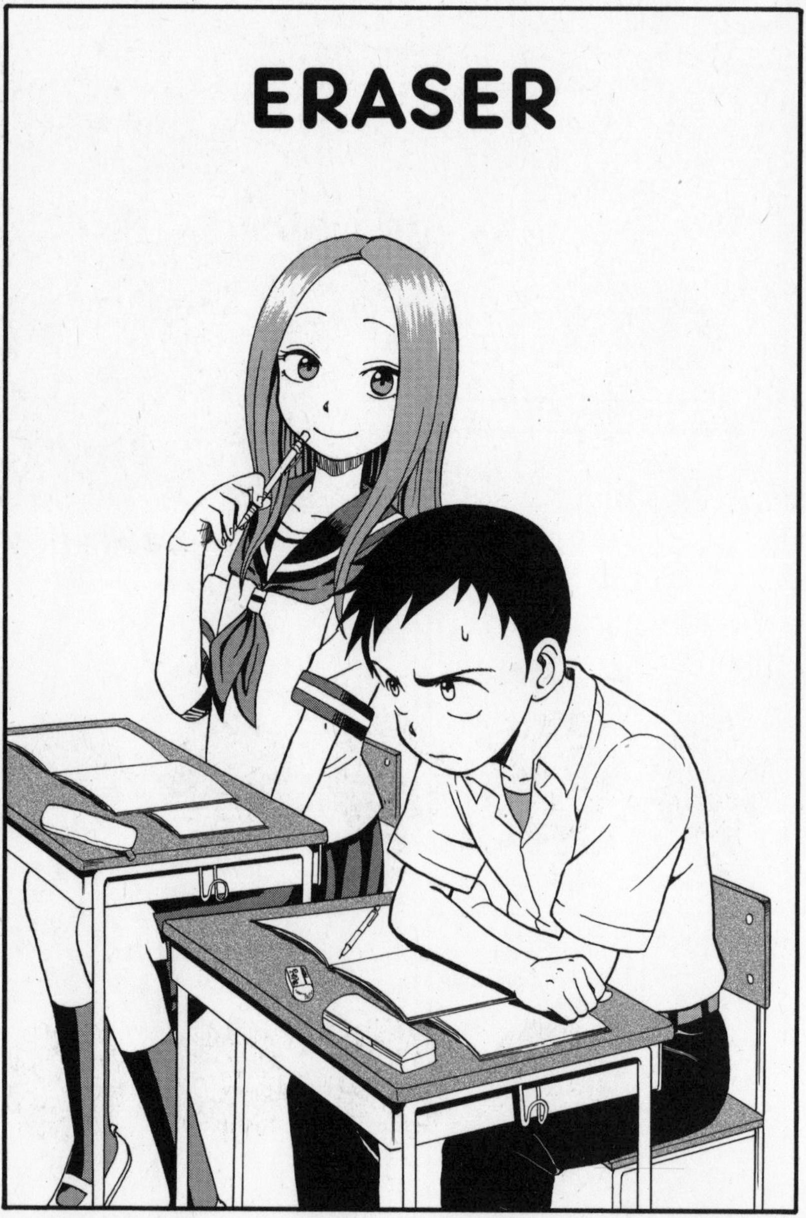
ERASER

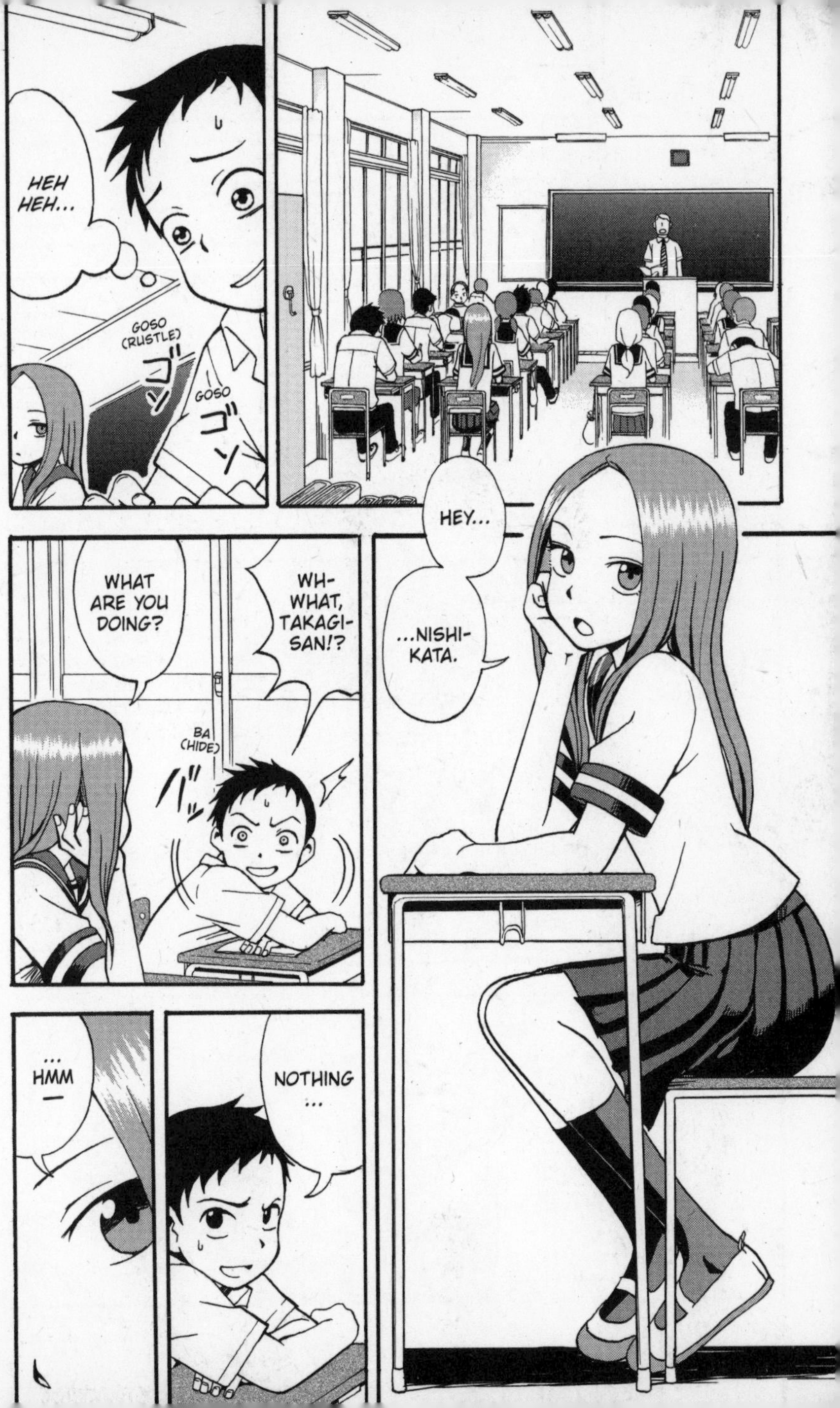
HEH HEH...
GOSO (RUSTLE)
GOSO
HEY...
...NISHI-KATA.
WH-WHAT, TAKAGI-SAN!?
WHAT ARE YOU DOING?
BA (HIDE)
NOTHING...
... HMM —

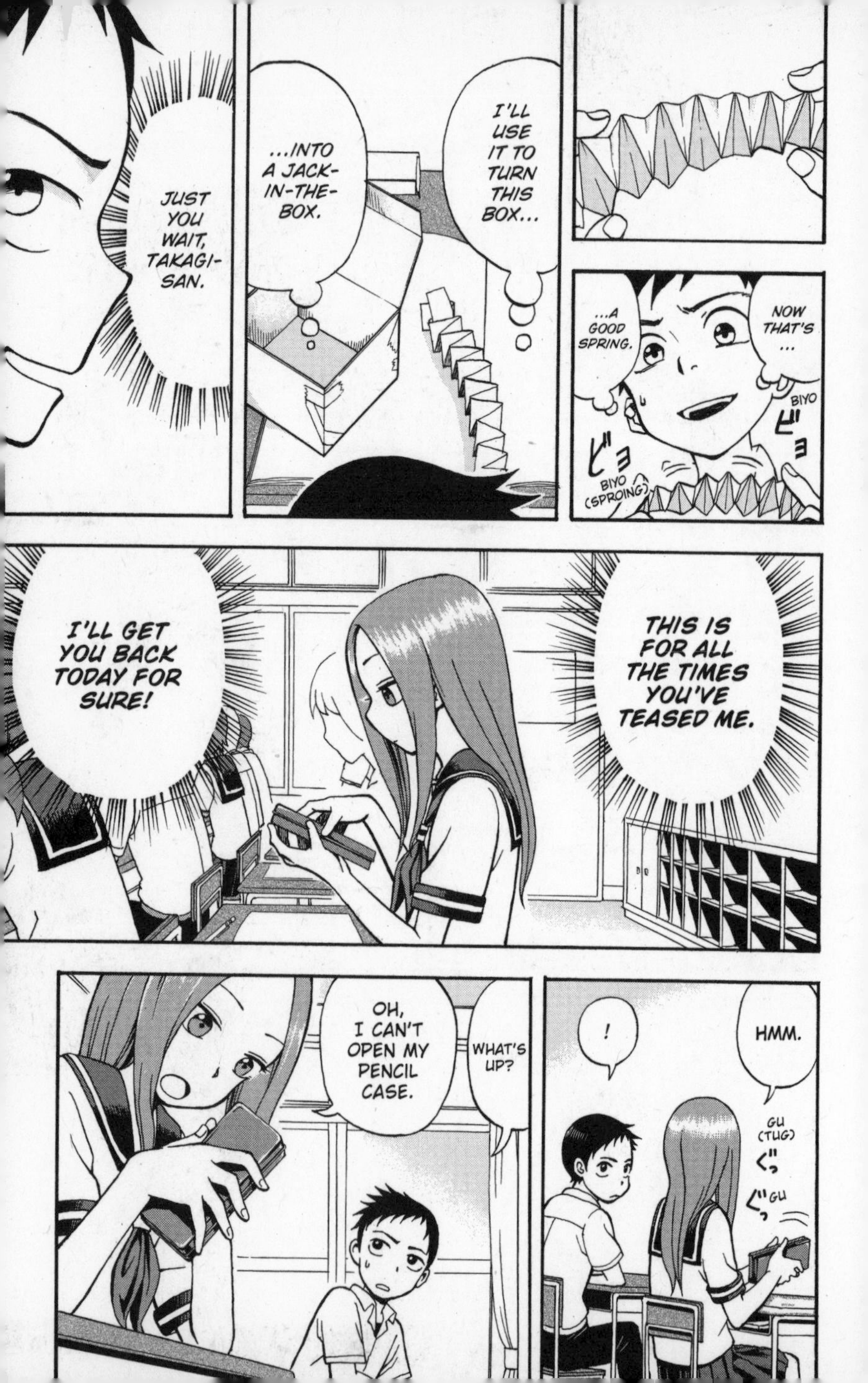
NOW THAT'S ...
...A GOOD SPRING.
BIYO ビヨ
ビヨ BIYO (SPROING)
I'LL USE IT TO TURN THIS BOX...
...INTO A JACK-IN-THE-BOX.
JUST YOU WAIT, TAKAGI-SAN.
THIS IS FOR ALL THE TIMES YOU'VE TEASED ME.
I'LL GET YOU BACK TODAY FOR SURE!
HMM.
!
GU (TUG) ぐっ
ぐっ GU
WHAT'S UP?
OH, I CAN'T OPEN MY PENCIL CASE.

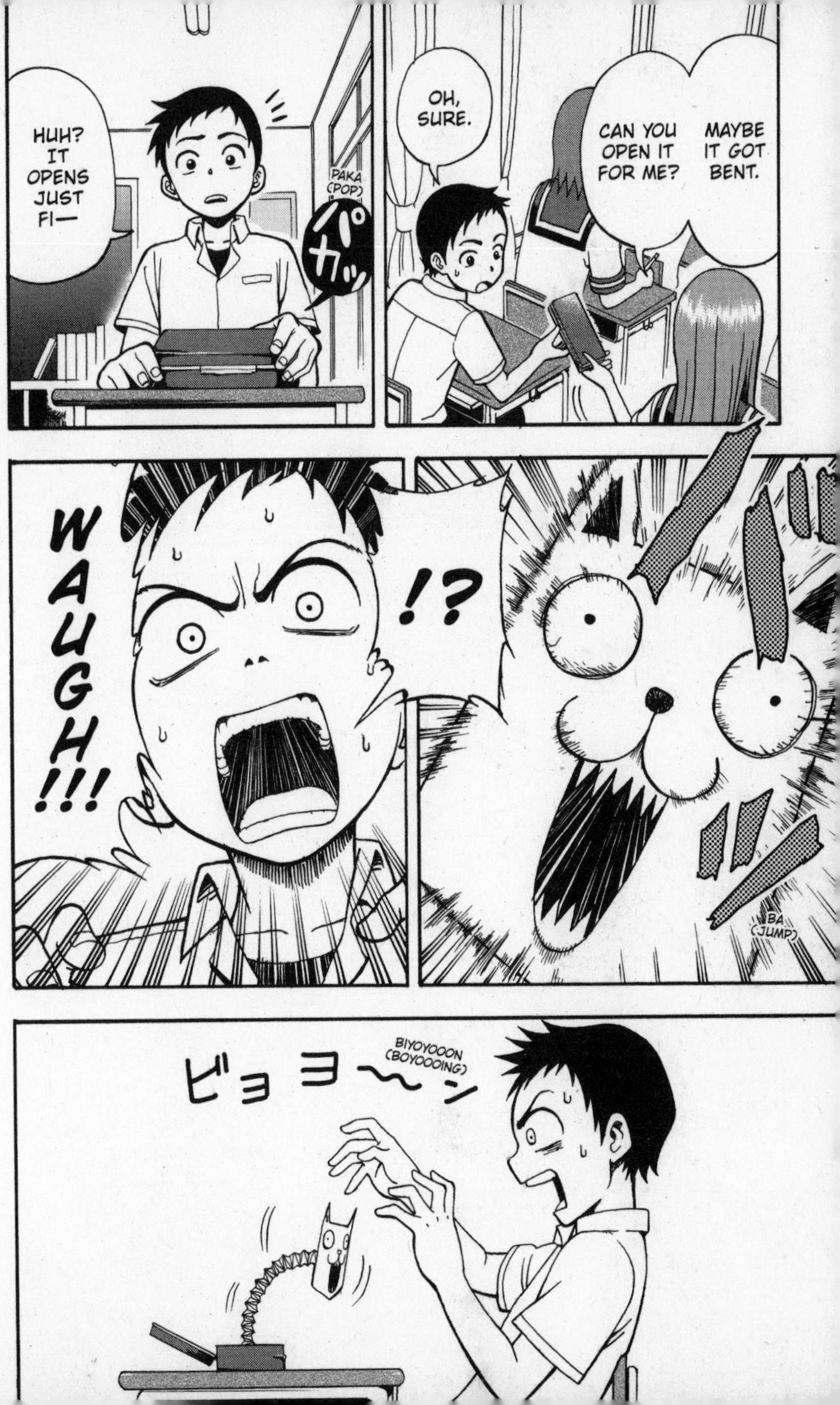
MAYBE IT GOT BENT.
CAN YOU OPEN IT FOR ME?
OH, SURE.
パカッ
PAKA (POP)
HUH? IT OPENS JUST FI—
BA (JUMP)
!?
WAUGH!!!
ビョヨ〜〜ン
BIYOYOOON (BOYOOOING)

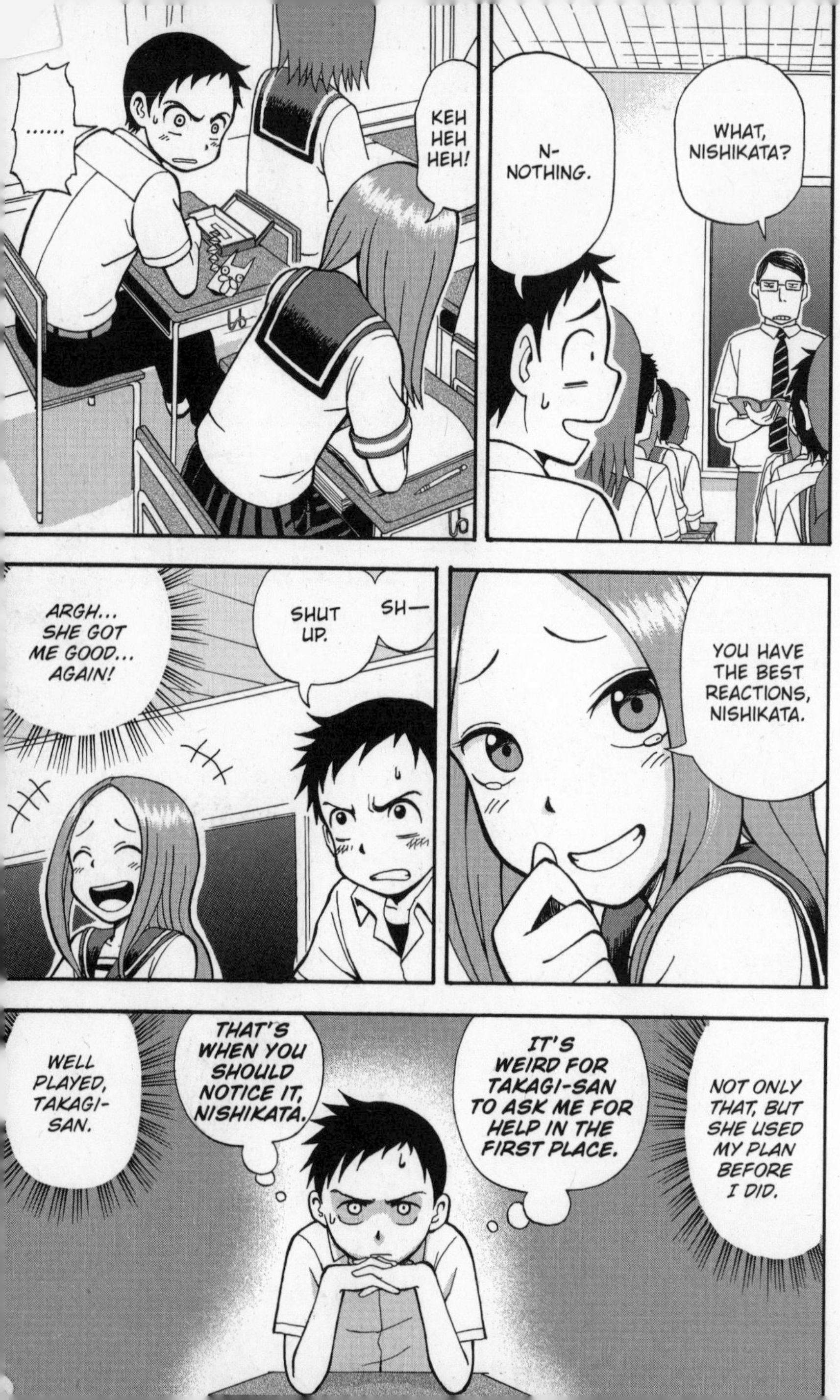
WHAT, NISHIKATA?
N- NOTHING.
KEH HEH HEH!
......
YOU HAVE THE BEST REACTIONS, NISHIKATA.
SH—
SHUT UP.
ARGH... SHE GOT ME GOOD... AGAIN!
NOT ONLY THAT, BUT SHE USED MY PLAN BEFORE I DID.
IT'S WEIRD FOR TAKAGI-SAN TO ASK ME FOR HELP IN THE FIRST PLACE.
THAT'S WHEN YOU SHOULD NOTICE IT, NISHIKATA.
WELL PLAYED, TAKAGI-SAN.

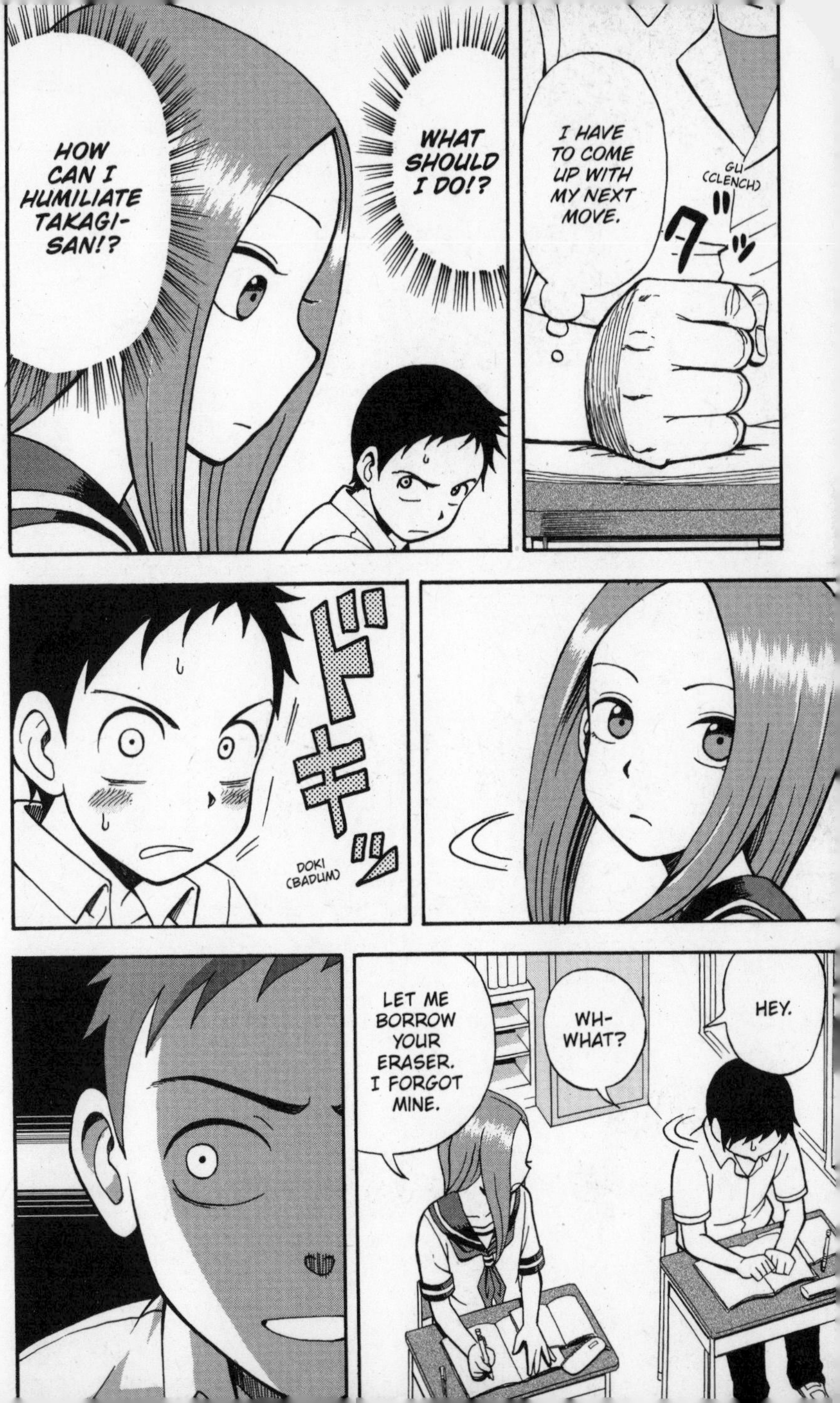
I HAVE TO COME UP WITH MY NEXT MOVE.
GU (CLENCH)
WHAT SHOULD I DO!?
HOW CAN I HUMILIATE TAKAGI-SAN!?
DOKI (BADUM)
HEY.
WH- WHAT?
LET ME BORROW YOUR ERASER. I FORGOT MINE.

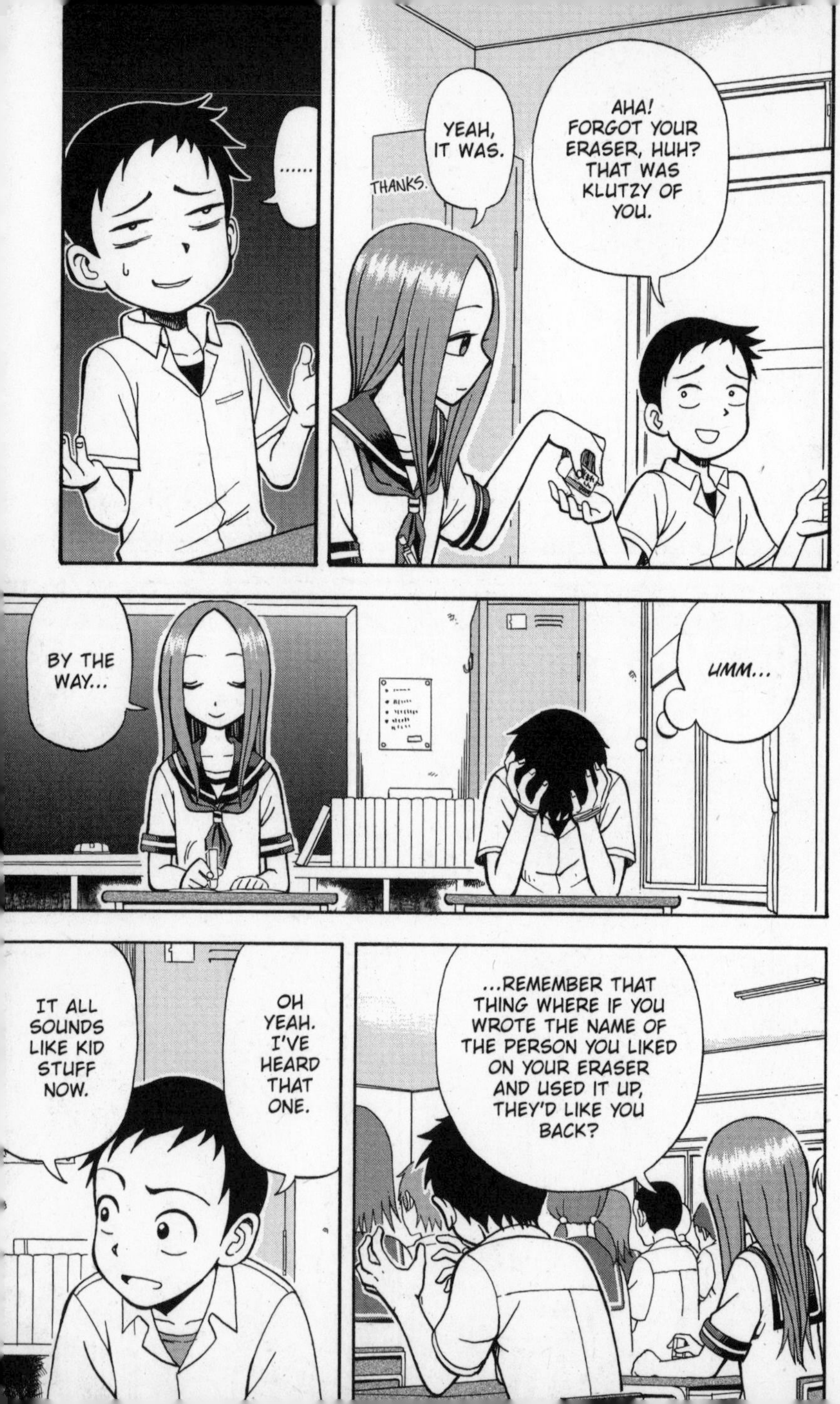
AHA! FORGOT YOUR ERASER, HUH? THAT WAS KLUTZY OF YOU.
YEAH, IT WAS.
THANKS.
......
UMM...
BY THE WAY...
...REMEMBER THAT THING WHERE IF YOU WROTE THE NAME OF THE PERSON YOU LIKED ON YOUR ERASER AND USED IT UP, THEY'D LIKE YOU BACK?
OH YEAH. I'VE HEARD THAT ONE.
IT ALL SOUNDS LIKE KID STUFF NOW.

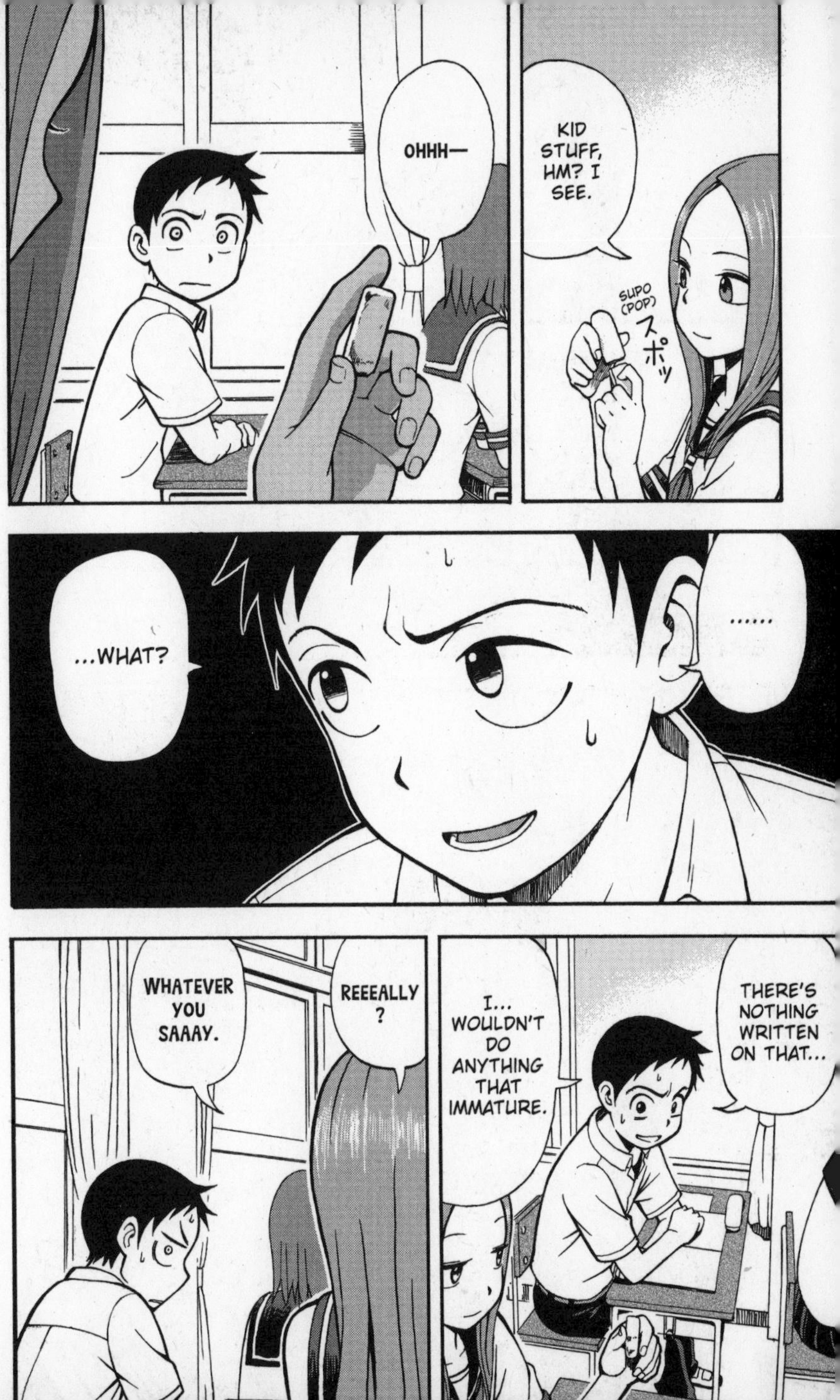
KID STUFF, HM? I SEE.
SUPO (POP)
スポッ
OHHH—
......
...WHAT?
THERE'S NOTHING WRITTEN ON THAT...
I... WOULDN'T DO ANYTHING THAT IMMATURE.
REEEALLY?
WHATEVER YOU SAAAY.

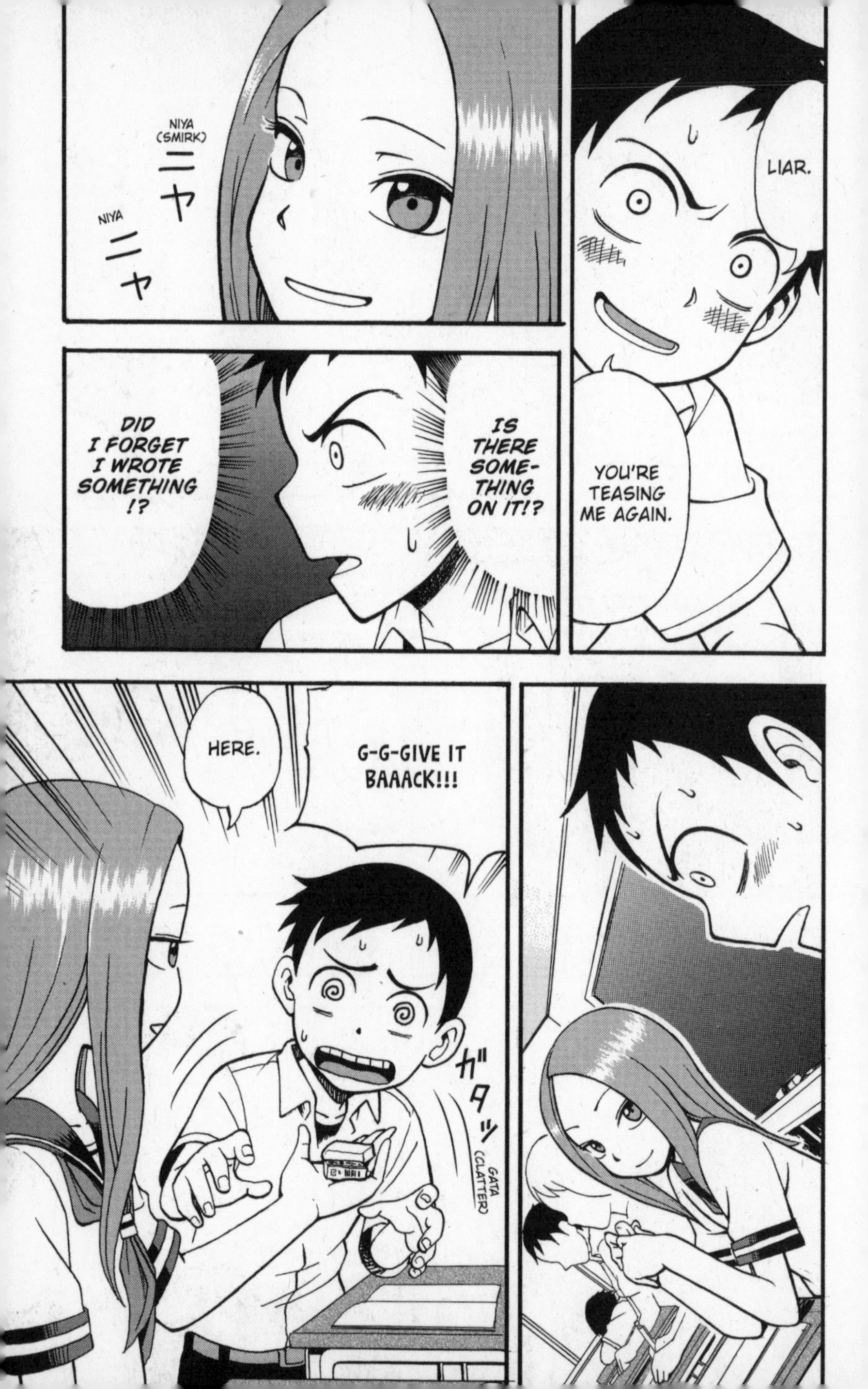
LIAR.
YOU'RE TEASING ME AGAIN.
NIYA (SMIRK) ニヤ
NIYA ニヤ
IS THERE SOMETHING ON IT!?
DID I FORGET I WROTE SOMETHING!?
G-G-GIVE IT BAAACK!!!
HERE.
ガタッ GATA (CLATTER)

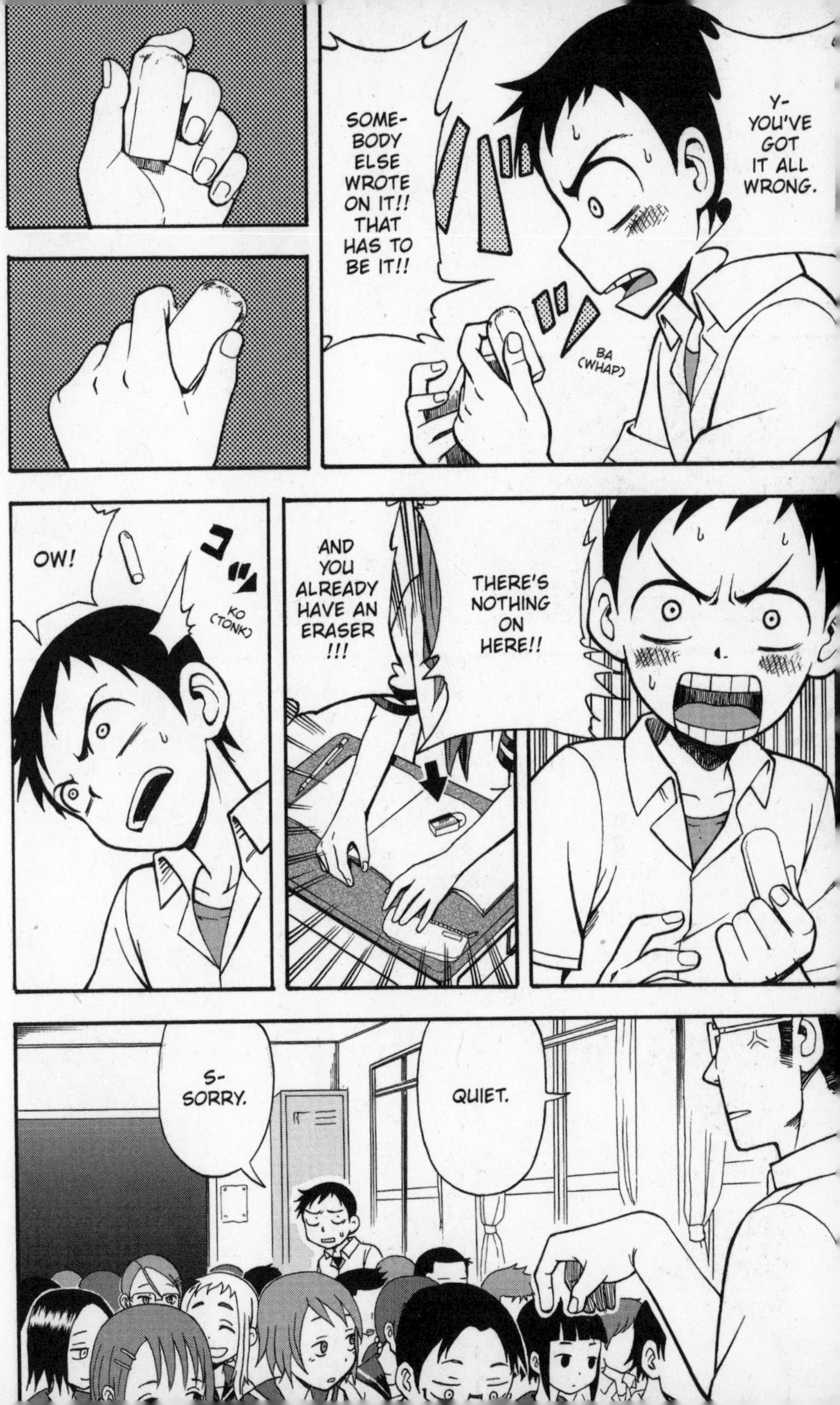
Y- YOU'VE GOT IT ALL WRONG.
SOME-BODY ELSE WROTE ON IT!! THAT HAS TO BE IT!!
BA (WHAP)
THERE'S NOTHING ON HERE!!
AND YOU ALREADY HAVE AN ERASER!!!
KO (TONK)
OW!
QUIET.
S- SORRY.

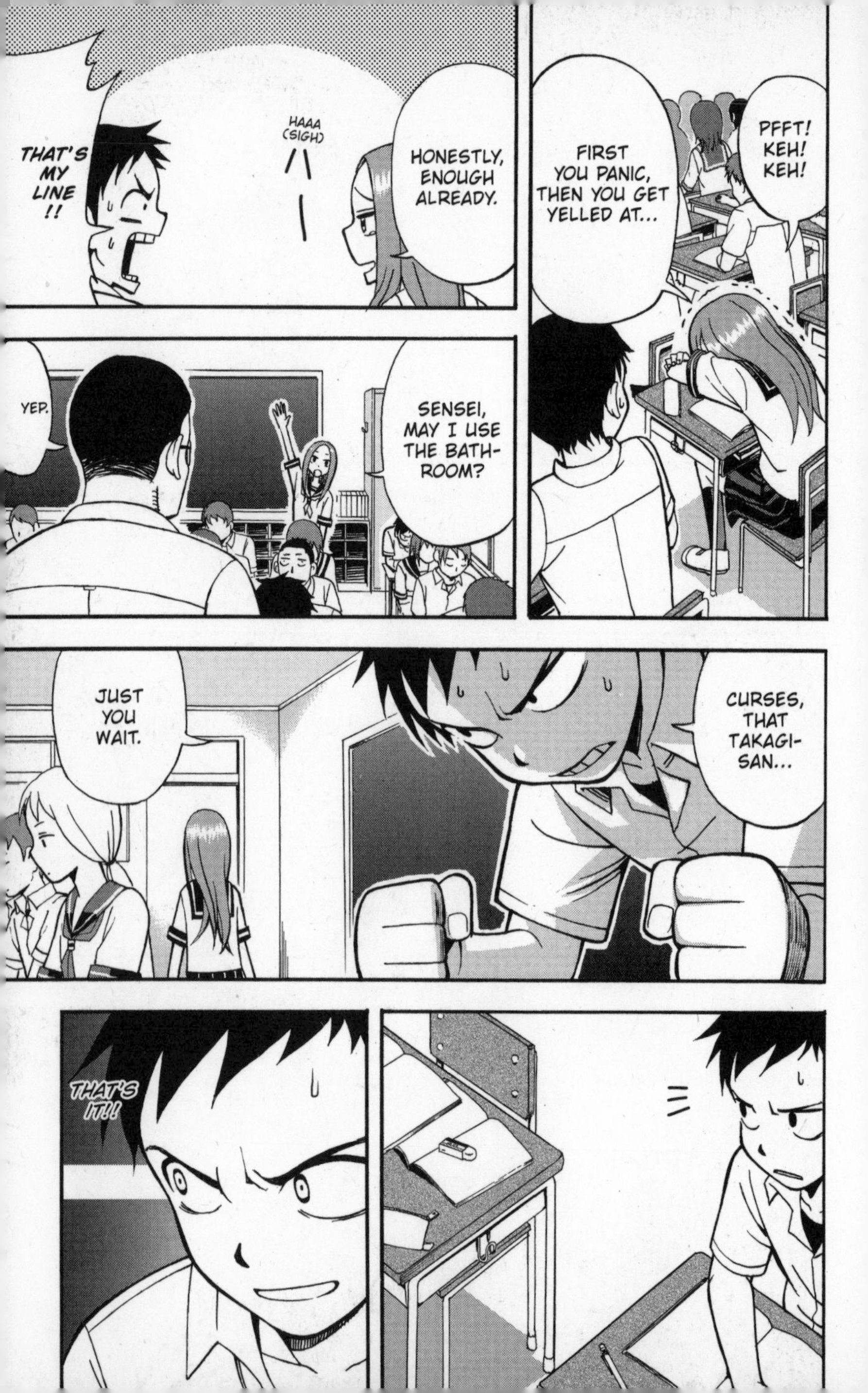
PFFT! KEH! KEH!
FIRST YOU PANIC, THEN YOU GET YELLED AT...
HONESTLY, ENOUGH ALREADY.
HAAA (SIGH)
THAT'S MY LINE !!
SENSEI, MAY I USE THE BATH-ROOM?
YEP.
CURSES, THAT TAKAGI-SAN...
JUST YOU WAIT.
THAT'S IT!!

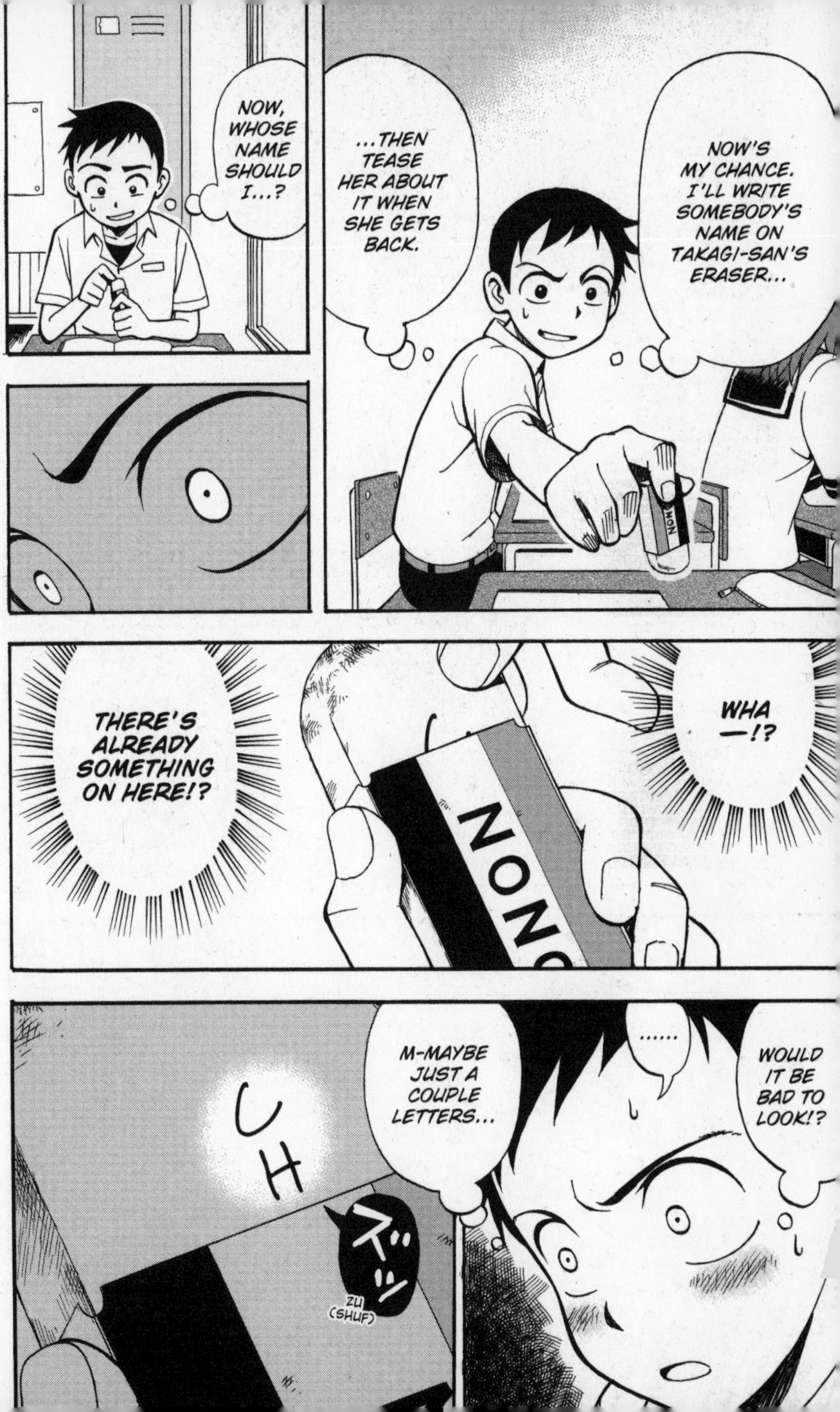
NOW'S MY CHANCE. I'LL WRITE SOMEBODY'S NAME ON TAKAGI-SAN'S ERASER...
...THEN TEASE HER ABOUT IT WHEN SHE GETS BACK.
NOW, WHOSE NAME SHOULD I...?
WHA—!?
THERE'S ALREADY SOMETHING ON HERE!?
WOULD IT BE BAD TO LOOK!?
......
M-MAYBE JUST A COUPLE LETTERS...
ズッ
ZU (SHUF)

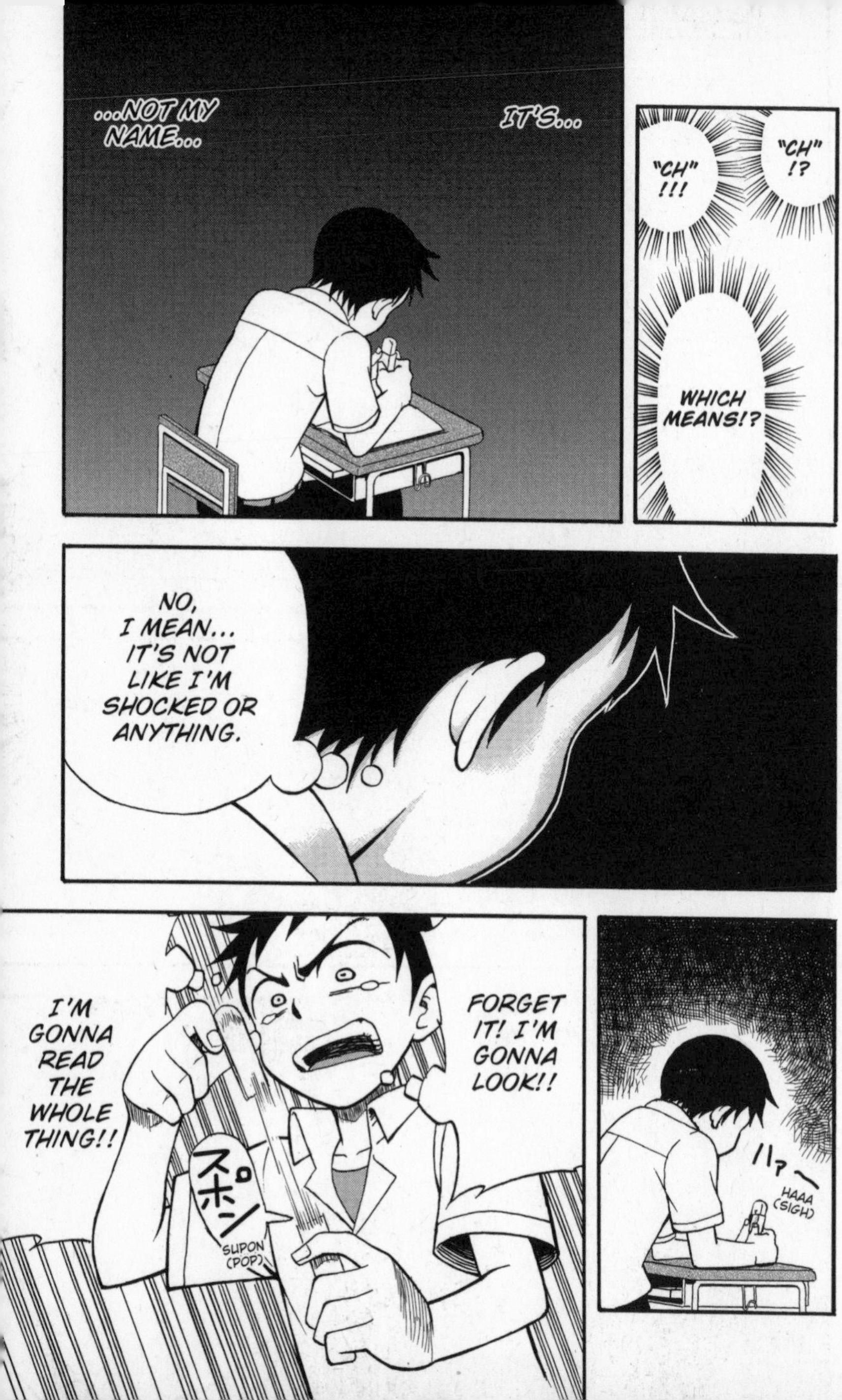
"CH" !?
"CH" !!!
WHICH MEANS!?
IT'S...
...NOT MY NAME...
NO, I MEAN... IT'S NOT LIKE I'M SHOCKED OR ANYTHING.
ハァ～
HAAA (SIGH)
FORGET IT! I'M GONNA LOOK!!
I'M GONNA READ THE WHOLE THING!!
スポン
SUPON (POP)

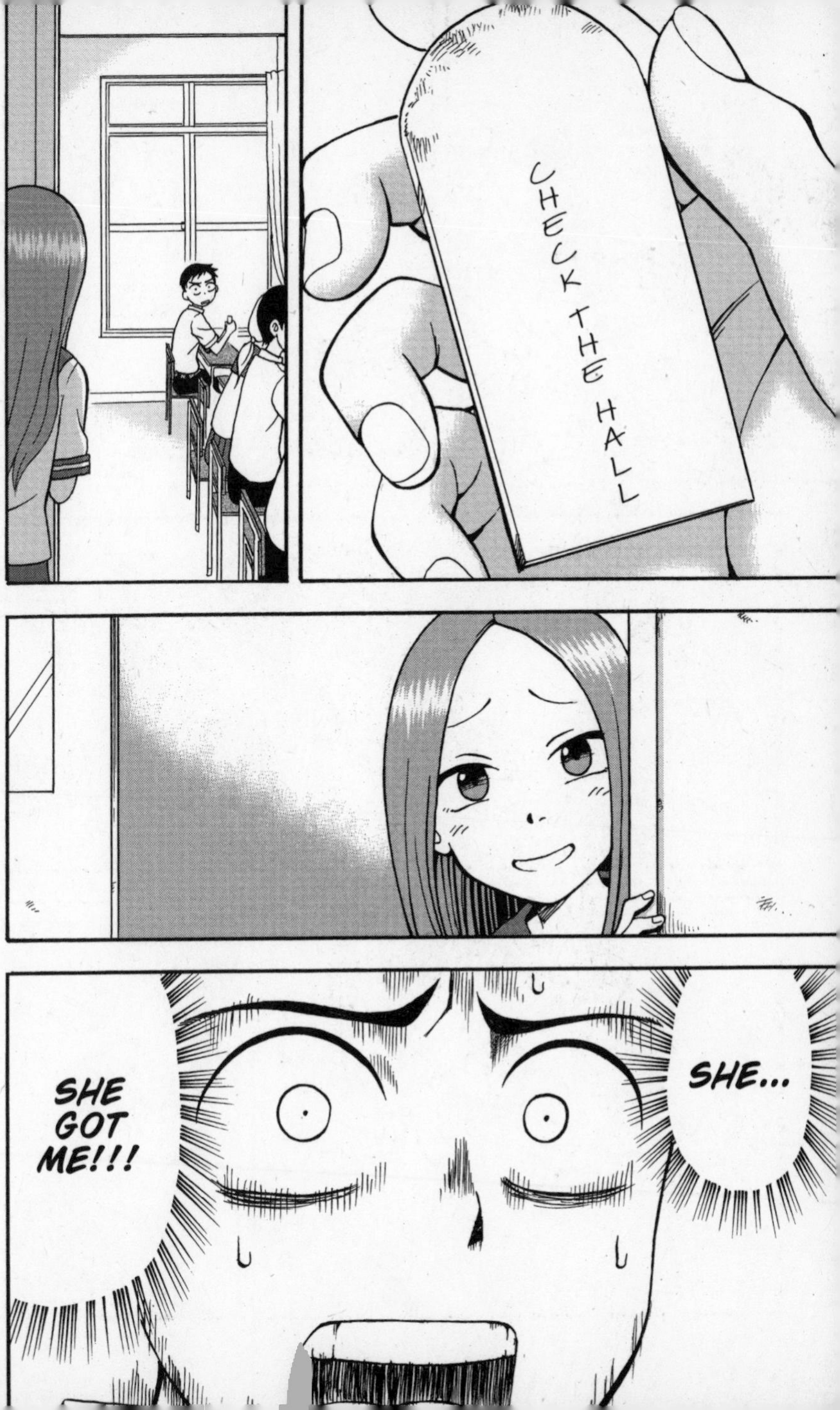
CHECK THE HALL
SHE...
SHE GOT ME!!!

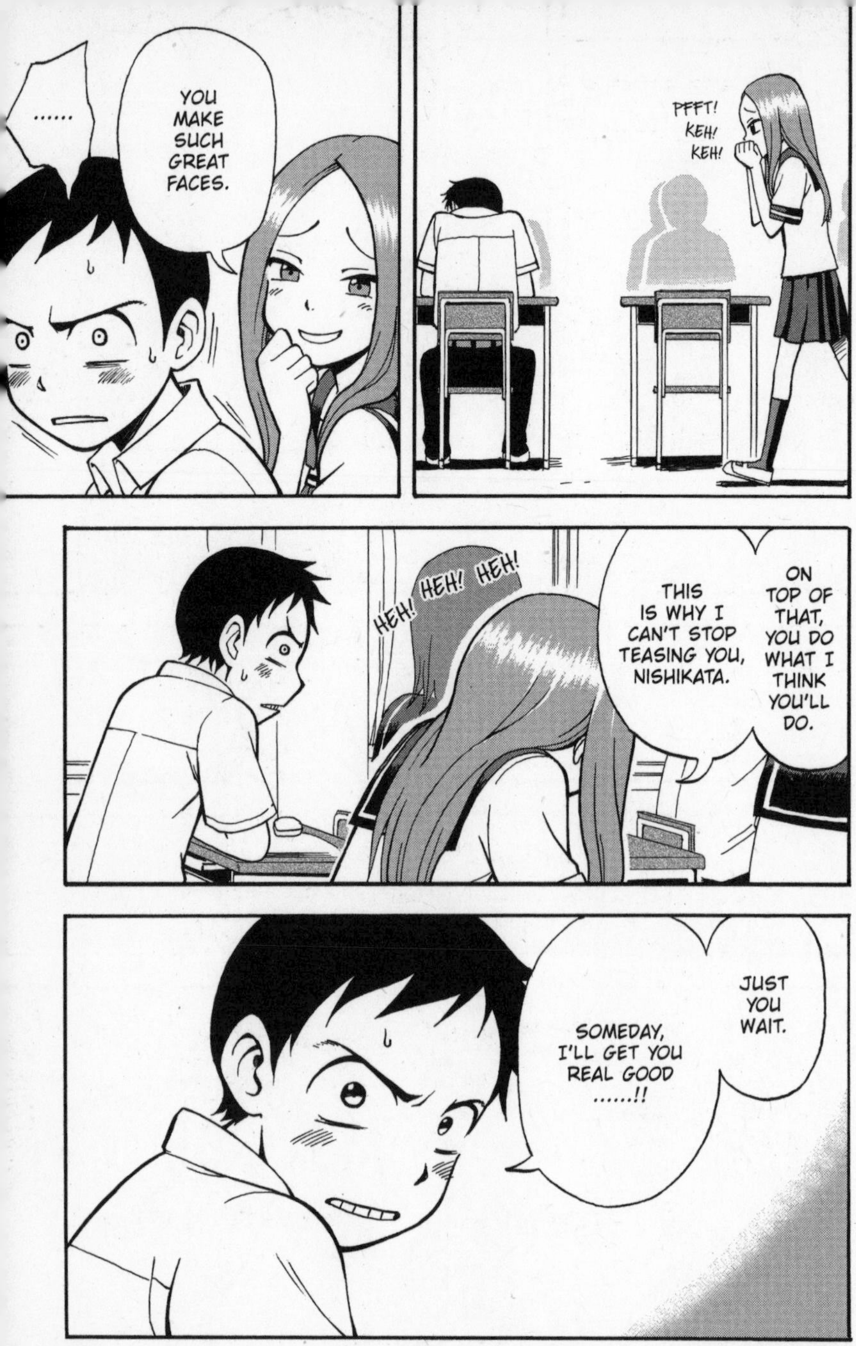
PFFT! KEH! KEH!
YOU MAKE SUCH GREAT FACES.
......
ON TOP OF THAT, YOU DO WHAT I THINK YOU'LL DO.
THIS IS WHY I CAN'T STOP TEASING YOU, NISHIKATA.
HEH! HEH! HEH!
JUST YOU WAIT.
SOMEDAY, I'LL GET YOU REAL GOOD ......!!

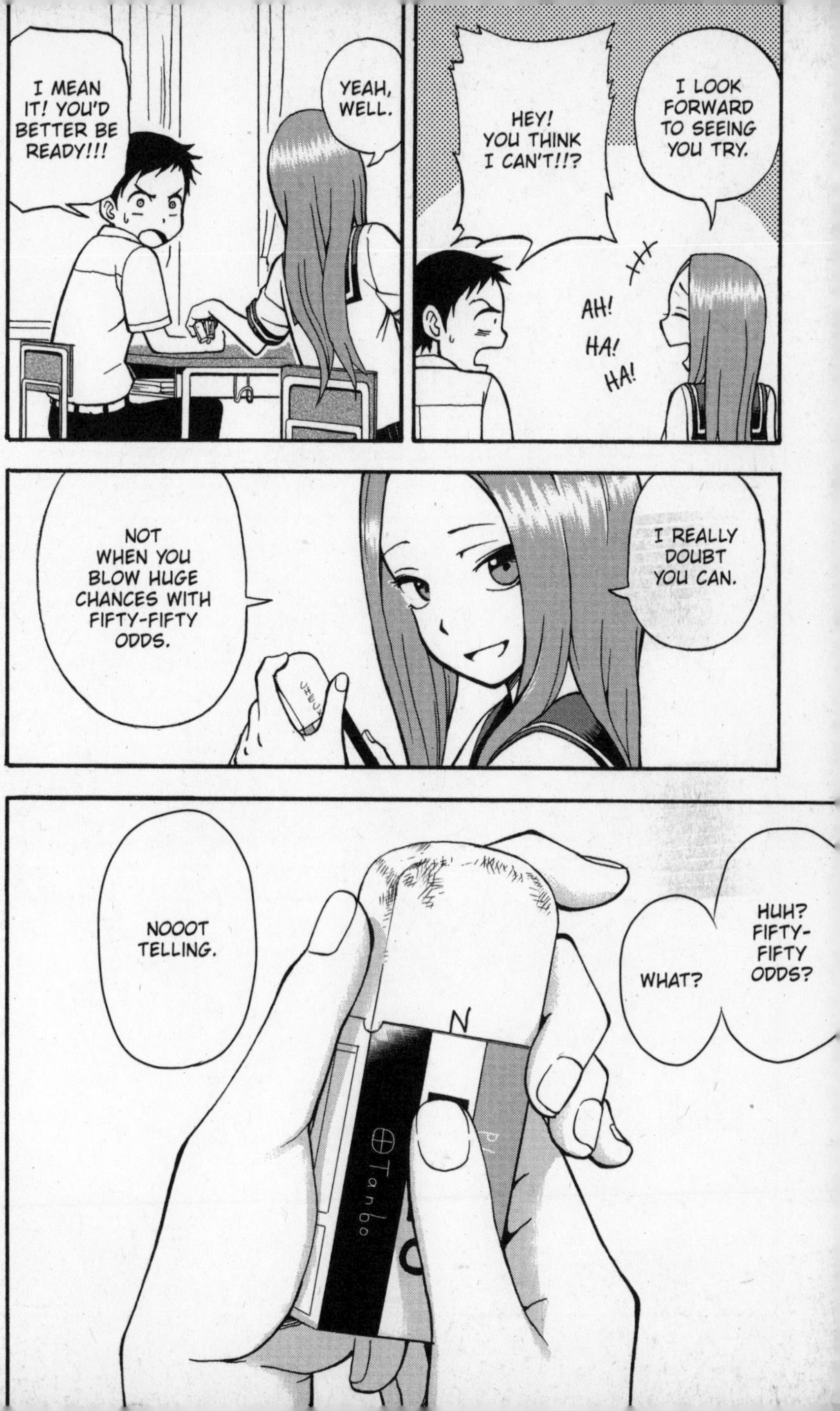
I LOOK FORWARD TO SEEING YOU TRY.
HEY! YOU THINK I CAN'T!!?
AH! HA! HA!
YEAH, WELL.
I MEAN IT! YOU'D BETTER BE READY!!!
I REALLY DOUBT YOU CAN.
NOT WHEN YOU BLOW HUGE CHANCES WITH FIFTY-FIFTY ODDS.
HUH? FIFTY-FIFTY ODDS?
WHAT?
NOOOT TELLING.
N
Tanbo

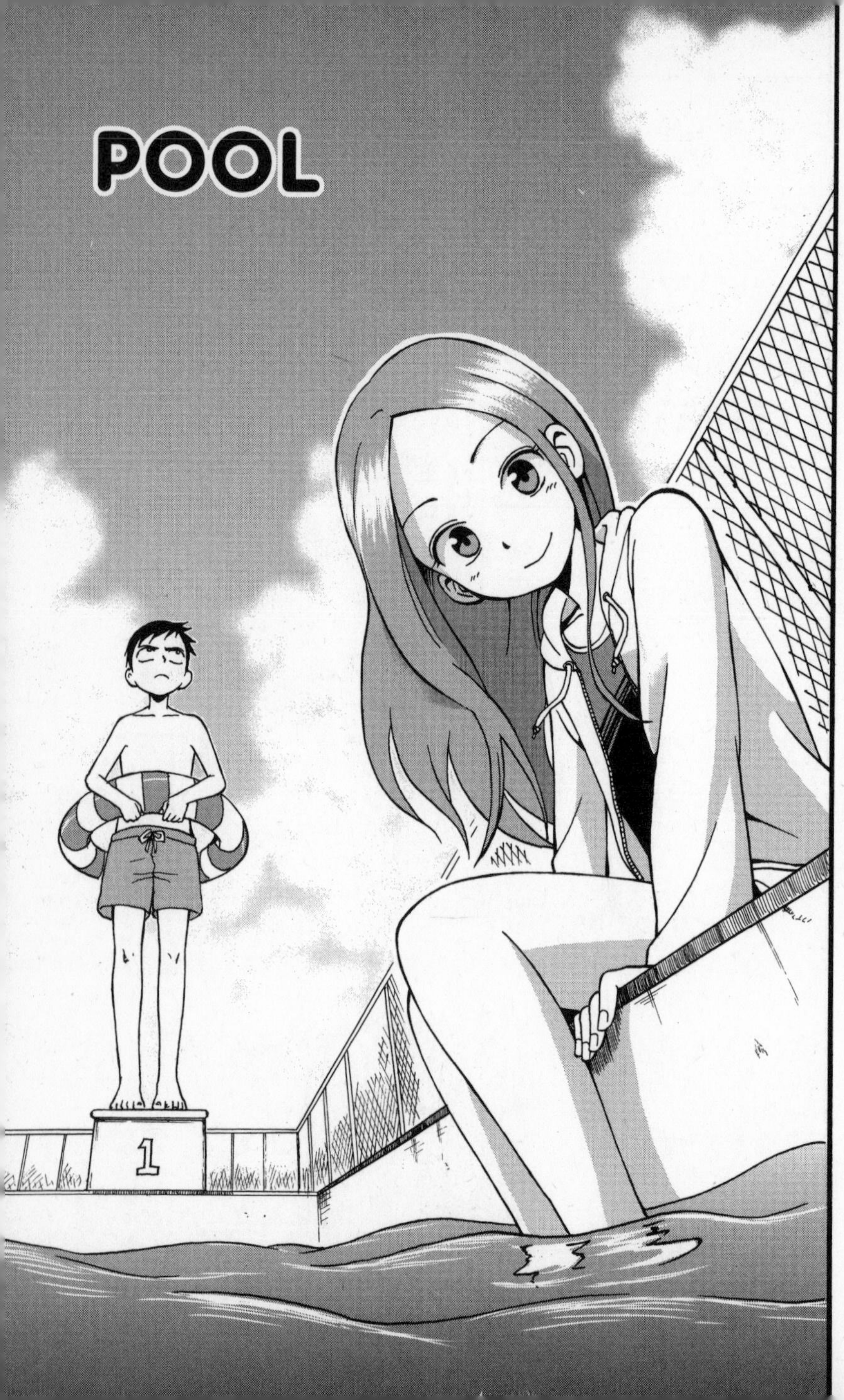
POOL
1

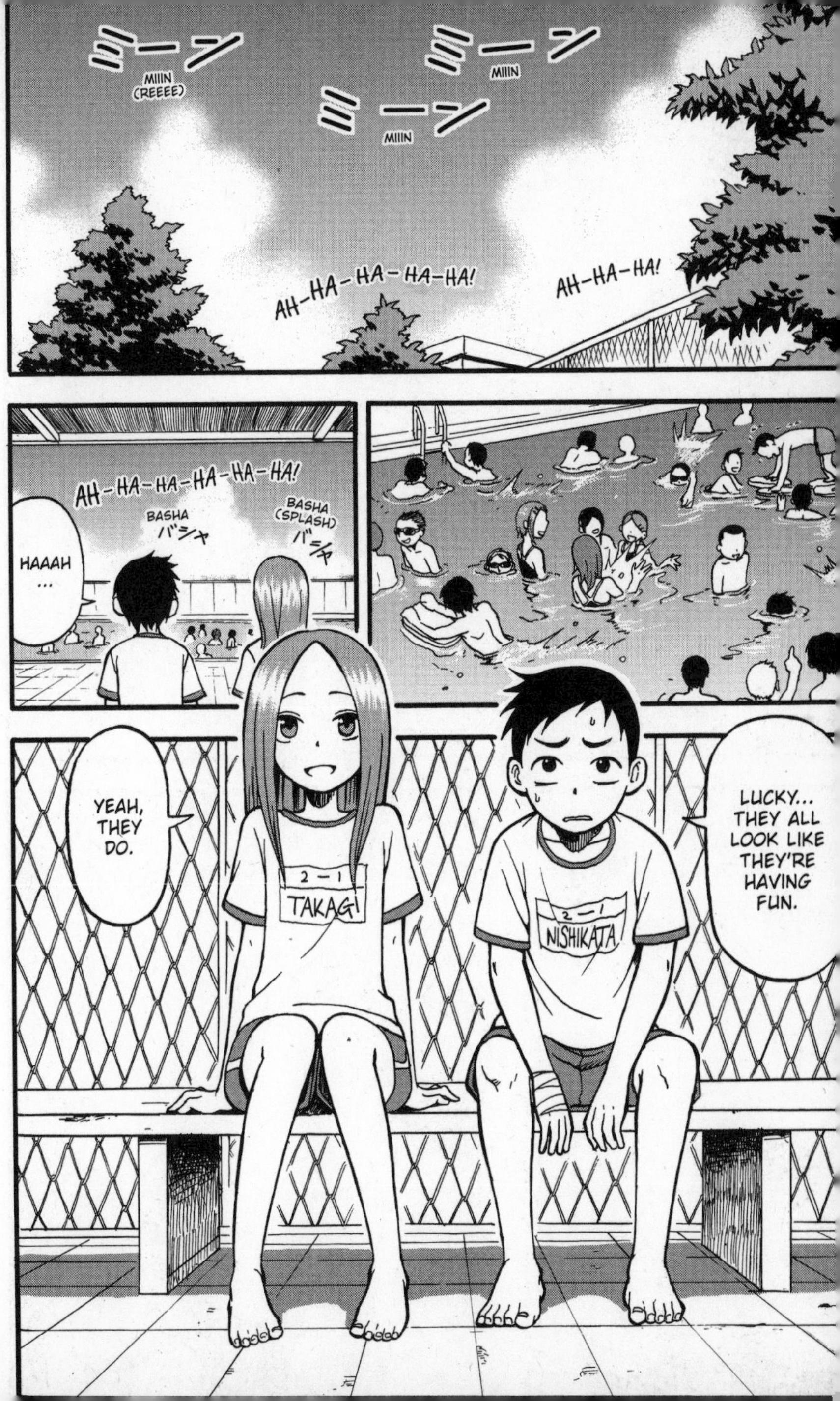

ミーン
MIIN
ミーン
MIIN (REEEE)
ミーン
MIIN
AH-HA-HA!
AH-HA-HA-HA-HA!
AH-HA-HA-HA-HA-HA!
BASHA (SPLASH)
バシャ
BASHA
バシャ
HAAAH ...
LUCKY... THEY ALL LOOK LIKE THEY'RE HAVING FUN.
2-1
NISHIKATA
YEAH, THEY DO.
2-1
TAKAGI

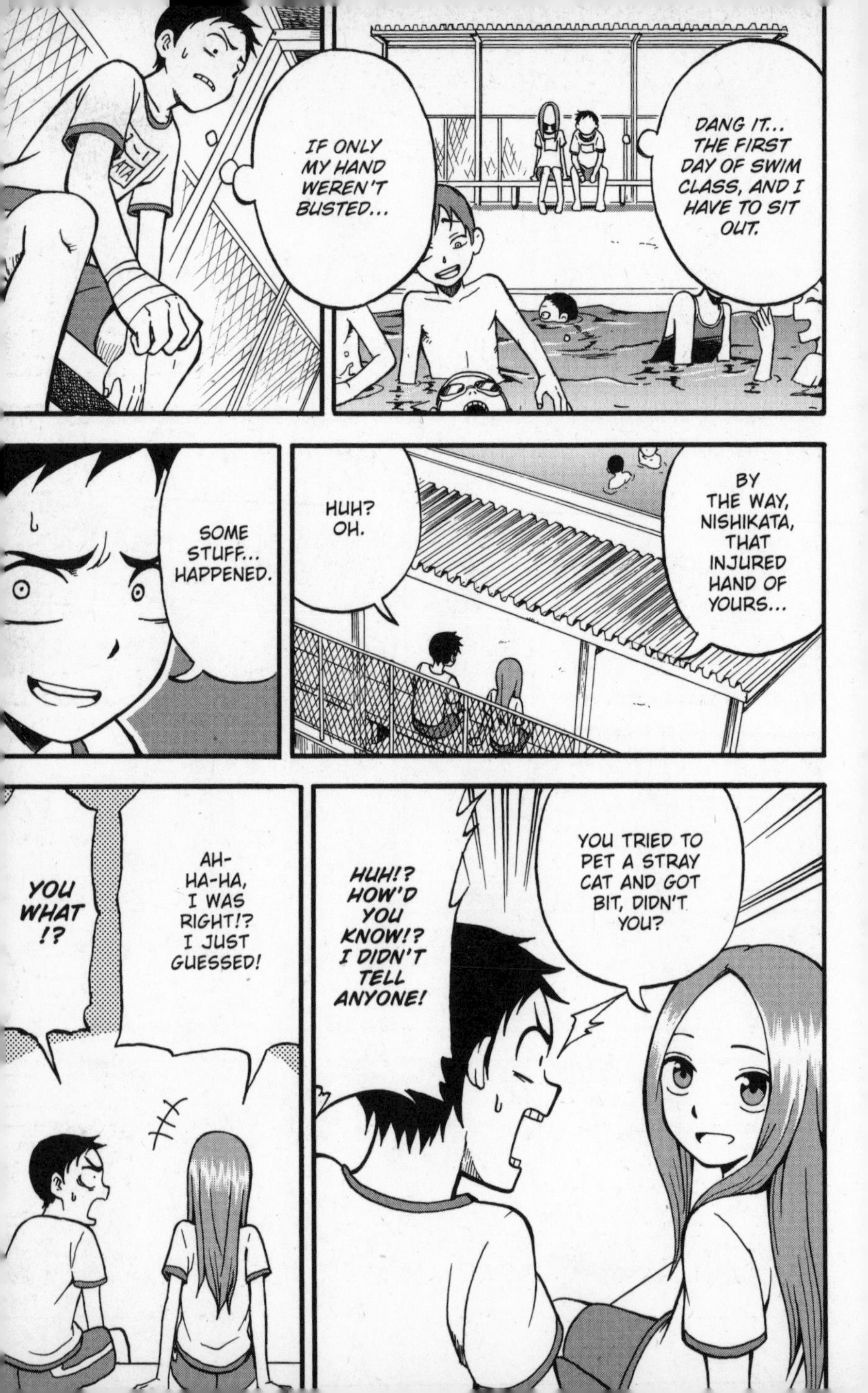
DANG IT... THE FIRST DAY OF SWIM CLASS, AND I HAVE TO SIT OUT.
IF ONLY MY HAND WEREN'T BUSTED...
BY THE WAY, NISHIKATA, THAT INJURED HAND OF YOURS...
HUH? OH.
SOME STUFF... HAPPENED.
YOU TRIED TO PET A STRAY CAT AND GOT BIT, DIDN'T YOU?
HUH!? HOW'D YOU KNOW!? I DIDN'T TELL ANYONE!
AH-HA-HA, I WAS RIGHT!? I JUST GUESSED!
YOU WHAT!?

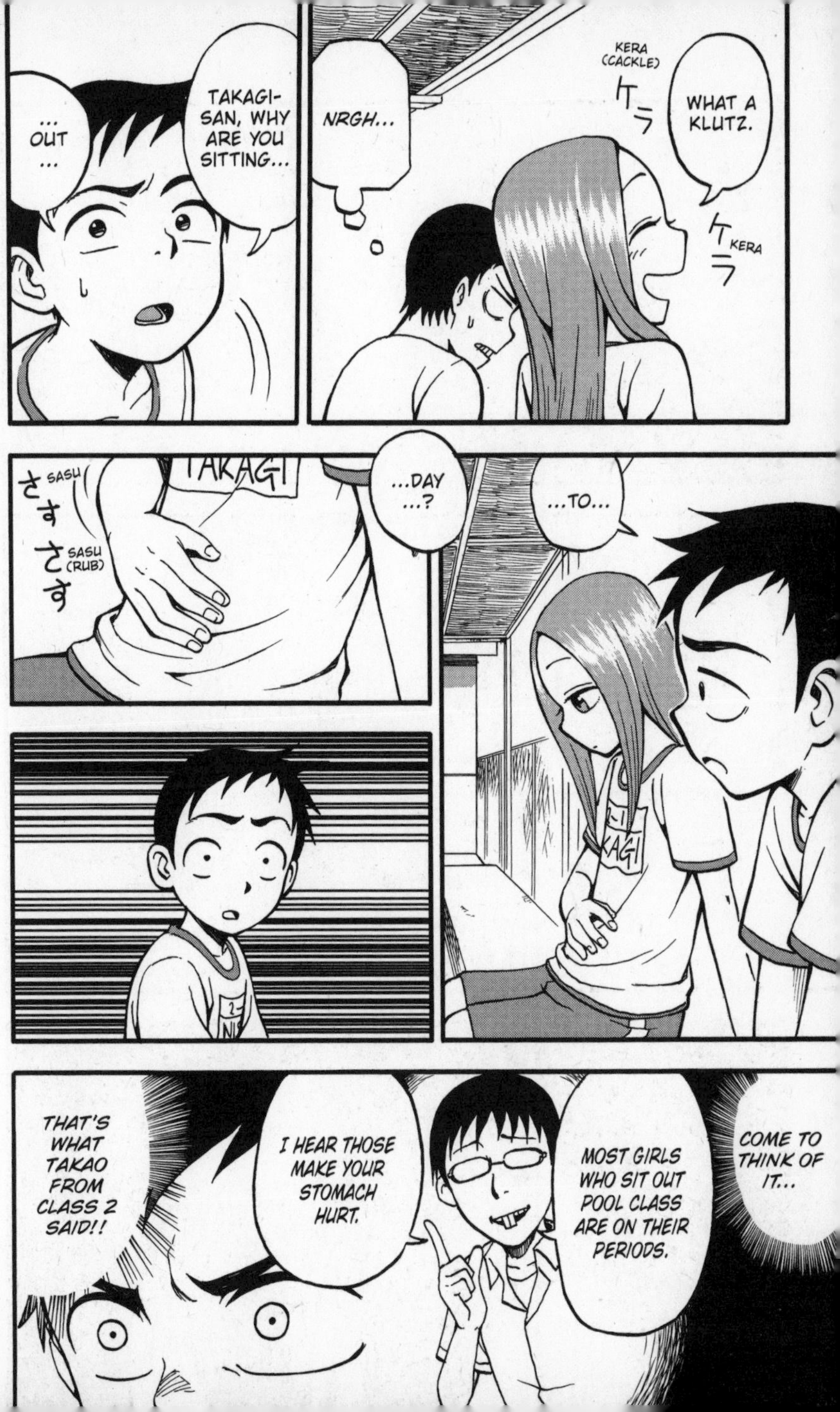
KERA (CACKLE)
ケラ
WHAT A KLUTZ.
ケラ KERA
NRGH...
TAKAGI-SAN, WHY ARE YOU SITTING...
... OUT ...
...TO...
...DAY ...?
TAKAGI
さす SASU
さす SASU (RUB)
COME TO THINK OF IT...
MOST GIRLS WHO SIT OUT POOL CLASS ARE ON THEIR PERIODS.
I HEAR THOSE MAKE YOUR STOMACH HURT.
THAT'S WHAT TAKAO FROM CLASS 2 SAID!!

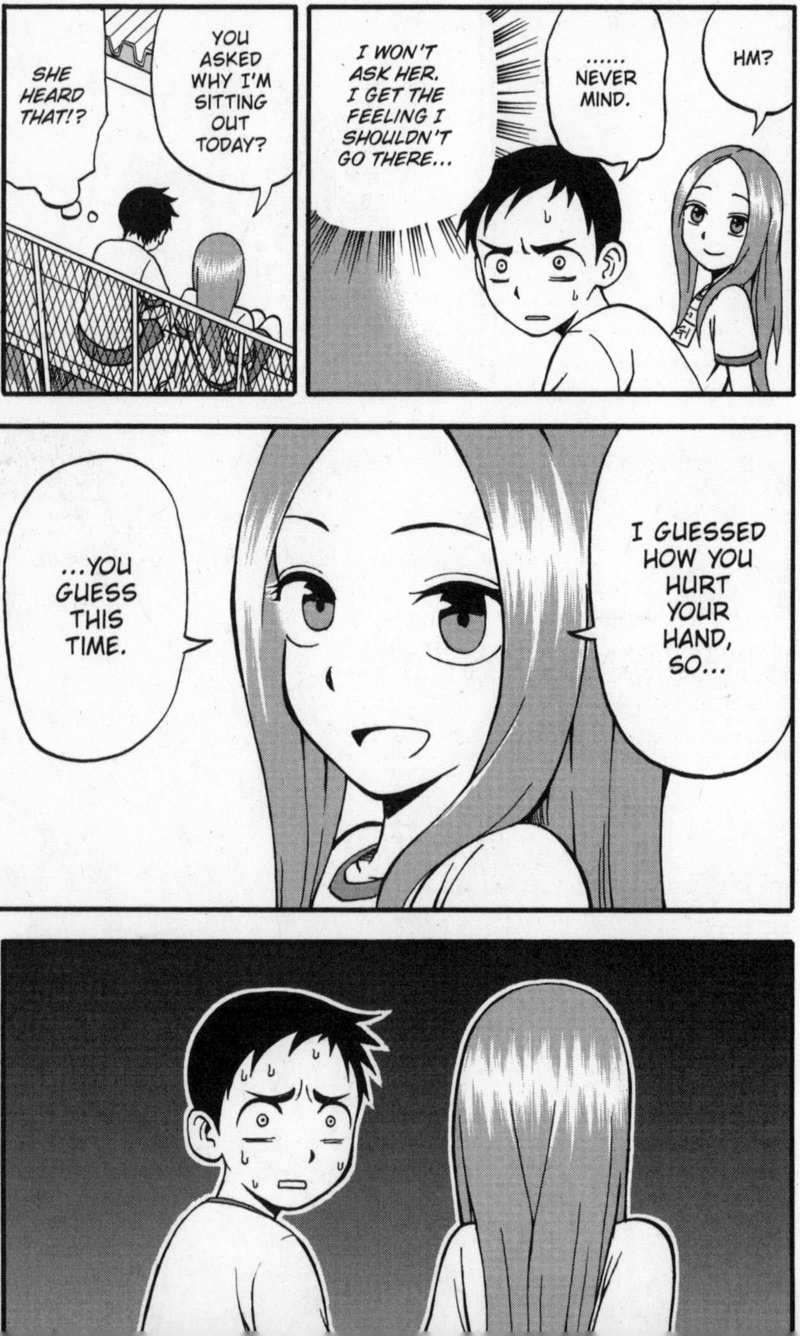
HM?
......NEVER MIND.
I WON'T ASK HER. I GET THE FEELING I SHOULDN'T GO THERE...
YOU ASKED WHY I'M SITTING OUT TODAY?
SHE HEARD THAT!?
I GUESSED HOW YOU HURT YOUR HAND, SO...
...YOU GUESS THIS TIME.

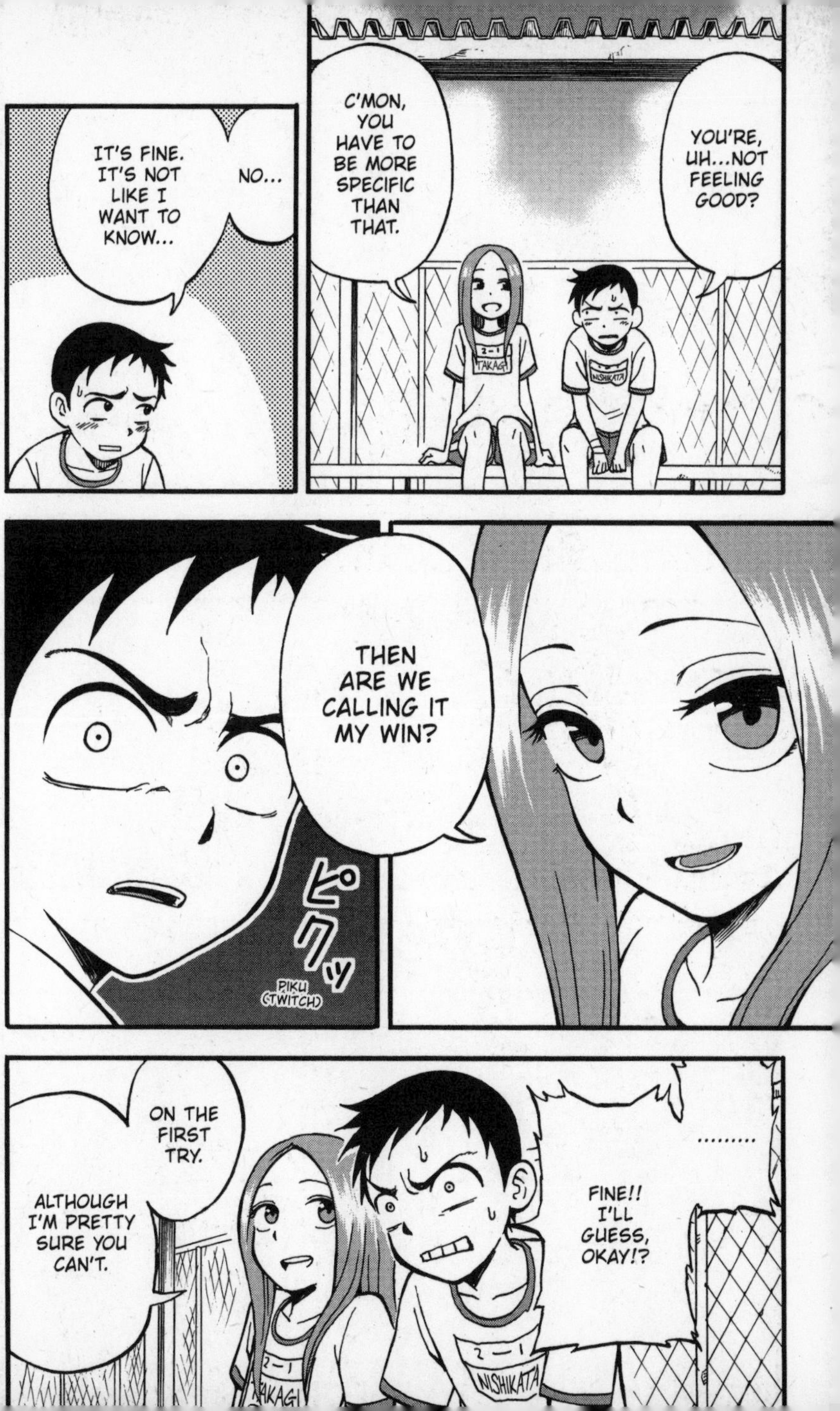

YOU'RE, UH...NOT FEELING GOOD?
C'MON, YOU HAVE TO BE MORE SPECIFIC THAN THAT.
NO...
IT'S FINE. IT'S NOT LIKE I WANT TO KNOW...
THEN ARE WE CALLING IT MY WIN?
ピクッ
PIKU (TWITCH)
....
FINE!! I'LL GUESS, OKAY!?
ON THE FIRST TRY.
ALTHOUGH I'M PRETTY SURE YOU CAN'T.

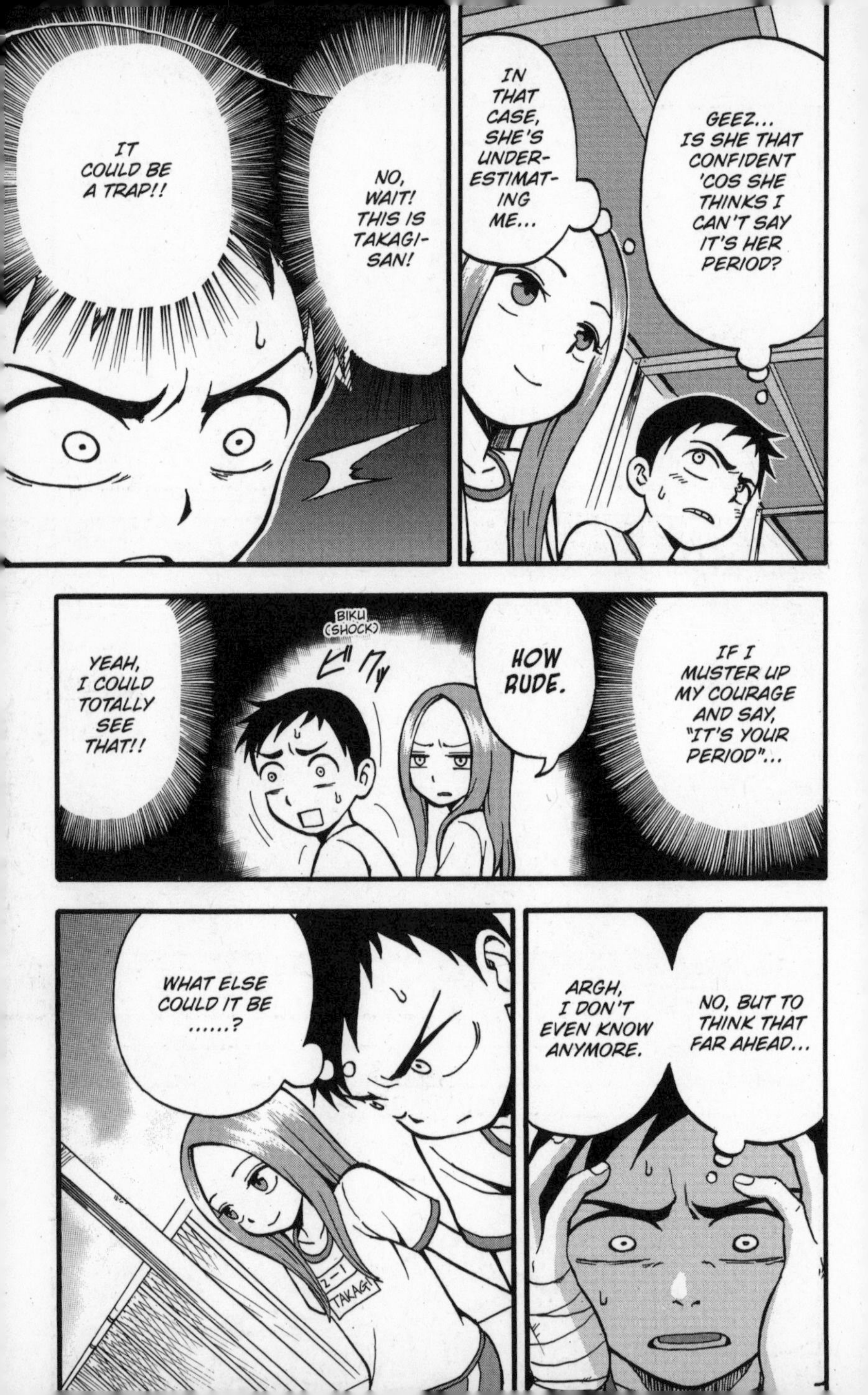
GEEZ... IS SHE THAT CONFIDENT 'COS SHE THINKS I CAN'T SAY IT'S HER PERIOD?
IN THAT CASE, SHE'S UNDER-ESTIMAT-ING ME...
NO, WAIT! THIS IS TAKAGI-SAN!
IT COULD BE A TRAP!!
IF I MUSTER UP MY COURAGE AND SAY, "IT'S YOUR PERIOD"...
HOW RUDE.
BIKU (SHOCK)
YEAH, I COULD TOTALLY SEE THAT!!
NO, BUT TO THINK THAT FAR AHEAD...
ARGH, I DON'T EVEN KNOW ANYMORE.
WHAT ELSE COULD IT BE ......?
2-1 TAKAGI

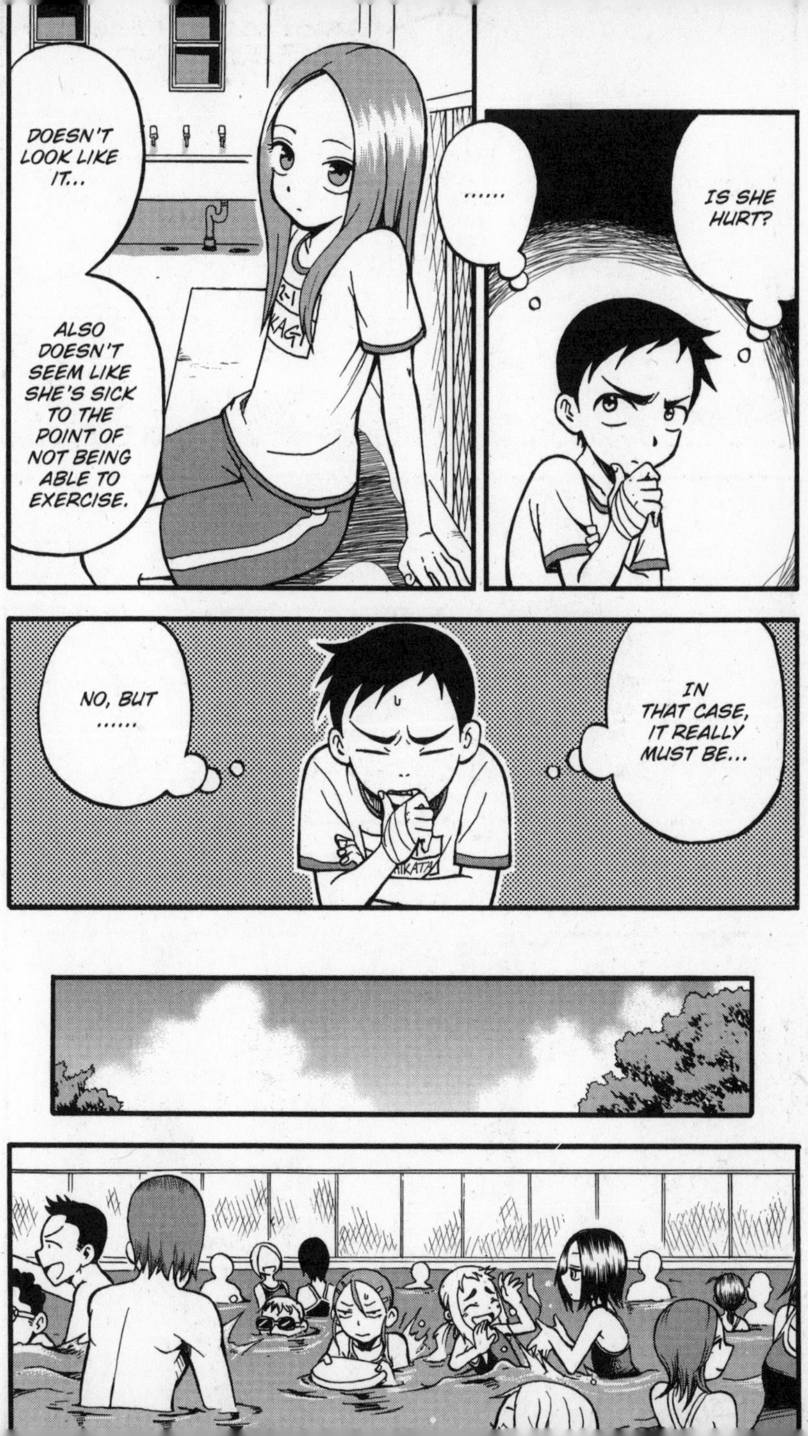
IS SHE HURT?
......
DOESN'T LOOK LIKE IT...
ALSO DOESN'T SEEM LIKE SHE'S SICK TO THE POINT OF NOT BEING ABLE TO EXERCISE.
IN THAT CASE, IT REALLY MUST BE...
NO, BUT ......

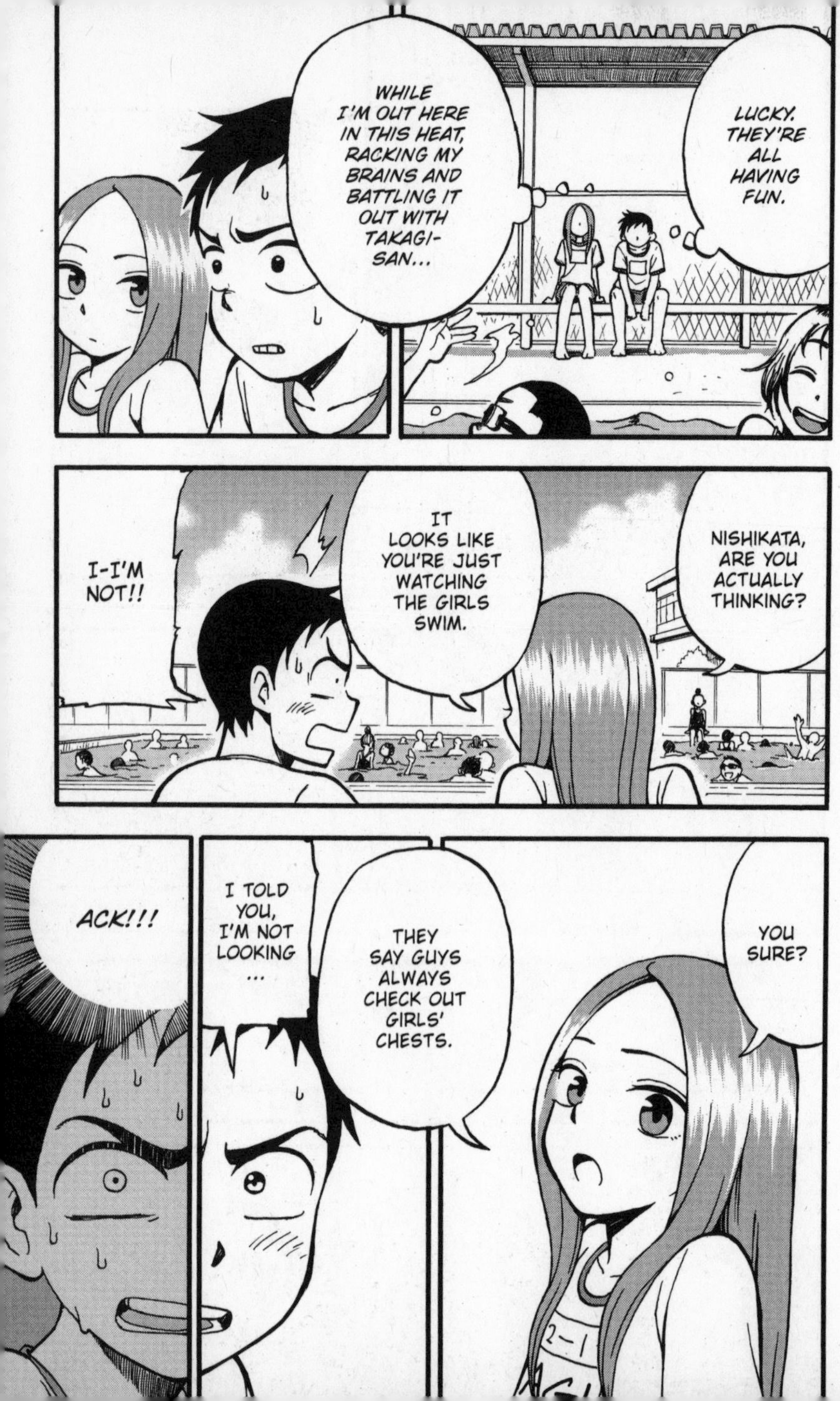
LUCKY. THEY'RE ALL HAVING FUN.
WHILE I'M OUT HERE IN THIS HEAT, RACKING MY BRAINS AND BATTLING IT OUT WITH TAKAGI-SAN...
NISHIKATA, ARE YOU ACTUALLY THINKING?
IT LOOKS LIKE YOU'RE JUST WATCHING THE GIRLS SWIM.
I-I'M NOT!!
YOU SURE?
THEY SAY GUYS ALWAYS CHECK OUT GIRLS' CHESTS.
I TOLD YOU, I'M NOT LOOKING ...
ACK!!!

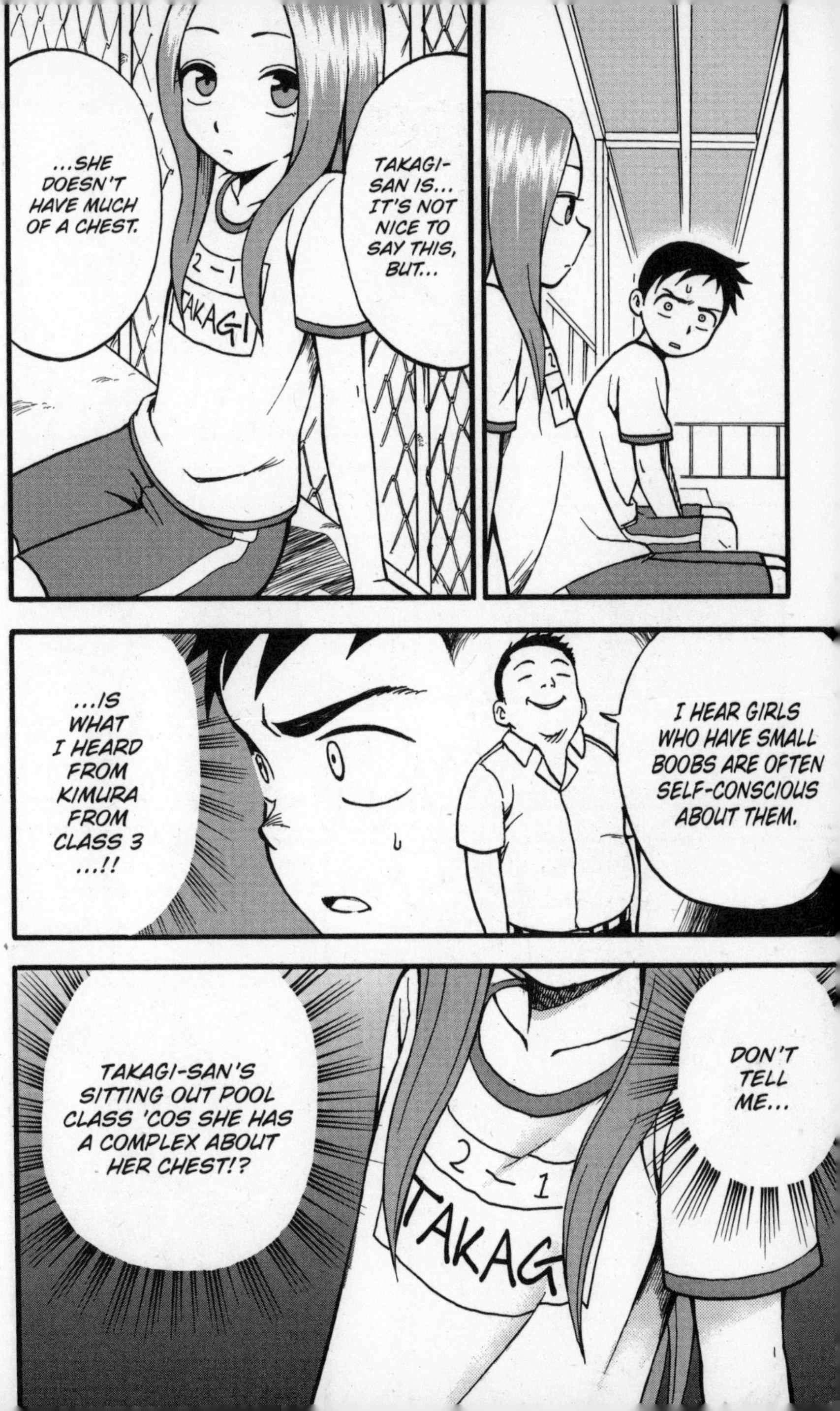
TAKAGI-SAN IS... IT'S NOT NICE TO SAY THIS, BUT...
...SHE DOESN'T HAVE MUCH OF A CHEST.
2-1
TAKAGI
I HEAR GIRLS WHO HAVE SMALL BOOBS ARE OFTEN SELF-CONSCIOUS ABOUT THEM.
...IS WHAT I HEARD FROM KIMURA FROM CLASS 3 ...!!
DON'T TELL ME...
TAKAGI-SAN'S SITTING OUT POOL CLASS 'COS SHE HAS A COMPLEX ABOUT HER CHEST!?
2-1
TAKAGI

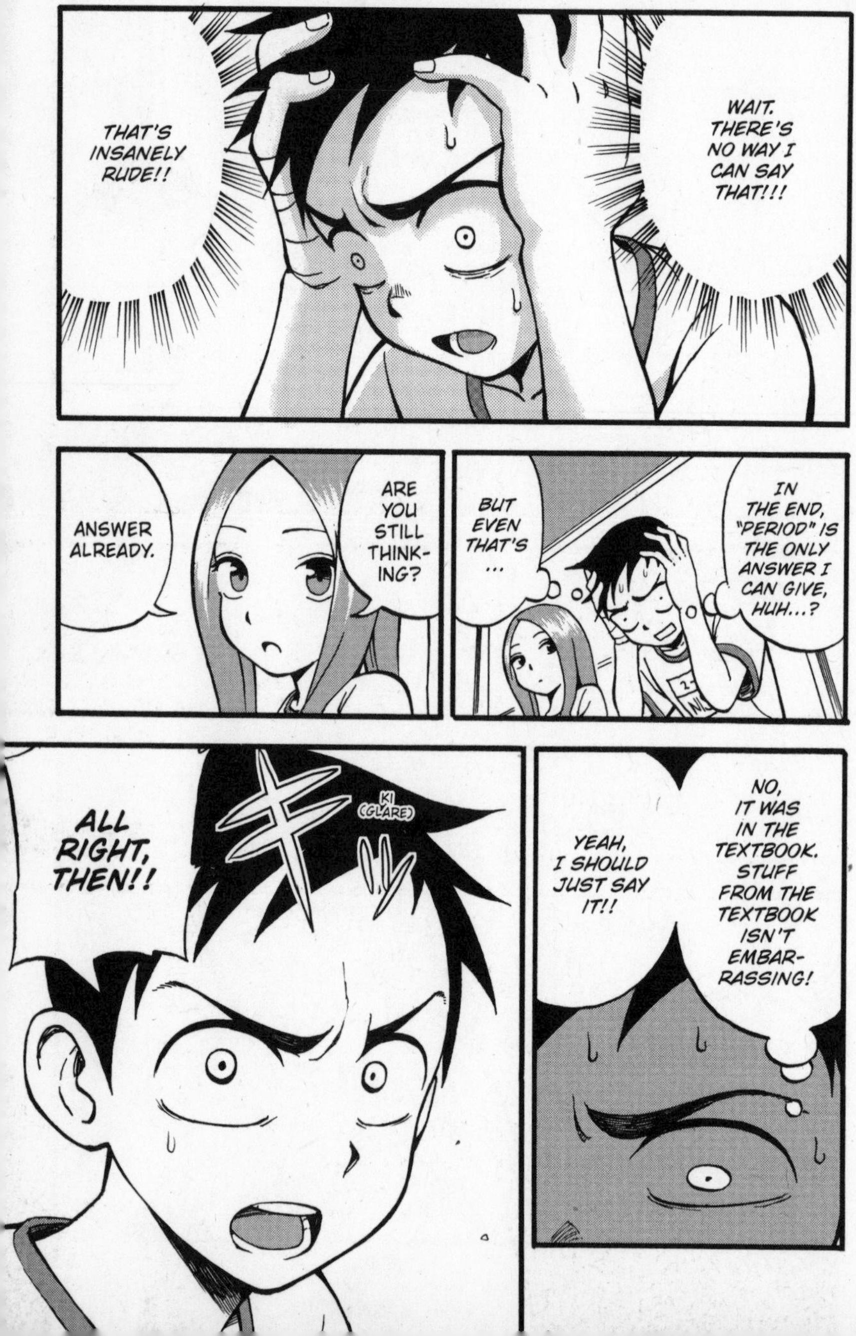
WAIT. THERE'S NO WAY I CAN SAY THAT!!!
THAT'S INSANELY RUDE!!
IN THE END, "PERIOD" IS THE ONLY ANSWER I CAN GIVE, HUH...?
BUT EVEN THAT'S ...
ARE YOU STILL THINK-ING?
ANSWER ALREADY.
NO, IT WAS IN THE TEXTBOOK. STUFF FROM THE TEXTBOOK ISN'T EMBAR-RASSING!
YEAH, I SHOULD JUST SAY IT!!
KI (GLARE)
ALL RIGHT, THEN!!

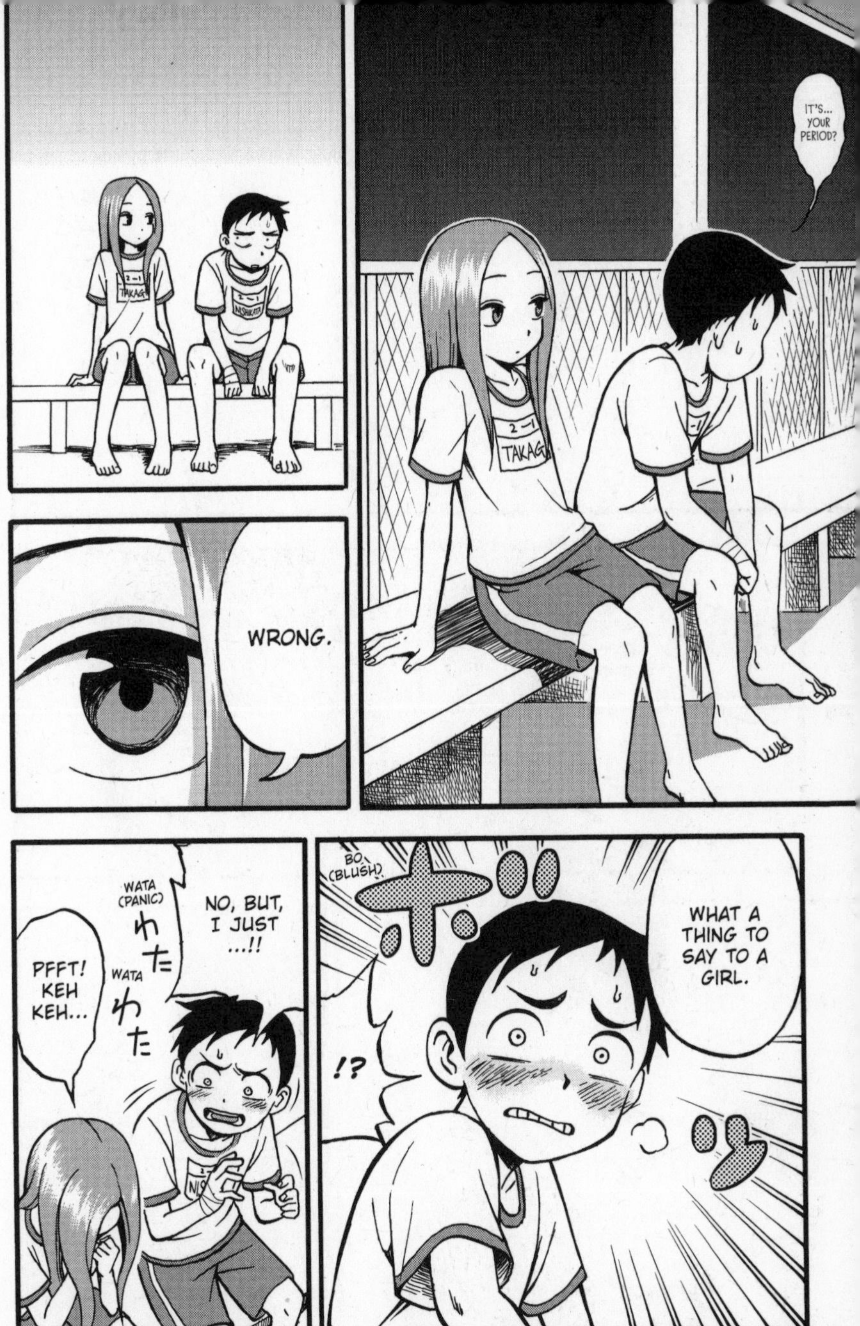
IT'S... YOUR PERIOD?
WRONG.
BO (BLUSH)
WHAT A THING TO SAY TO A GIRL.
!?
NO, BUT, I JUST ...!!
WATA (PANIC) わた
WATA わた
PFFT! KEH KEH...

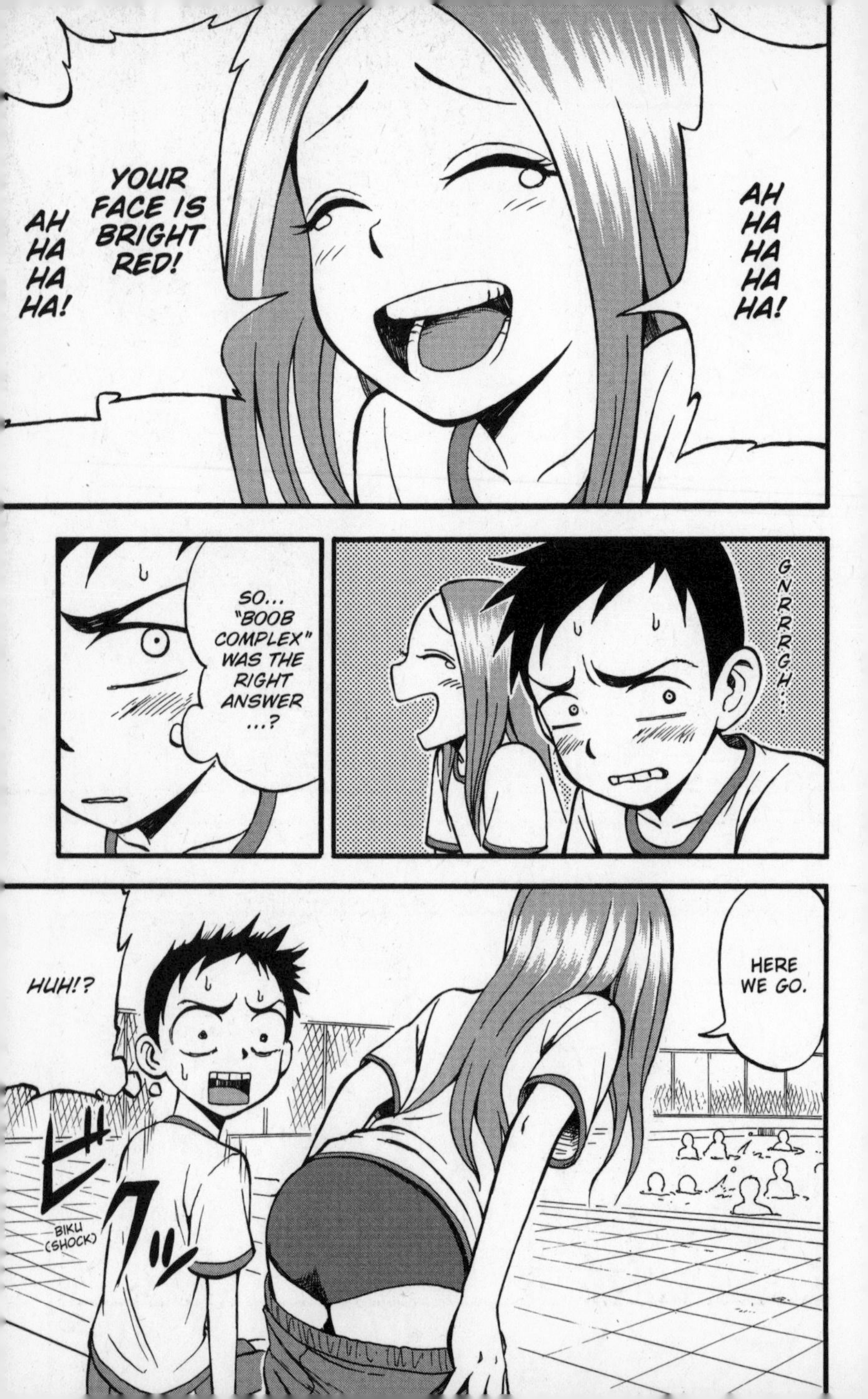
AH HA HA HA HA HA!
YOUR FACE IS BRIGHT RED!
AH HA HA HA!
GNRRRGH...
SO... "BOOB COMPLEX" WAS THE RIGHT ANSWER ...?
HERE WE GO.
HUH!?
BIKU (SHOCK)

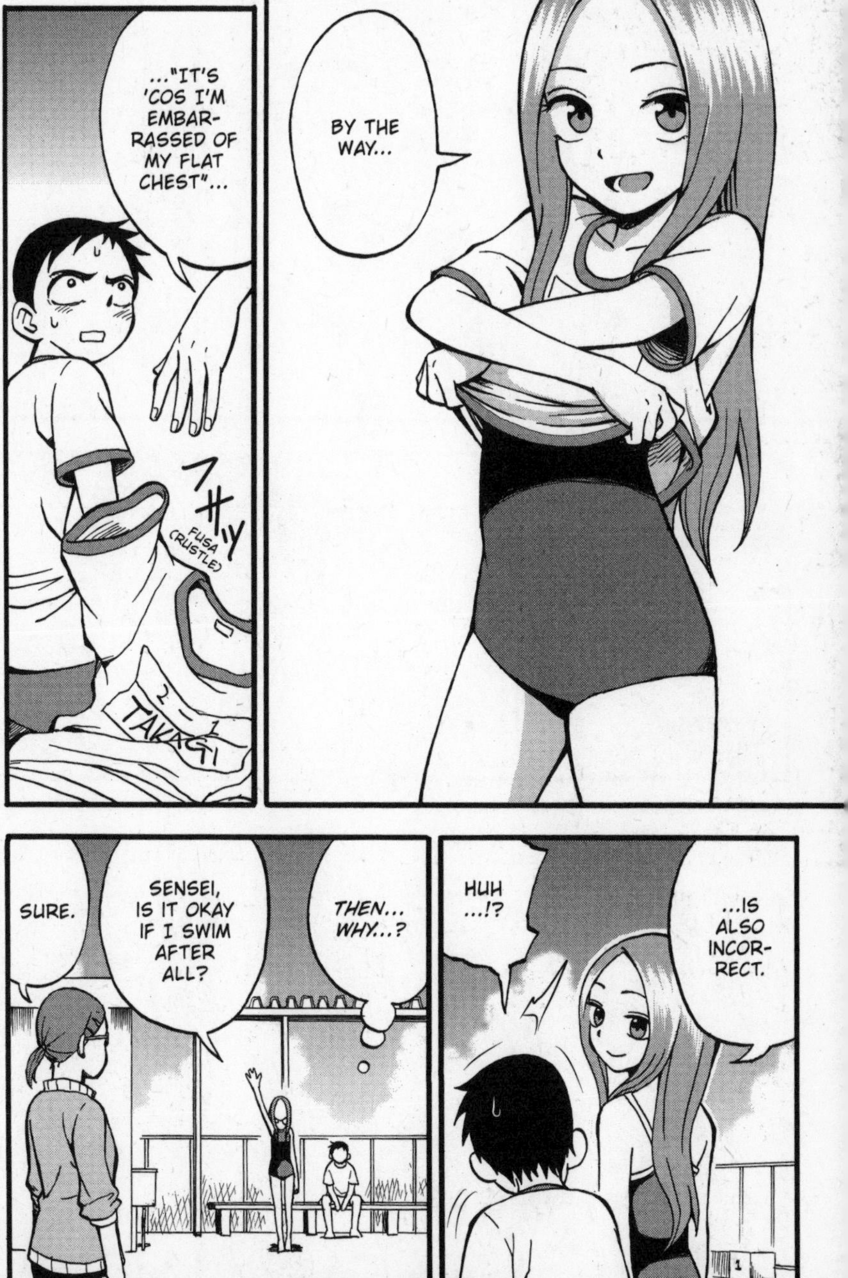
BY THE WAY...
..."IT'S 'COS I'M EMBARRASSED OF MY FLAT CHEST"...
FUSA (RUSTLE)
2-1 TAKAGI
...IS ALSO INCORRECT.
HUH ...!?
THEN... WHY...?
SENSEI, IS IT OKAY IF I SWIM AFTER ALL?
SURE.

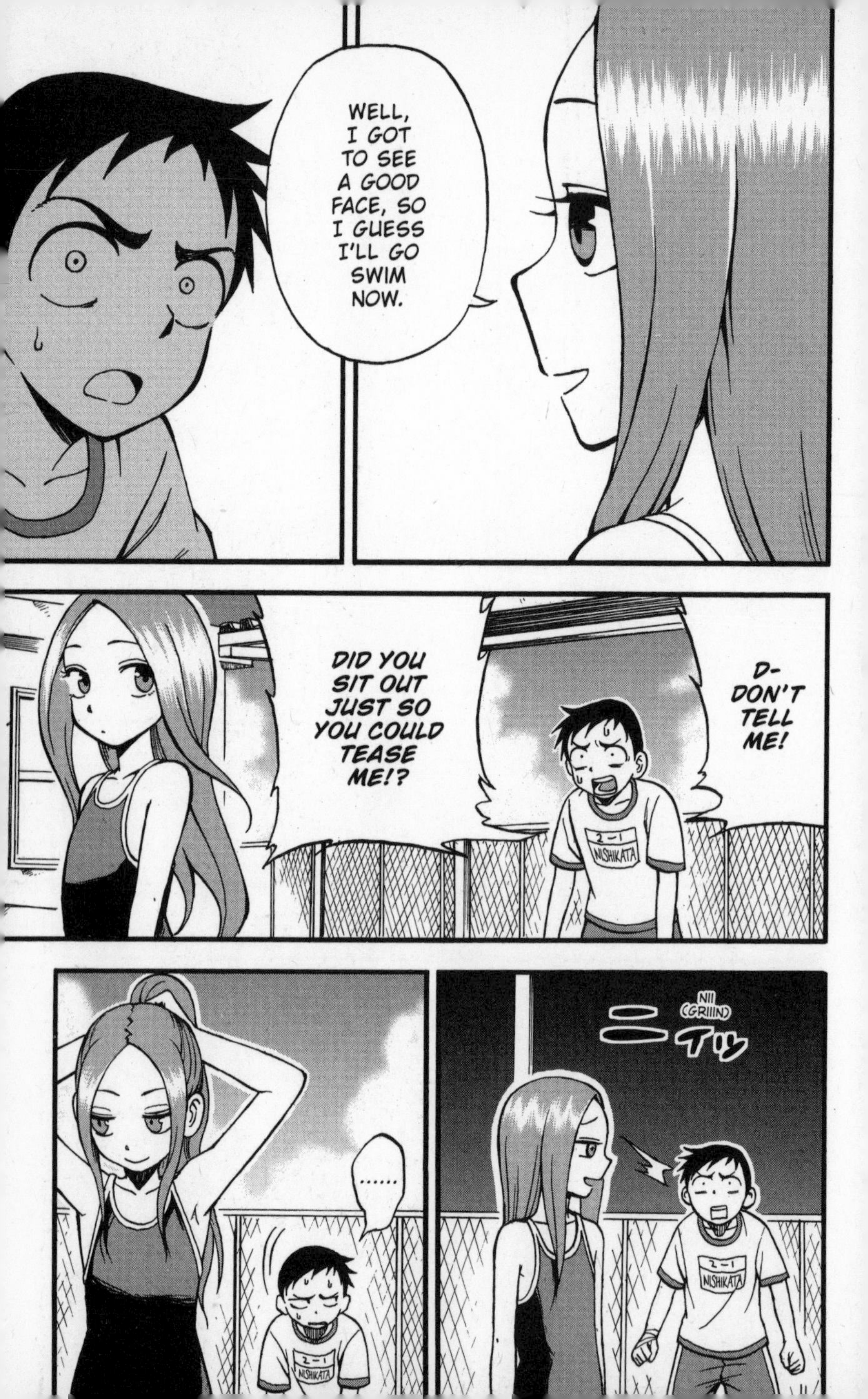
WELL, I GOT TO SEE A GOOD FACE, SO I GUESS I'LL GO SWIM NOW.
D-DON'T TELL ME!
DID YOU SIT OUT JUST SO YOU COULD TEASE ME!?
2-1 NISHIKATA
NII (GRIIN)
2-1 NISHIKATA
......
2-1 NISHIKATA

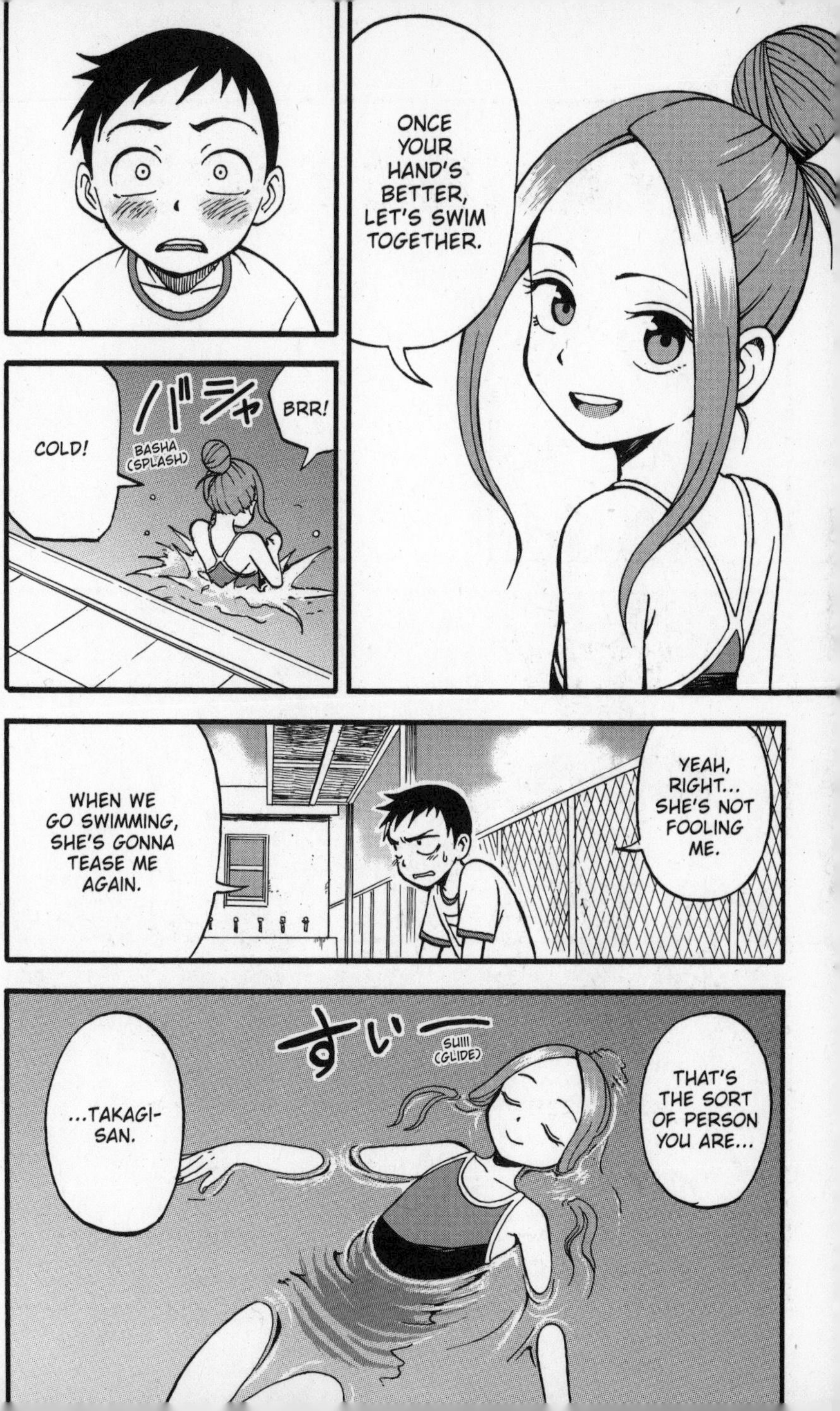
ONCE YOUR HAND'S BETTER, LET'S SWIM TOGETHER.
BRR!
バシャ
BASHA (SPLASH)
COLD!
YEAH, RIGHT... SHE'S NOT FOOLING ME.
WHEN WE GO SWIMMING, SHE'S GONNA TEASE ME AGAIN.
THAT'S THE SORT OF PERSON YOU ARE...
すいー
SUIII (GLIDE)
...TAKAGI-SAN.

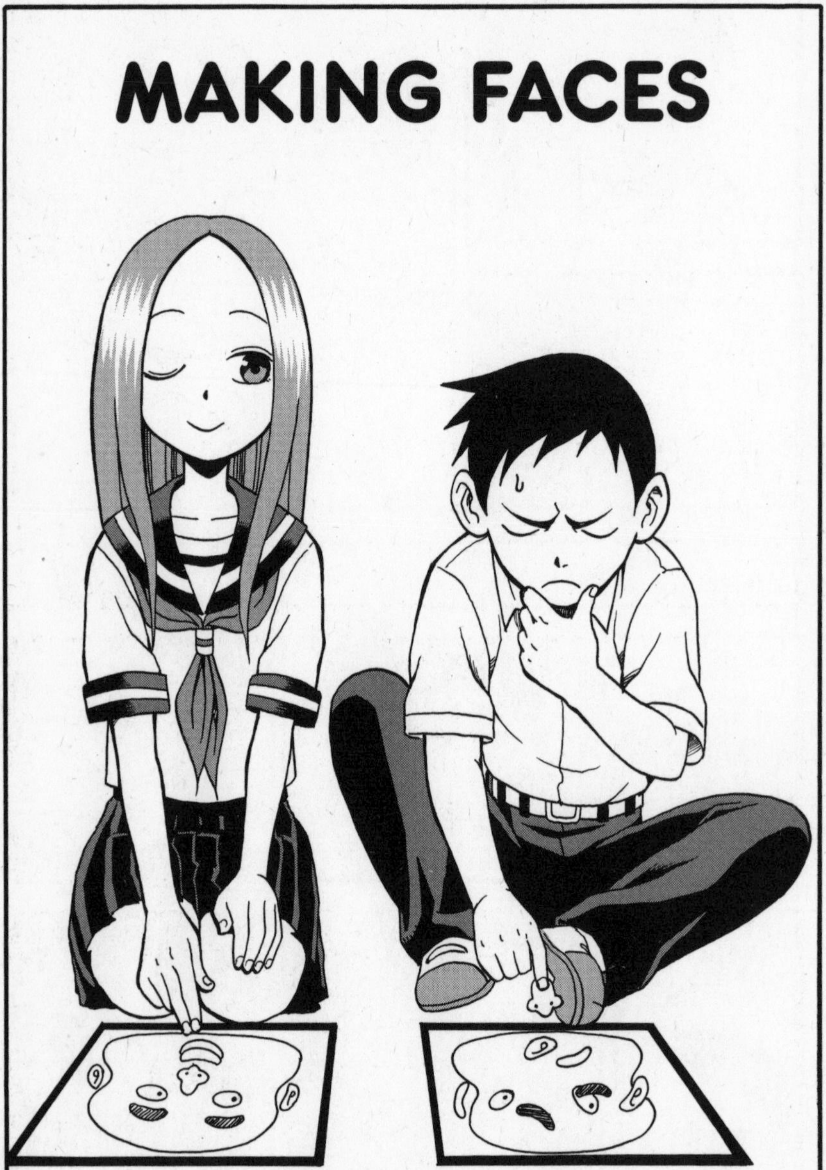
MAKING FACES

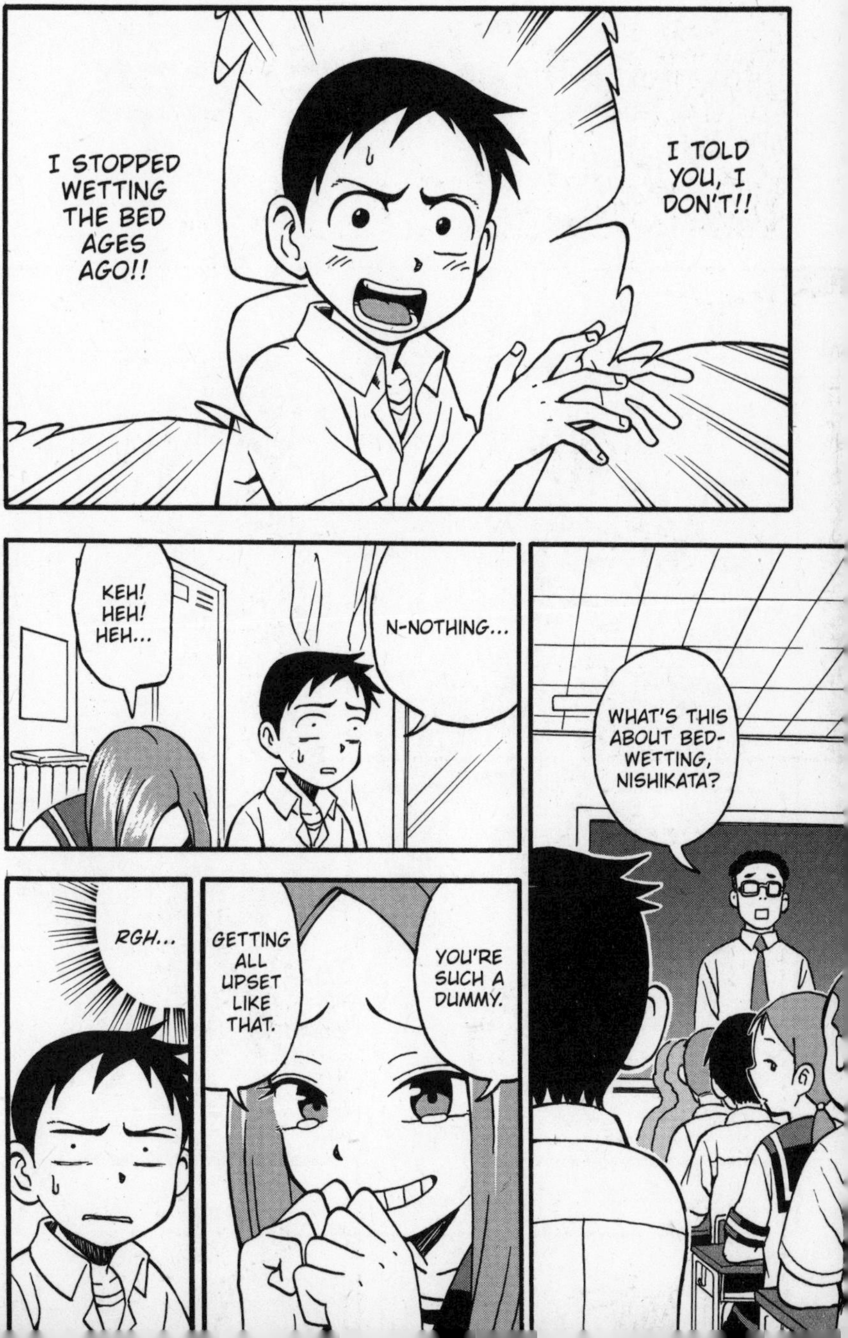
I TOLD YOU, I DON'T!!
I STOPPED WETTING THE BED AGES AGO!!
WHAT'S THIS ABOUT BED-WETTING, NISHIKATA?
N-NOTHING...
KEH! HEH! HEH...
YOU'RE SUCH A DUMMY.
GETTING ALL UPSET LIKE THAT.
RGH...

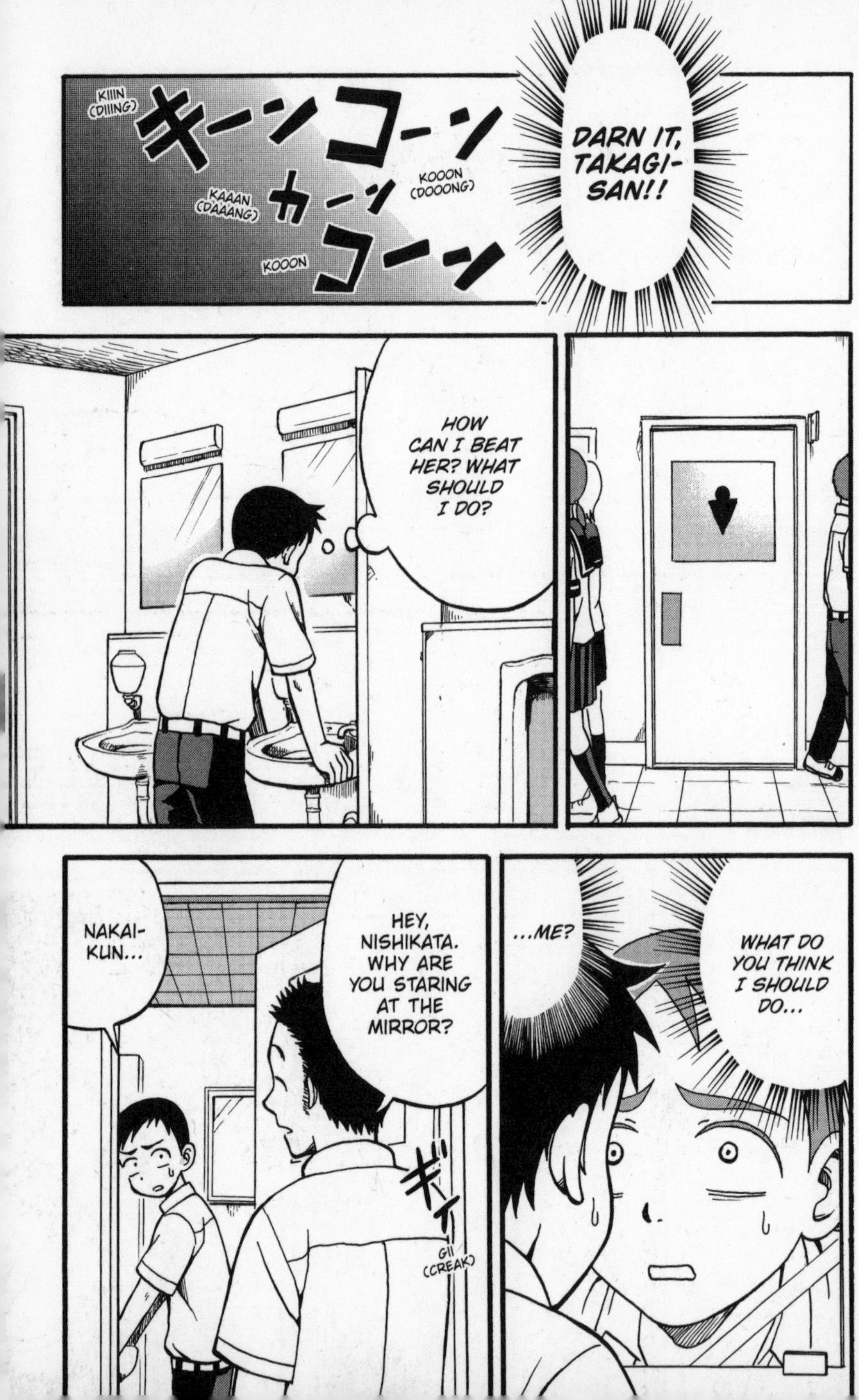
DARN IT, TAKAGI-SAN!!
KIIIN (DIIING)
KOOON (DOOONG)
KAAAN (DAAANG)
KOOON
HOW CAN I BEAT HER? WHAT SHOULD I DO?
WHAT DO YOU THINK I SHOULD DO...
...ME?
HEY, NISHIKATA. WHY ARE YOU STARING AT THE MIRROR?
GII (CREAK)
NAKAI-KUN...

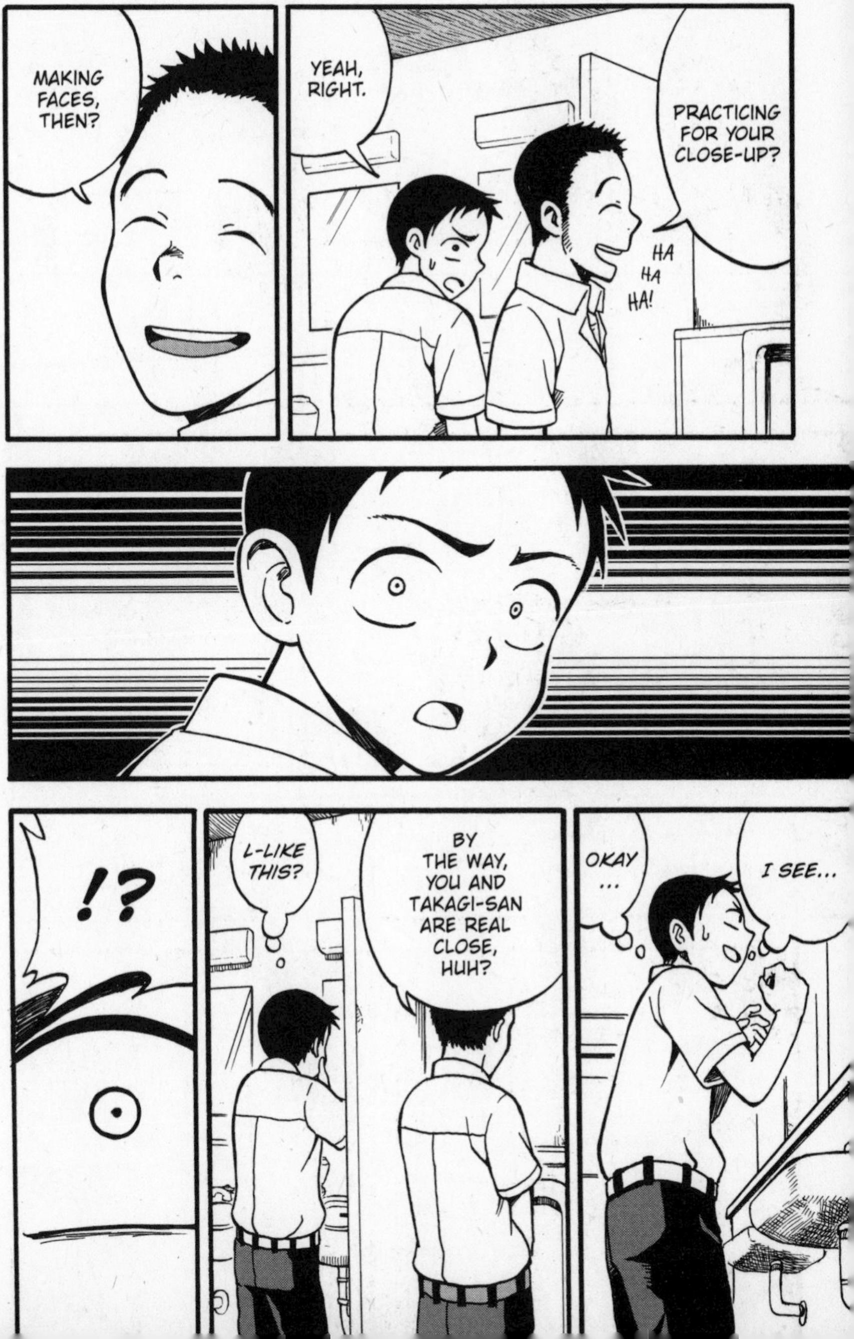
PRACTICING FOR YOUR CLOSE-UP?
HA HA HA!
YEAH, RIGHT.
MAKING FACES, THEN?
I SEE...
OKAY ...
BY THE WAY, YOU AND TAKAGI-SAN ARE REAL CLOSE, HUH?
L-LIKE THIS?
!?

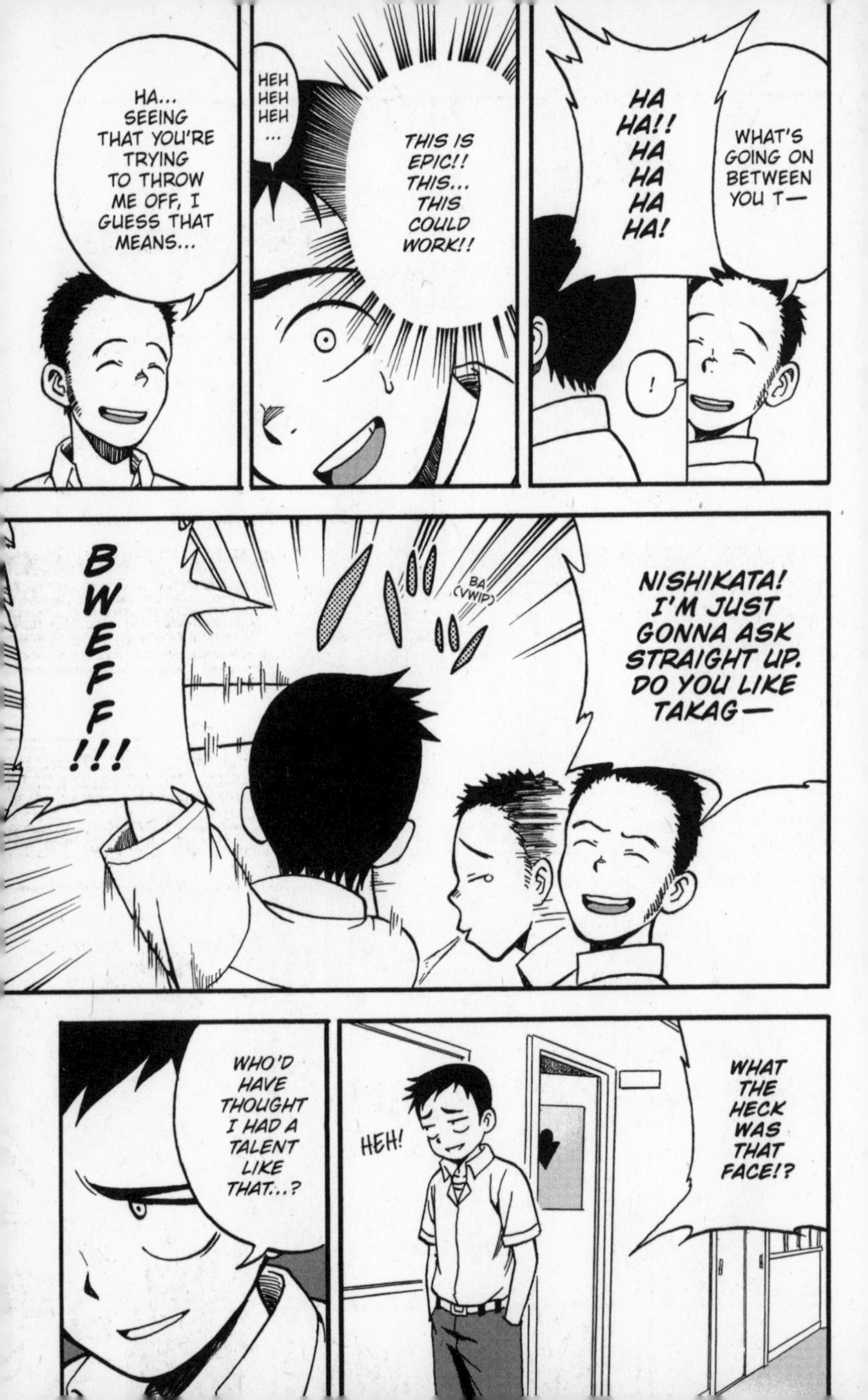
WHAT'S GOING ON BETWEEN YOU T—
HA HA!! HA HA HA HA!
!
HEH HEH HEH ...
THIS IS EPIC!! THIS... THIS COULD WORK!!
HA... SEEING THAT YOU'RE TRYING TO THROW ME OFF, I GUESS THAT MEANS...
NISHIKATA! I'M JUST GONNA ASK STRAIGHT UP. DO YOU LIKE TAKAG—
BA (VWIP)
BWEFF!!!
WHAT THE HECK WAS THAT FACE!?
HEH!
WHO'D HAVE THOUGHT I HAD A TALENT LIKE THAT...?

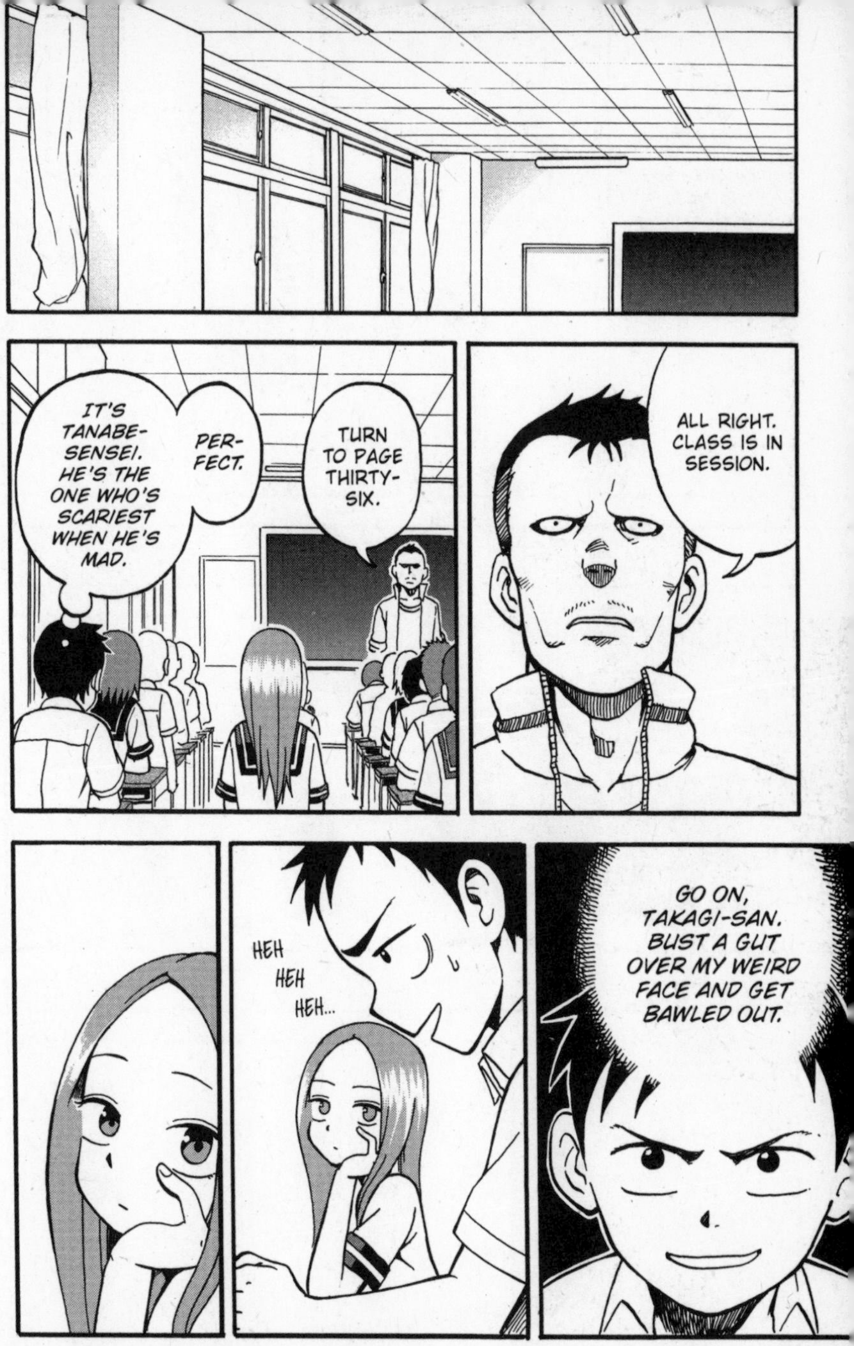
ALL RIGHT. CLASS IS IN SESSION.
TURN TO PAGE THIRTY-SIX.
PER-FECT.
IT'S TANABE-SENSEI. HE'S THE ONE WHO'S SCARIEST WHEN HE'S MAD.
GO ON, TAKAGI-SAN. BUST A GUT OVER MY WEIRD FACE AND GET BAWLED OUT.
HEH HEH HEH...

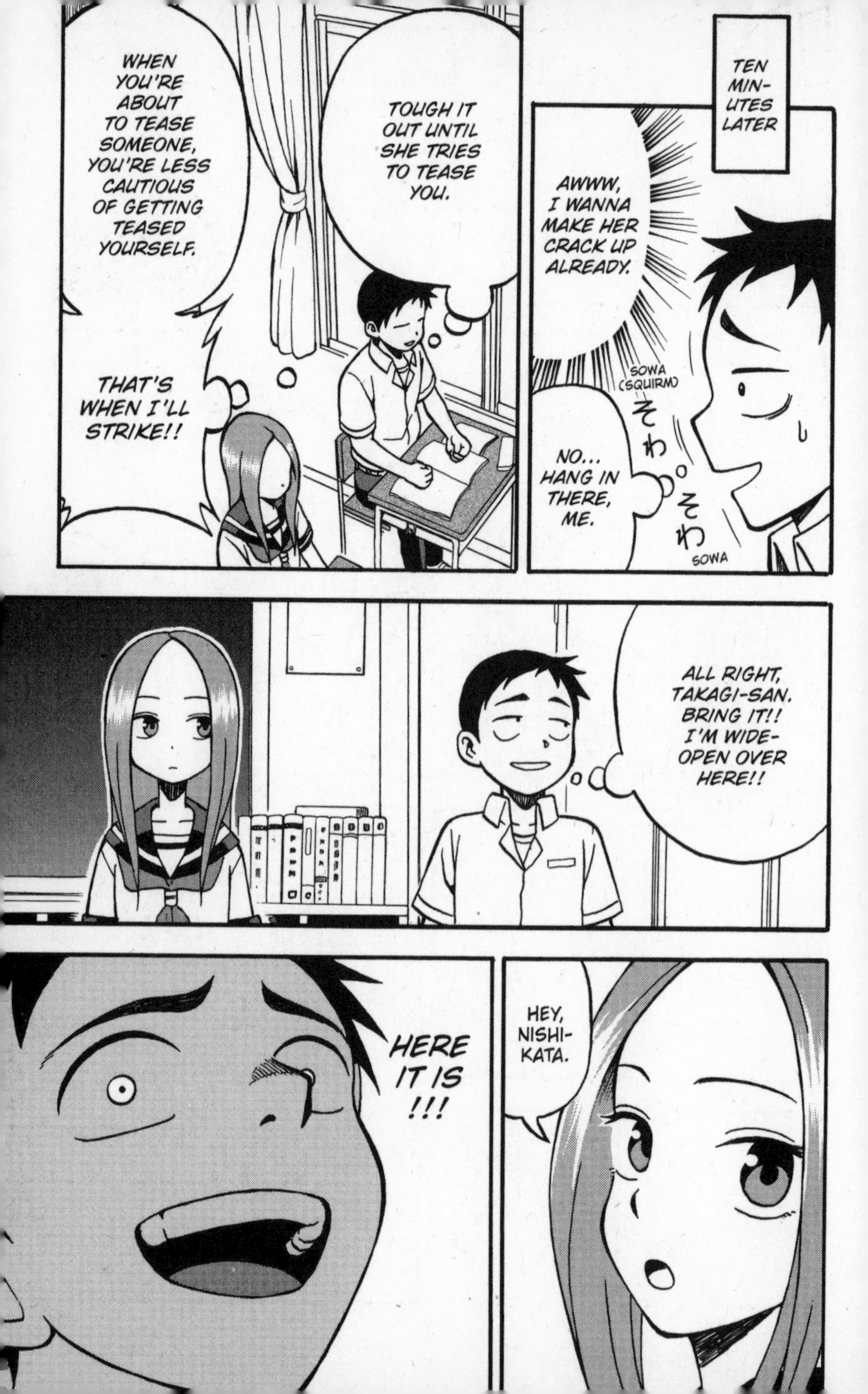
TEN MIN-UTES LATER
AWWW, I WANNA MAKE HER CRACK UP ALREADY.
SOWA (SQUIRM)
そわ
そわ
SOWA
NO... HANG IN THERE, ME.
TOUGH IT OUT UNTIL SHE TRIES TO TEASE YOU.
WHEN YOU'RE ABOUT TO TEASE SOMEONE, YOU'RE LESS CAUTIOUS OF GETTING TEASED YOURSELF.
THAT'S WHEN I'LL STRIKE!!
ALL RIGHT, TAKAGI-SAN. BRING IT!! I'M WIDE-OPEN OVER HERE!!
HEY, NISHI-KATA.
HERE IT IS !!!

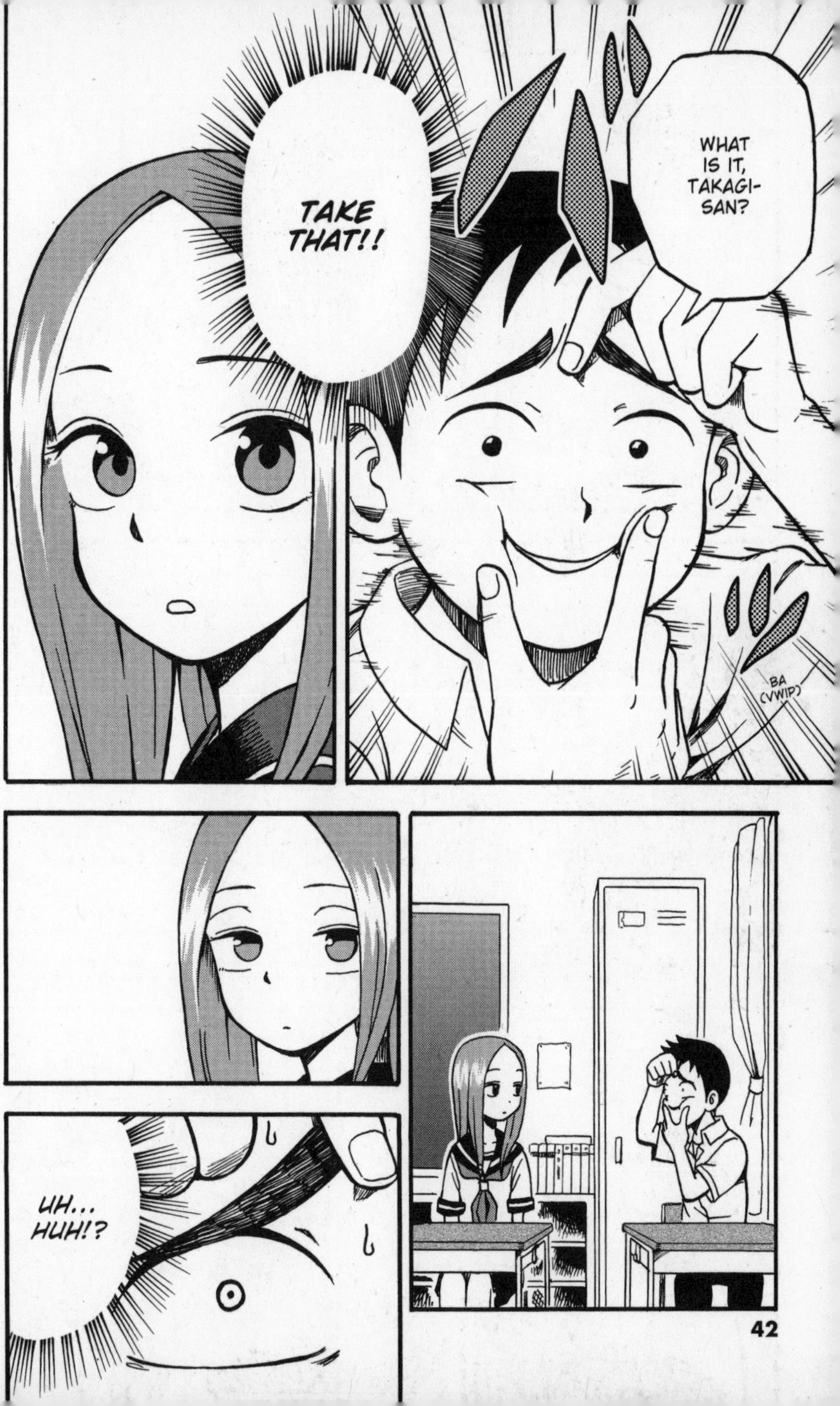
WHAT IS IT, TAKAGI-SAN?
BA (VWIP)
TAKE THAT!!
UH... HUH!?

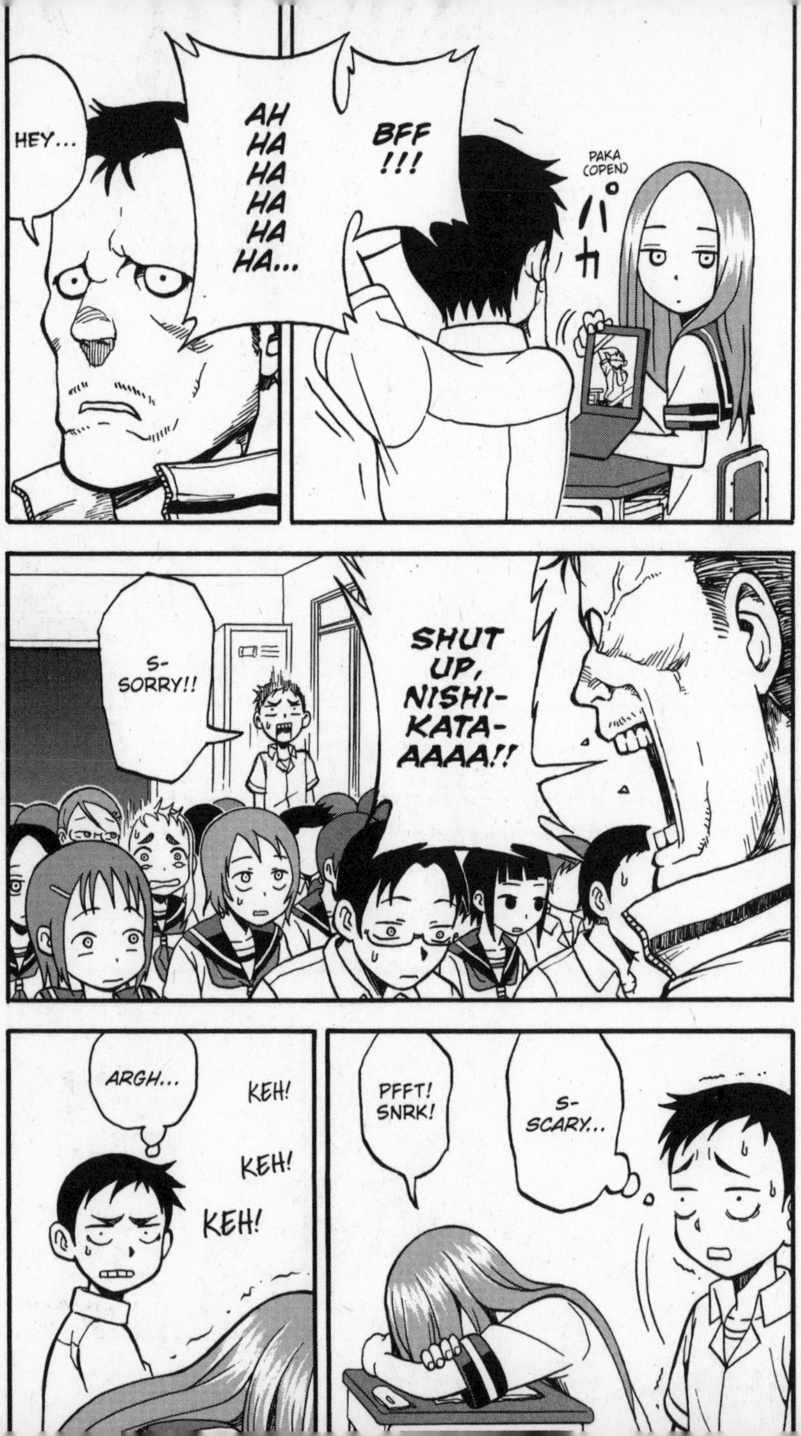
PAKA (OPEN)
パカ
BFF!!!
AH HA HA HA HA HA...
HEY...
SHUT UP, NISHI-KATA-AAAA!!
S-SORRY!!
S-SCARY...
PFFT! SNRK!
KEH!
KEH!
KEH!
ARGH...

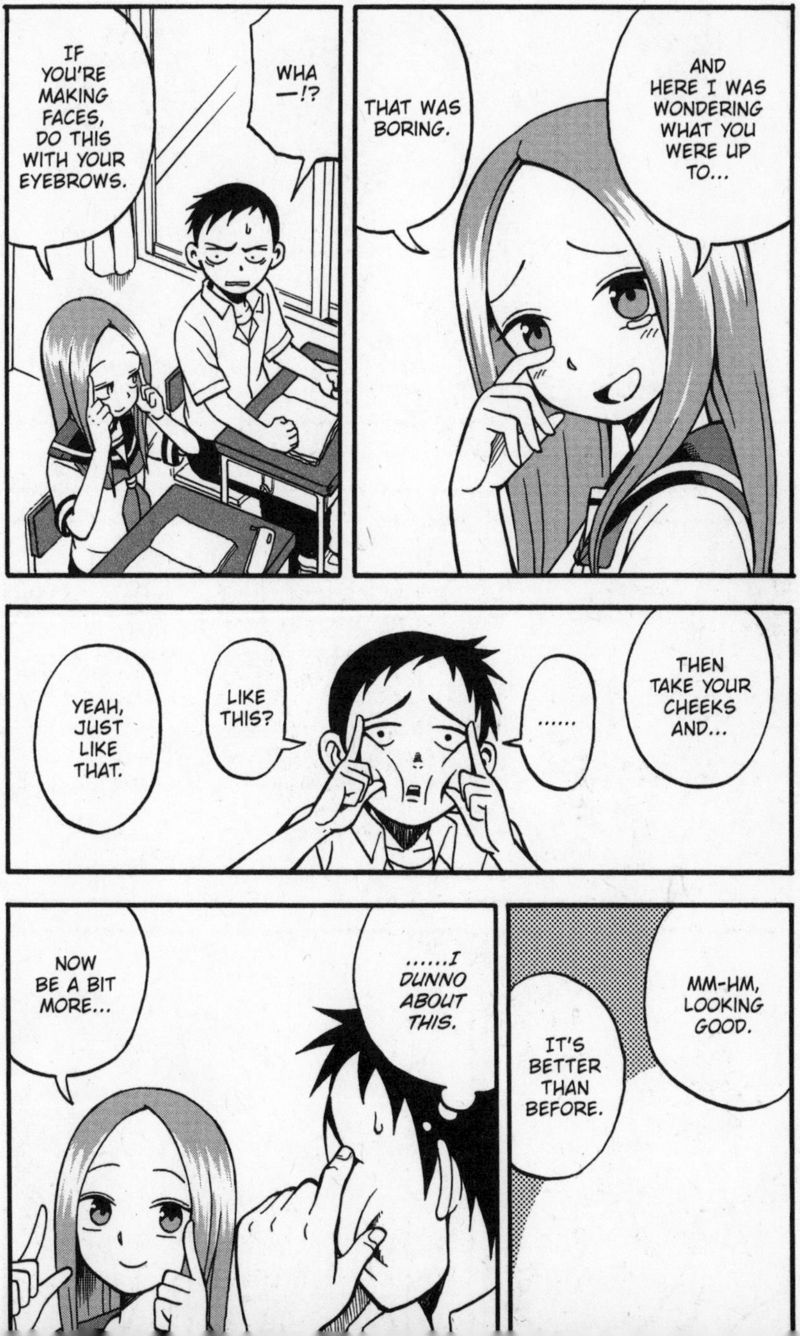
AND HERE I WAS WONDERING WHAT YOU WERE UP TO...
THAT WAS BORING.
WHA—!?
IF YOU'RE MAKING FACES, DO THIS WITH YOUR EYEBROWS.
THEN TAKE YOUR CHEEKS AND...
......
LIKE THIS?
YEAH, JUST LIKE THAT.
MM-HM, LOOKING GOOD.
IT'S BETTER THAN BEFORE.
......I DUNNO ABOUT THIS.
NOW BE A BIT MORE...

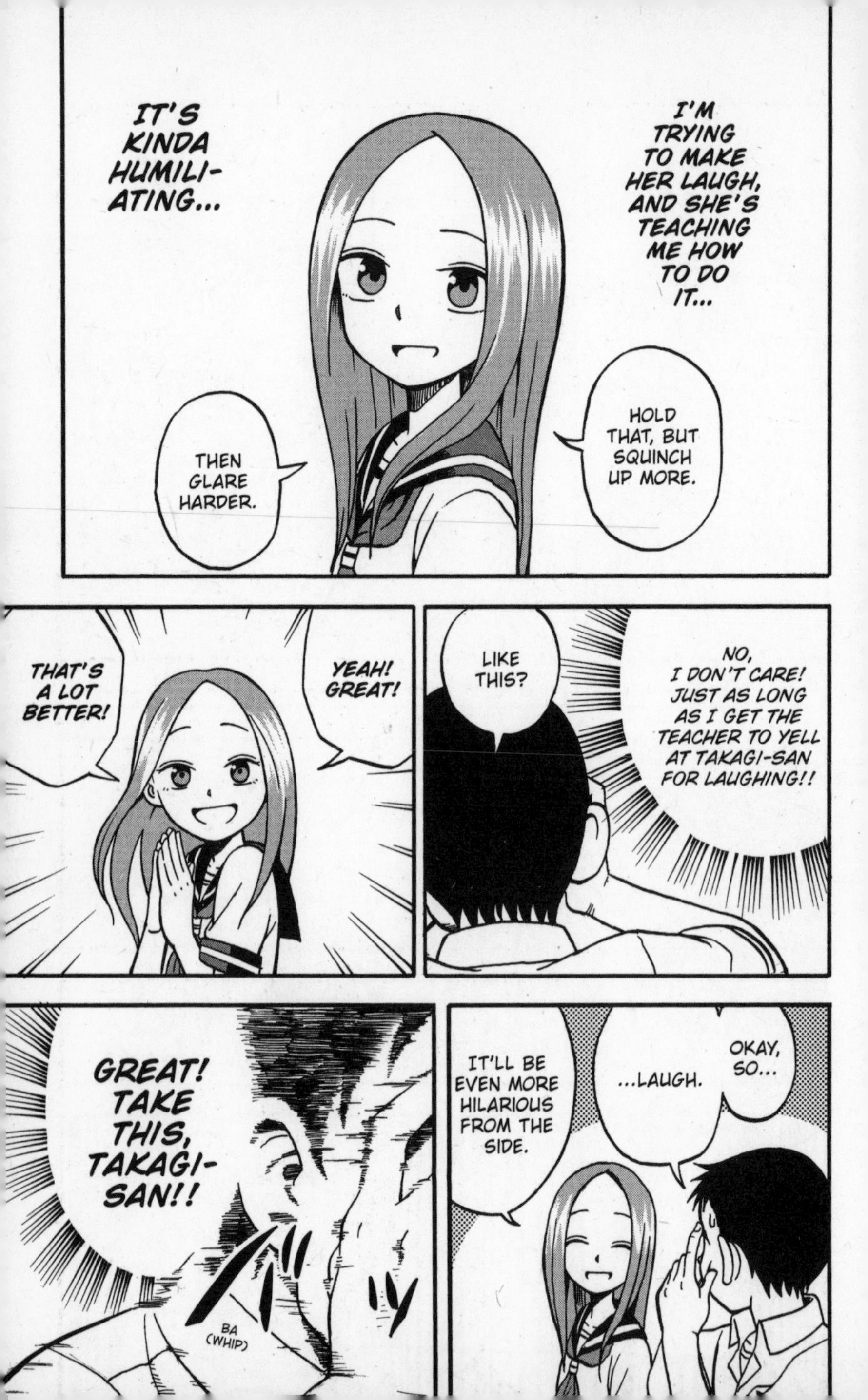
I'M TRYING TO MAKE HER LAUGH, AND SHE'S TEACHING ME HOW TO DO IT...
IT'S KINDA HUMILIATING...
HOLD THAT, BUT SQUINCH UP MORE.
THEN GLARE HARDER.
NO, I DON'T CARE! JUST AS LONG AS I GET THE TEACHER TO YELL AT TAKAGI-SAN FOR LAUGHING!!
LIKE THIS?
YEAH! GREAT!
THAT'S A LOT BETTER!
OKAY, SO...
...LAUGH.
IT'LL BE EVEN MORE HILARIOUS FROM THE SIDE.
GREAT! TAKE THIS, TAKAGI-SAN!!
BA (WHIP)

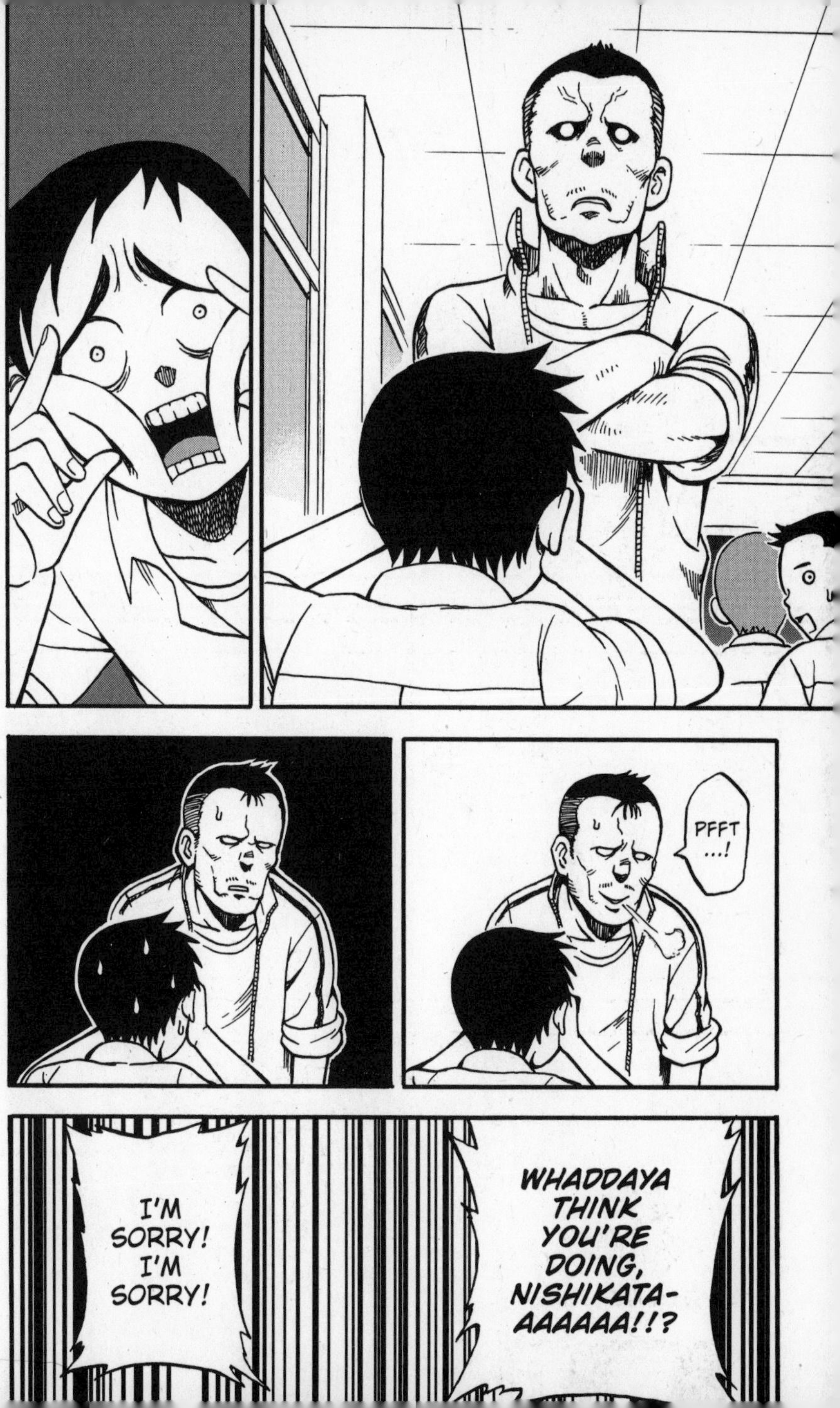
PFFT ...!
WHADDAYA THINK YOU'RE DOING, NISHIKATA-AAAAAA!!?
I'M SORRY! I'M SORRY!

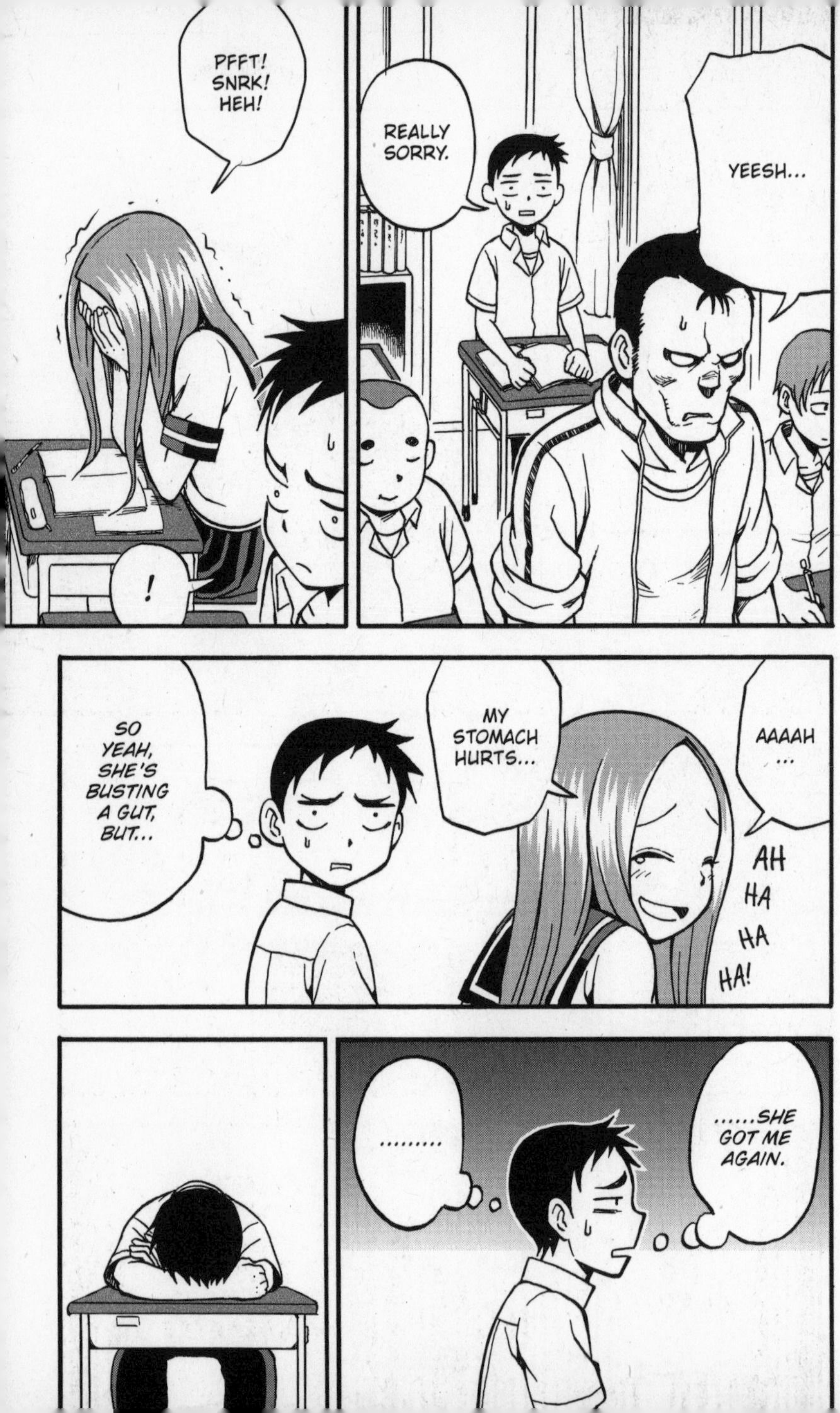
YEESH...
REALLY SORRY.
PFFT! SNRK! HEH!
!
AAAAH...
AH HA HA HA!
MY STOMACH HURTS...
SO YEAH, SHE'S BUSTING A GUT, BUT...
......SHE GOT ME AGAIN.
....

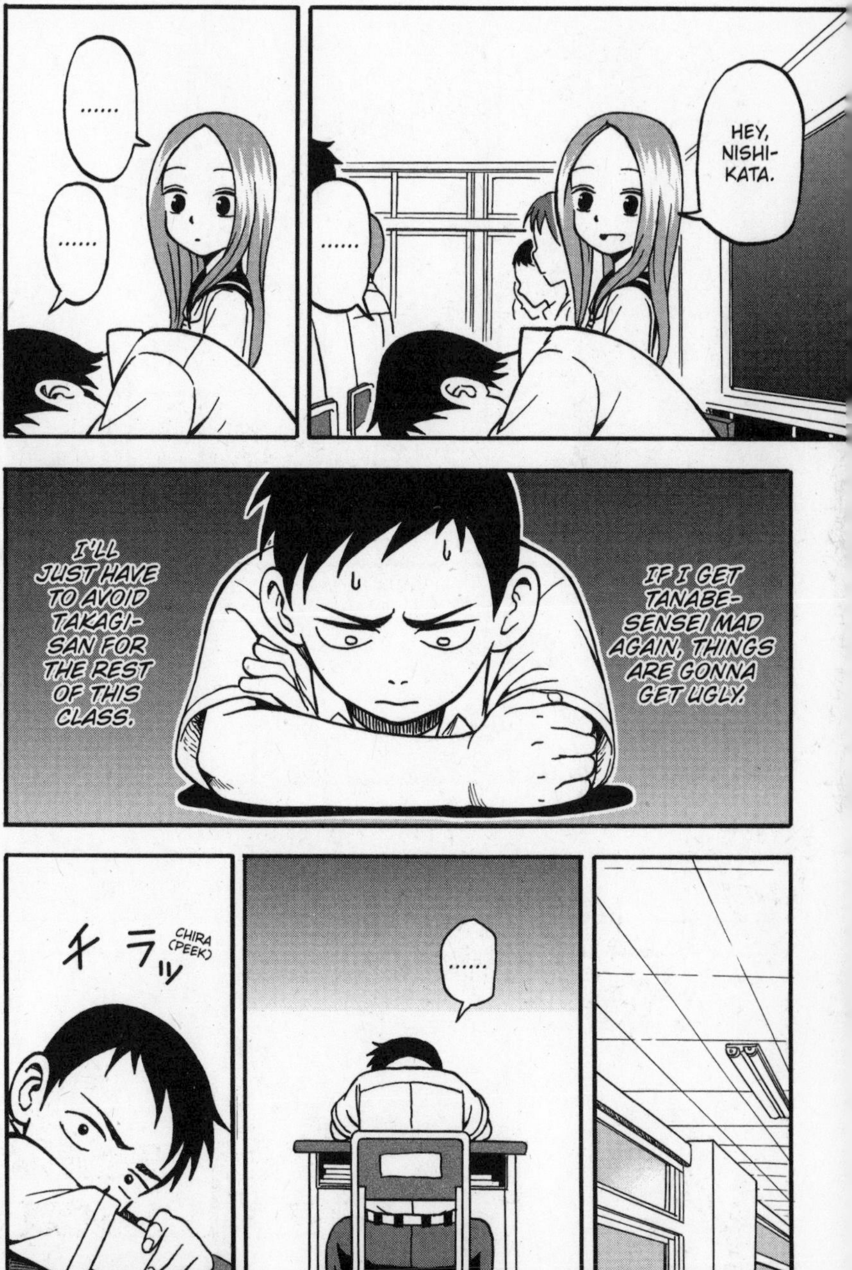

HEY, NISHI-KATA.
......
......
......
IF I GET TANABE-SENSEI MAD AGAIN, THINGS ARE GONNA GET UGLY.
I'LL JUST HAVE TO AVOID TAKAGI-SAN FOR THE REST OF THIS CLASS.
......
チラッ
CHIRA (PEEK)

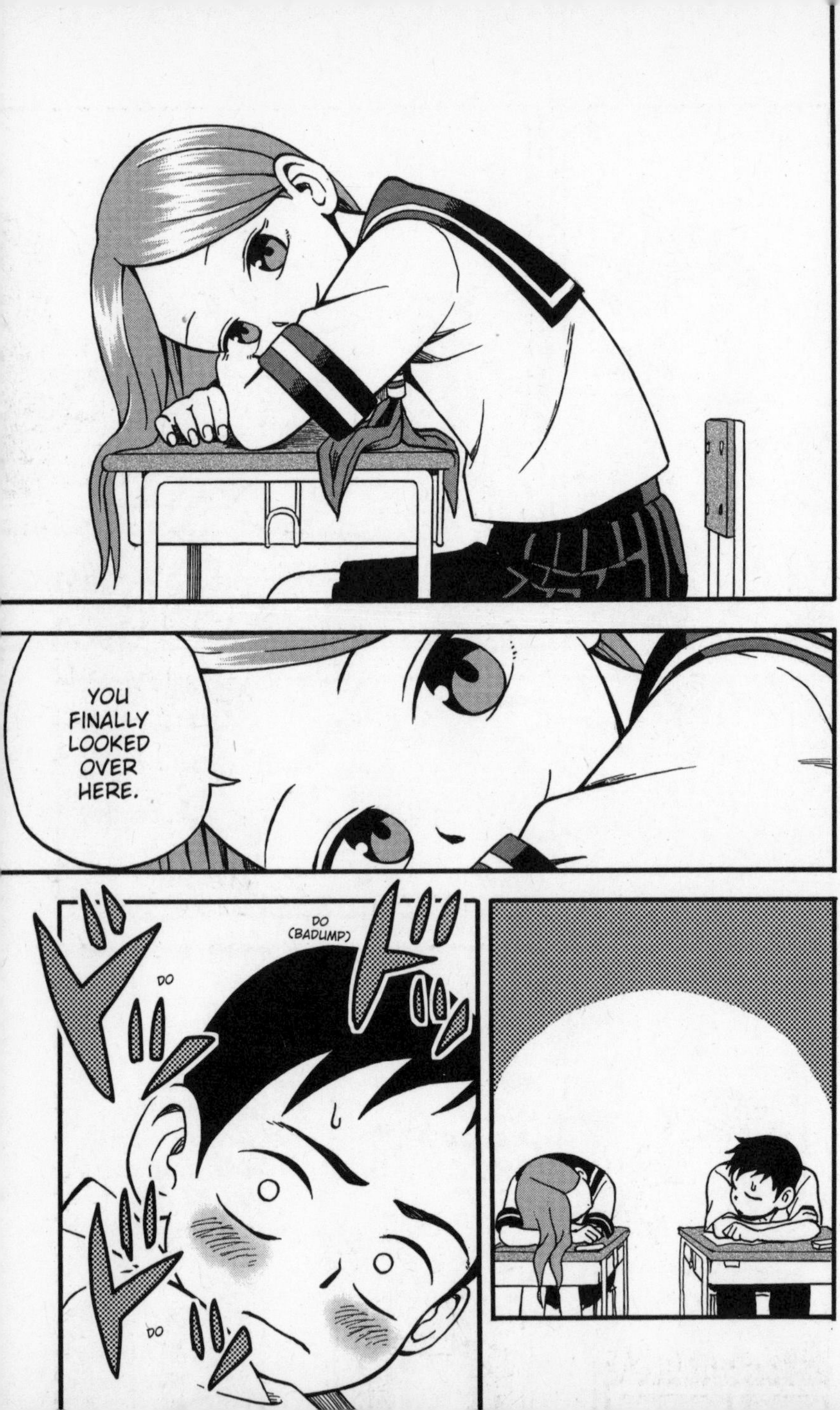
YOU FINALLY LOOKED OVER HERE.
DO (BADUMP)
DO
DO

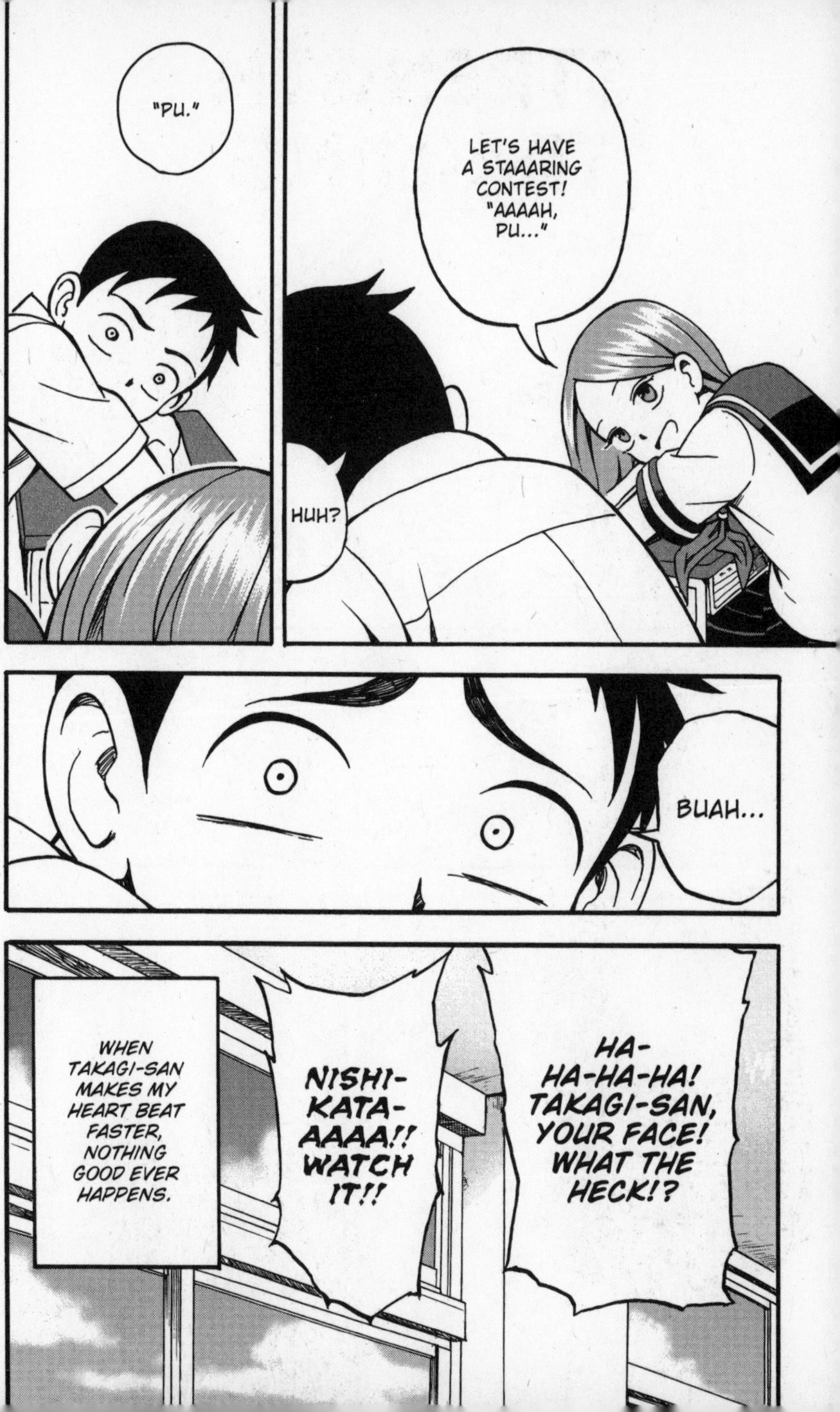
LET'S HAVE A STAAARING CONTEST! "AAAAH, PU..."
HUH?
"PU."
BUAH...
HA-HA-HA-HA! TAKAGI-SAN, YOUR FACE! WHAT THE HECK!?
NISHI-KATA-AAAA!! WATCH IT!!
WHEN TAKAGI-SAN MAKES MY HEART BEAT FASTER, NOTHING GOOD EVER HAPPENS.

STRENGTH TRAINING

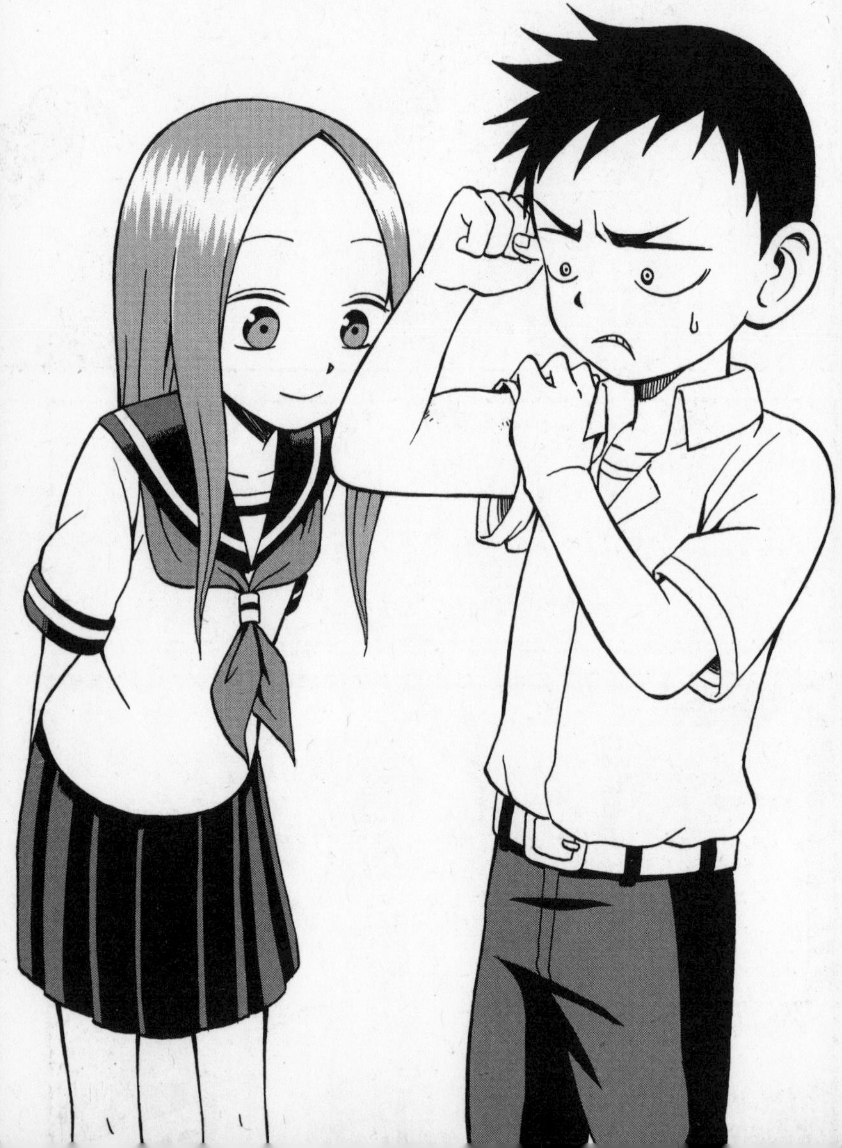

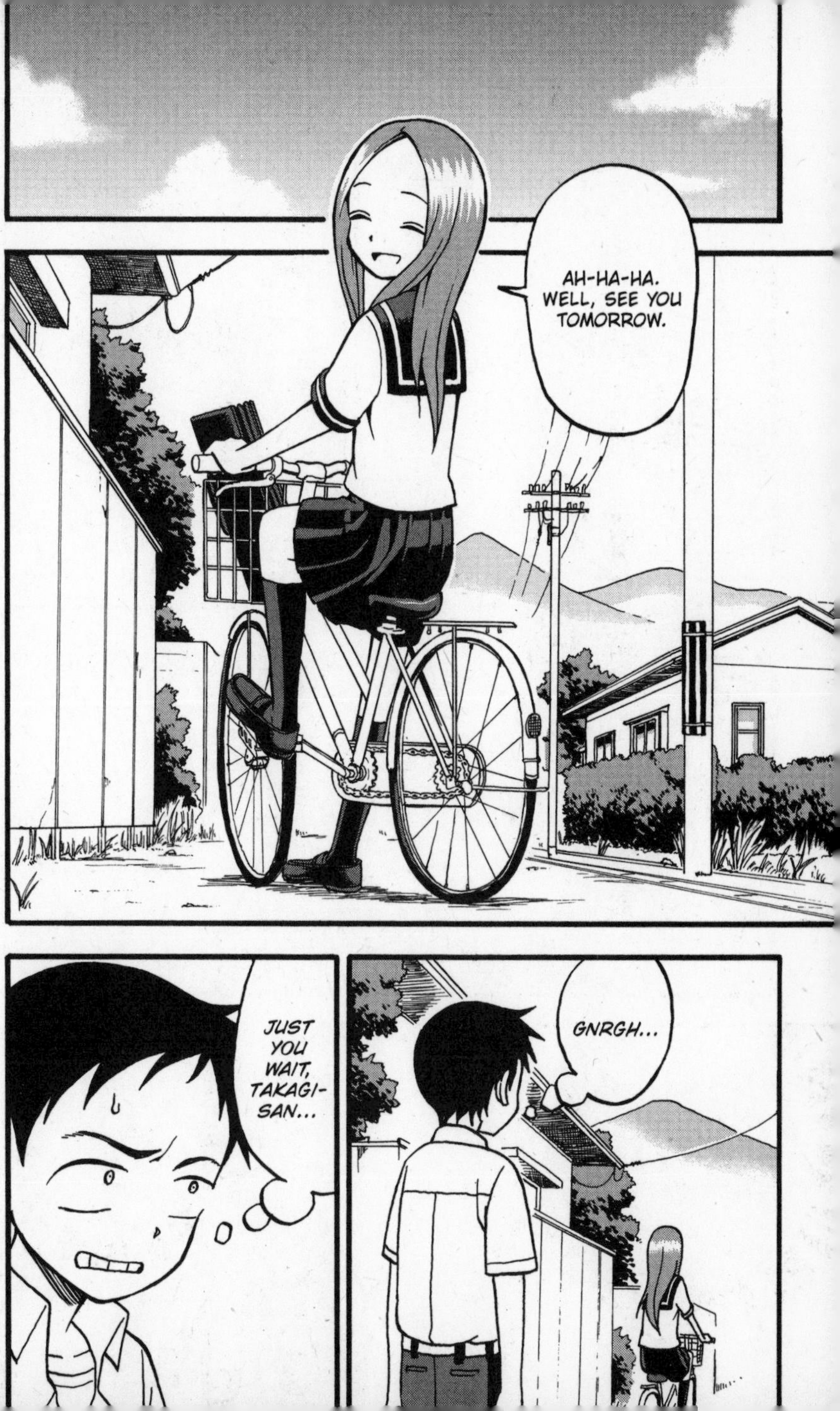
AH-HA-HA. WELL, SEE YOU TOMORROW.
GNRGH...
JUST YOU WAIT, TAKAGI-SAN...

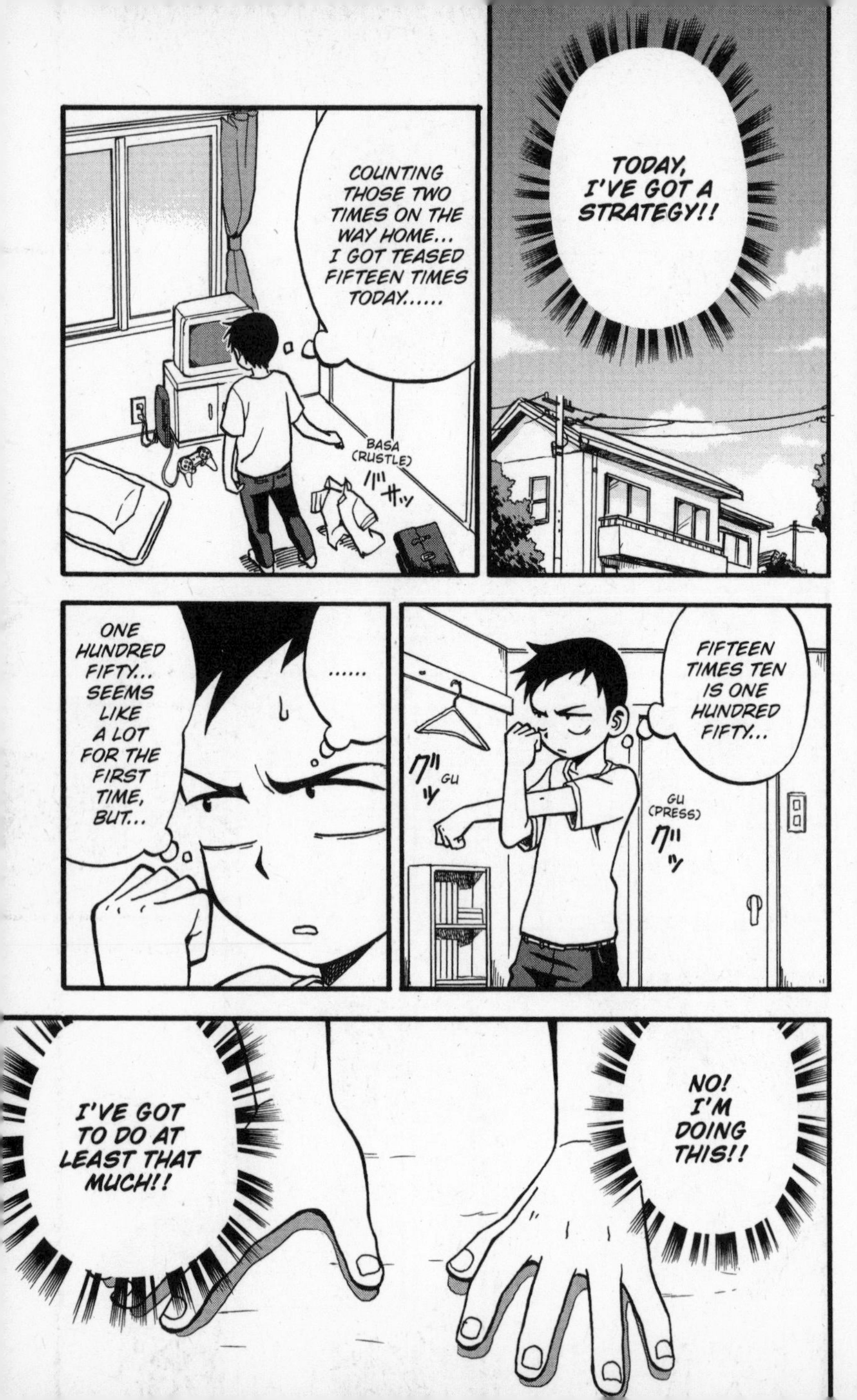
TODAY, I'VE GOT A STRATEGY!!
COUNTING THOSE TWO TIMES ON THE WAY HOME... I GOT TEASED FIFTEEN TIMES TODAY......
BASA (RUSTLE)
バサッ
FIFTEEN TIMES TEN IS ONE HUNDRED FIFTY...
GU (PRESS)
グッ
GU
グッ
......
ONE HUNDRED FIFTY... SEEMS LIKE A LOT FOR THE FIRST TIME, BUT...
NO! I'M DOING THIS!!
I'VE GOT TO DO AT LEAST THAT MUCH!!

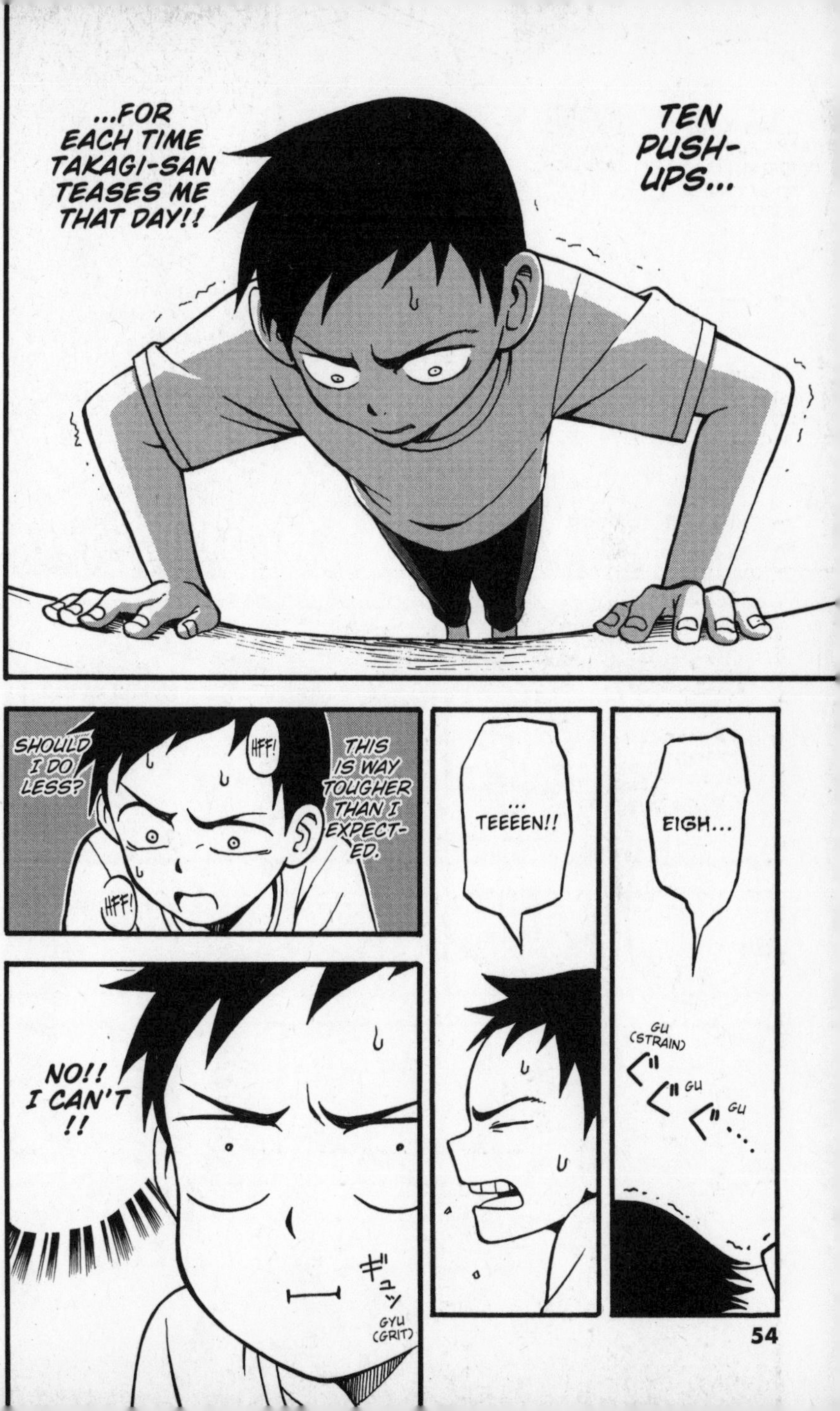

TEN PUSH-UPS...
...FOR EACH TIME TAKAGI-SAN TEASES ME THAT DAY!!
EIGH...
GU (STRAIN)
GU
GU
...TEEEEN!!
THIS IS WAY TOUGHER THAN I EXPECTED.
HFF!
HFF!
SHOULD I DO LESS?
NO!! I CAN'T!!
GYU (GRIT)

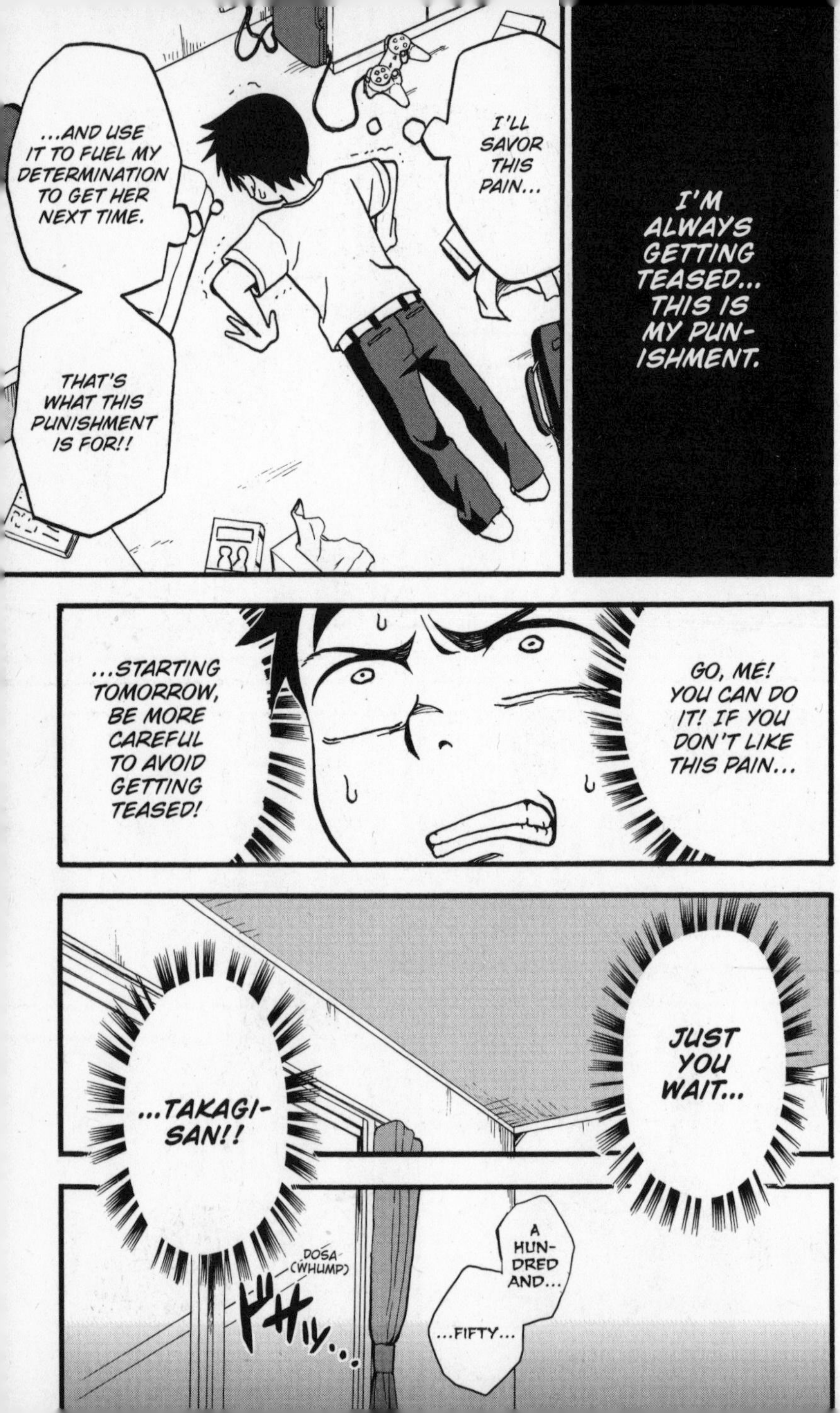
I'M ALWAYS GETTING TEASED... THIS IS MY PUN-ISHMENT.
I'LL SAVOR THIS PAIN...
...AND USE IT TO FUEL MY DETERMINATION TO GET HER NEXT TIME.
THAT'S WHAT THIS PUNISHMENT IS FOR!!
GO, ME! YOU CAN DO IT! IF YOU DON'T LIKE THIS PAIN...
...STARTING TOMORROW, BE MORE CAREFUL TO AVOID GETTING TEASED!
JUST YOU WAIT...
...TAKAGI-SAN!!
A HUN-DRED AND...
...FIFTY...
DOSA (WHUMP)

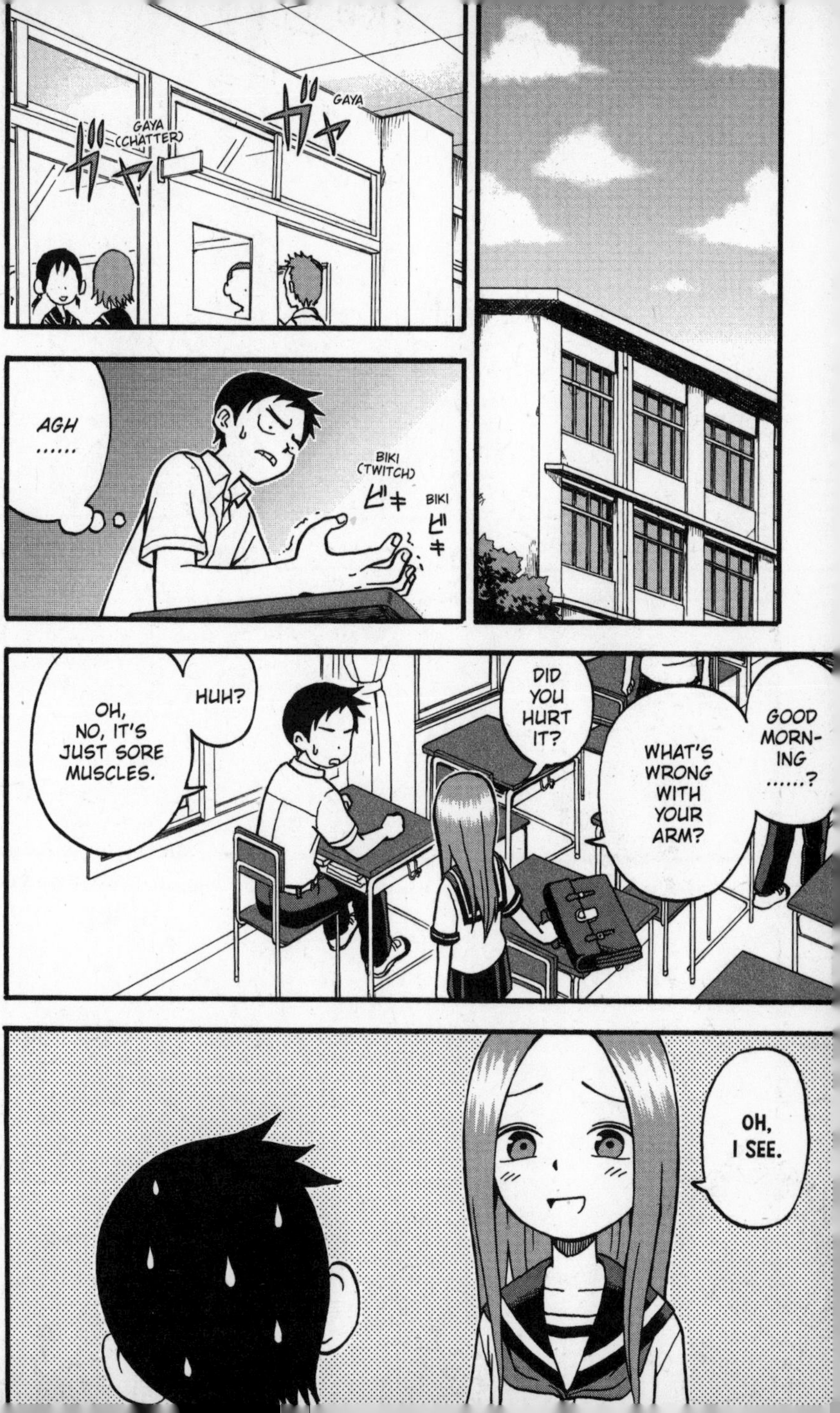
GAYA
ガヤ
GAYA (CHATTER)
ガヤ
AGH ......
BIKI (TWITCH)
ビキ
BIKI
ビキ
GOOD MORNING ......?
WHAT'S WRONG WITH YOUR ARM?
DID YOU HURT IT?
HUH?
OH, NO, IT'S JUST SORE MUSCLES.
OH, I SEE.

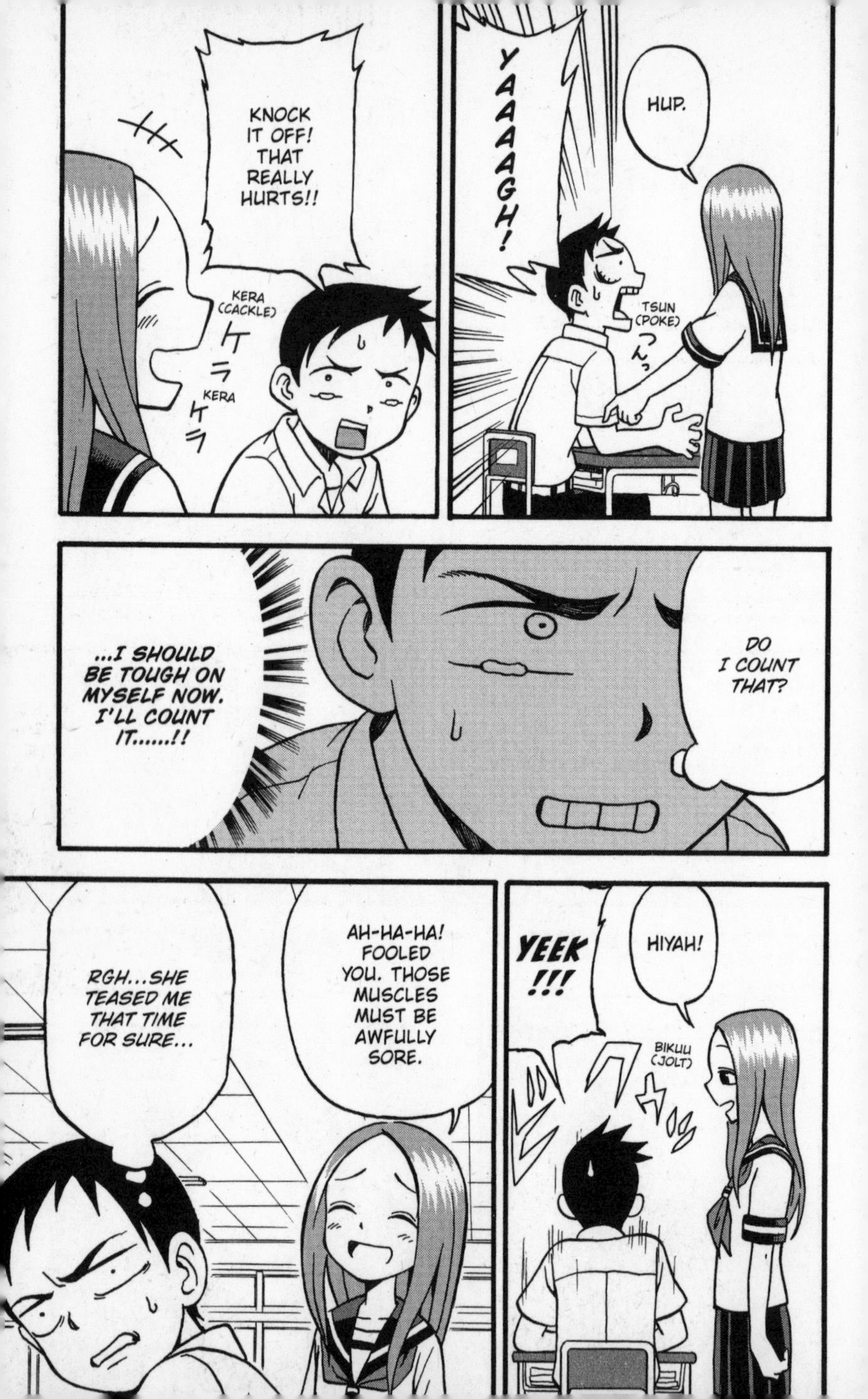
HUP.
TSUN (POKE)
YAAAAAGH!
KNOCK IT OFF! THAT REALLY HURTS!!
KERA (CACKLE)
KERA
DO I COUNT THAT?
...I SHOULD BE TOUGH ON MYSELF NOW. I'LL COUNT IT......!!
HIYAH!
YEEK!!!
BIKUU (JOLT)
AH-HA-HA! FOOLED YOU. THOSE MUSCLES MUST BE AWFULLY SORE.
RGH...SHE TEASED ME THAT TIME FOR SURE...

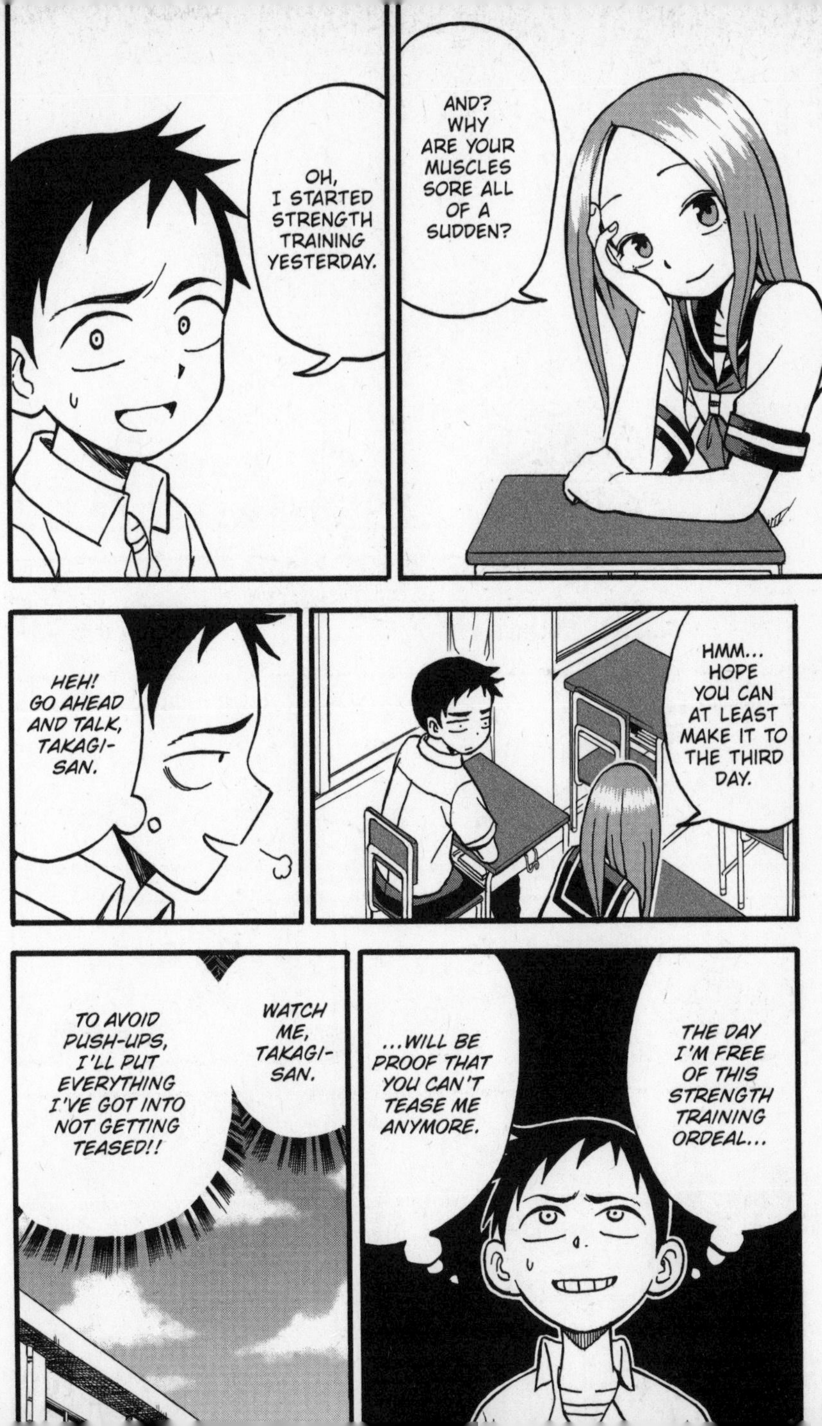
AND? WHY ARE YOUR MUSCLES SORE ALL OF A SUDDEN?
OH, I STARTED STRENGTH TRAINING YESTERDAY.
HMM... HOPE YOU CAN AT LEAST MAKE IT TO THE THIRD DAY.
HEH! GO AHEAD AND TALK, TAKAGI-SAN.
THE DAY I'M FREE OF THIS STRENGTH TRAINING ORDEAL...
...WILL BE PROOF THAT YOU CAN'T TEASE ME ANYMORE.
WATCH ME, TAKAGI-SAN.
TO AVOID PUSH-UPS, I'LL PUT EVERYTHING I'VE GOT INTO NOT GETTING TEASED!!

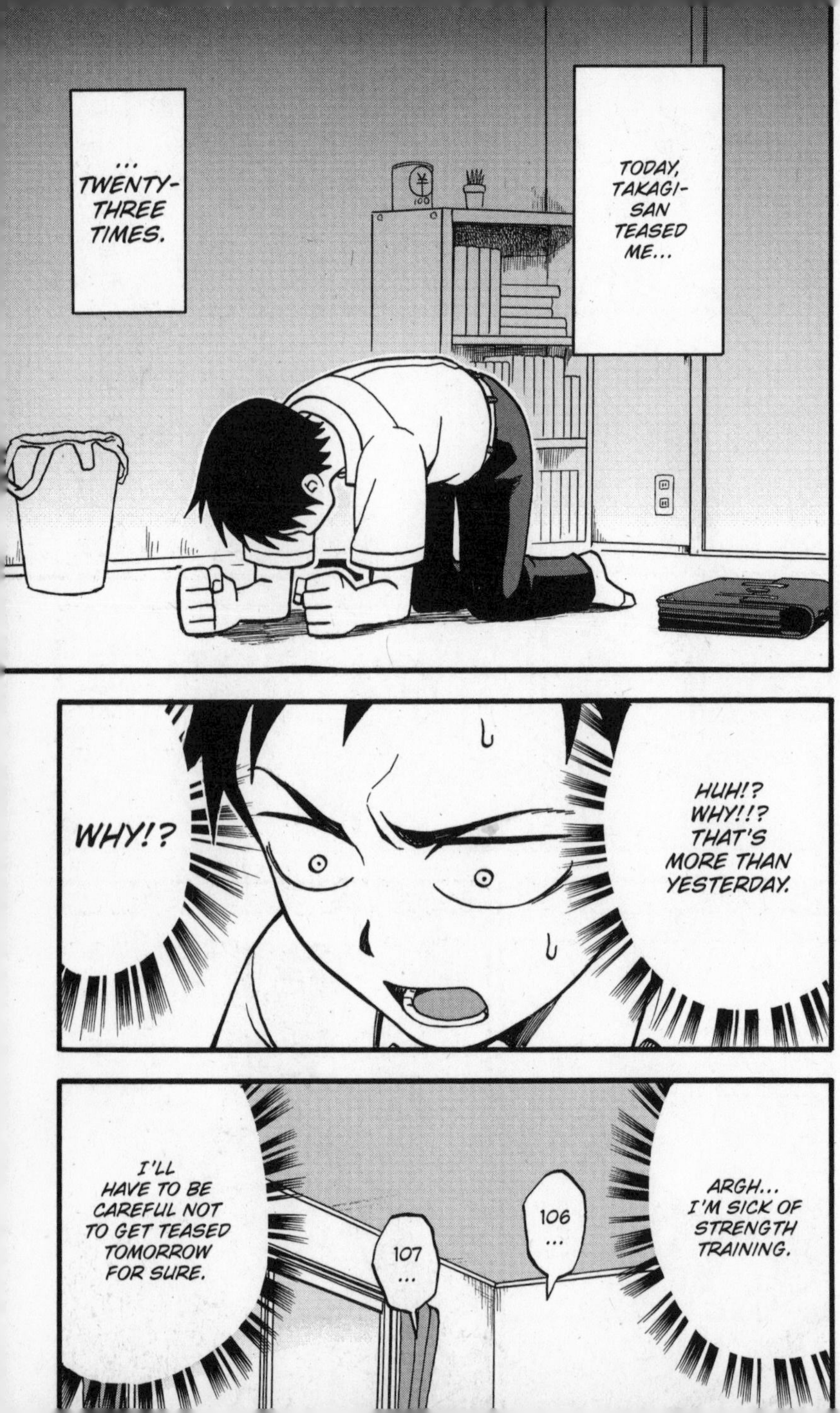
TODAY, TAKAGI-SAN TEASED ME...
...TWENTY-THREE TIMES.
HUH!? WHY!!? THAT'S MORE THAN YESTERDAY.
WHY!?
ARGH... I'M SICK OF STRENGTH TRAINING.
106 ...
107 ...
I'LL HAVE TO BE CAREFUL NOT TO GET TEASED TOMORROW FOR SURE.

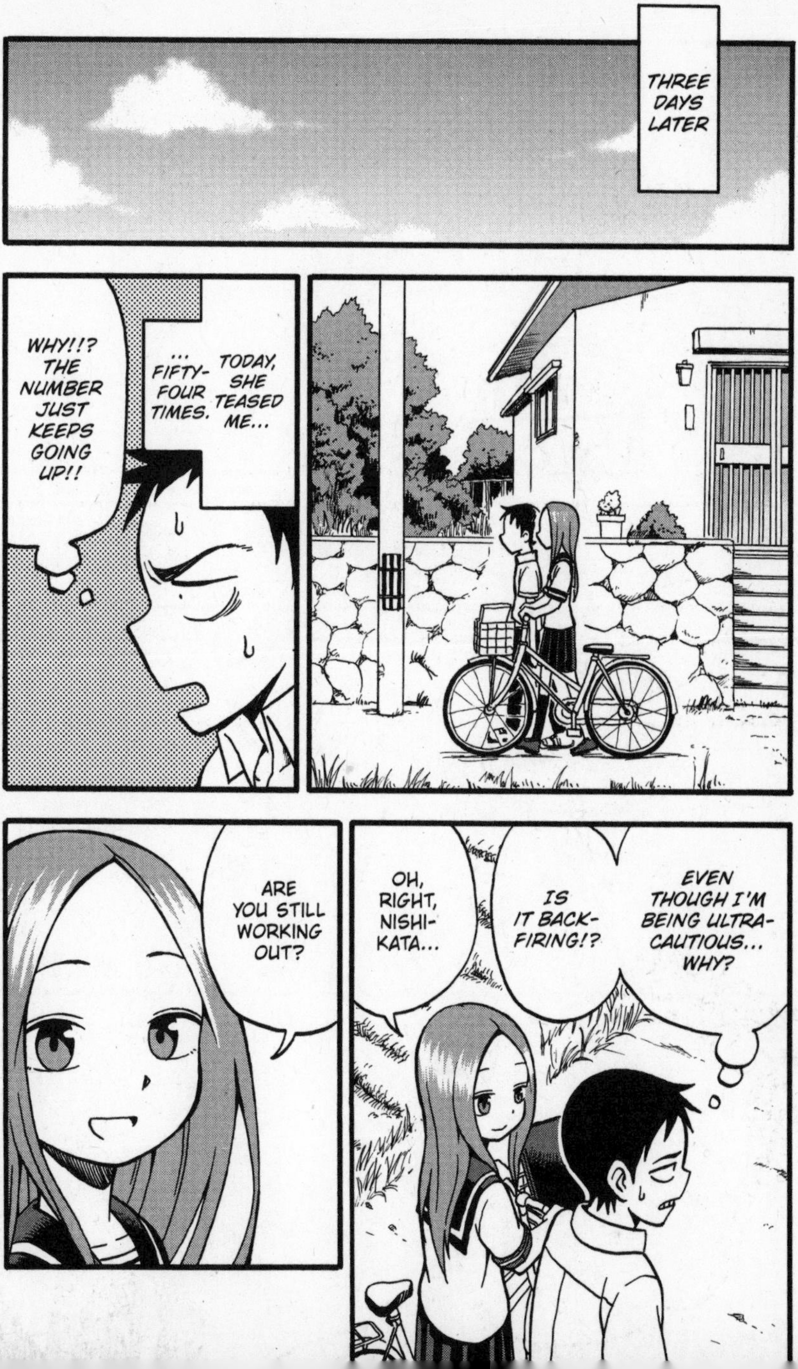
THREE DAYS LATER
TODAY, SHE TEASED ME...
...FIFTY-FOUR TIMES.
WHY!!? THE NUMBER JUST KEEPS GOING UP!!
EVEN THOUGH I'M BEING ULTRA-CAUTIOUS... WHY?
IS IT BACK-FIRING!?
OH, RIGHT, NISHI-KATA...
ARE YOU STILL WORKING OUT?

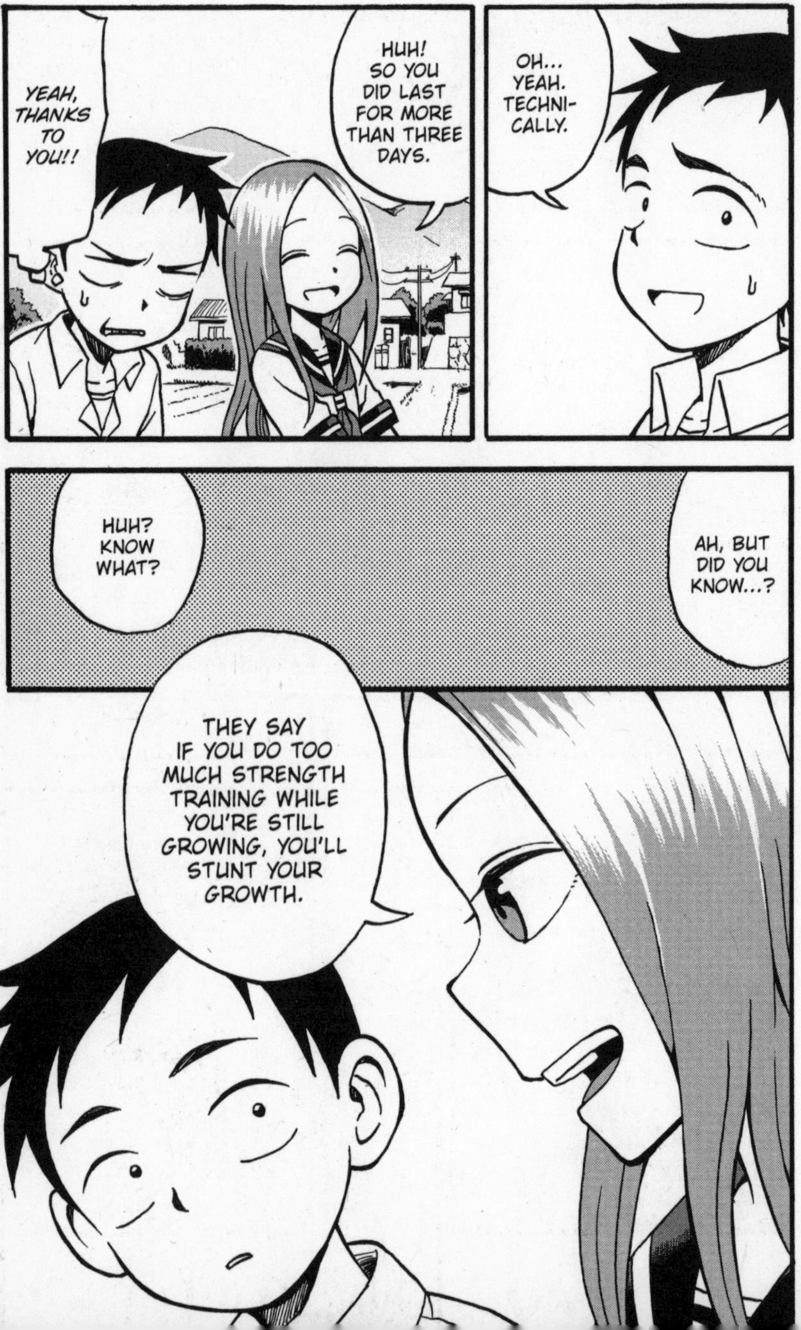
OH... YEAH. TECHNICALLY.
HUH! SO YOU DID LAST FOR MORE THAN THREE DAYS.
YEAH, THANKS TO YOU!!
AH, BUT DID YOU KNOW...?
HUH? KNOW WHAT?
THEY SAY IF YOU DO TOO MUCH STRENGTH TRAINING WHILE YOU'RE STILL GROWING, YOU'LL STUNT YOUR GROWTH.

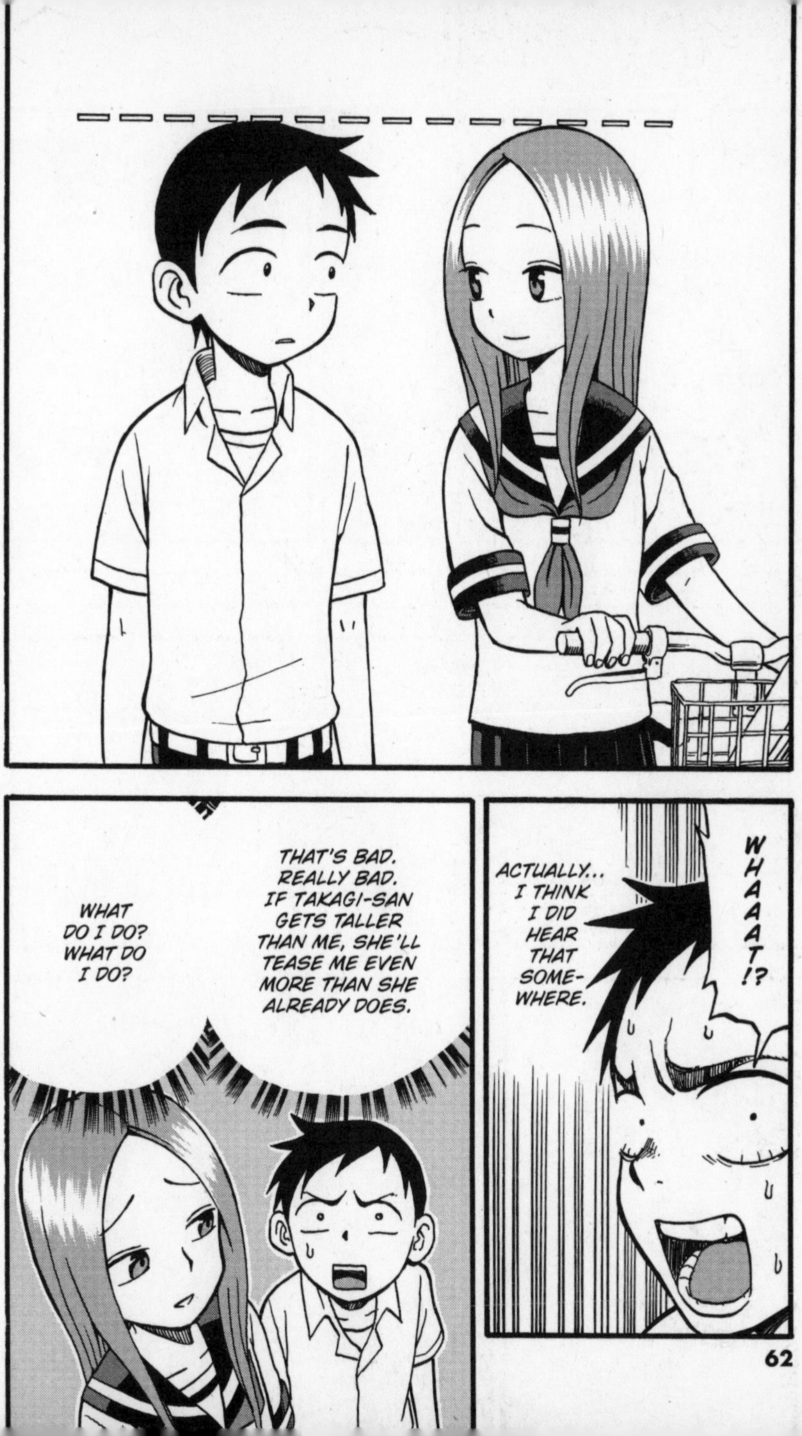
WHAAAAT!?
ACTUALLY... I THINK I DID HEAR THAT SOMEWHERE.
THAT'S BAD. REALLY BAD. IF TAKAGI-SAN GETS TALLER THAN ME, SHE'LL TEASE ME EVEN MORE THAN SHE ALREADY DOES.
WHAT DO I DO? WHAT DO I DO?

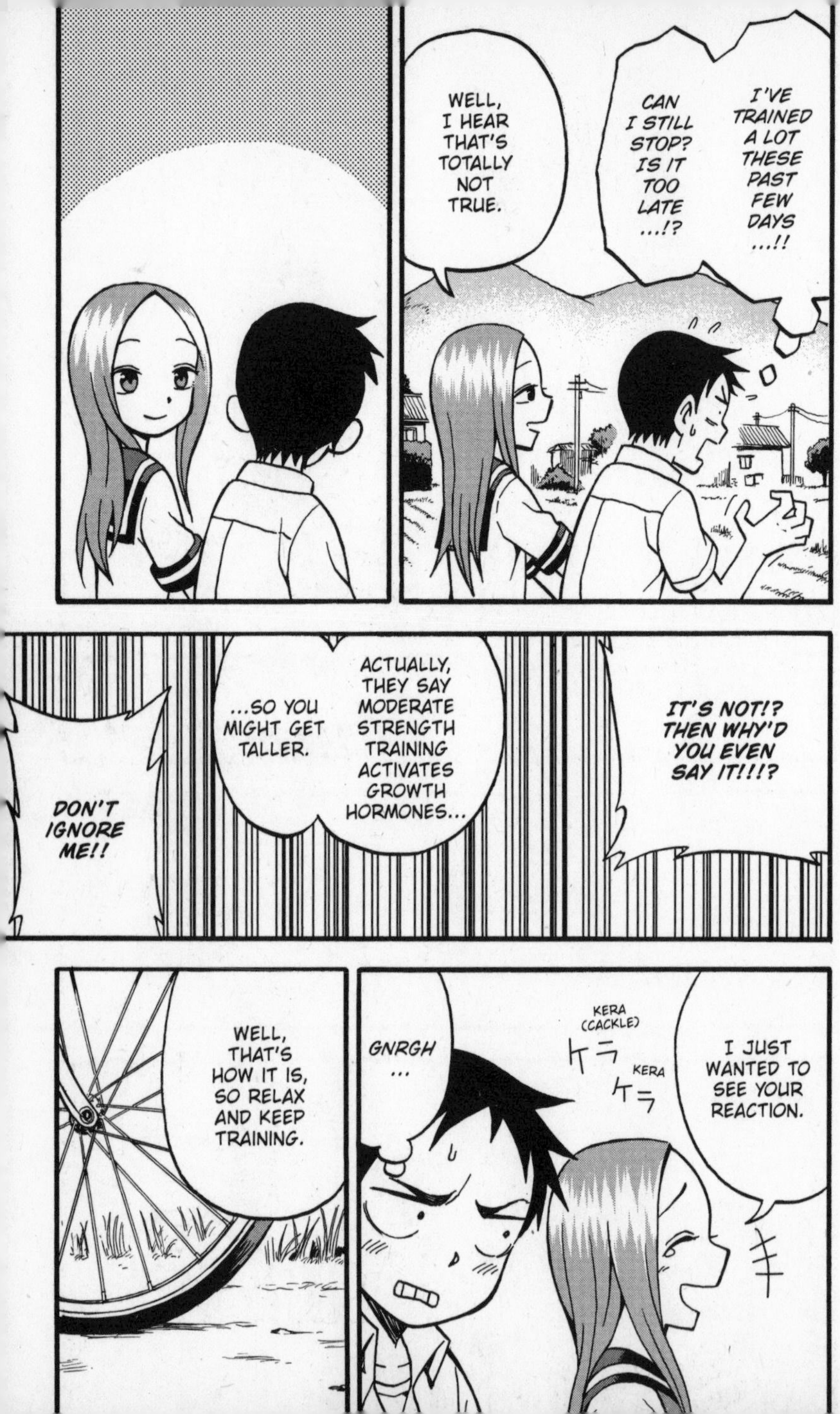
I'VE TRAINED A LOT THESE PAST FEW DAYS ...!!
CAN I STILL STOP? IS IT TOO LATE ...!?
WELL, I HEAR THAT'S TOTALLY NOT TRUE.
IT'S NOT!? THEN WHY'D YOU EVEN SAY IT!!!?
ACTUALLY, THEY SAY MODERATE STRENGTH TRAINING ACTIVATES GROWTH HORMONES...
...SO YOU MIGHT GET TALLER.
DON'T IGNORE ME!!
I JUST WANTED TO SEE YOUR REACTION.
KERA (CACKLE)
ケラ
KERA
ケラ
GNRGH ...
WELL, THAT'S HOW IT IS, SO RELAX AND KEEP TRAINING.

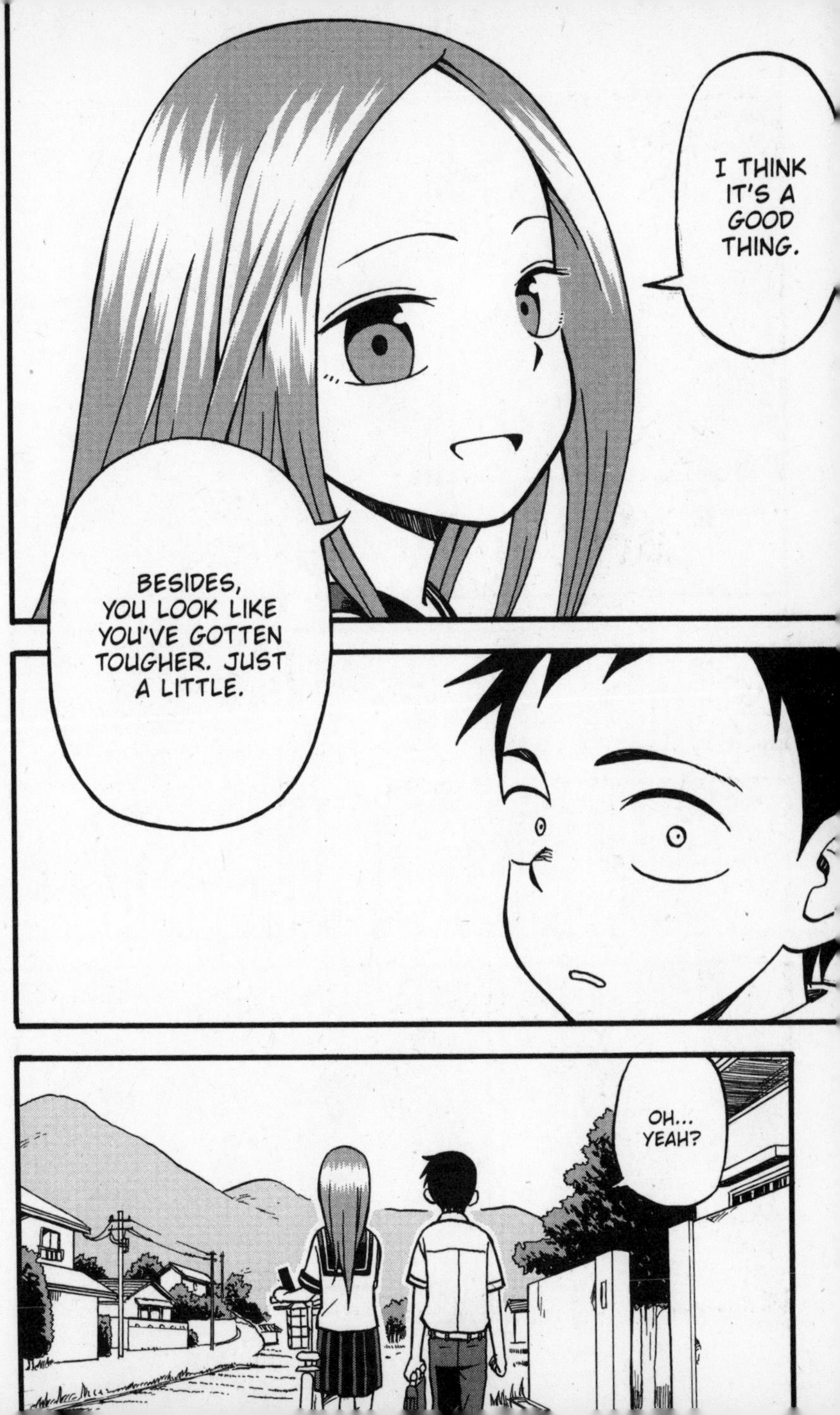
I THINK IT'S A GOOD THING.
BESIDES, YOU LOOK LIKE YOU'VE GOTTEN TOUGHER. JUST A LITTLE.
OH... YEAH?

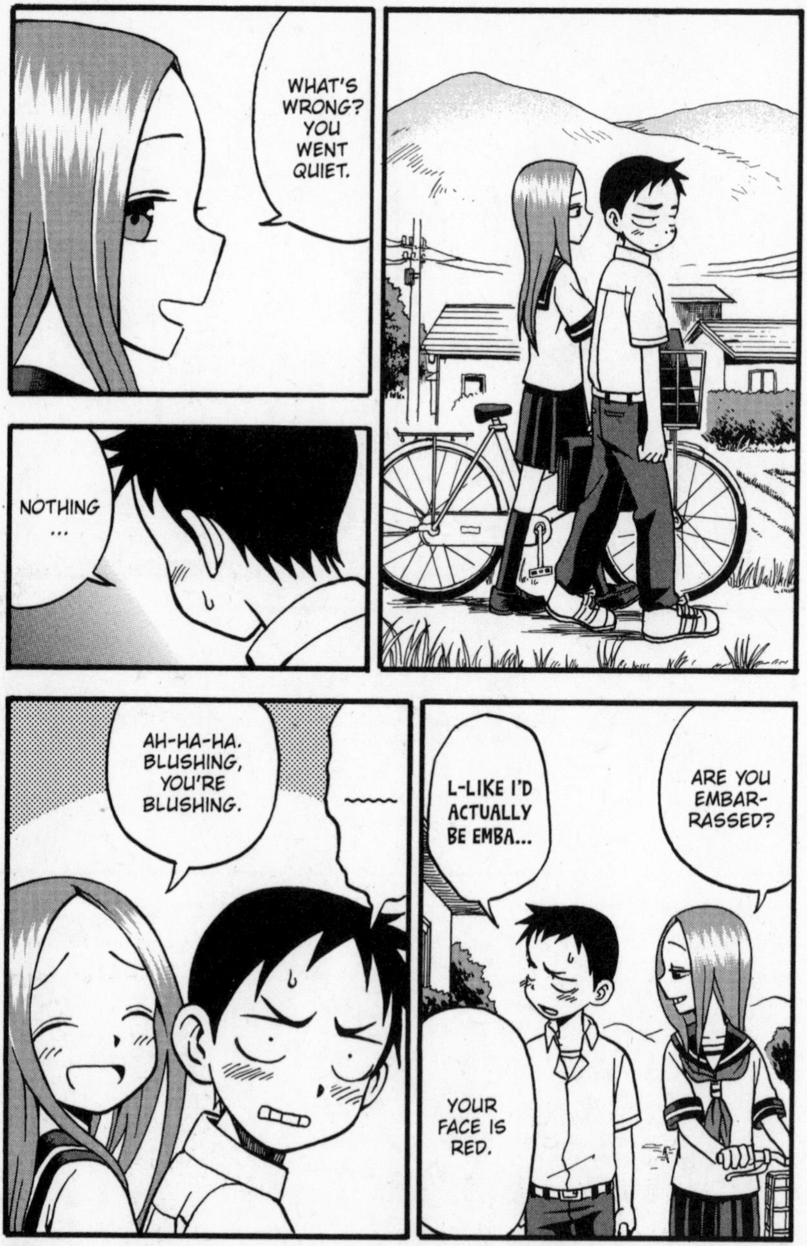
WHAT'S WRONG? YOU WENT QUIET.
NOTHING ...
ARE YOU EMBAR-RASSED?
L-LIKE I'D ACTUALLY BE EMBA...
YOUR FACE IS RED.
~~~~
AH-HA-HA. BLUSHING, YOU'RE BLUSHING.
~~~~

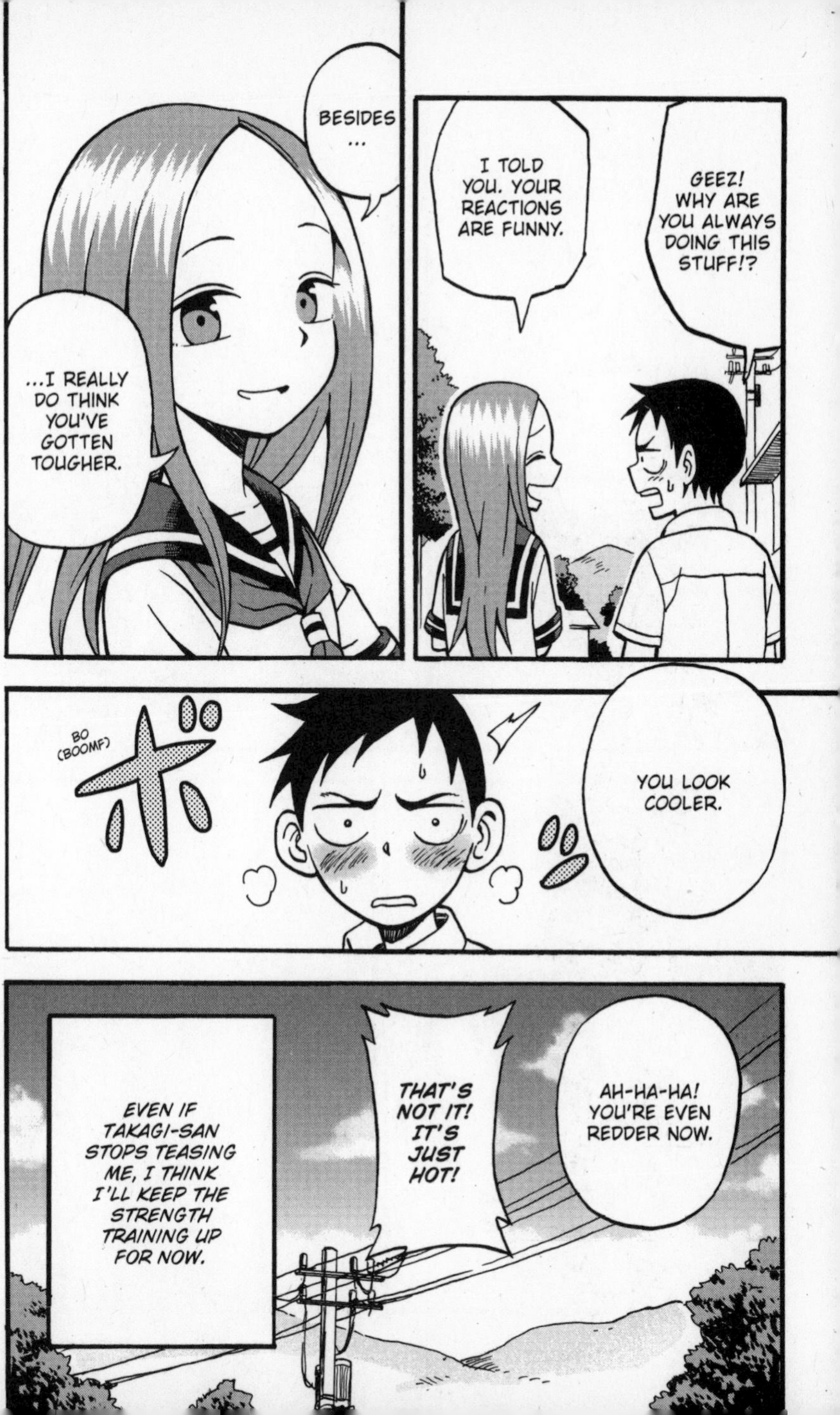
GEEZ! WHY ARE YOU ALWAYS DOING THIS STUFF!?
I TOLD YOU. YOUR REACTIONS ARE FUNNY.
BESIDES...
...I REALLY DO THINK YOU'VE GOTTEN TOUGHER.
YOU LOOK COOLER.
BO (BOOMF)
AH-HA-HA! YOU'RE EVEN REDDER NOW.
THAT'S NOT IT! IT'S JUST HOT!
EVEN IF TAKAGI-SAN STOPS TEASING ME, I THINK I'LL KEEP THE STRENGTH TRAINING UP FOR NOW.

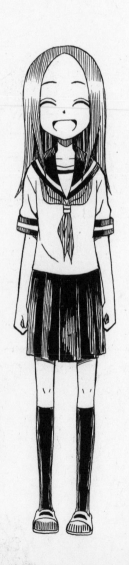

Teasing Master
Takagi-san

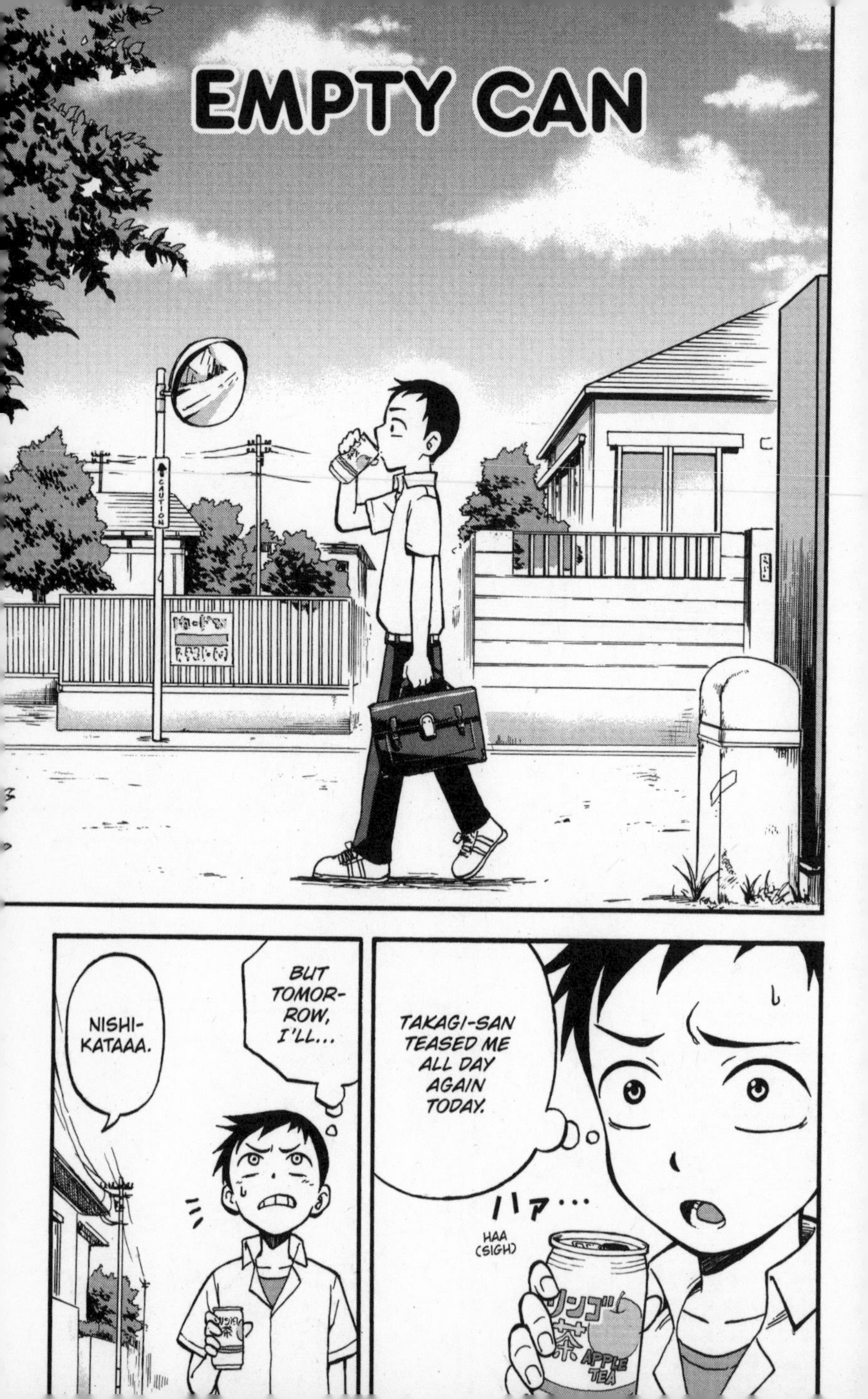
EMPTY CAN
CAUTION
TAKAGI-SAN TEASED ME ALL DAY AGAIN TODAY.
ハァ…
HAA (SIGH)
リンゴ茶
APPLE TEA
BUT TOMORROW, I'LL...
NISHI-KATAAA.

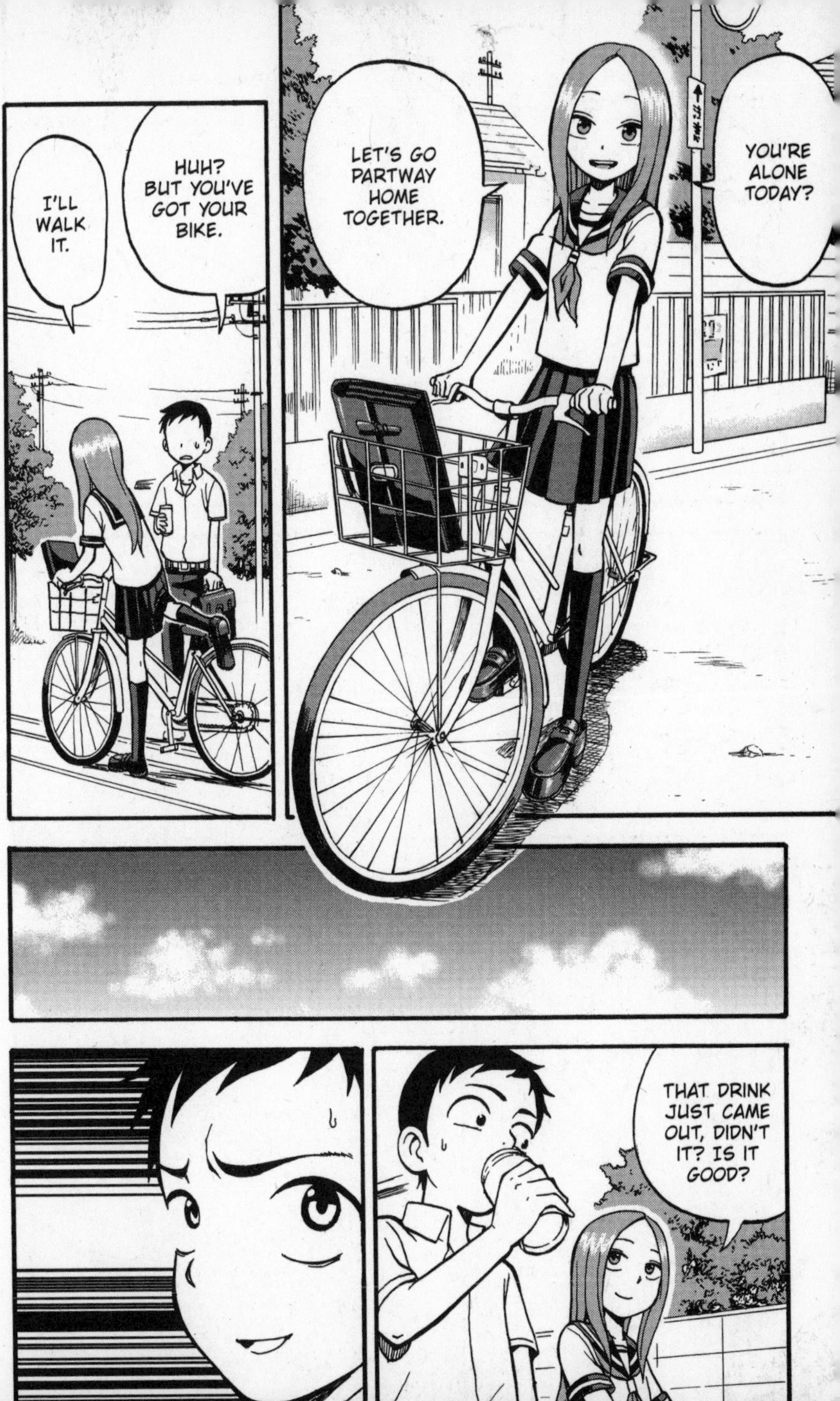
YOU'RE ALONE TODAY?
LET'S GO PARTWAY HOME TOGETHER.
HUH? BUT YOU'VE GOT YOUR BIKE.
I'LL WALK IT.
THAT DRINK JUST CAME OUT, DIDN'T IT? IS IT GOOD?

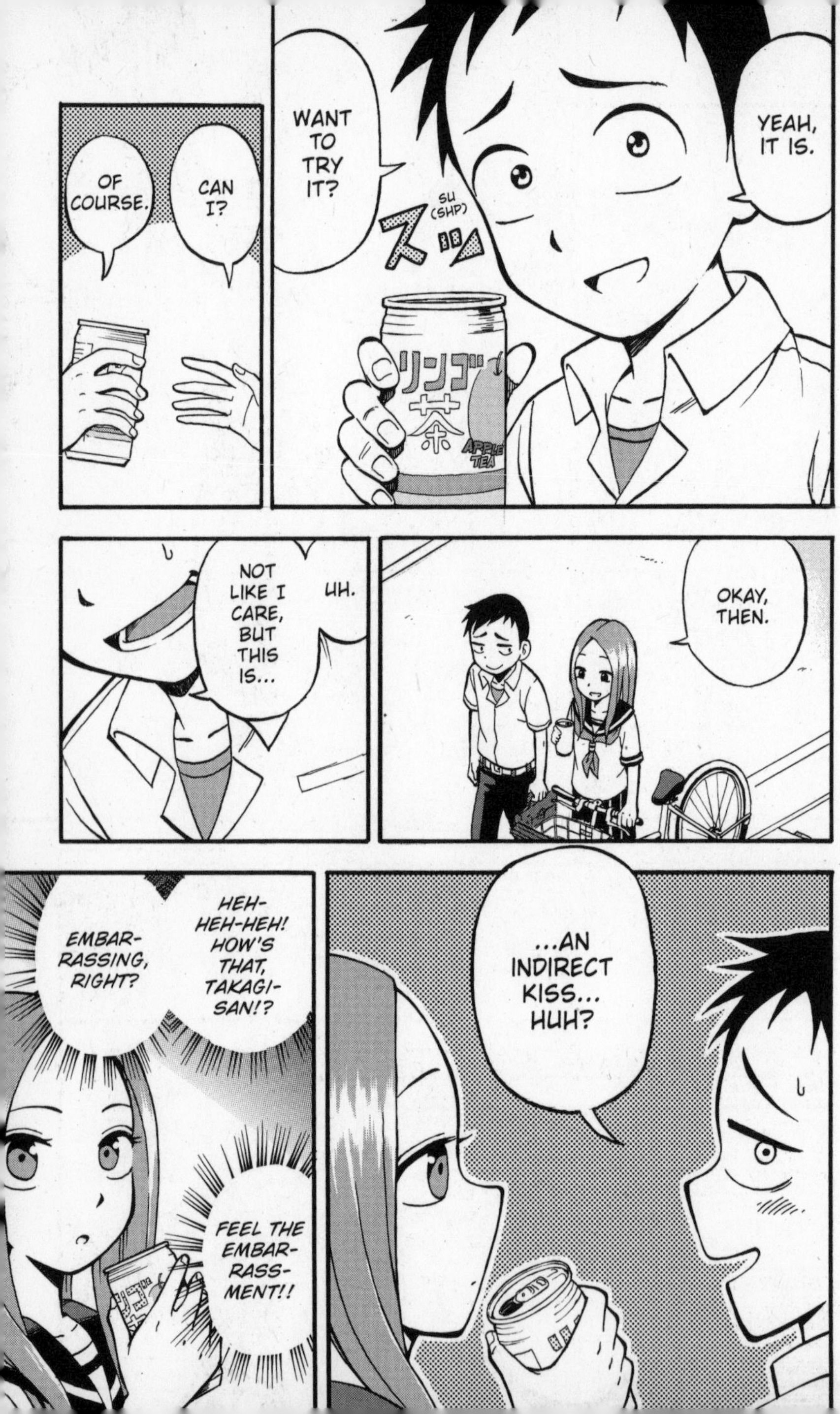
YEAH, IT IS.
WANT TO TRY IT?
SU (SHP)
リンゴ茶 APPLE TEA
CAN I?
OF COURSE.
OKAY, THEN.
UH.
NOT LIKE I CARE, BUT THIS IS...
...AN INDIRECT KISS... HUH?
HEH-HEH-HEH! HOW'S THAT, TAKAGI-SAN!?
EMBAR-RASSING, RIGHT?
FEEL THE EMBAR-RASS-MENT!!

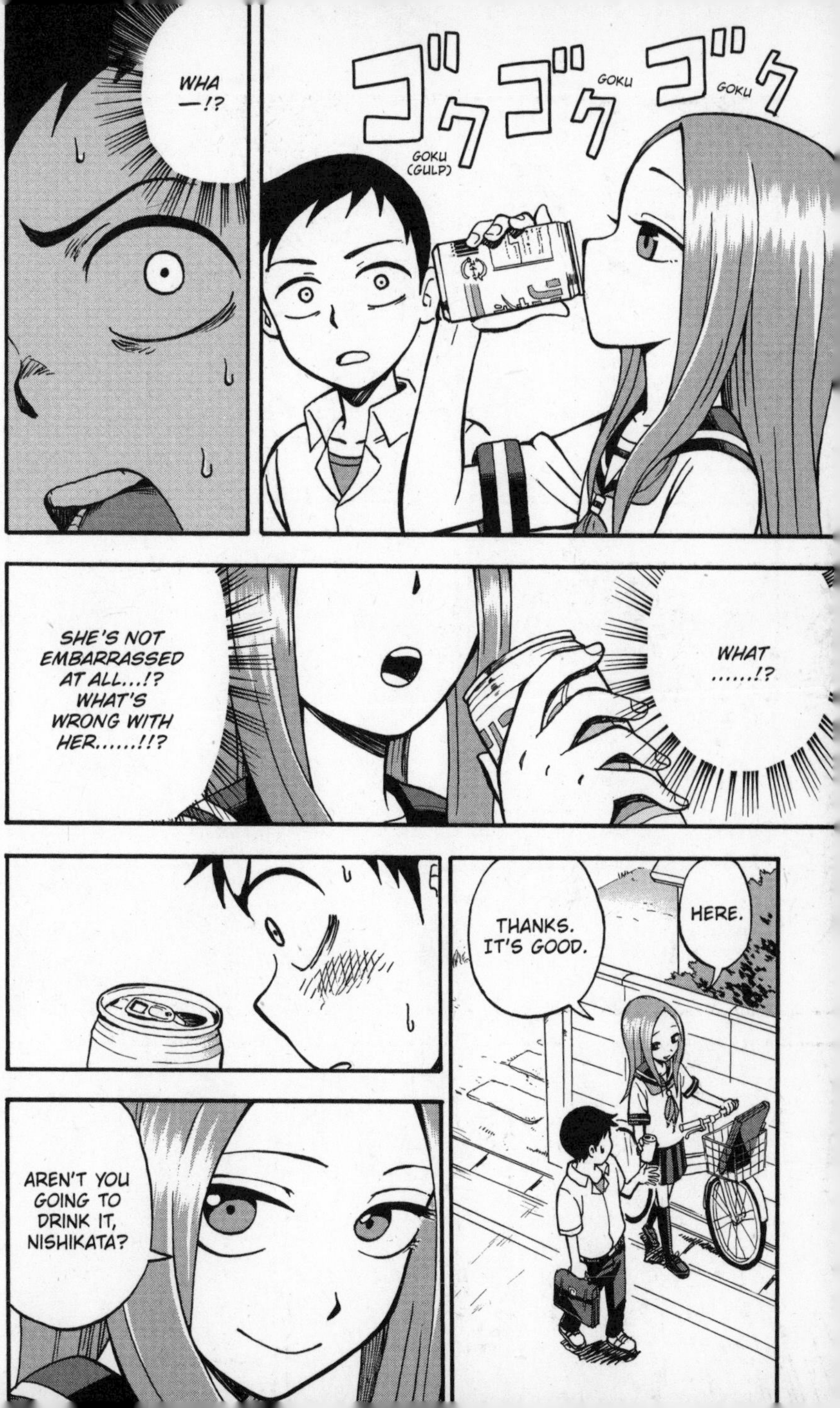
ゴクゴクゴク
GOKU
GOKU
GOKU (GULP)
WHA—!?
WHAT ......!?
SHE'S NOT EMBARRASSED AT ALL...!? WHAT'S WRONG WITH HER......!!?
HERE.
THANKS. IT'S GOOD.
AREN'T YOU GOING TO DRINK IT, NISHIKATA?

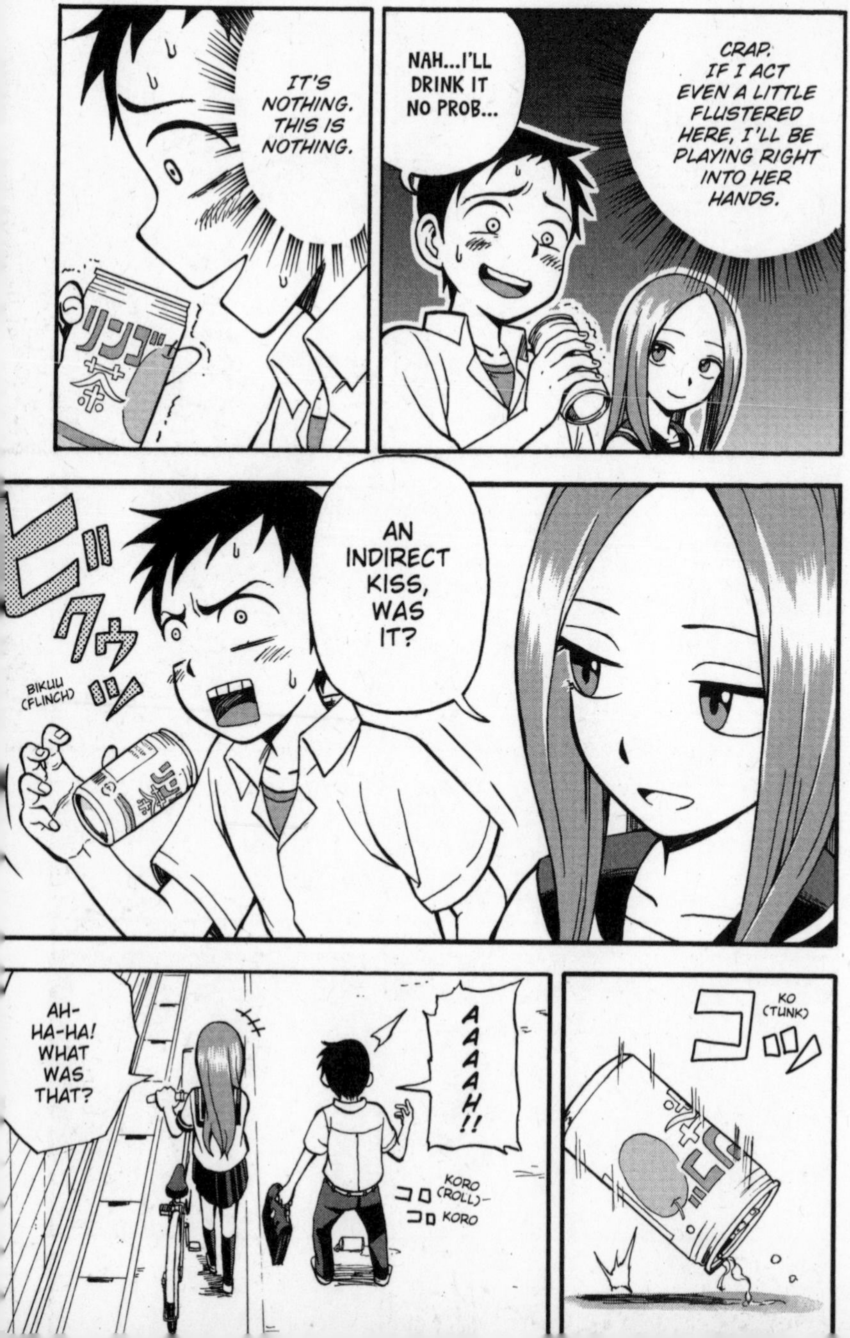
CRAP. IF I ACT EVEN A LITTLE FLUSTERED HERE, I'LL BE PLAYING RIGHT INTO HER HANDS.
NAH...I'LL DRINK IT NO PROB...
IT'S NOTHING. THIS IS NOTHING.
AN INDIRECT KISS, WAS IT?
BIKUU (FLINCH)
KO (TUNK)
AAAAAH!!
AH-HA-HA! WHAT WAS THAT?
KORO (ROLL)- KORO

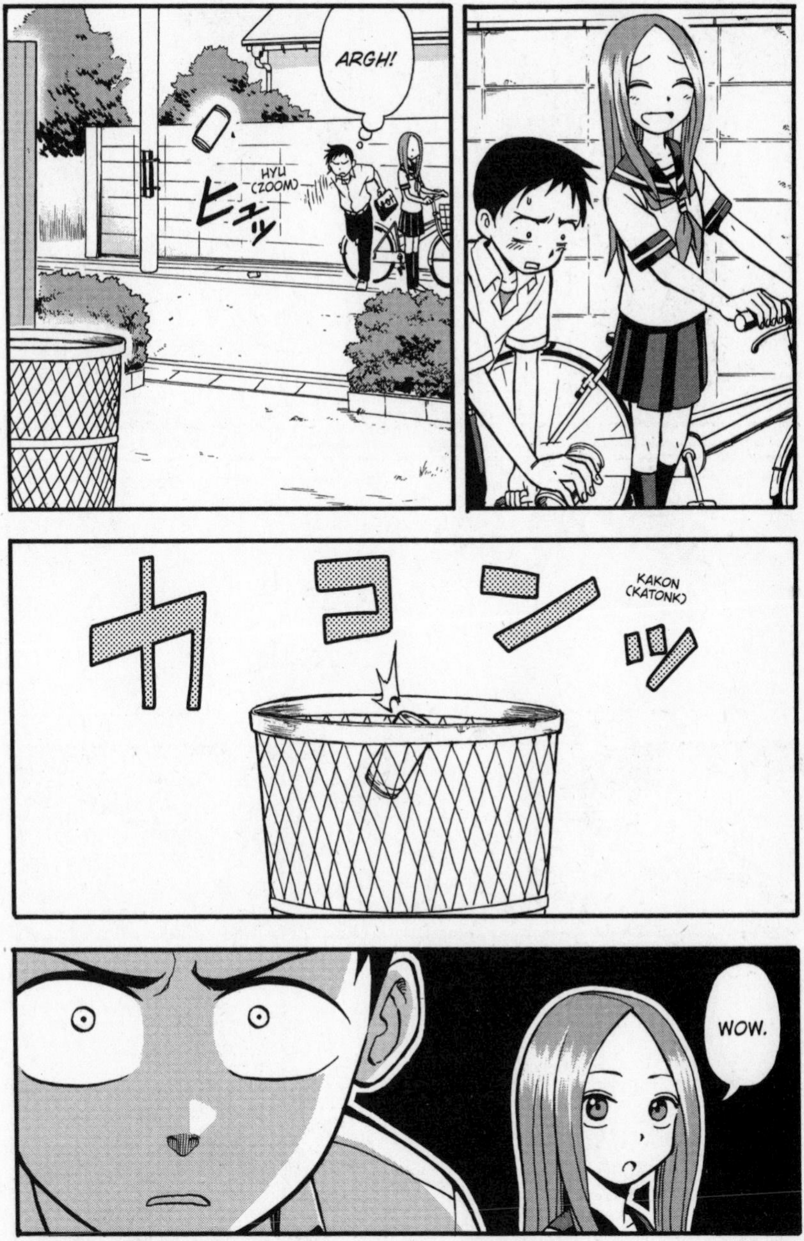
ARGH!
ヒュッ
HYU (ZOOM)
カコンッ
KAKON (KATONK)
WOW.

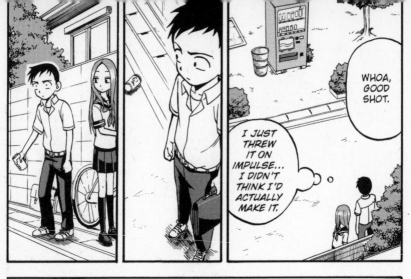

WHOA, GOOD SHOT.

I JUST THREW IT ON IMPULSE... I DIDN'T THINK I'D ACTUALLY MAKE IT.

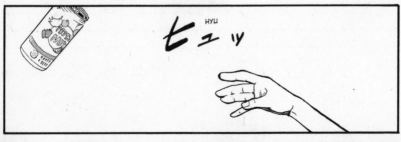

HYU

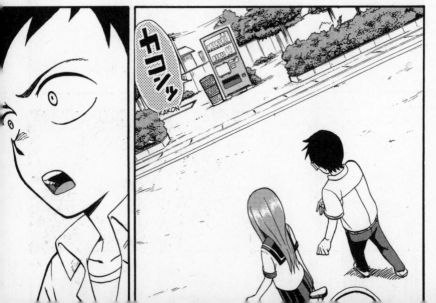

KAKON

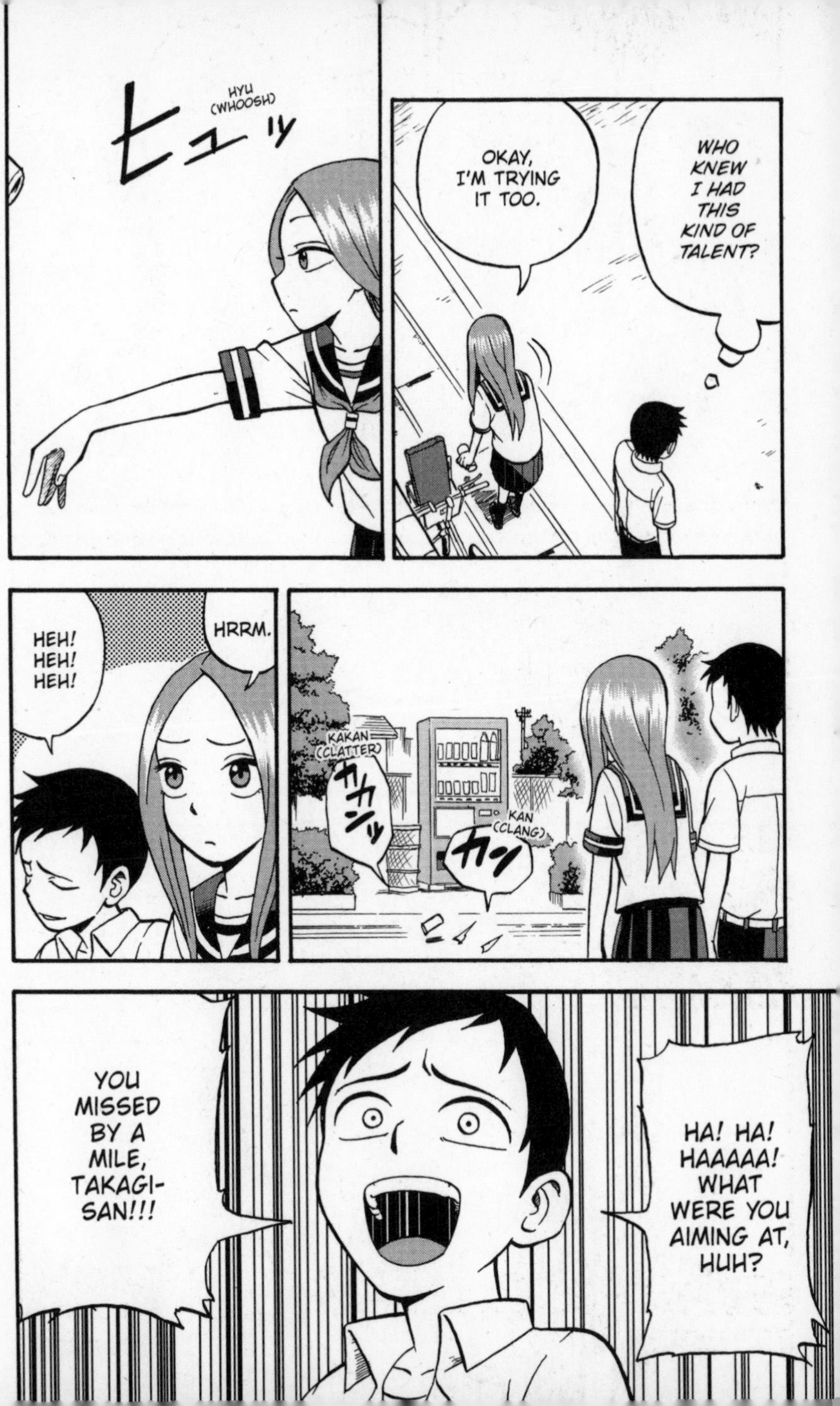
WHO KNEW I HAD THIS KIND OF TALENT?
OKAY, I'M TRYING IT TOO.
HYU (WHOOSH)
ヒュッ
KAKAN (CLATTER)
カカンッ
KAN (CLANG)
カン
HRRM.
HEH! HEH! HEH!
HA! HA! HAAAAA! WHAT WERE YOU AIMING AT, HUH?
YOU MISSED BY A MILE, TAKAGI-SAN!!!

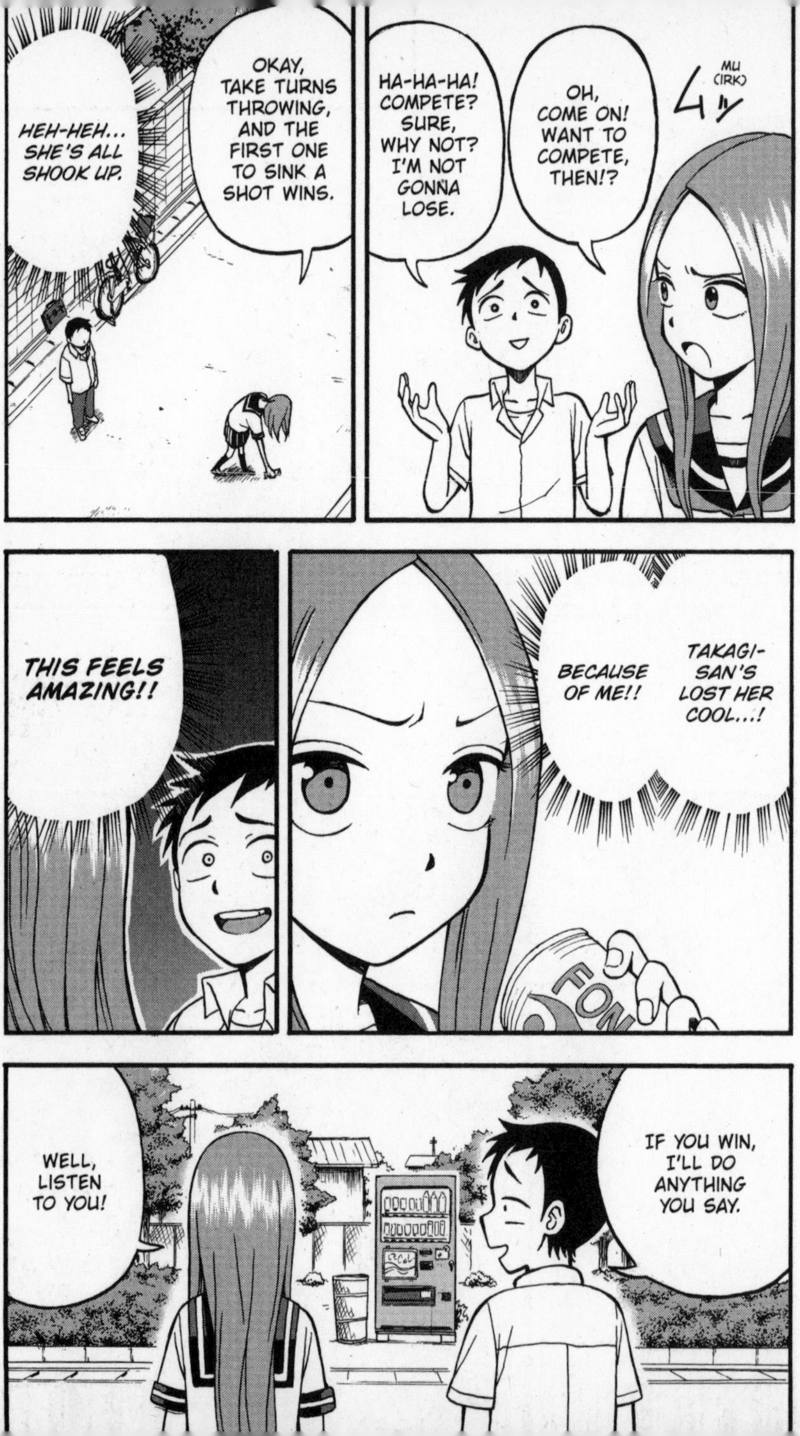
MU (IRK)
OH, COME ON! WANT TO COMPETE, THEN!?
HA-HA-HA! COMPETE? SURE, WHY NOT? I'M NOT GONNA LOSE.
OKAY, TAKE TURNS THROWING, AND THE FIRST ONE TO SINK A SHOT WINS.
HEH-HEH... SHE'S ALL SHOOK UP.
TAKAGI-SAN'S LOST HER COOL...!
BECAUSE OF ME!!
FON
THIS FEELS AMAZING!!
IF YOU WIN, I'LL DO ANYTHING YOU SAY.
WELL, LISTEN TO YOU!

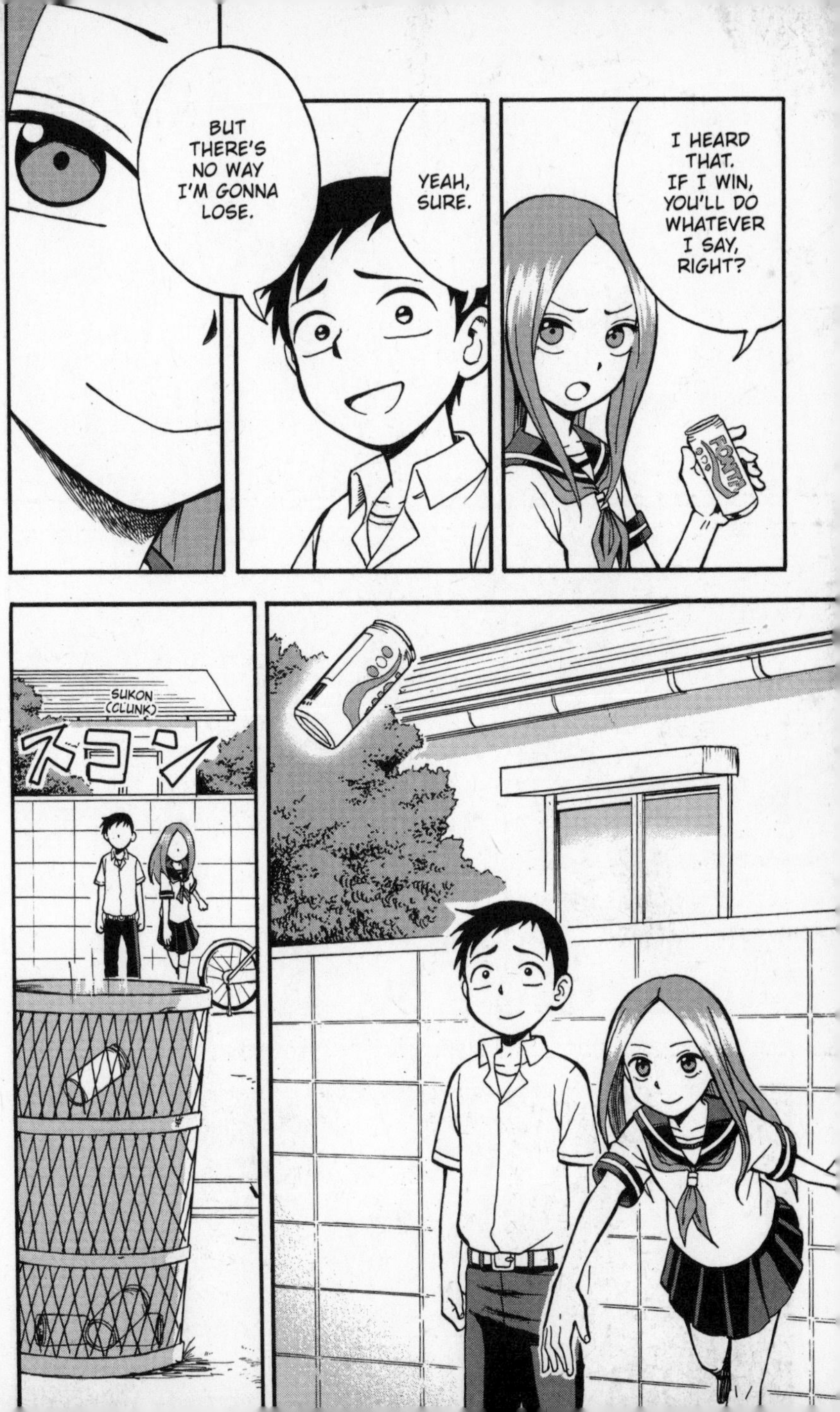
I HEARD THAT. IF I WIN, YOU'LL DO WHATEVER I SAY, RIGHT?
YEAH, SURE.
BUT THERE'S NO WAY I'M GONNA LOSE.
SUKON (CLUNK)
スコーン

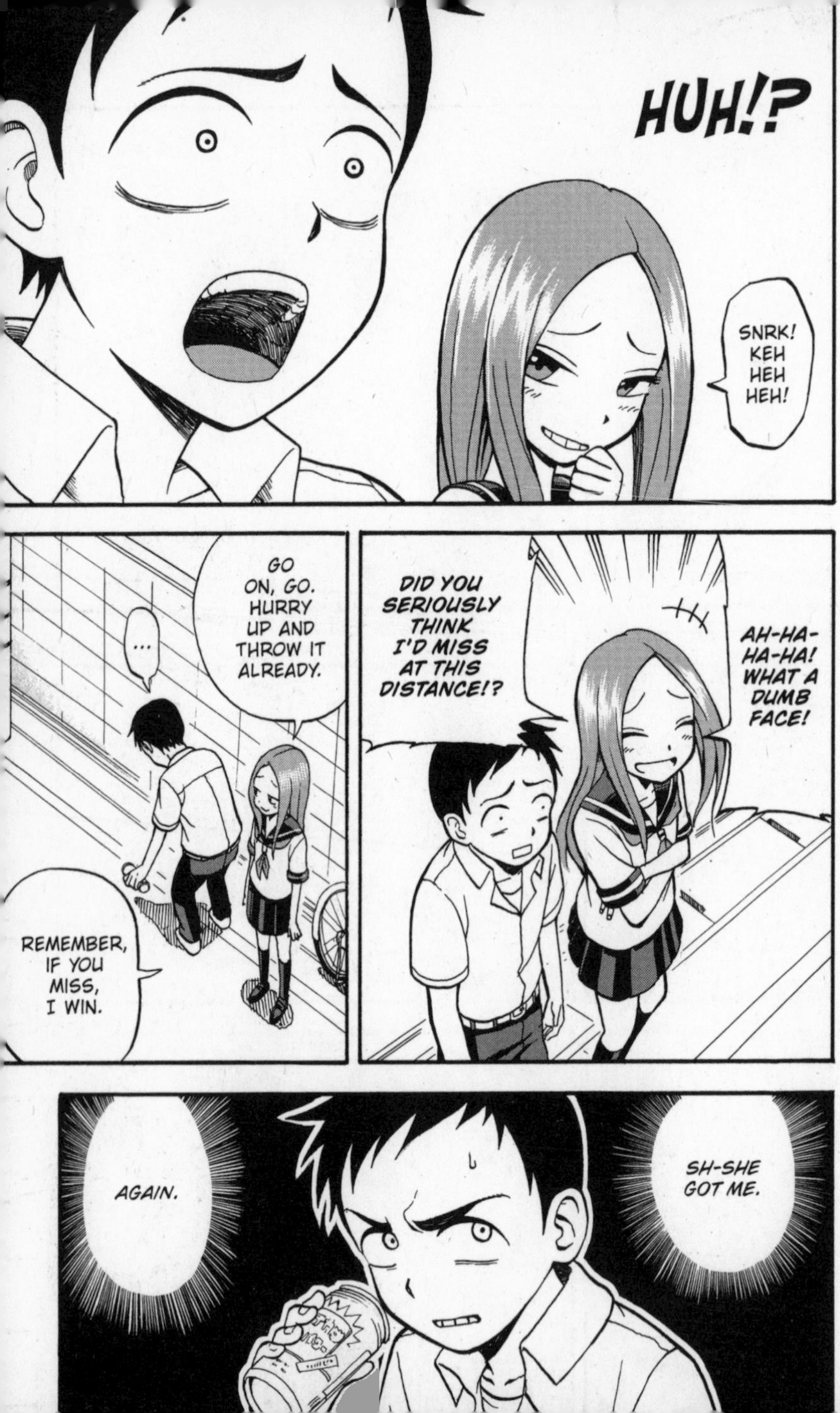
HUH!?
SNRK! KEH HEH HEH!
AH-HA-HA-HA! WHAT A DUMB FACE!
DID YOU SERIOUSLY THINK I'D MISS AT THIS DISTANCE!?
GO ON, GO. HURRY UP AND THROW IT ALREADY.
...
REMEMBER, IF YOU MISS, I WIN.
SH-SHE GOT ME.
AGAIN.

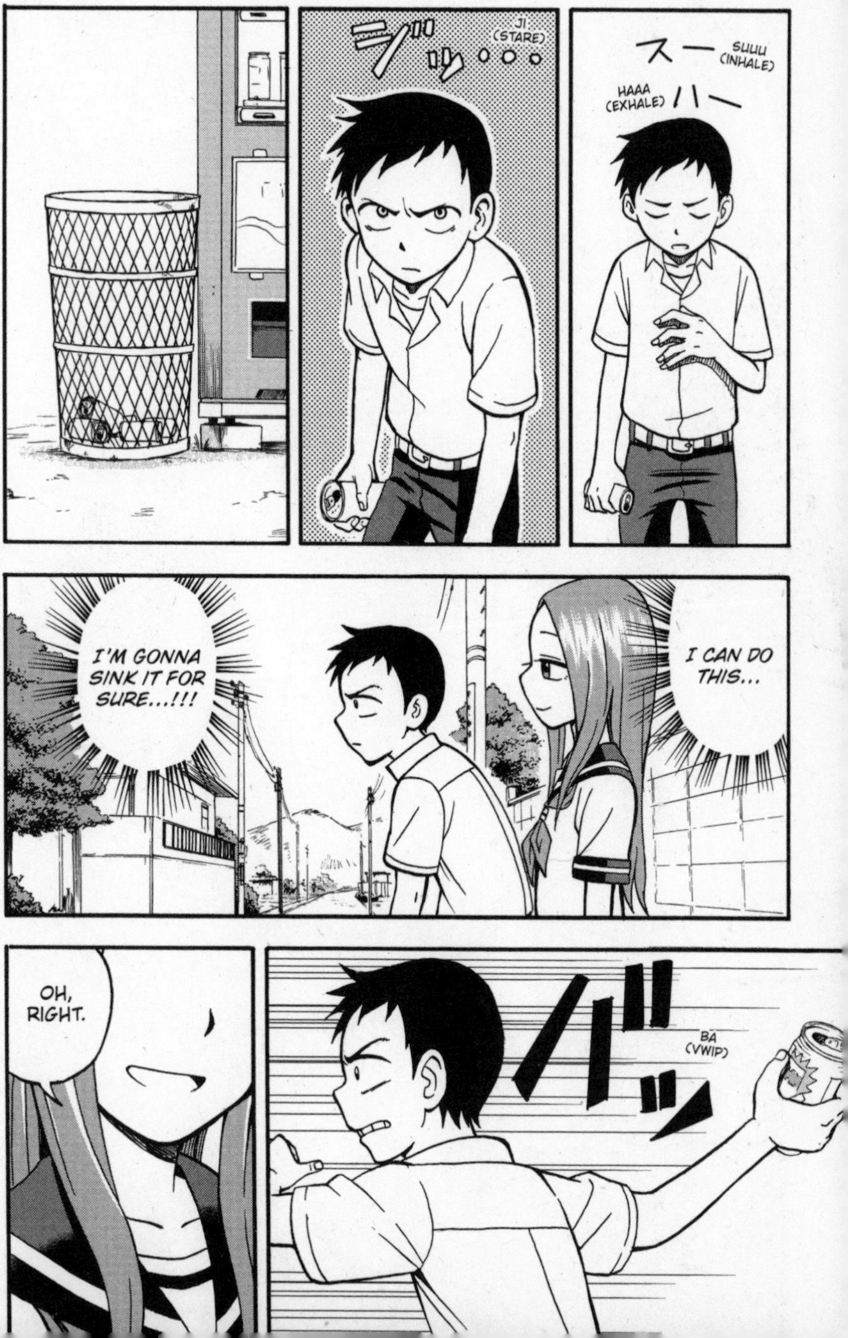
スー
SUUU (INHALE)
ハー
HAAA (EXHALE)
ジッ・・・
JI (STARE)
I CAN DO THIS...
I'M GONNA SINK IT FOR SURE...!!!
バッ
BA (VWIP)
OH, RIGHT.

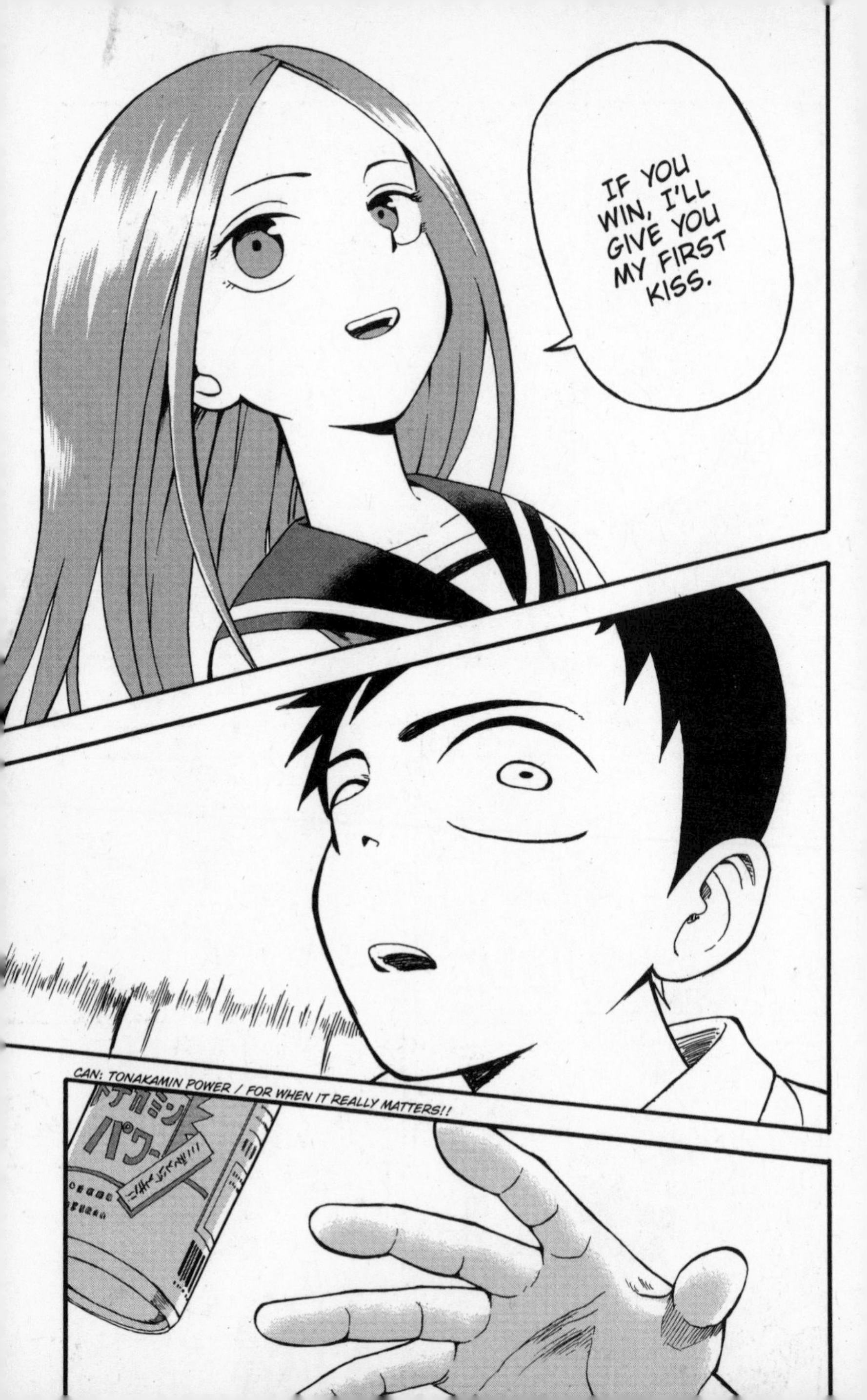
IF YOU WIN, I'LL GIVE YOU MY FIRST KISS.
CAN: TONAKAMIN POWER / FOR WHEN IT REALLY MATTERS!!

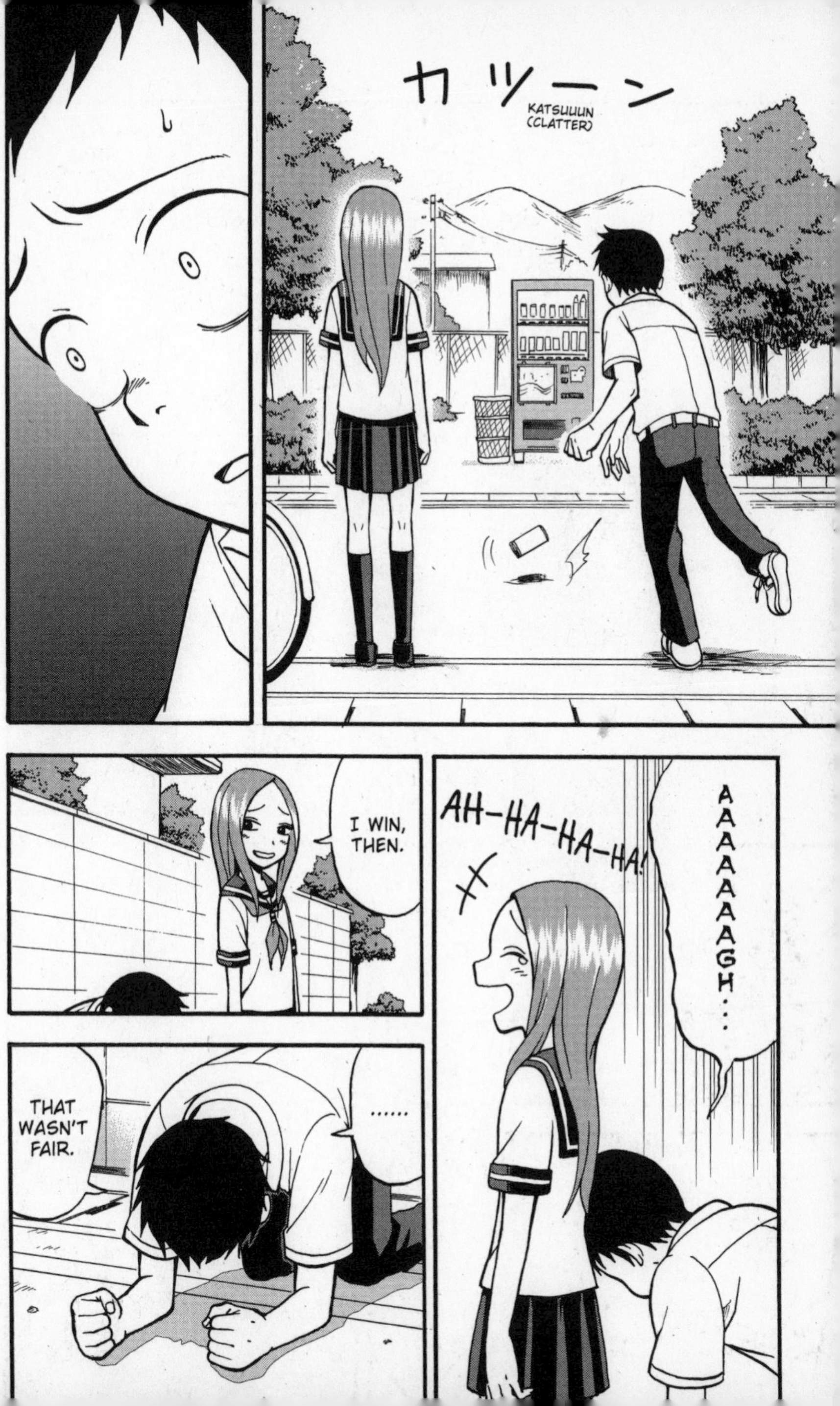
カツーン
KATSUUUN (CLATTER)
AAAAAAAGH...
AH-HA-HA-HA!
I WIN, THEN.
......
THAT WASN'T FAIR.

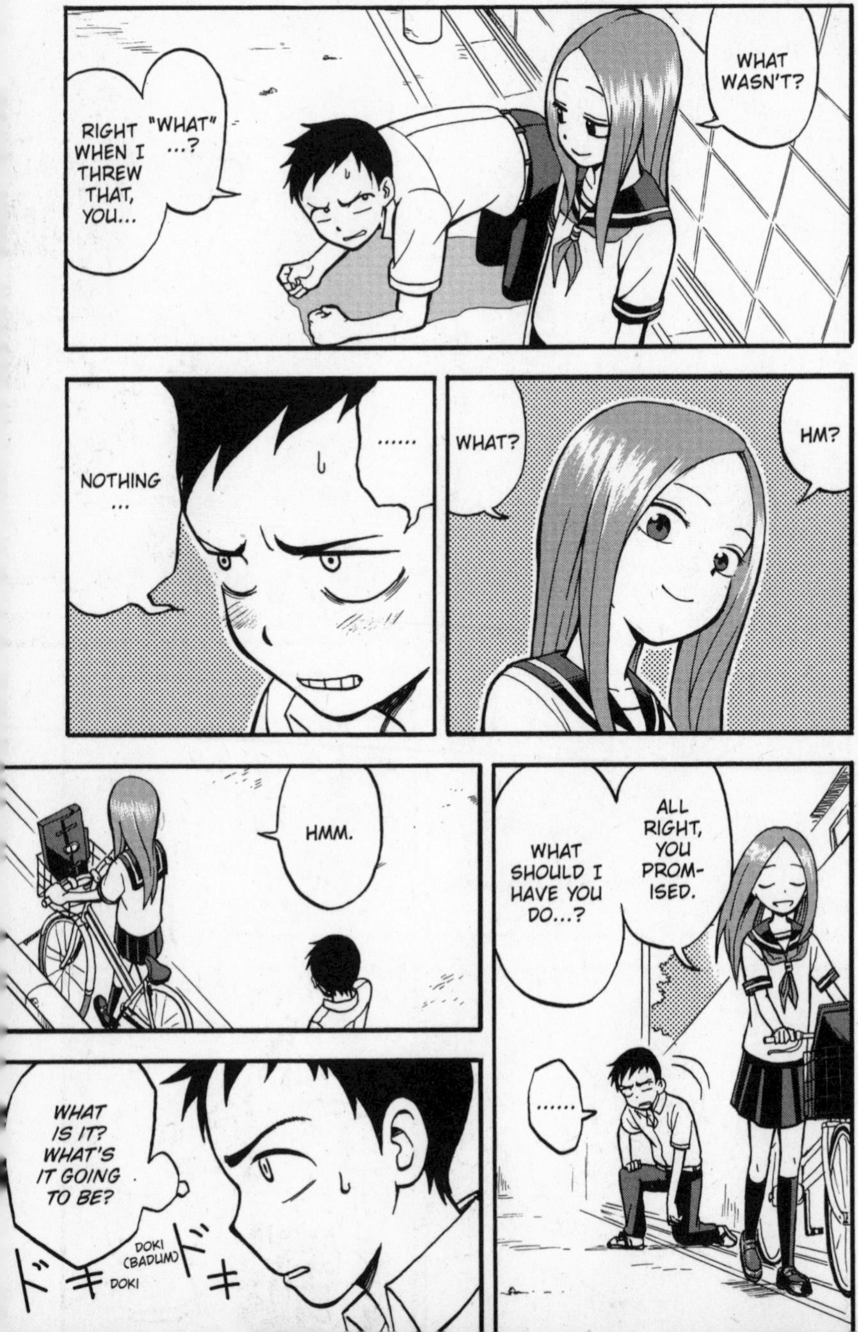
WHAT WASN'T?
RIGHT WHEN I THREW THAT, YOU...
"WHAT" ...?
HM?
WHAT?
......
NOTHING ...
ALL RIGHT, YOU PROMISED.
WHAT SHOULD I HAVE YOU DO...?
......
HMM.
WHAT IS IT? WHAT'S IT GOING TO BE?
DOKI (BADUM) DOKI

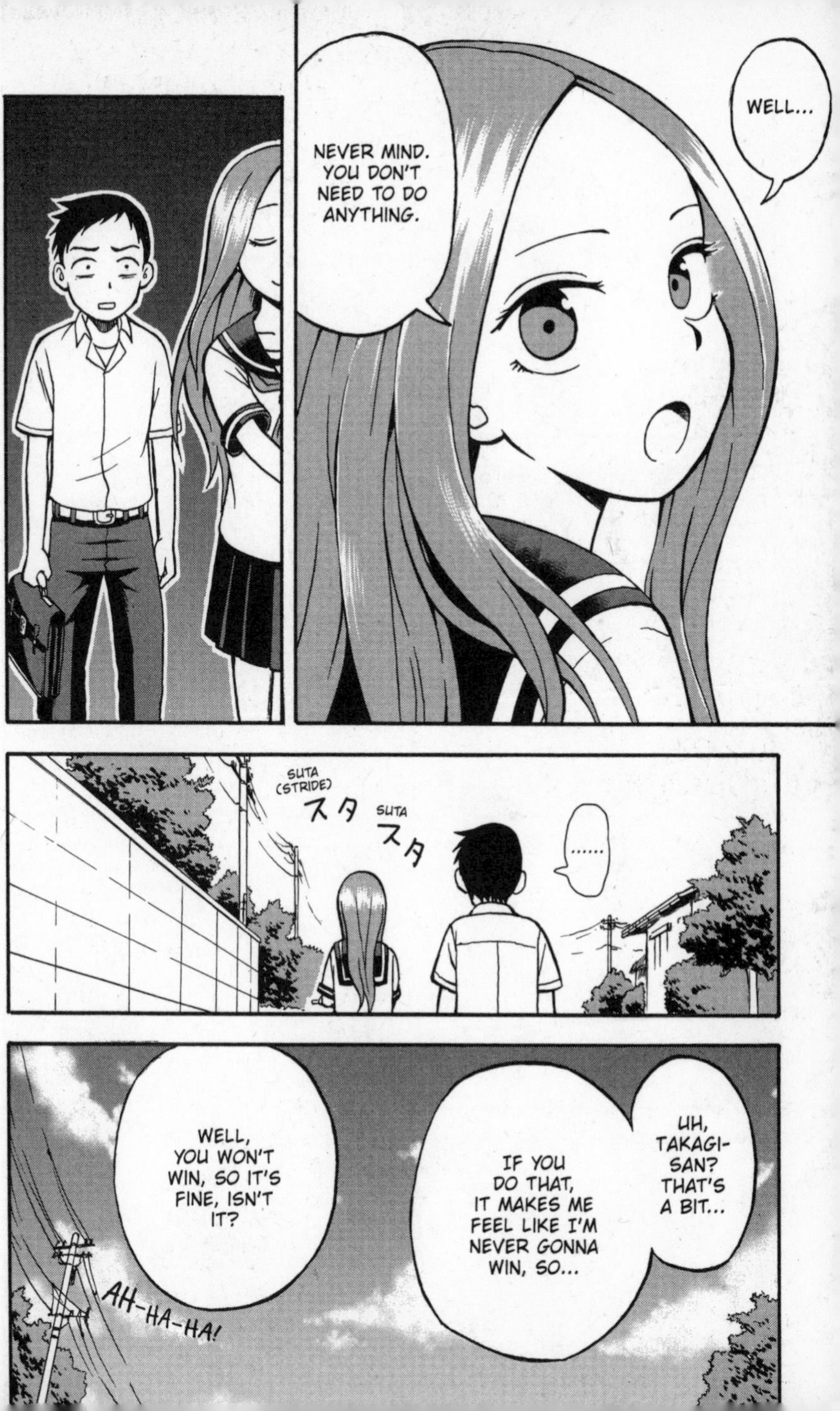
WELL...
NEVER MIND. YOU DON'T NEED TO DO ANYTHING.
SUTA (STRIDE)
スタ
SUTA
スタ
......
UH, TAKAGI-SAN? THAT'S A BIT...
IF YOU DO THAT, IT MAKES ME FEEL LIKE I'M NEVER GONNA WIN, SO...
WELL, YOU WON'T WIN, SO IT'S FINE, ISN'T IT?
AH-HA-HA!

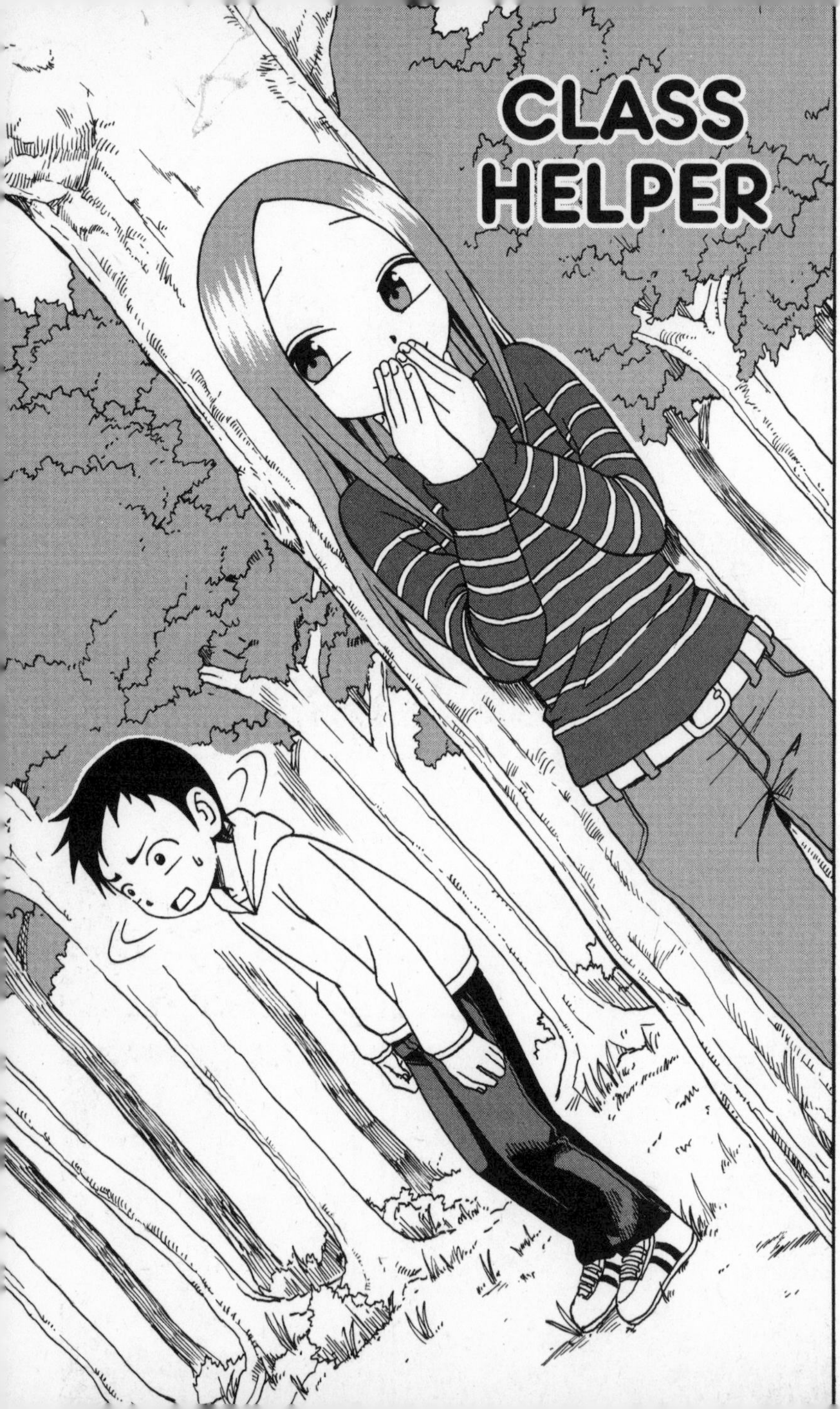
CLASS HELPER

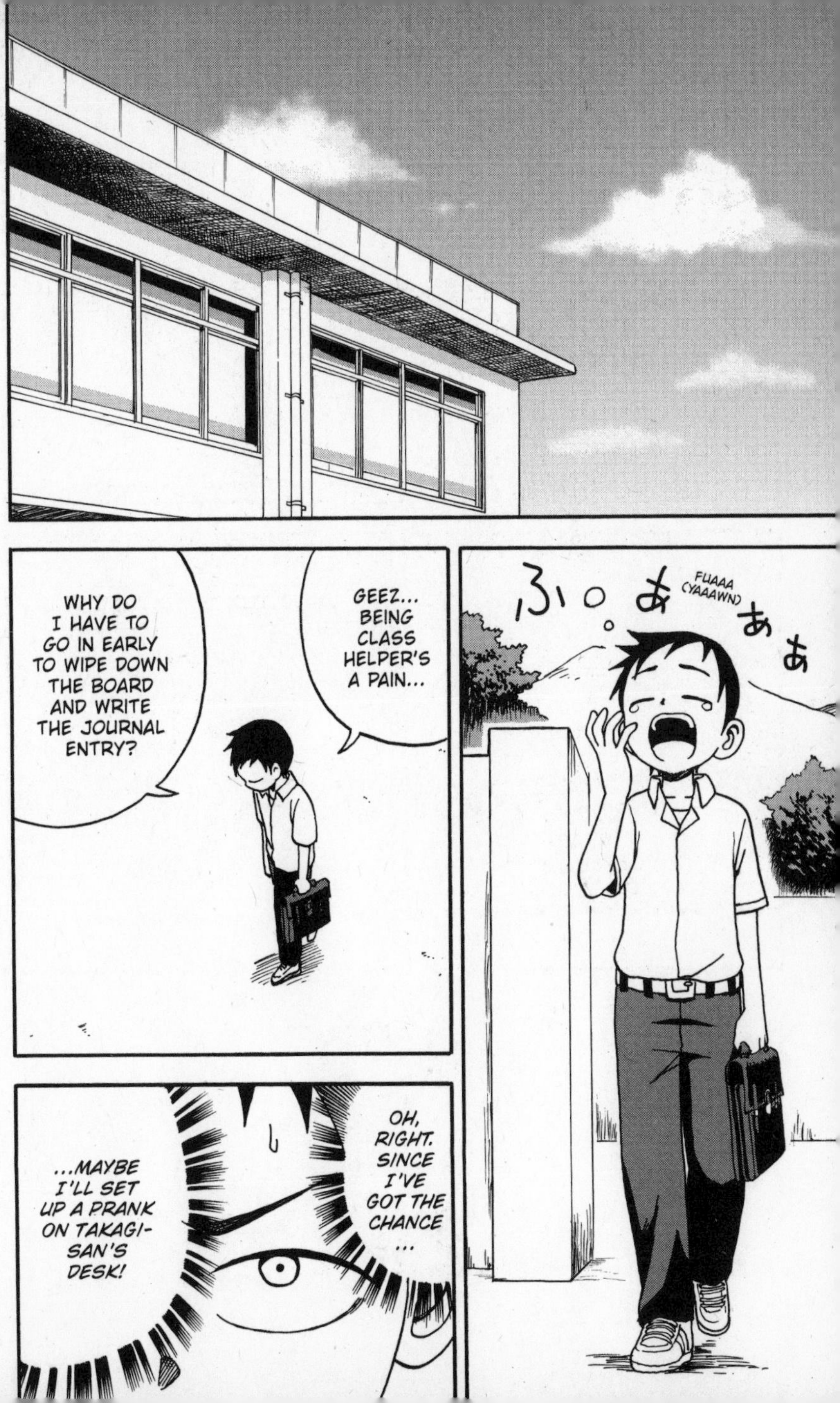
ふあああ
FUAAA (YAAAWN)
GEEZ... BEING CLASS HELPER'S A PAIN...
WHY DO I HAVE TO GO IN EARLY TO WIPE DOWN THE BOARD AND WRITE THE JOURNAL ENTRY?
OH, RIGHT. SINCE I'VE GOT THE CHANCE...
...MAYBE I'LL SET UP A PRANK ON TAKAGI-SAN'S DESK!

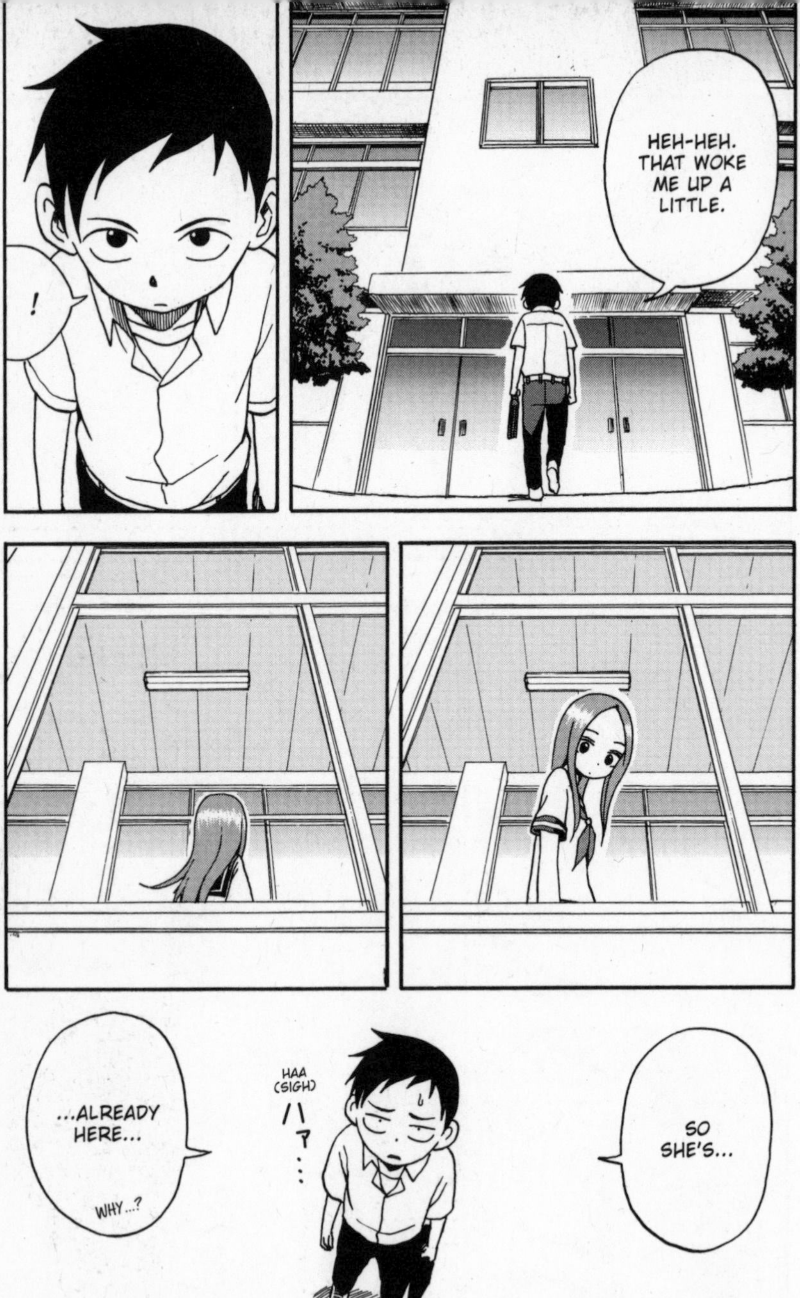
HEH-HEH. THAT WOKE ME UP A LITTLE.
!
SO SHE'S...
HAA (SIGH)
ハア…
...ALREADY HERE...
WHY...?

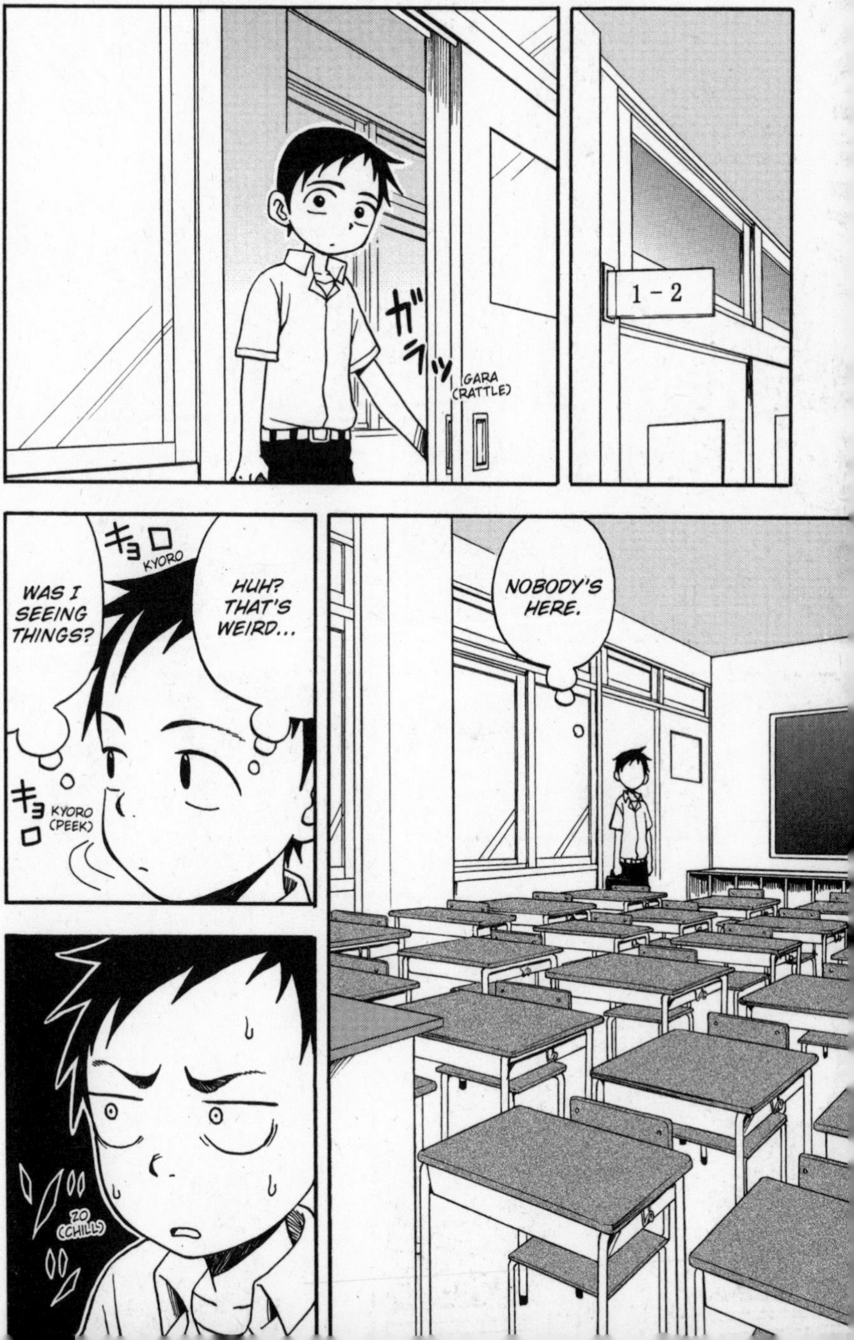

1 – 2
ガラッ
GARA (RATTLE)
NOBODY'S HERE.
HUH? THAT'S WEIRD...
キョロ
KYORO
WAS I SEEING THINGS?
キョロ
KYORO (PEEK)
ZO (CHILL)

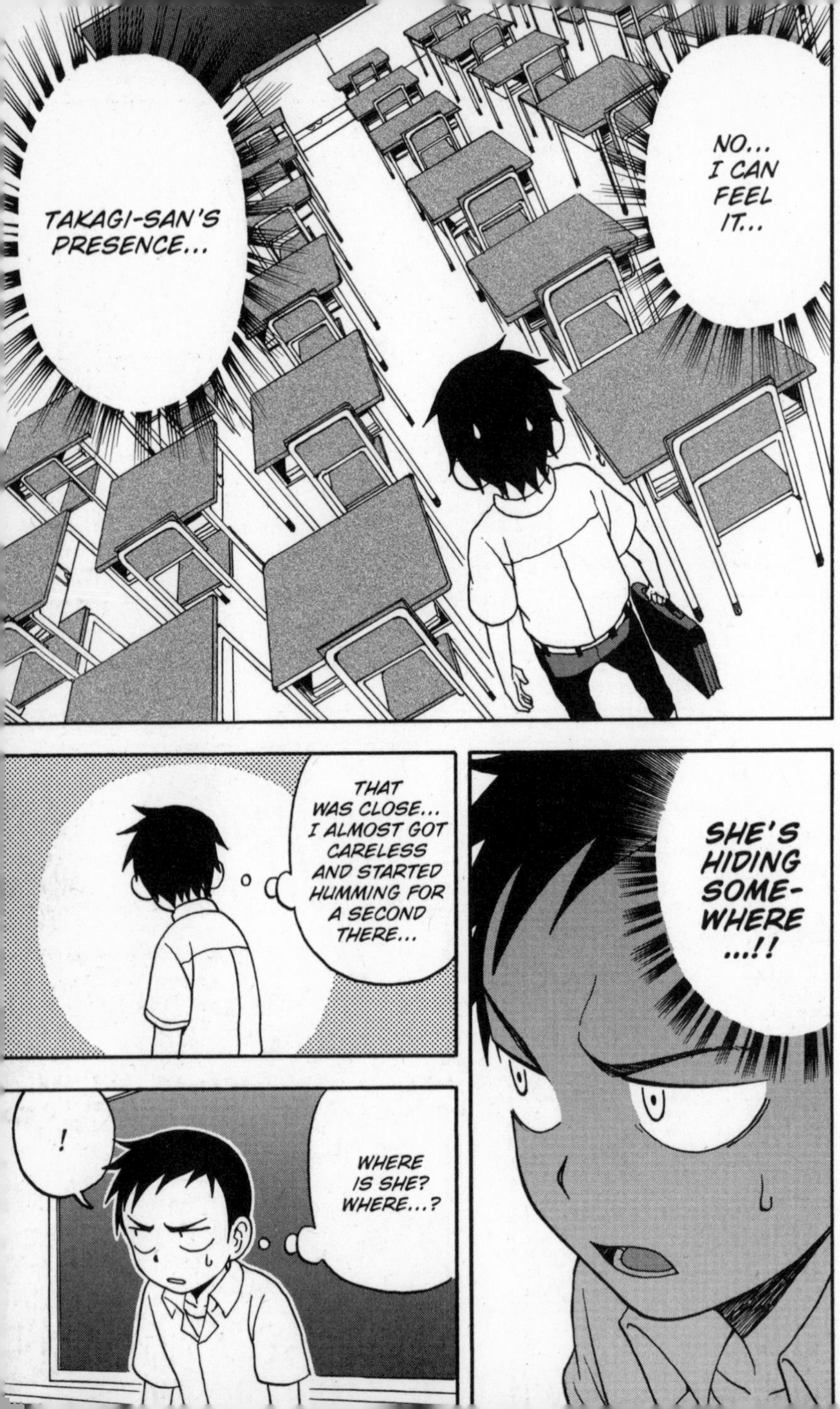
NO... I CAN FEEL IT...
TAKAGI-SAN'S PRESENCE...
SHE'S HIDING SOME-WHERE ...!!
THAT WAS CLOSE... I ALMOST GOT CARELESS AND STARTED HUMMING FOR A SECOND THERE...
WHERE IS SHE? WHERE...?
!

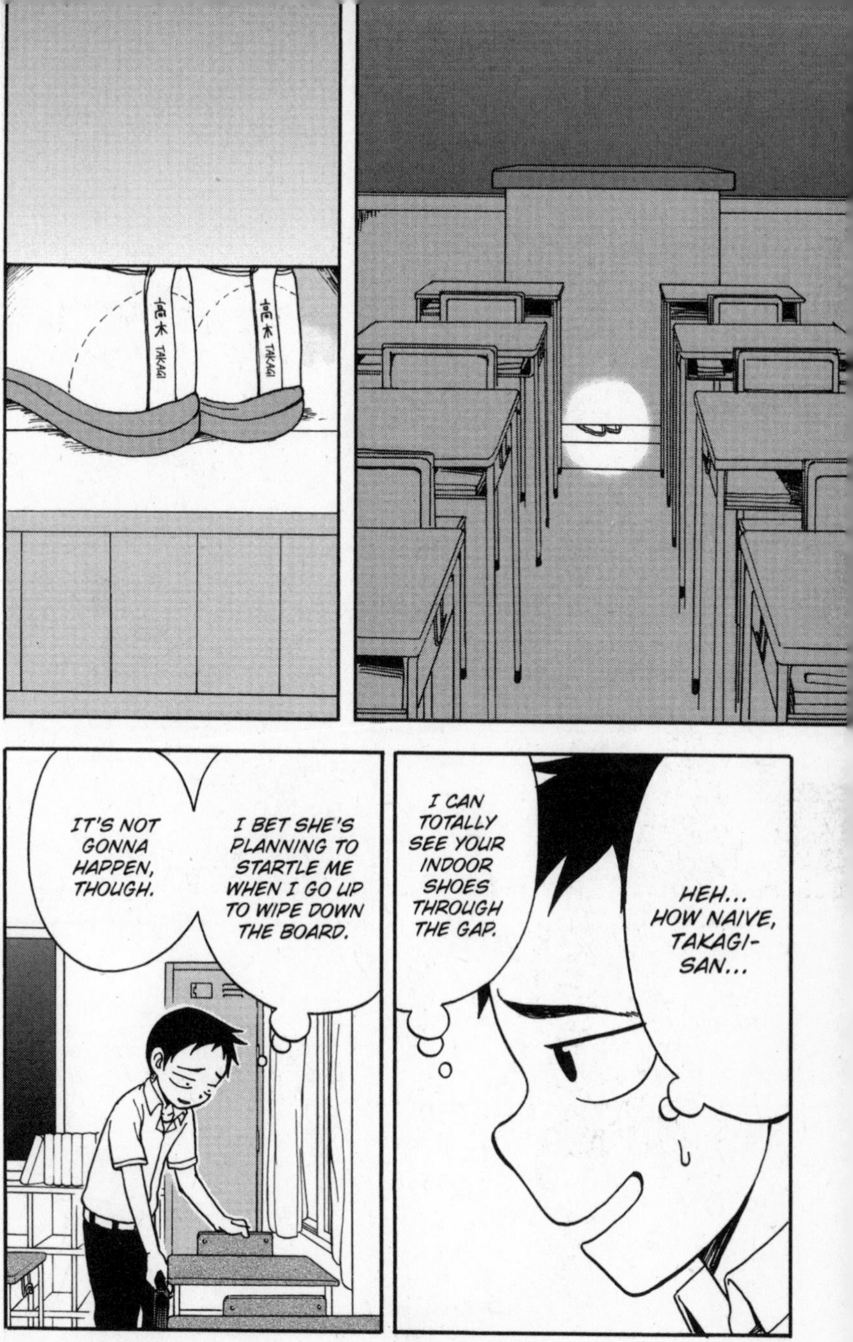
高木 TAKAGI
高木 TAKAGI
HEH... HOW NAIVE, TAKAGI-SAN...
I CAN TOTALLY SEE YOUR INDOOR SHOES THROUGH THE GAP.
I BET SHE'S PLANNING TO STARTLE ME WHEN I GO UP TO WIPE DOWN THE BOARD.
IT'S NOT GONNA HAPPEN, THOUGH.

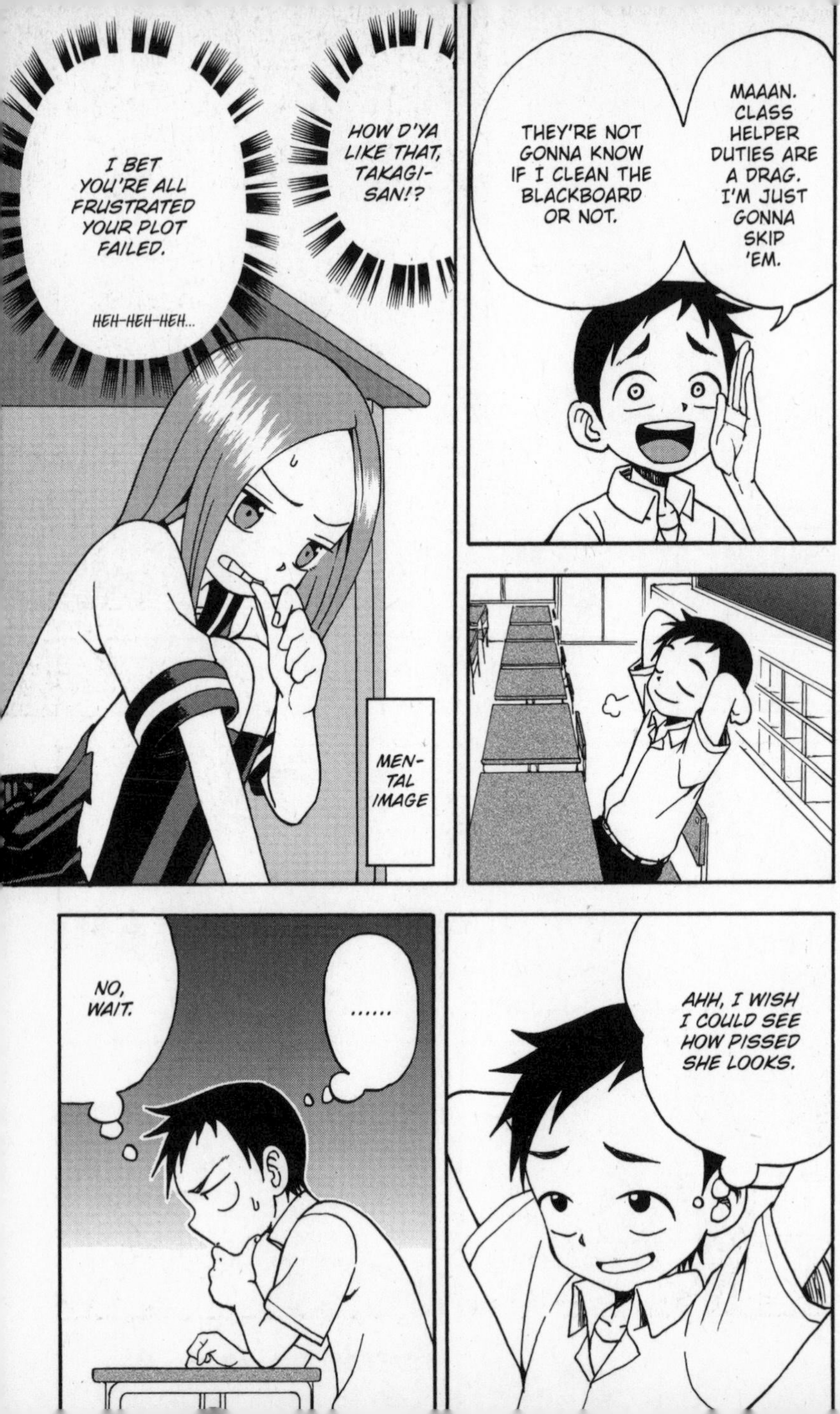
MAAAN. CLASS HELPER DUTIES ARE A DRAG. I'M JUST GONNA SKIP 'EM.
THEY'RE NOT GONNA KNOW IF I CLEAN THE BLACKBOARD OR NOT.
HOW D'YA LIKE THAT, TAKAGI-SAN!?
I BET YOU'RE ALL FRUSTRATED YOUR PLOT FAILED.
HEH-HEH-HEH...
MEN-TAL IMAGE
AHH, I WISH I COULD SEE HOW PISSED SHE LOOKS.
......
NO, WAIT.

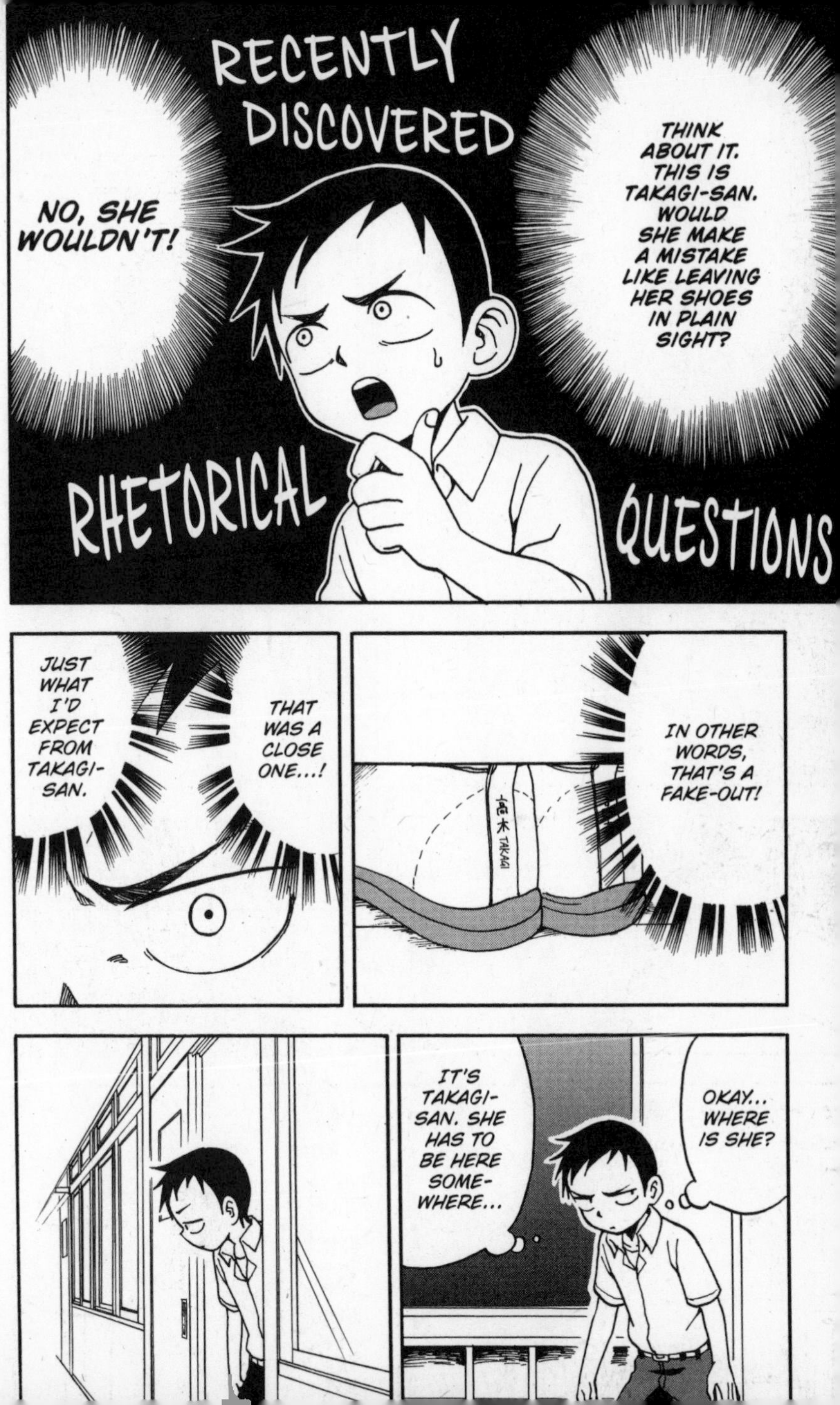
RECENTLY DISCOVERED
THINK ABOUT IT. THIS IS TAKAGI-SAN. WOULD SHE MAKE A MISTAKE LIKE LEAVING HER SHOES IN PLAIN SIGHT?
NO, SHE WOULDN'T!
RHETORICAL QUESTIONS
IN OTHER WORDS, THAT'S A FAKE-OUT!
高木 TAKAGI
THAT WAS A CLOSE ONE...!
JUST WHAT I'D EXPECT FROM TAKAGI-SAN.
OKAY... WHERE IS SHE?
IT'S TAKAGI-SAN. SHE HAS TO BE HERE SOMEWHERE...

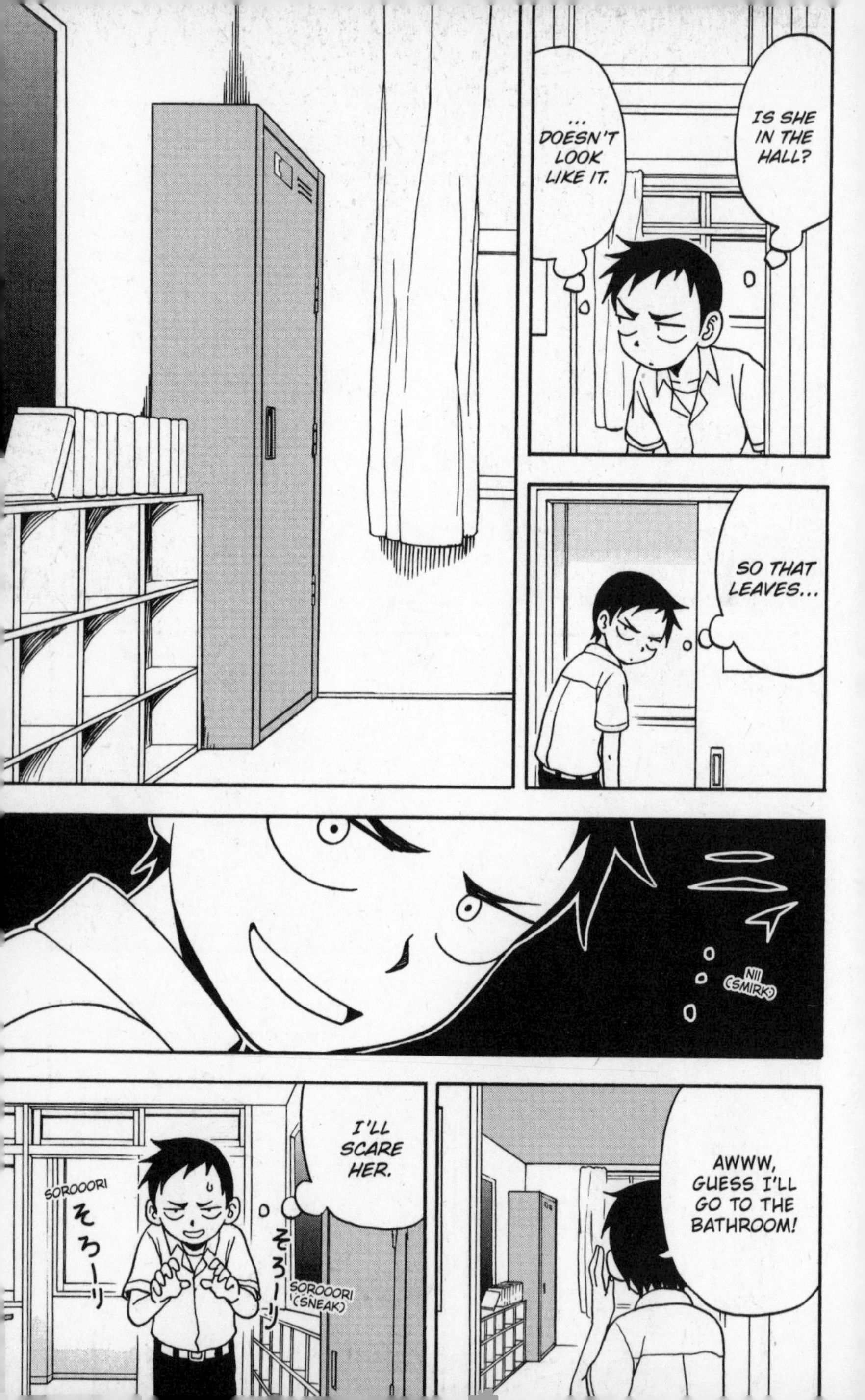
IS SHE IN THE HALL?
... DOESN'T LOOK LIKE IT.
SO THAT LEAVES...
NII (SMIRK)
AWWW, GUESS I'LL GO TO THE BATHROOM!
I'LL SCARE HER.
そろーり
SOROOORI (SNEAK)
SOROOORI
そろーり

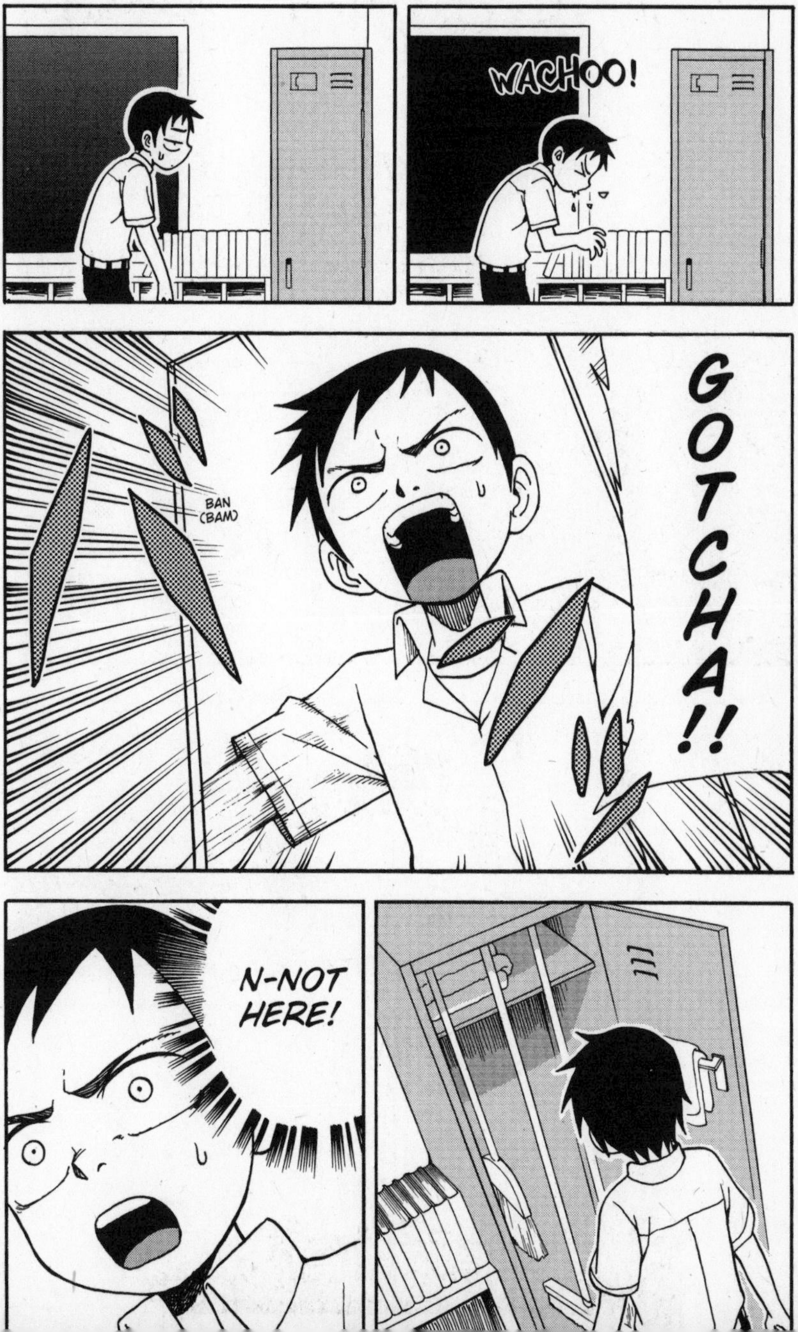
WACHOO!
GOTCHA!!
BAN (BAM)
N-NOT HERE!

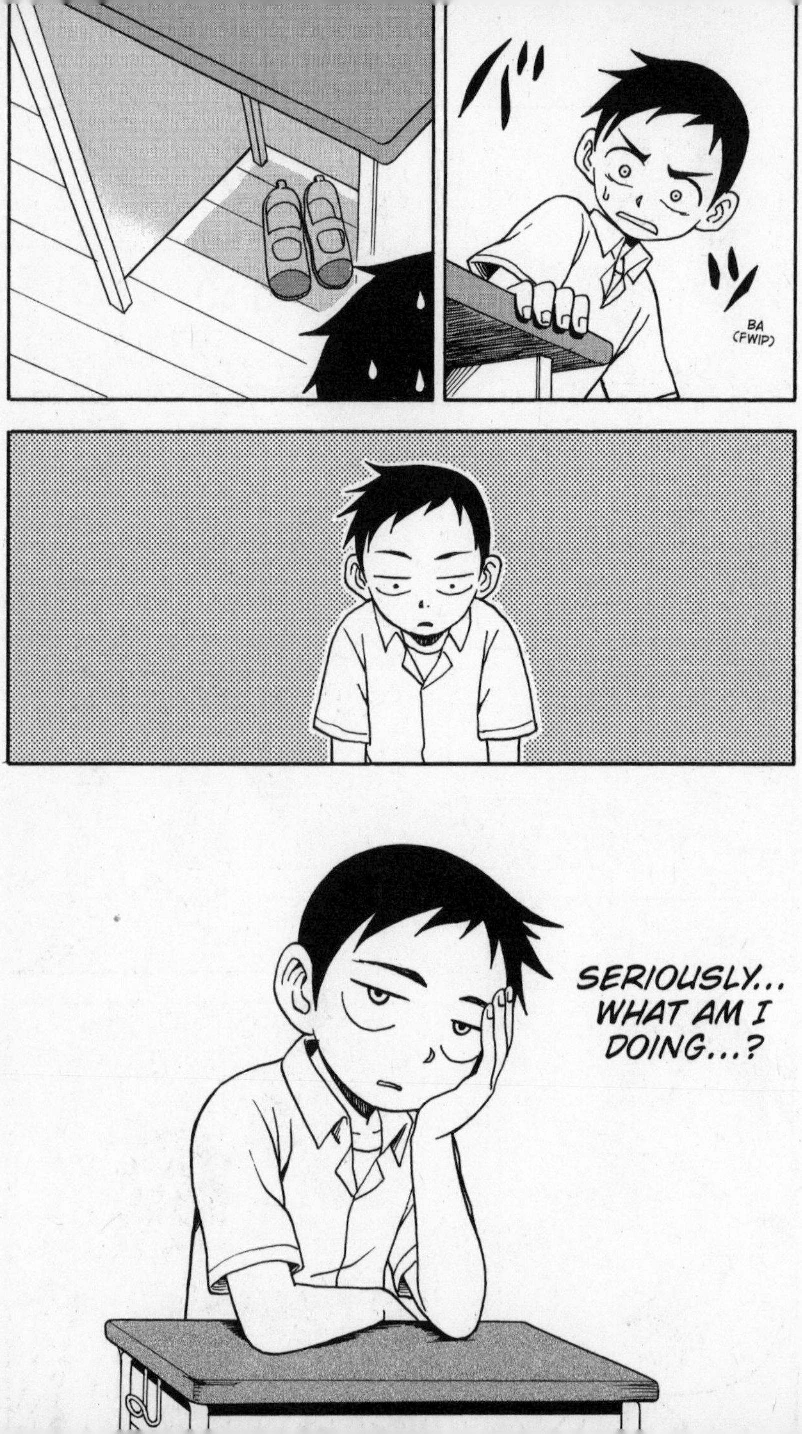
BA (FWIP)
SERIOUSLY... WHAT AM I DOING...?

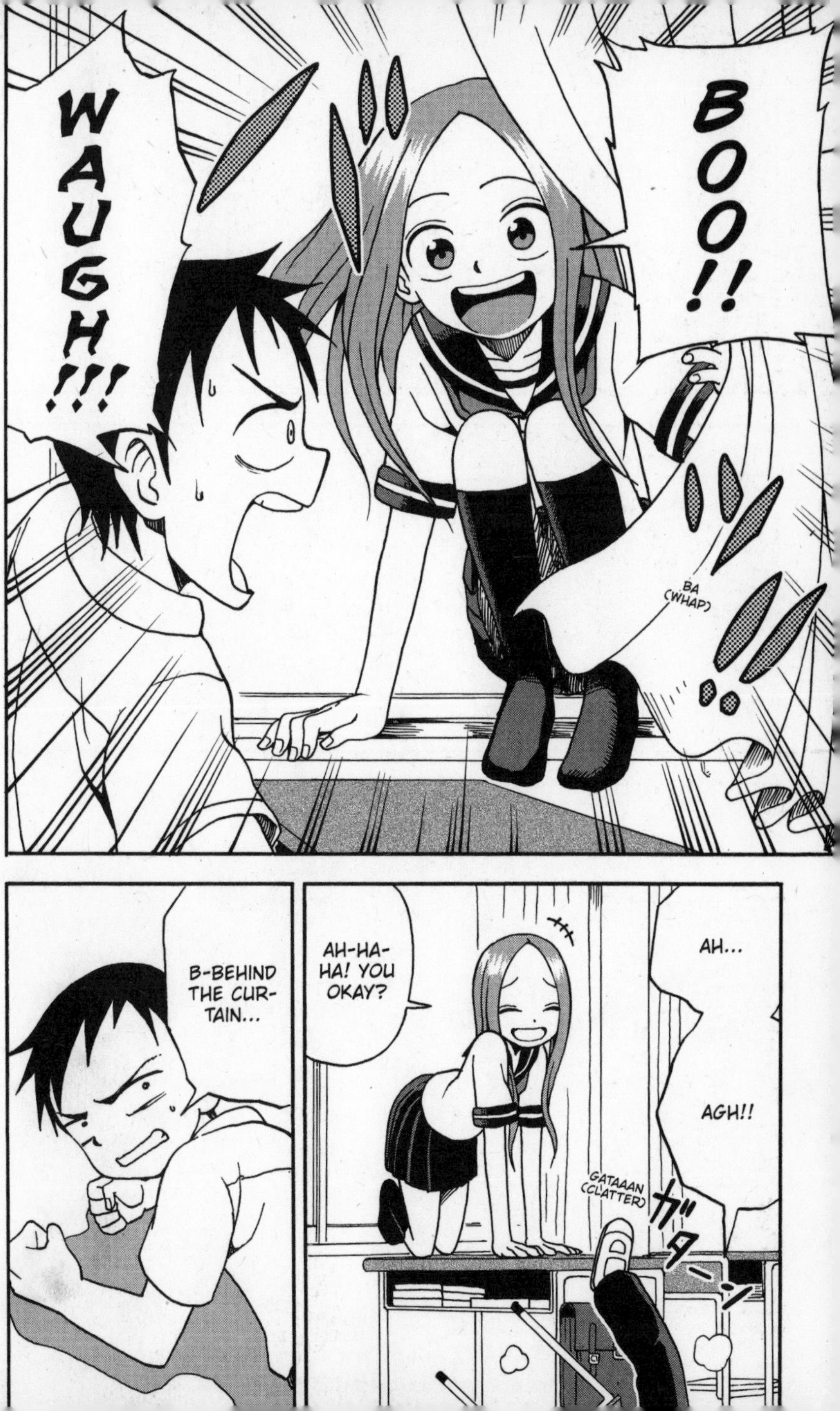
BOO!!
WAUGH!!!
BA (WHAP)
AH...
AGH!!
GATAAAN (CLATTER)
AH-HA-HA! YOU OKAY?
B-BEHIND THE CUR-TAIN...

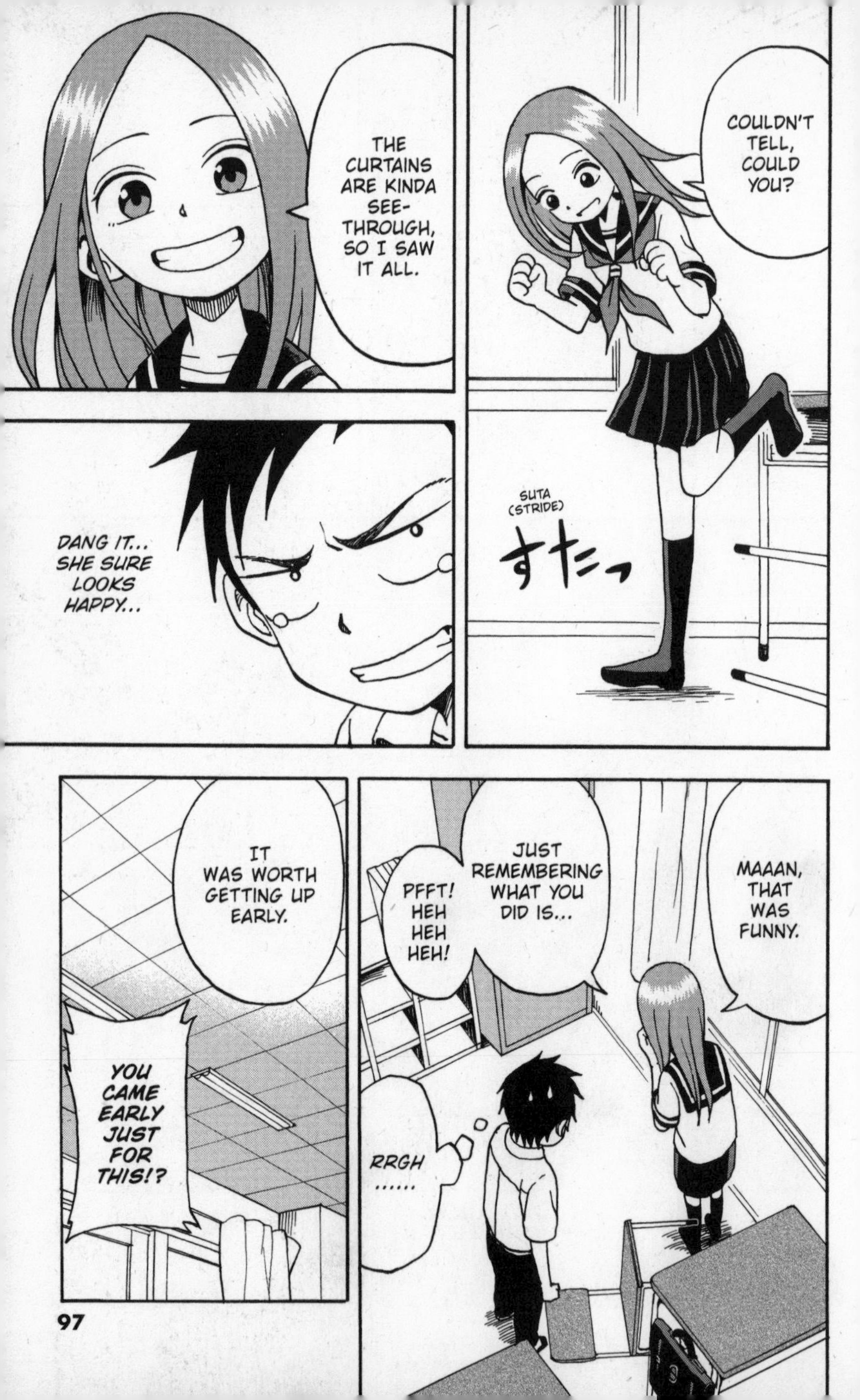
COULDN'T TELL, COULD YOU?
SUTA (STRIDE)
すたっ
THE CURTAINS ARE KINDA SEE-THROUGH, SO I SAW IT ALL.
DANG IT... SHE SURE LOOKS HAPPY...
MAAAN, THAT WAS FUNNY.
JUST REMEMBERING WHAT YOU DID IS...
PFFT! HEH HEH HEH!
RRGH ......
IT WAS WORTH GETTING UP EARLY.
YOU CAME EARLY JUST FOR THIS!?

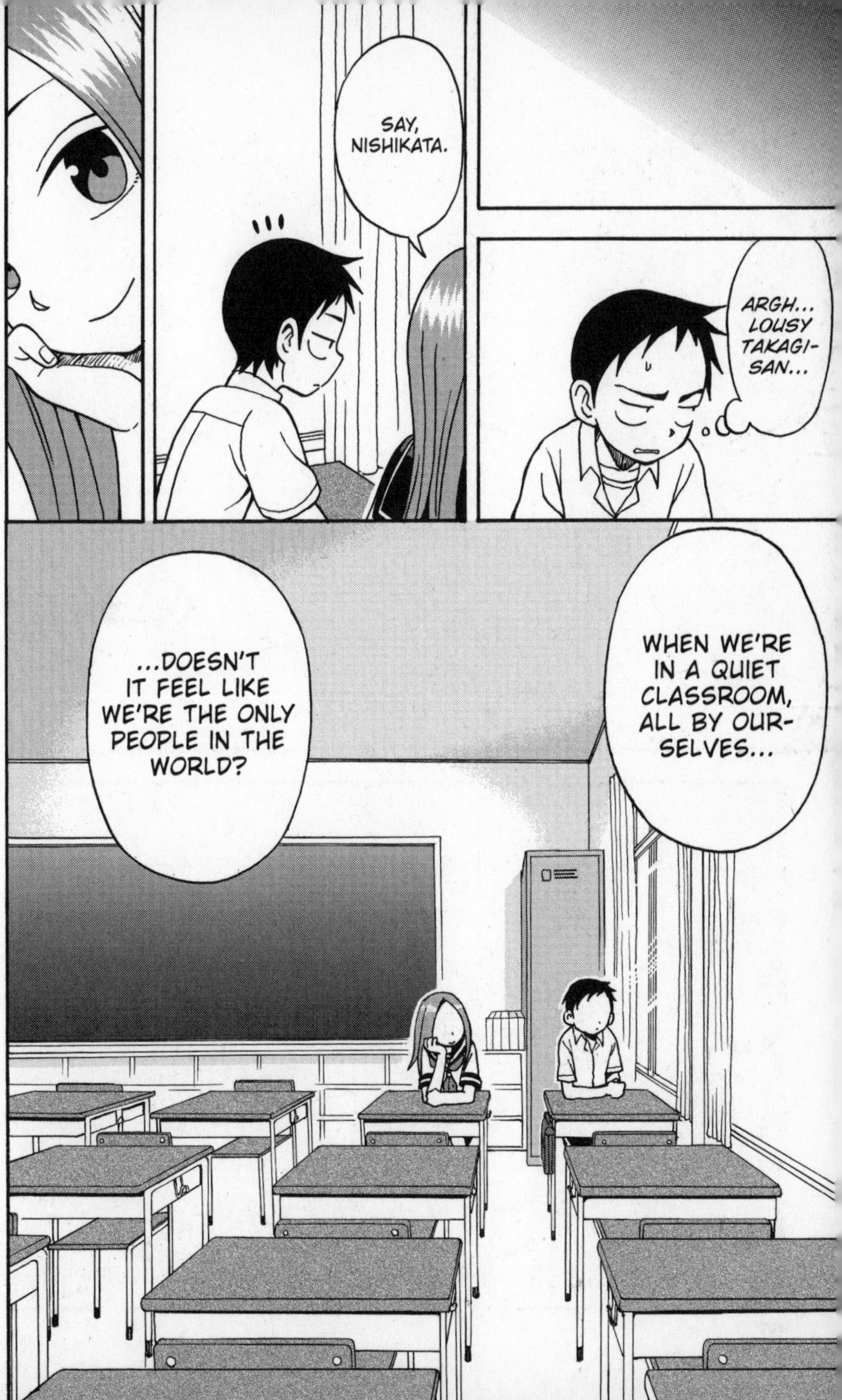
ARGH... LOUSY TAKAGI-SAN...
SAY, NISHIKATA.
WHEN WE'RE IN A QUIET CLASSROOM, ALL BY OURSELVES...
...DOESN'T IT FEEL LIKE WE'RE THE ONLY PEOPLE IN THE WORLD?

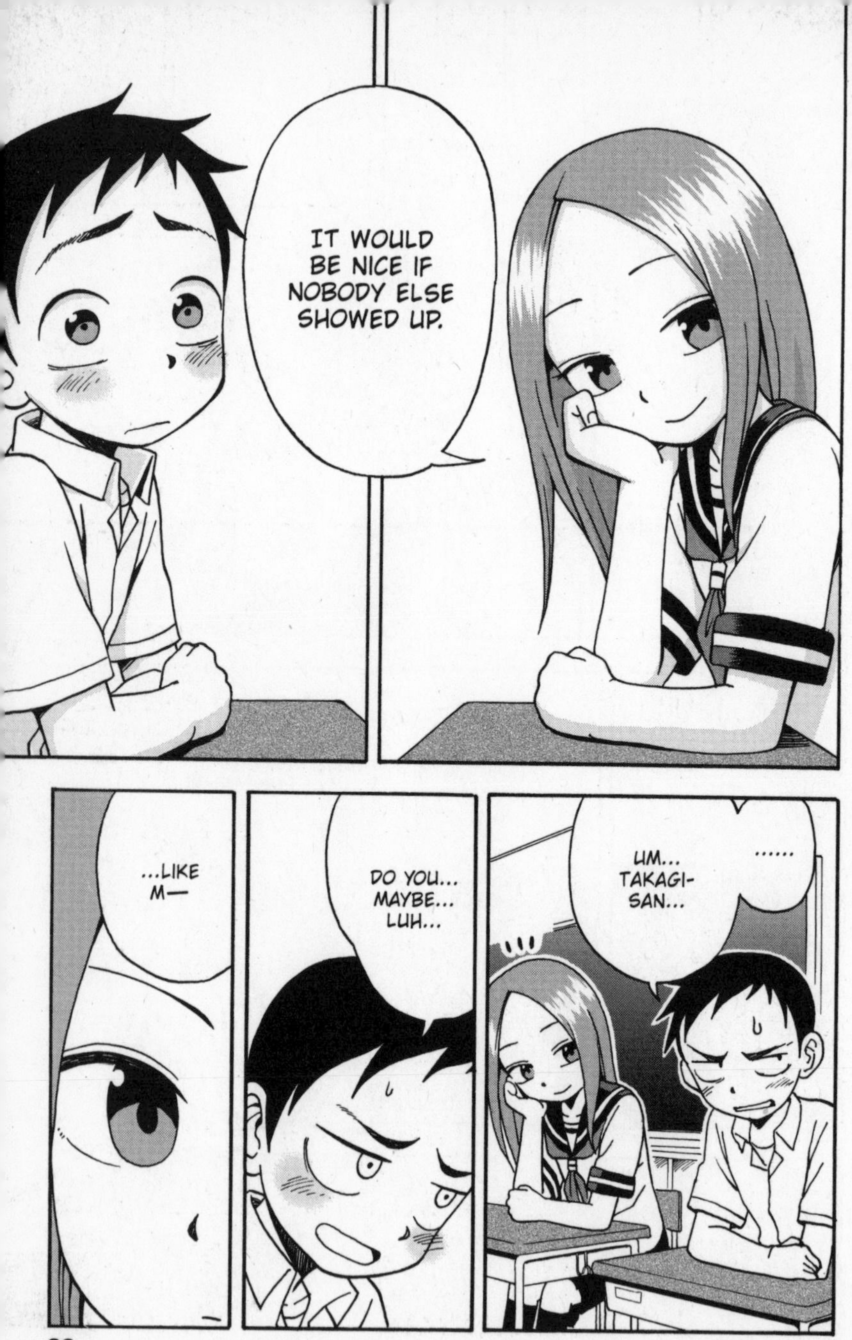
IT WOULD BE NICE IF NOBODY ELSE SHOWED UP.
......
UM... TAKAGI-SAN...
DO YOU... MAYBE... LUH...
...LIKE M—

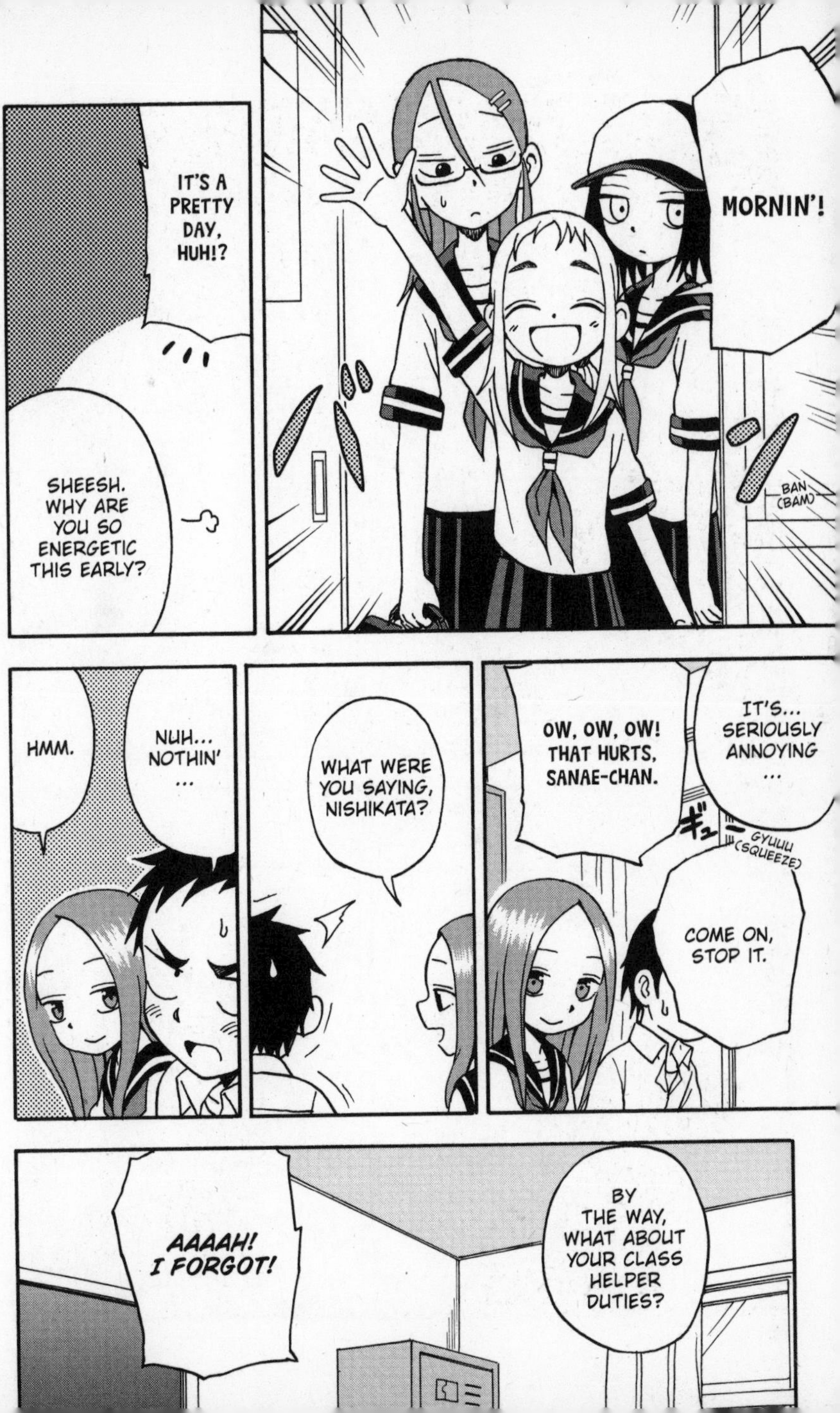
MORNIN'!
BAN (BAM)
IT'S A PRETTY DAY, HUH!?
SHEESH. WHY ARE YOU SO ENERGETIC THIS EARLY?
IT'S... SERIOUSLY ANNOYING...
OW, OW, OW! THAT HURTS, SANAE-CHAN.
ギュー GYUUU (SQUEEZE)
COME ON, STOP IT.
WHAT WERE YOU SAYING, NISHIKATA?
NUH... NOTHIN'...
HMM.
BY THE WAY, WHAT ABOUT YOUR CLASS HELPER DUTIES?
AAAAH! I FORGOT!

UMBRELLA

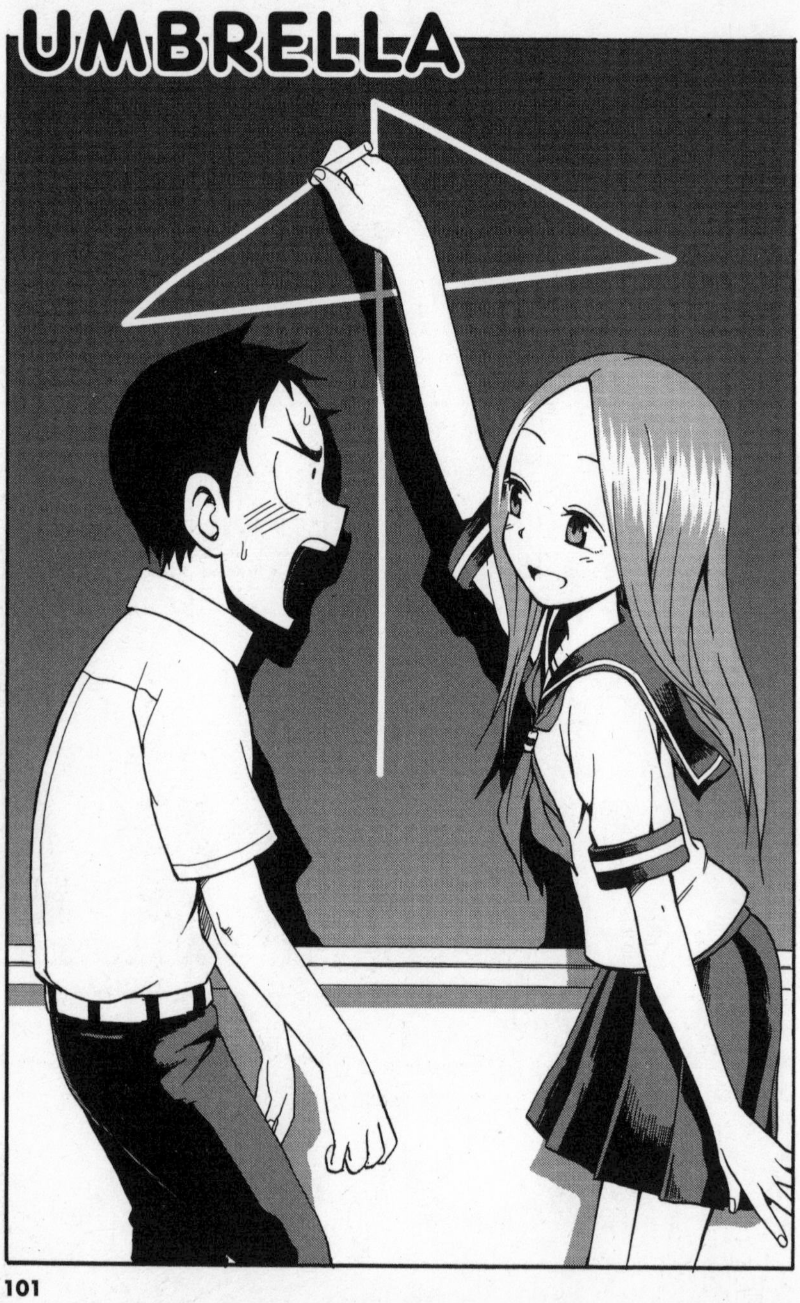

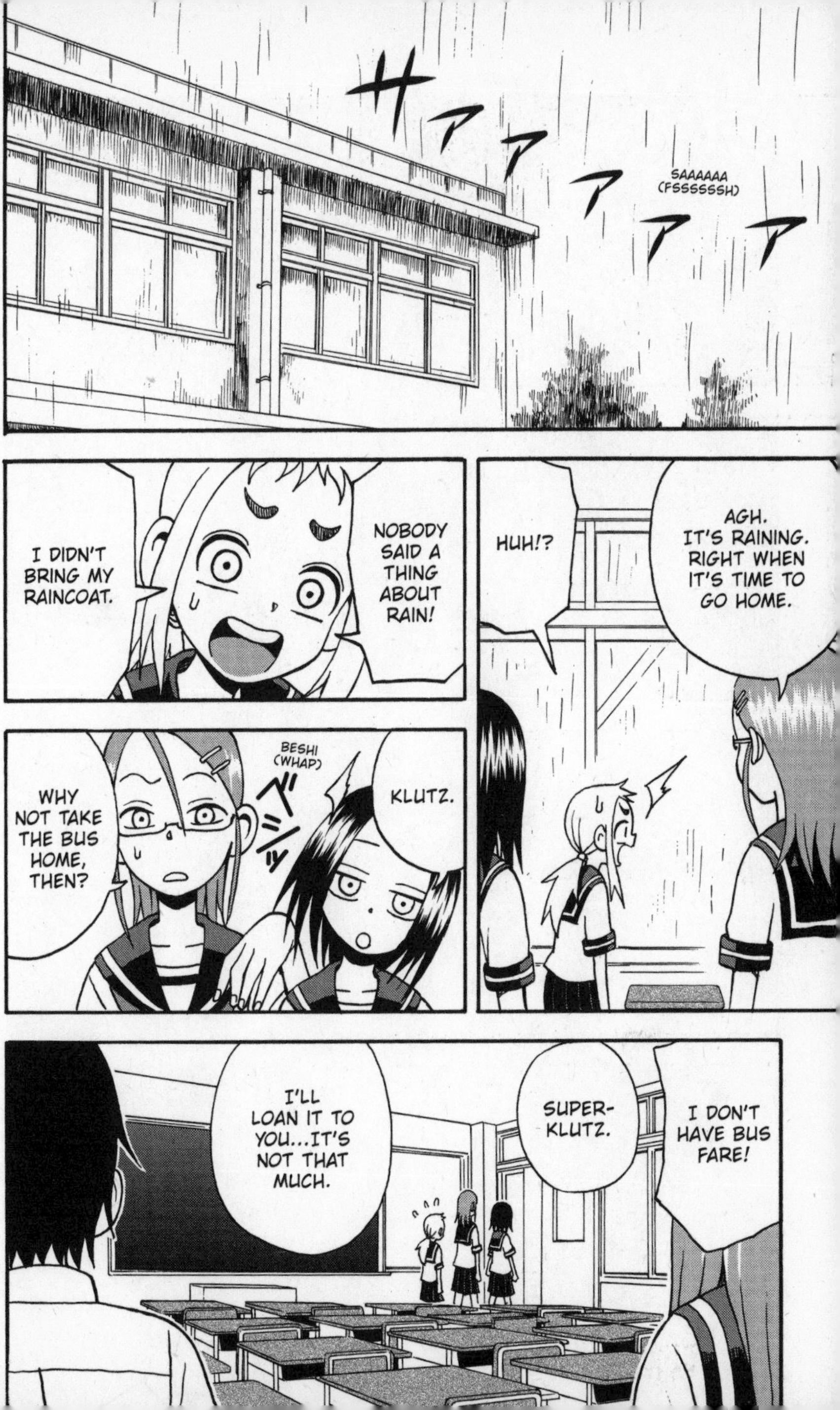
SAAAAAA (FSSSSSSH)
AGH. IT'S RAINING. RIGHT WHEN IT'S TIME TO GO HOME.
HUH!?
NOBODY SAID A THING ABOUT RAIN!
I DIDN'T BRING MY RAINCOAT.
KLUTZ.
BESHI (WHAP)
WHY NOT TAKE THE BUS HOME, THEN?
I DON'T HAVE BUS FARE!
SUPER-KLUTZ.
I'LL LOAN IT TO YOU...IT'S NOT THAT MUCH.

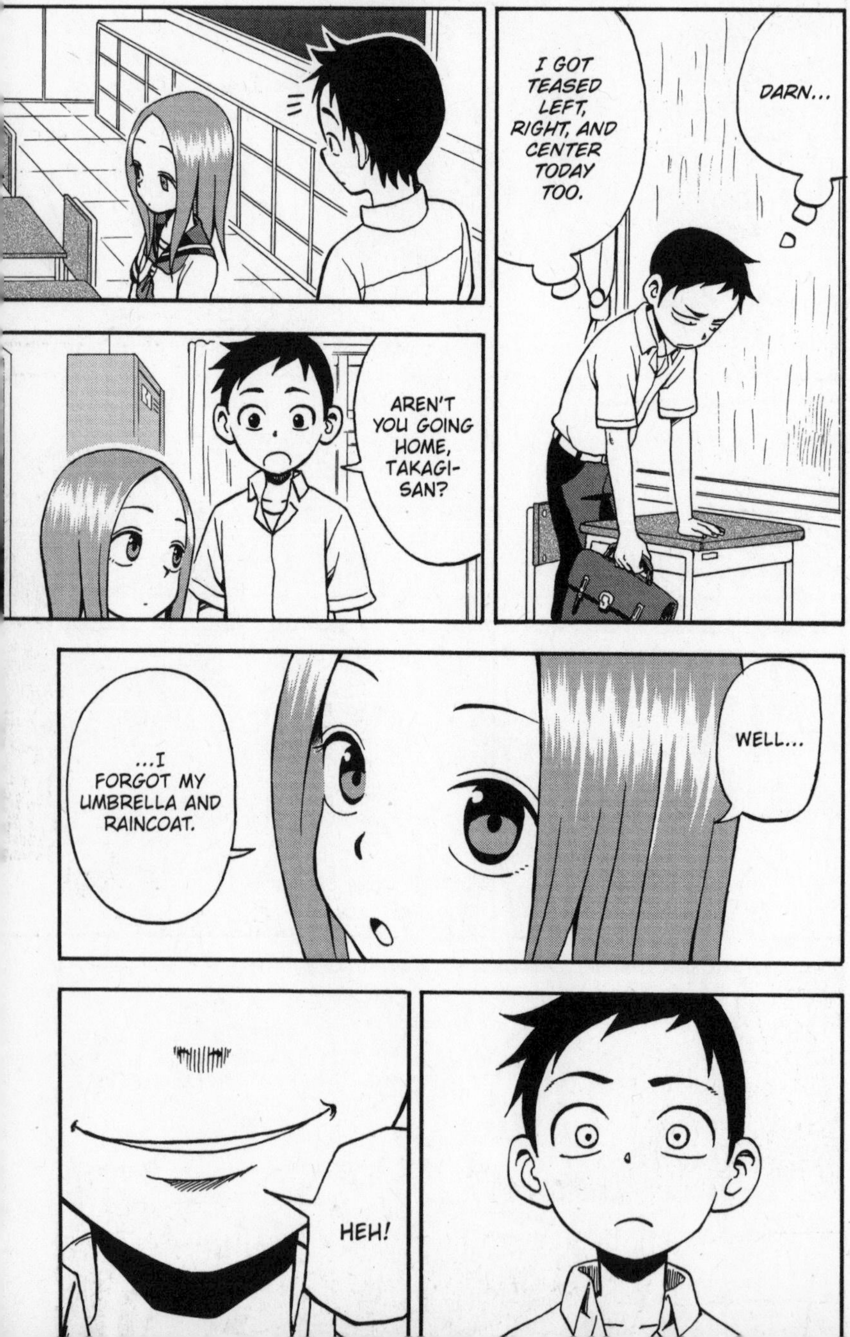
DARN...
I GOT TEASED LEFT, RIGHT, AND CENTER TODAY TOO.
AREN'T YOU GOING HOME, TAKAGI-SAN?
WELL...
...I FORGOT MY UMBRELLA AND RAINCOAT.
HEH!

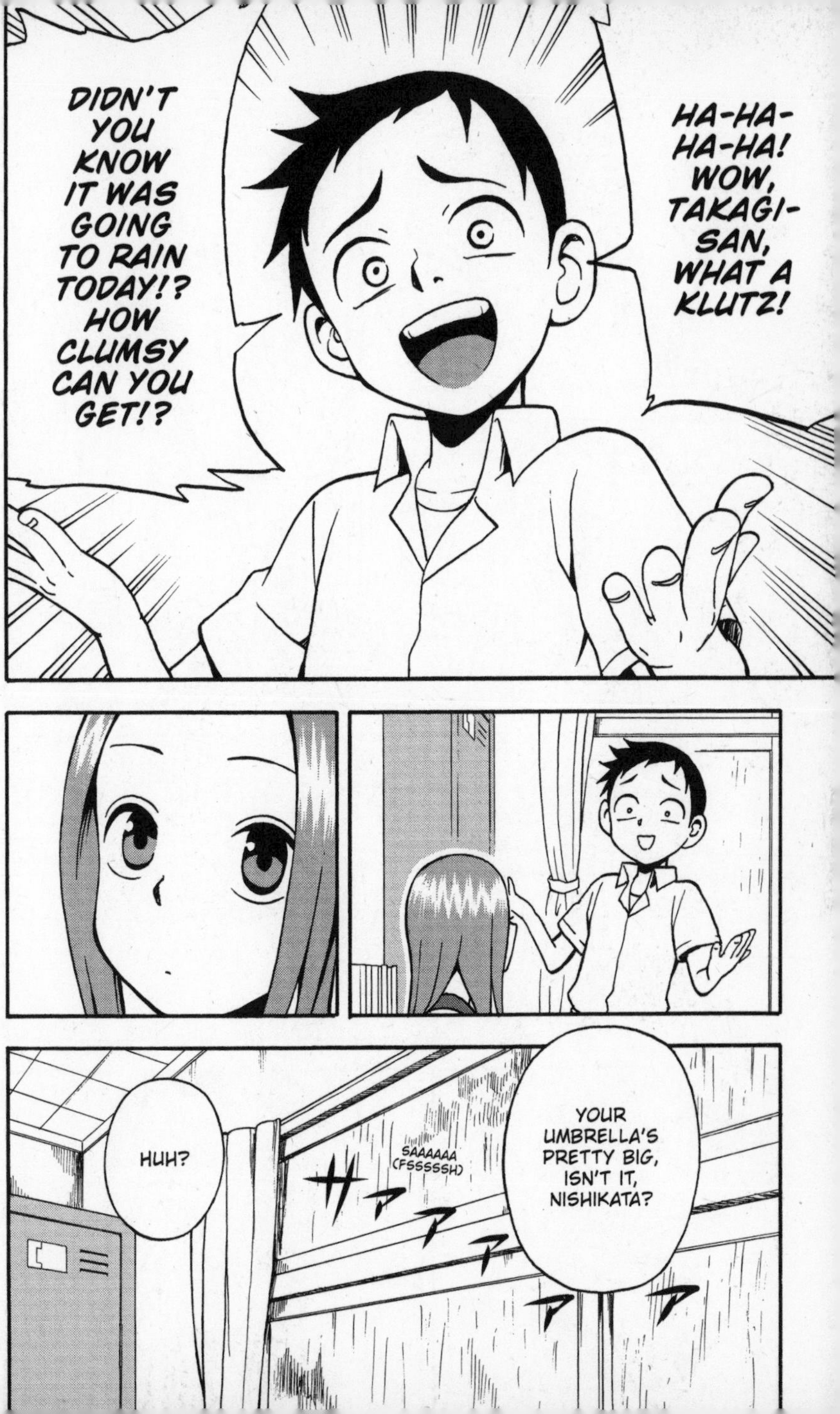
HA-HA-HA-HA! WOW, TAKAGI-SAN, WHAT A KLUTZ!
DIDN'T YOU KNOW IT WAS GOING TO RAIN TODAY!? HOW CLUMSY CAN YOU GET!?
YOUR UMBRELLA'S PRETTY BIG, ISN'T IT, NISHIKATA?
SAAAAAA (FSSSSSH)
HUH?

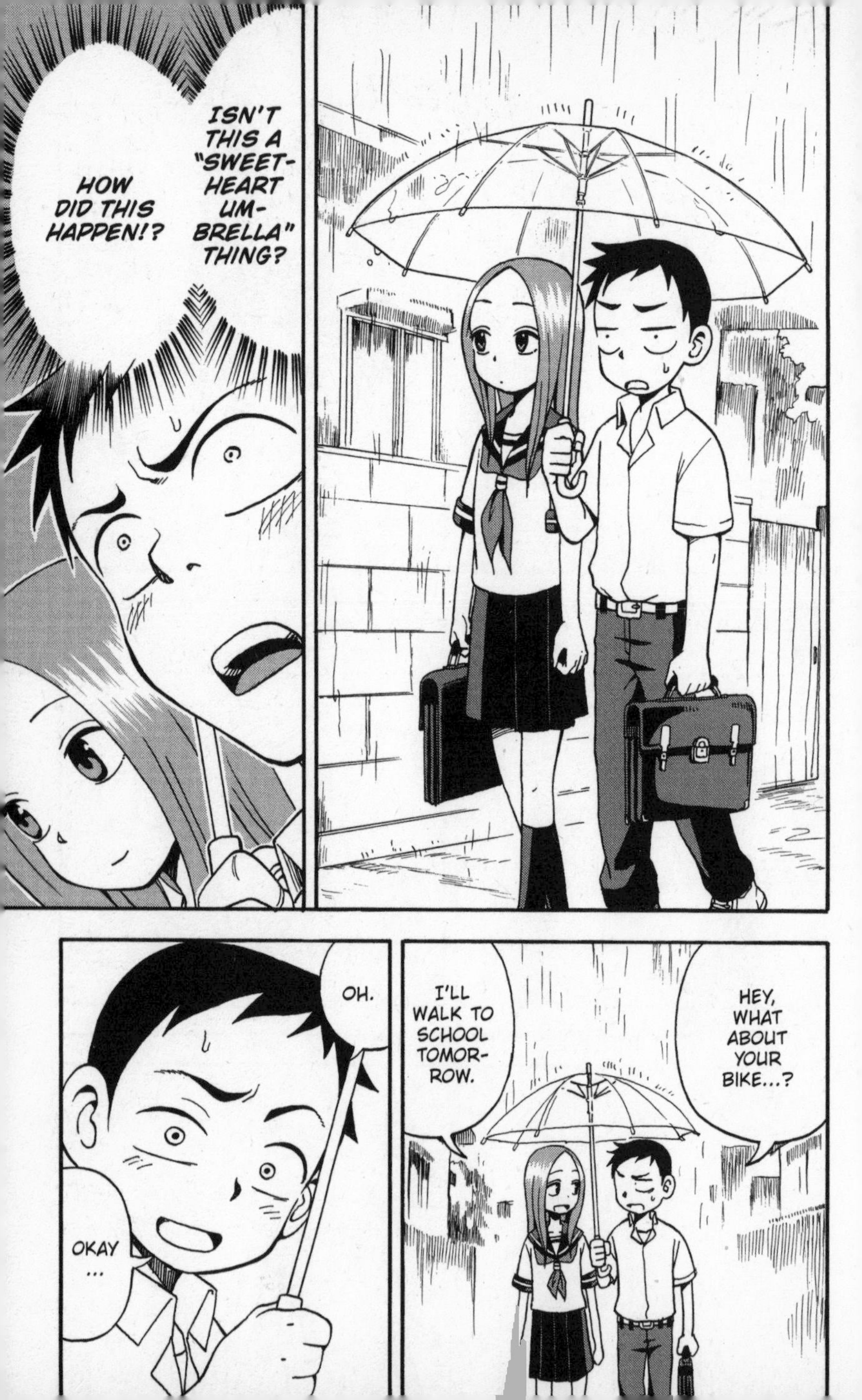
ISN'T THIS A "SWEET-HEART UM-BRELLA" THING?
HOW DID THIS HAPPEN!?
HEY, WHAT ABOUT YOUR BIKE...?
I'LL WALK TO SCHOOL TOMOR-ROW.
OH.
OKAY ...

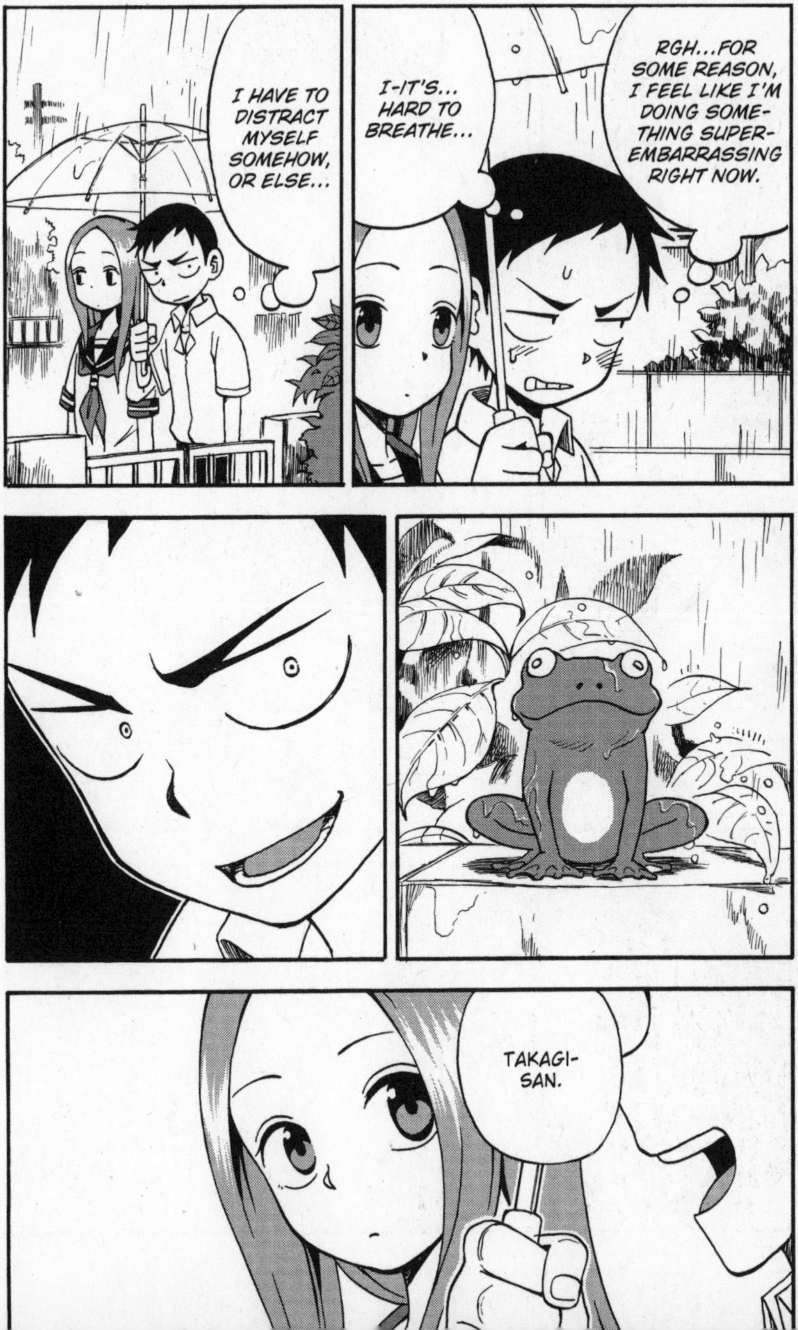
RGH...FOR SOME REASON, I FEEL LIKE I'M DOING SOME-THING SUPER-EMBARRASSING RIGHT NOW.
I-IT'S... HARD TO BREATHE...
I HAVE TO DISTRACT MYSELF SOMEHOW, OR ELSE...
TAKAGI-SAN.

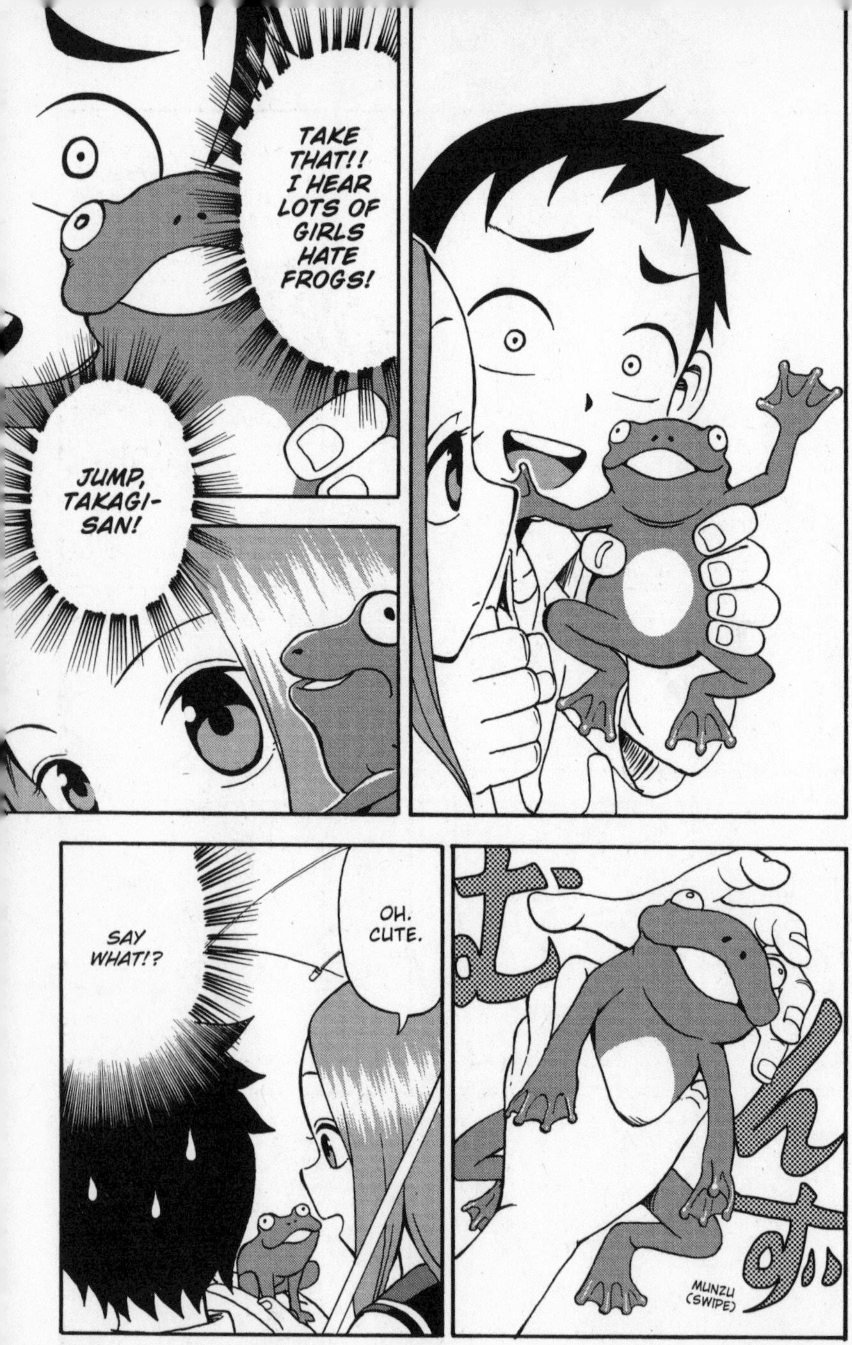
TAKE THAT!! I HEAR LOTS OF GIRLS HATE FROGS!
JUMP, TAKAGI-SAN!
MUNZU (SWIPE)
OH. CUTE.
SAY WHAT!?

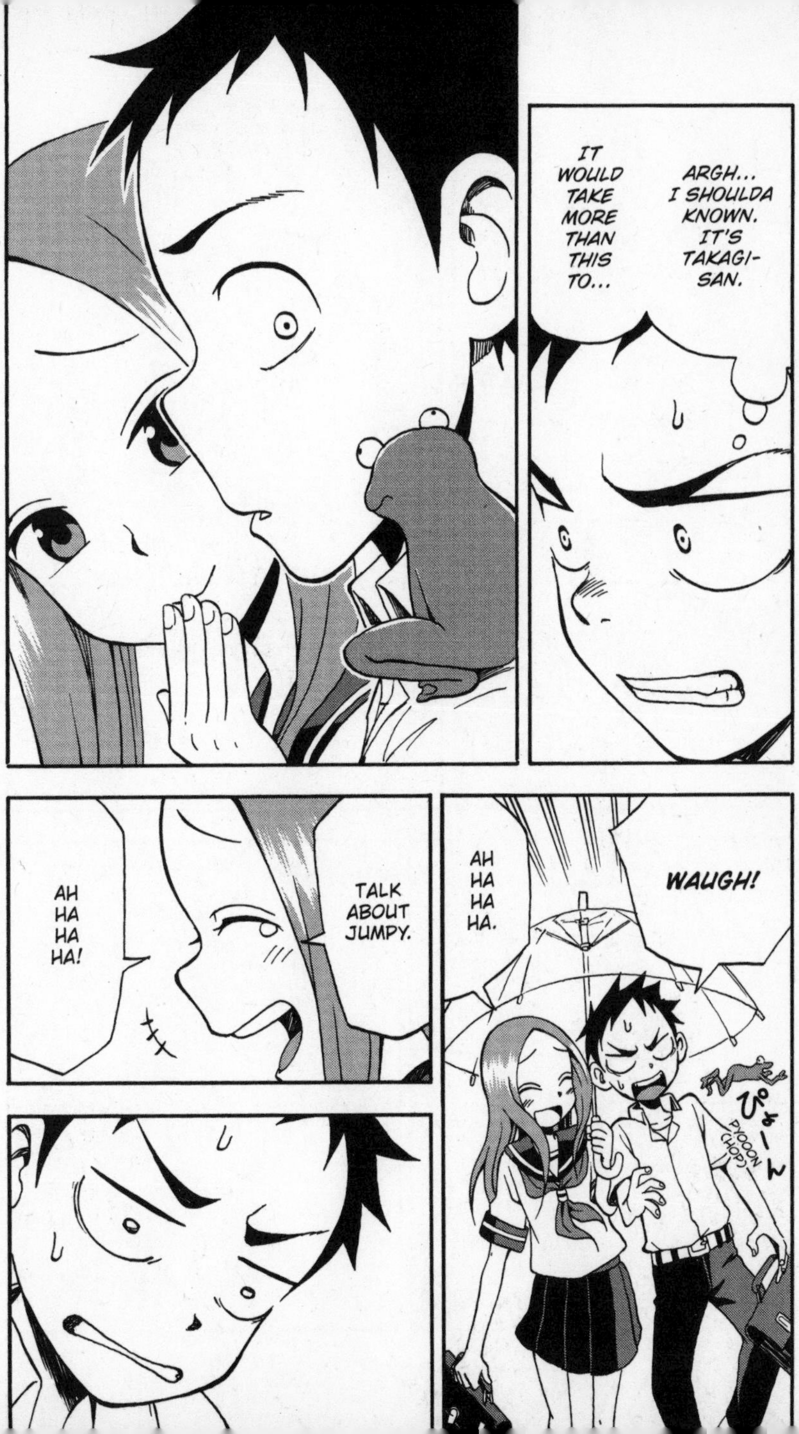
ARGH... I SHOULDA KNOWN. IT'S TAKAGI-SAN.
IT WOULD TAKE MORE THAN THIS TO...
WAUGH!
AH HA HA HA HA.
ぴょーん
PYOOON (HOP)
TALK ABOUT JUMPY.
AH HA HA HA!

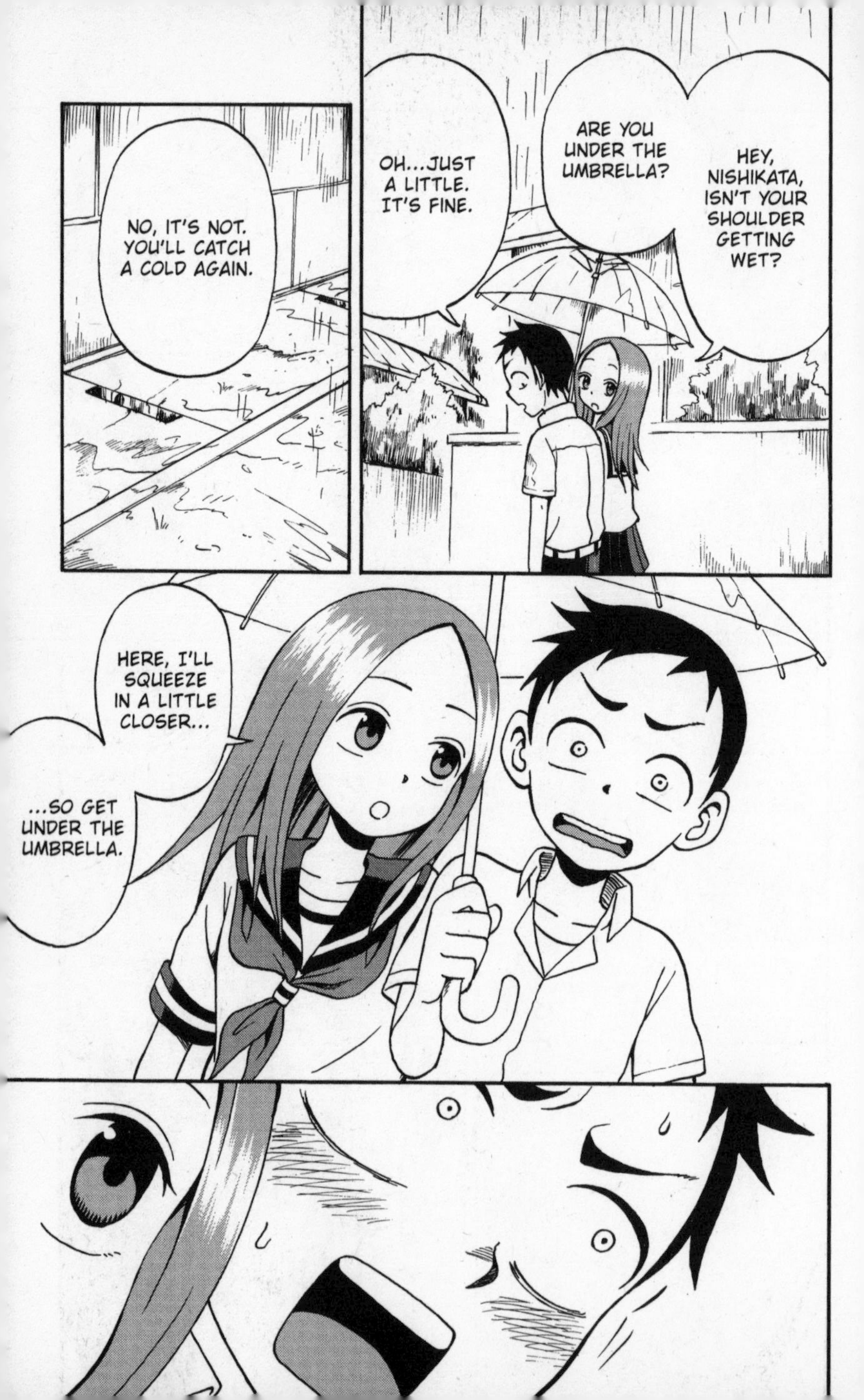
HEY, NISHIKATA, ISN'T YOUR SHOULDER GETTING WET?
ARE YOU UNDER THE UMBRELLA?
OH...JUST A LITTLE. IT'S FINE.
NO, IT'S NOT. YOU'LL CATCH A COLD AGAIN.
HERE, I'LL SQUEEZE IN A LITTLE CLOSER...
...SO GET UNDER THE UMBRELLA.

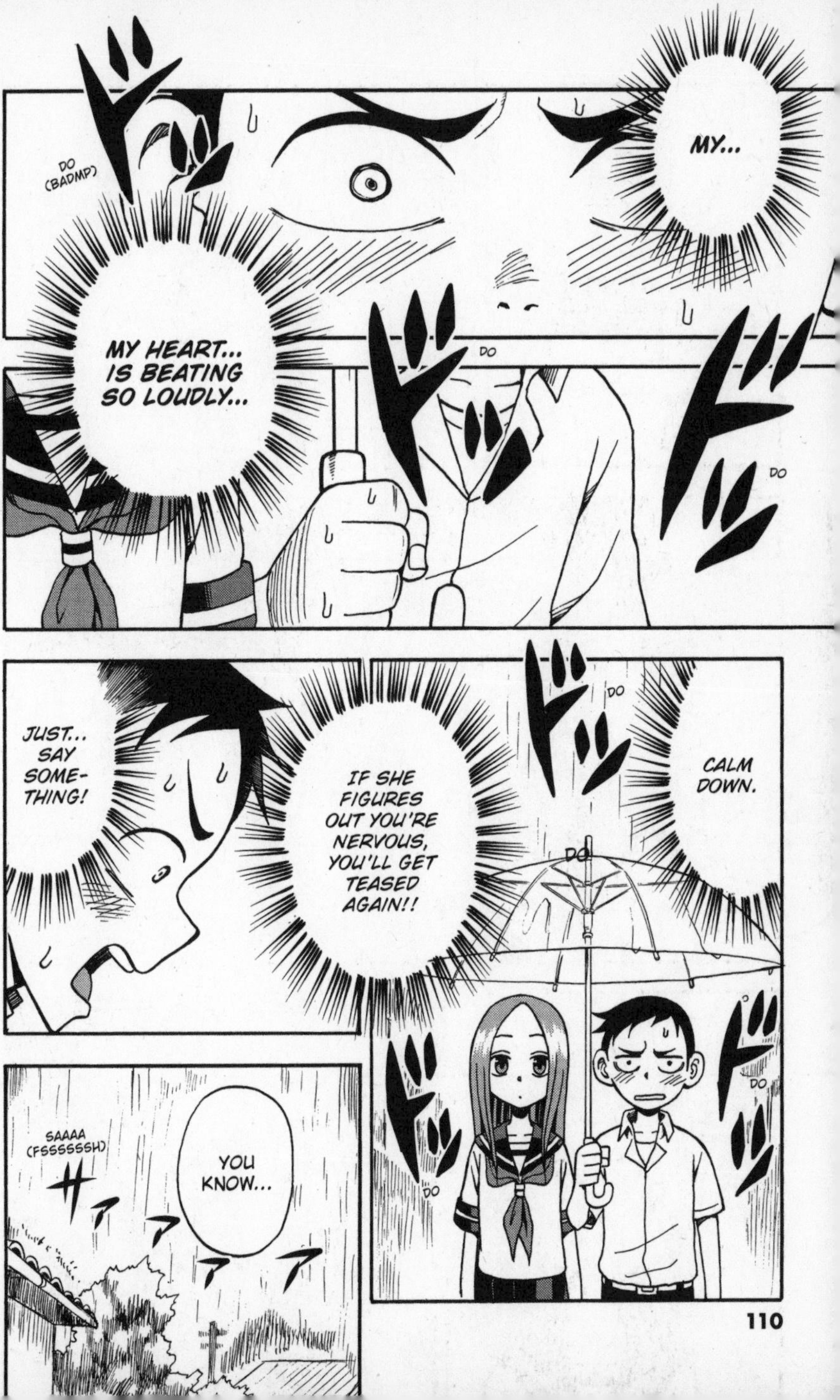
MY...
DO (BADMP)
DO
DO
MY HEART... IS BEATING SO LOUDLY...
DO
CALM DOWN.
IF SHE FIGURES OUT YOU'RE NERVOUS, YOU'LL GET TEASED AGAIN!!
DO
DO
DO
JUST... SAY SOME-THING!
SAAAA (FSSSSSSH)
YOU KNOW...

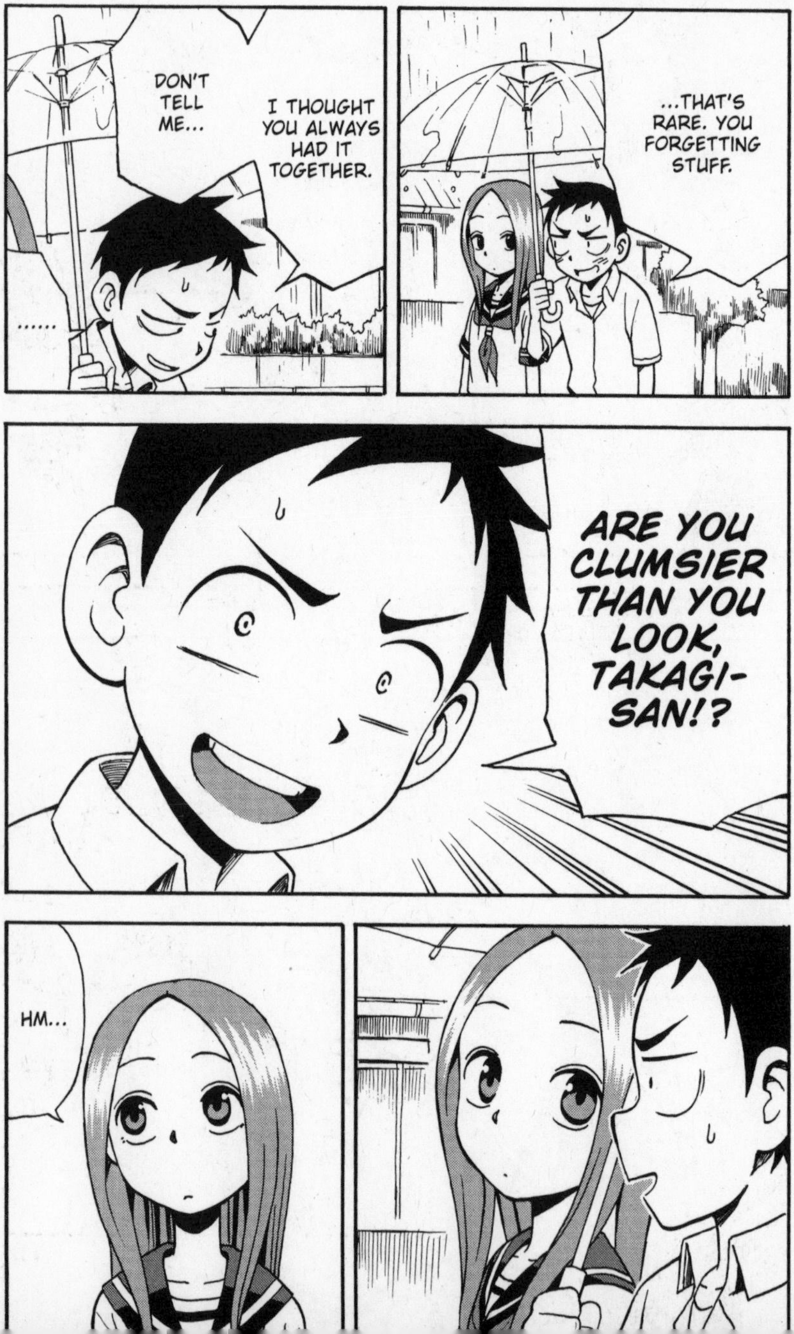
...THAT'S RARE. YOU FORGETTING STUFF.
I THOUGHT YOU ALWAYS HAD IT TOGETHER.
DON'T TELL ME...
......
ARE YOU CLUMSIER THAN YOU LOOK, TAKAGI-SAN!?
HM...

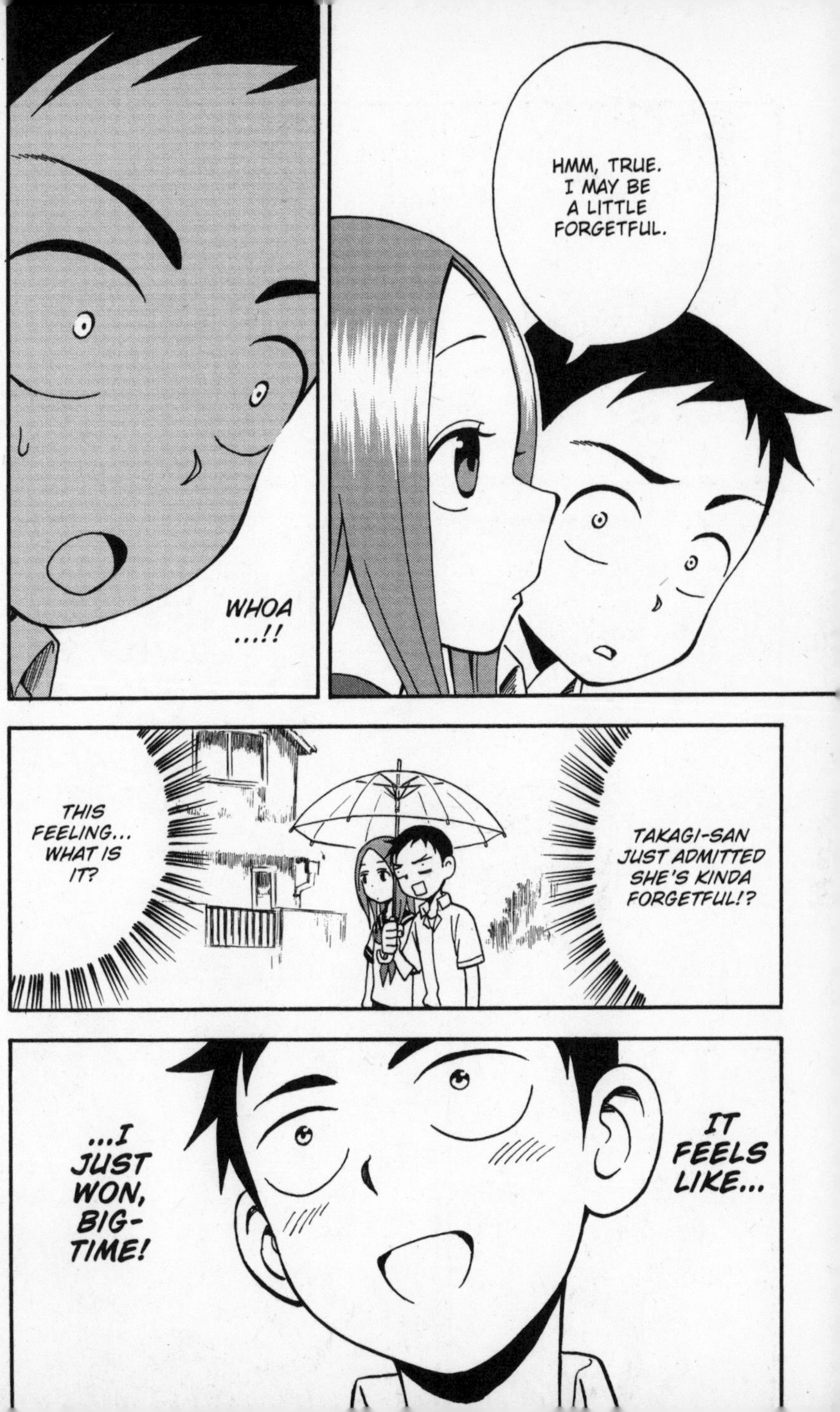
HMM, TRUE. I MAY BE A LITTLE FORGETFUL.
WHOA ...!!
TAKAGI-SAN JUST ADMITTED SHE'S KINDA FORGETFUL!?
THIS FEELING... WHAT IS IT?
IT FEELS LIKE...
...I JUST WON, BIG-TIME!

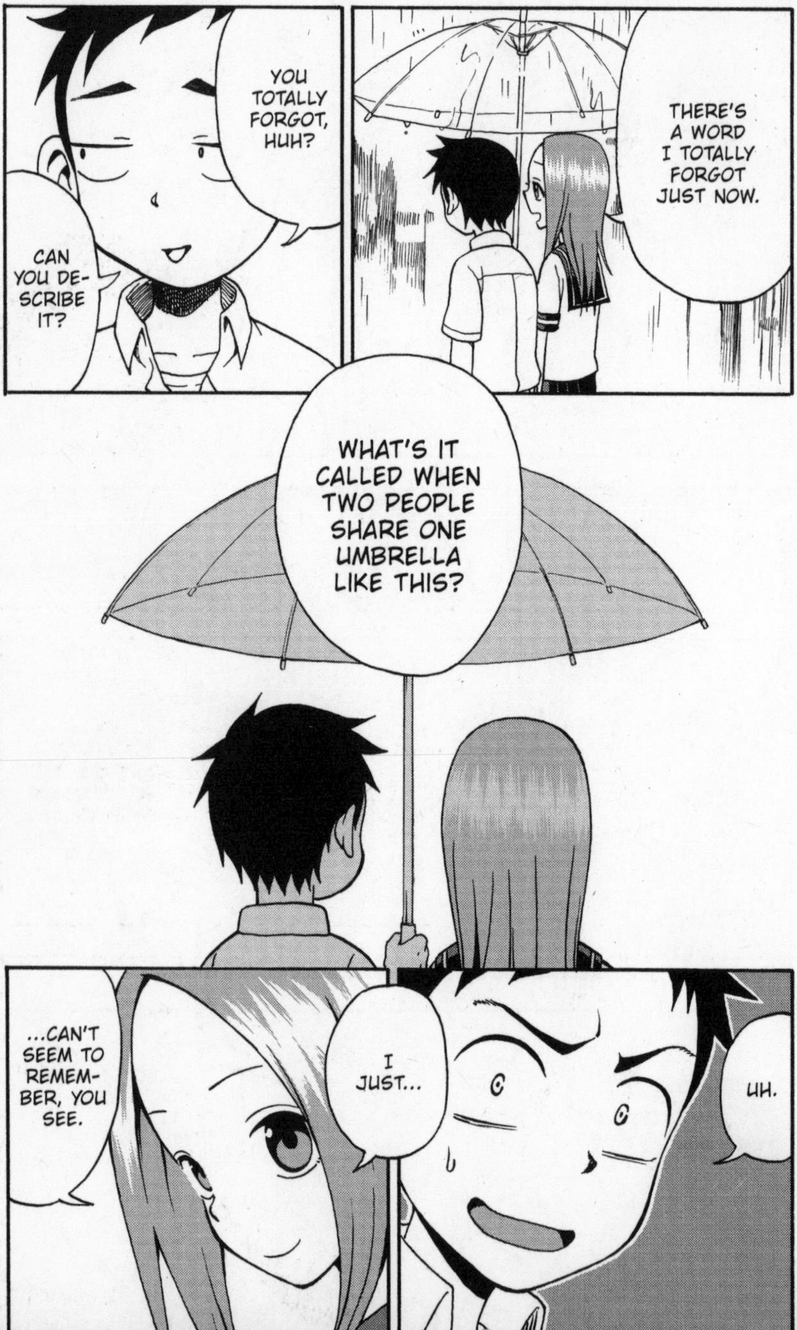
THERE'S A WORD I TOTALLY FORGOT JUST NOW.
YOU TOTALLY FORGOT, HUH?
CAN YOU DE-SCRIBE IT?
WHAT'S IT CALLED WHEN TWO PEOPLE SHARE ONE UMBRELLA LIKE THIS?
UH.
I JUST...
...CAN'T SEEM TO REMEMBER, YOU SEE.

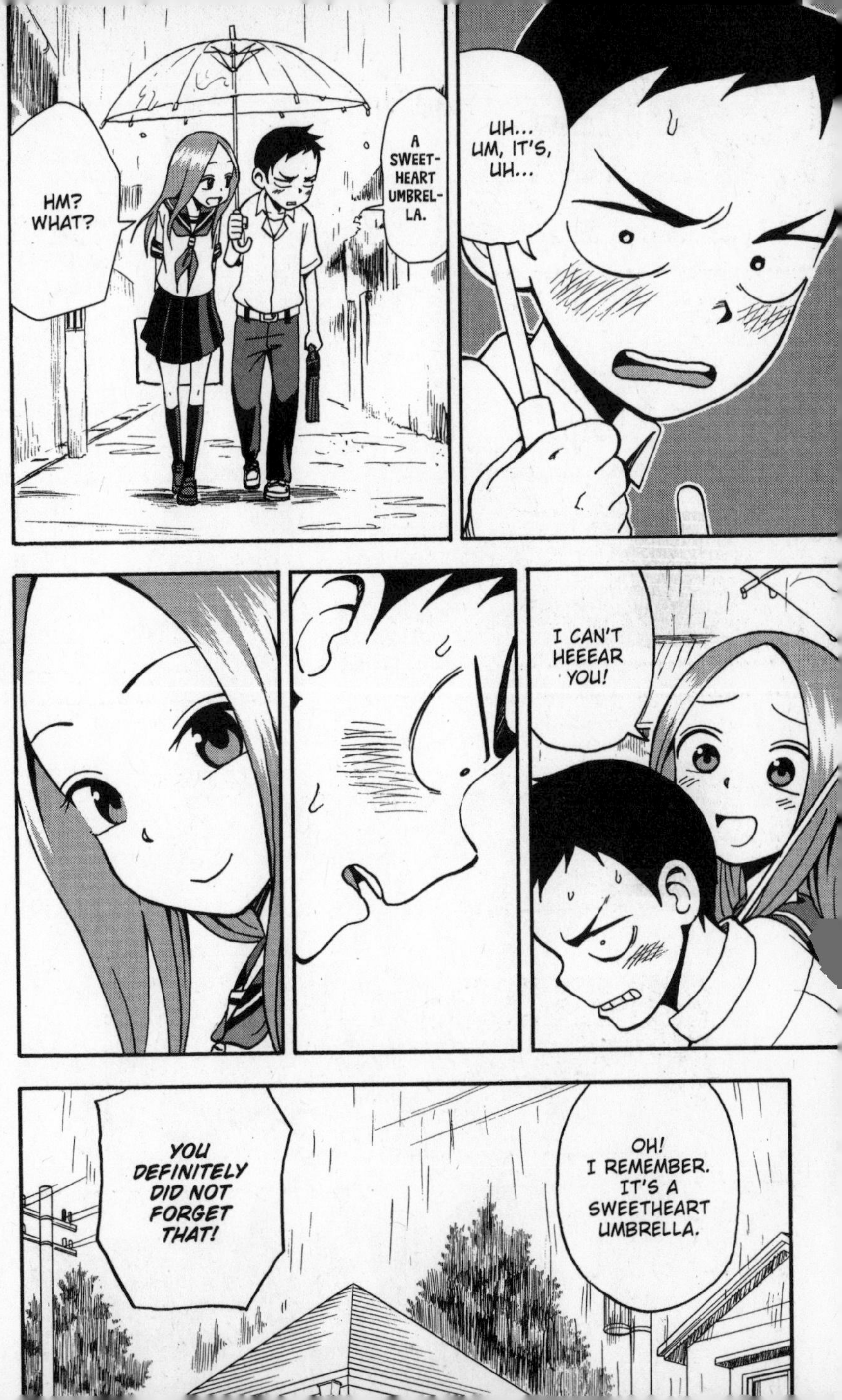
UH... UM, IT'S, UH...
A SWEET-HEART UMBREL-LA.
HM? WHAT?
I CAN'T HEEEAR YOU!
OH! I REMEMBER. IT'S A SWEETHEART UMBRELLA.
YOU DEFINITELY DID NOT FORGET THAT!

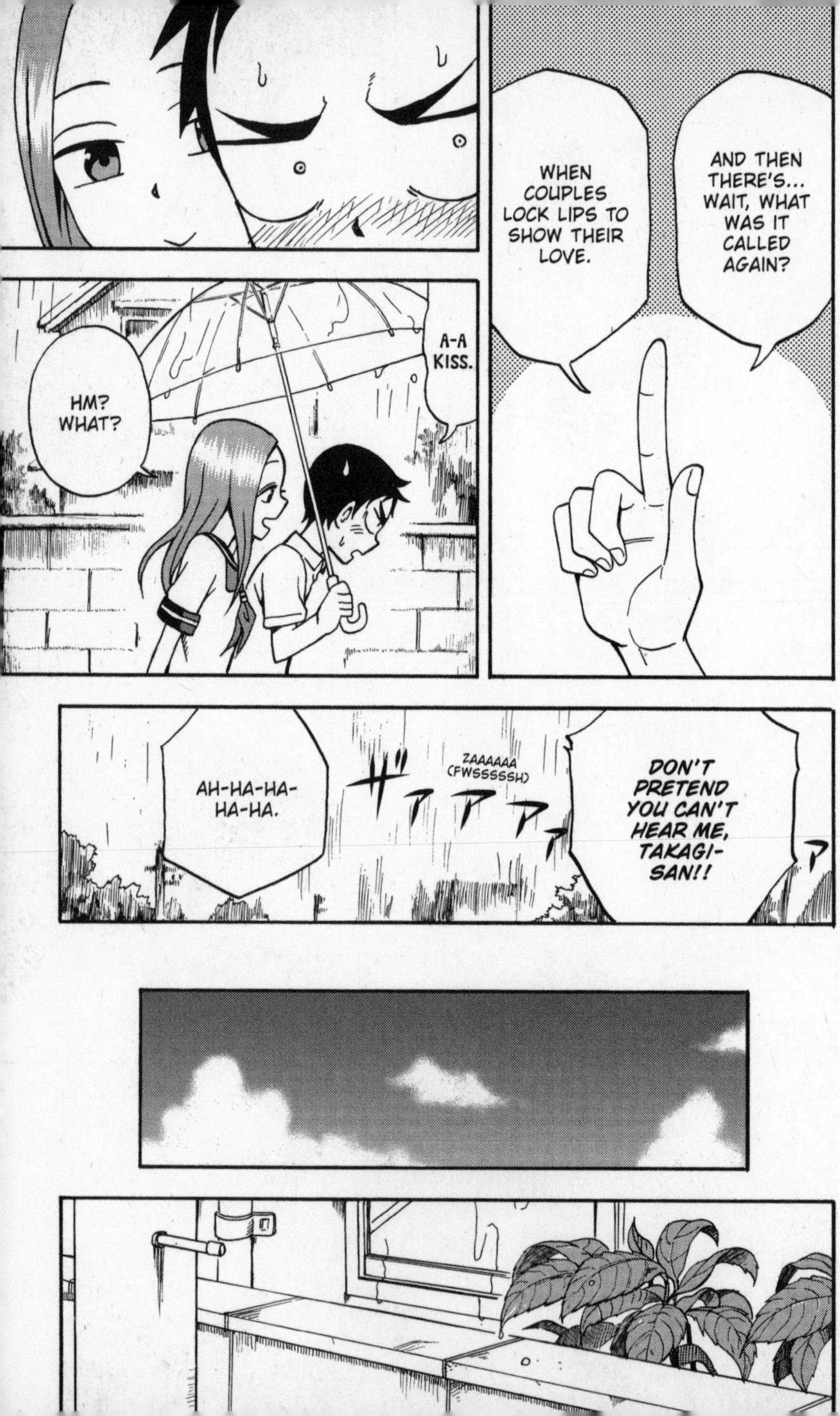
AND THEN THERE'S... WAIT, WHAT WAS IT CALLED AGAIN?
WHEN COUPLES LOCK LIPS TO SHOW THEIR LOVE.
A-A KISS.
HM? WHAT?
DON'T PRETEND YOU CAN'T HEAR ME, TAKAGI-SAN!!
ZAAAAAA (FWSSSSSH)
AH-HA-HA-HA-HA.

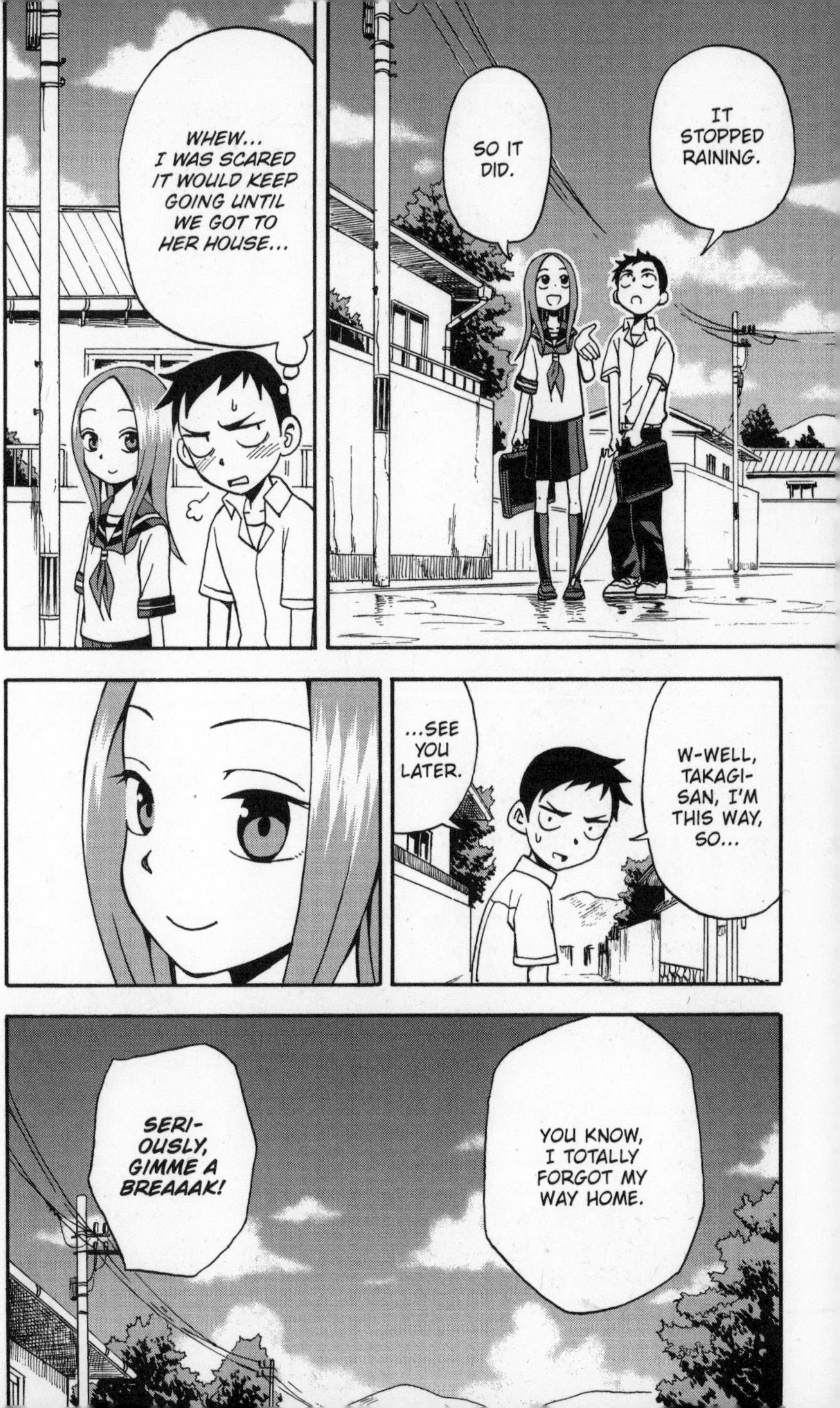
IT STOPPED RAINING.
SO IT DID.
WHEW... I WAS SCARED IT WOULD KEEP GOING UNTIL WE GOT TO HER HOUSE...
W-WELL, TAKAGI-SAN, I'M THIS WAY, SO...
...SEE YOU LATER.
YOU KNOW, I TOTALLY FORGOT MY WAY HOME.
SERI-OUSLY, GIMME A BREAAAK!

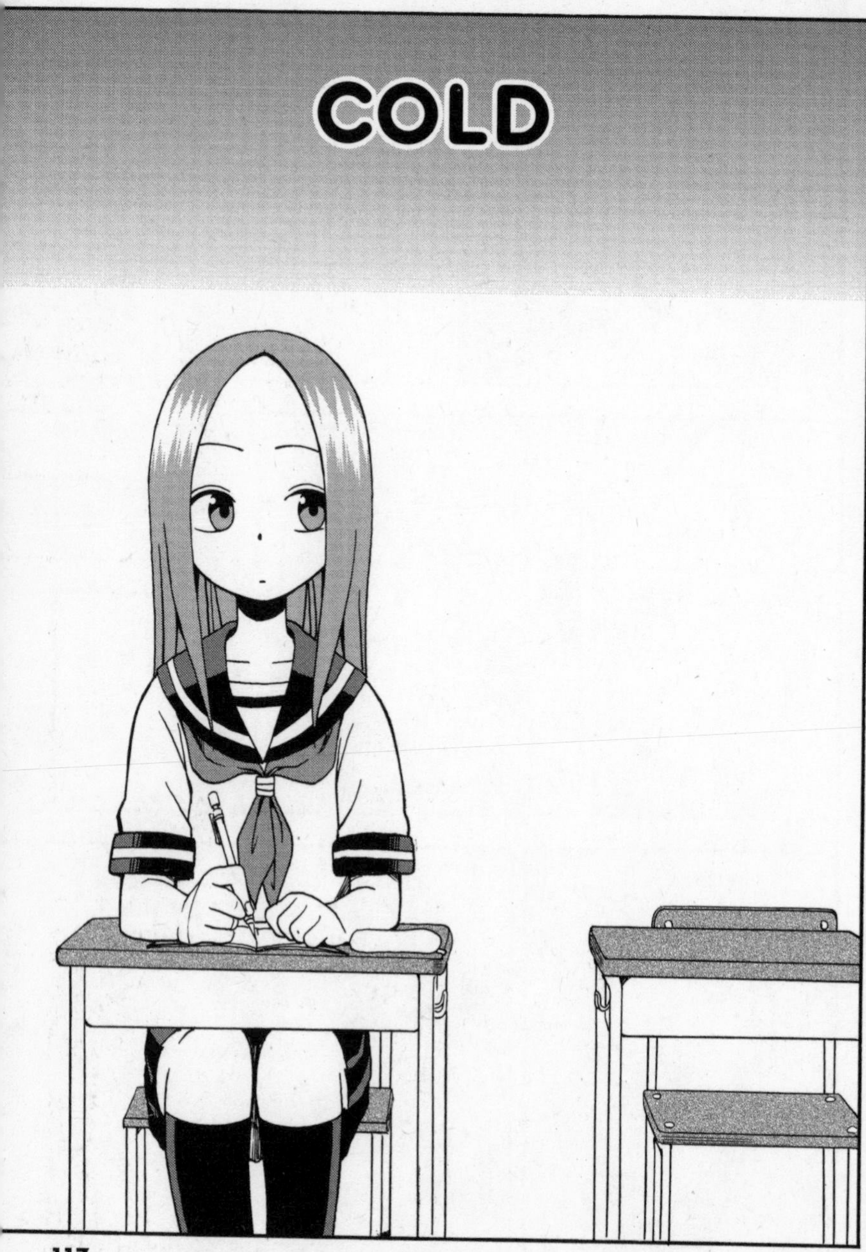
COLD

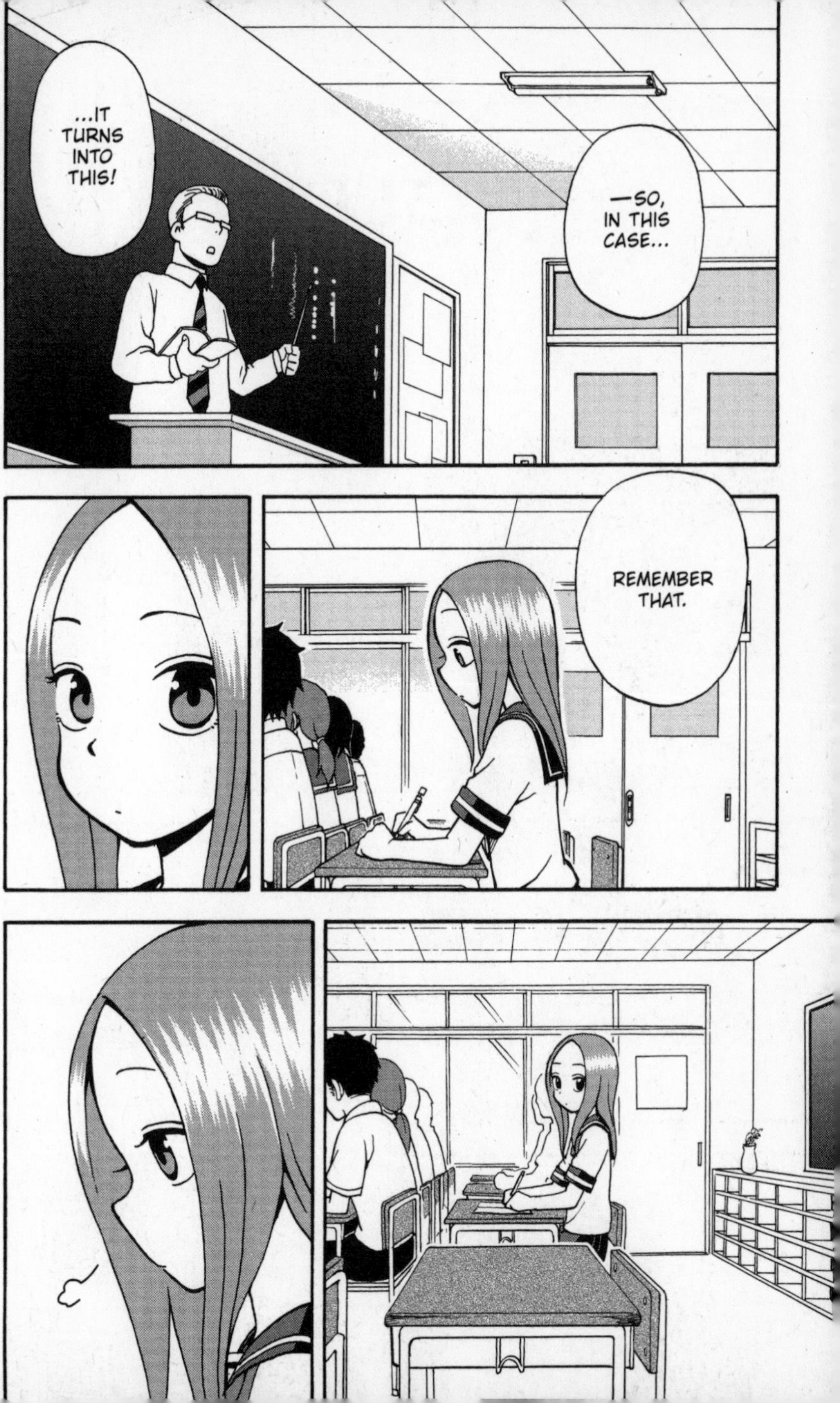
—SO, IN THIS CASE...
...IT TURNS INTO THIS!
REMEMBER THAT.

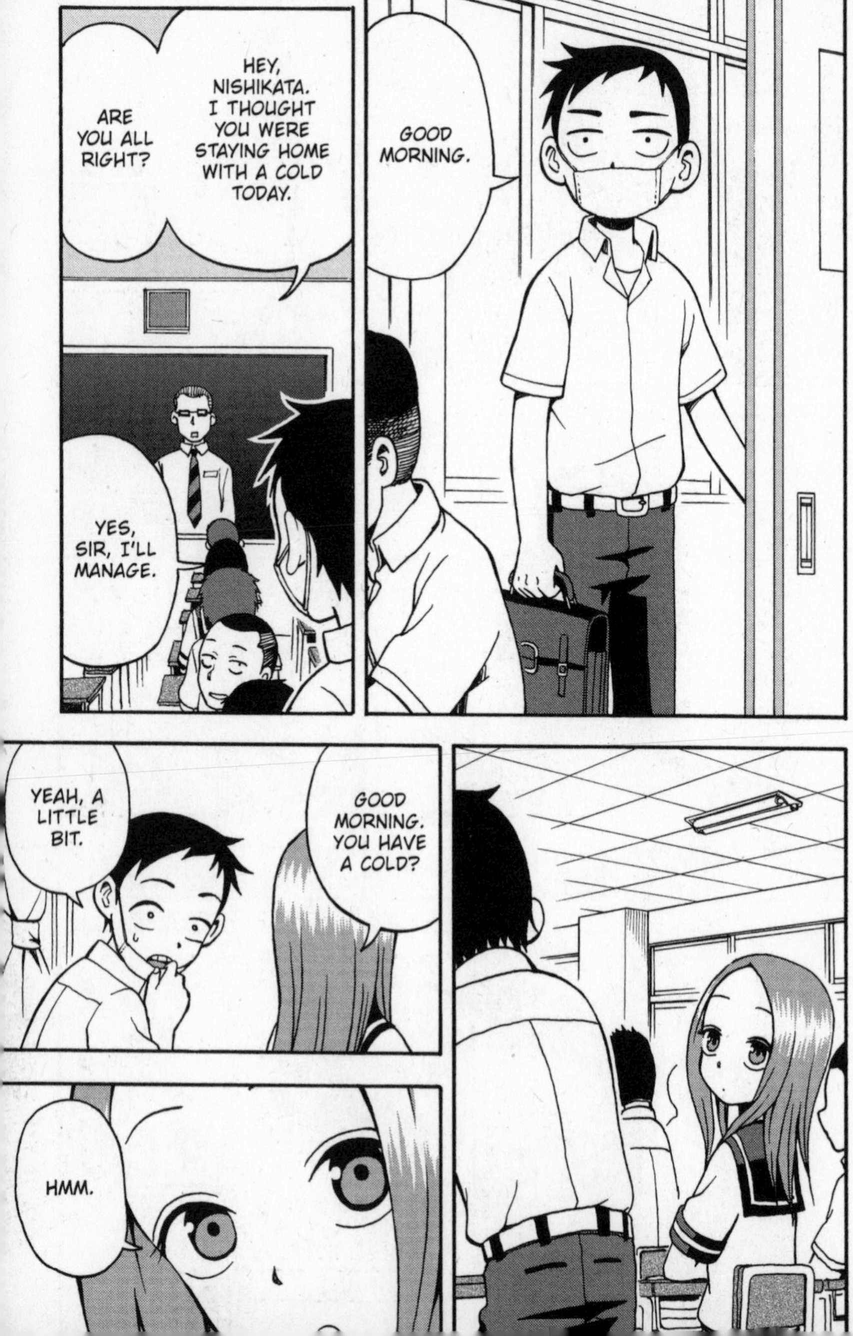
GOOD MORNING.
HEY, NISHIKATA. I THOUGHT YOU WERE STAYING HOME WITH A COLD TODAY.
ARE YOU ALL RIGHT?
YES, SIR, I'LL MANAGE.
GOOD MORNING. YOU HAVE A COLD?
YEAH, A LITTLE BIT.
HMM.

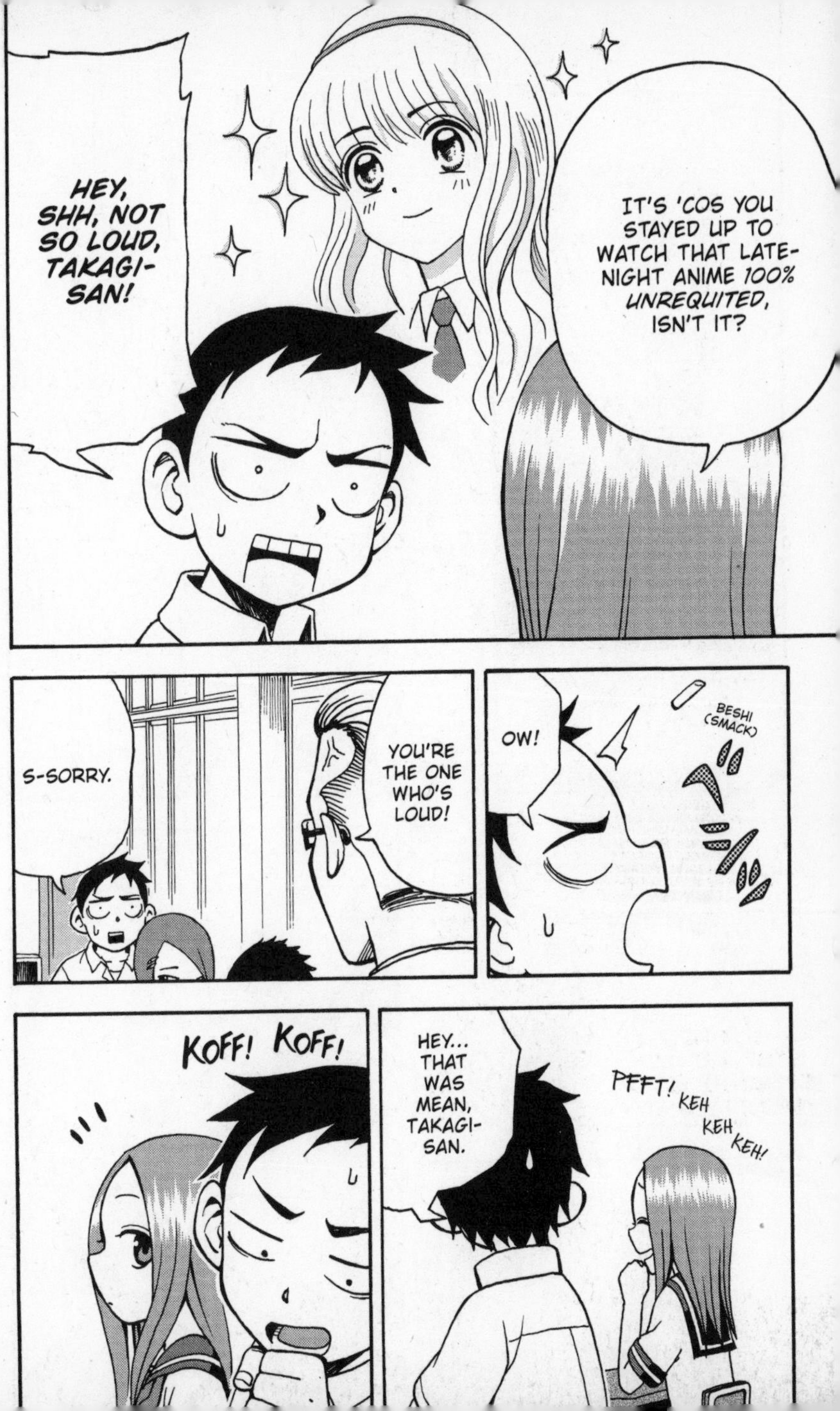
IT'S 'COS YOU STAYED UP TO WATCH THAT LATE-NIGHT ANIME *100% UNREQUITED*, ISN'T IT?
HEY, SHH, NOT SO LOUD, TAKAGI-SAN!
BESHI (SMACK)
OW!
YOU'RE THE ONE WHO'S LOUD!
S-SORRY.
PFFT! KEH KEH KEH!
HEY... THAT WAS MEAN, TAKAGI-SAN.
KOFF! KOFF!

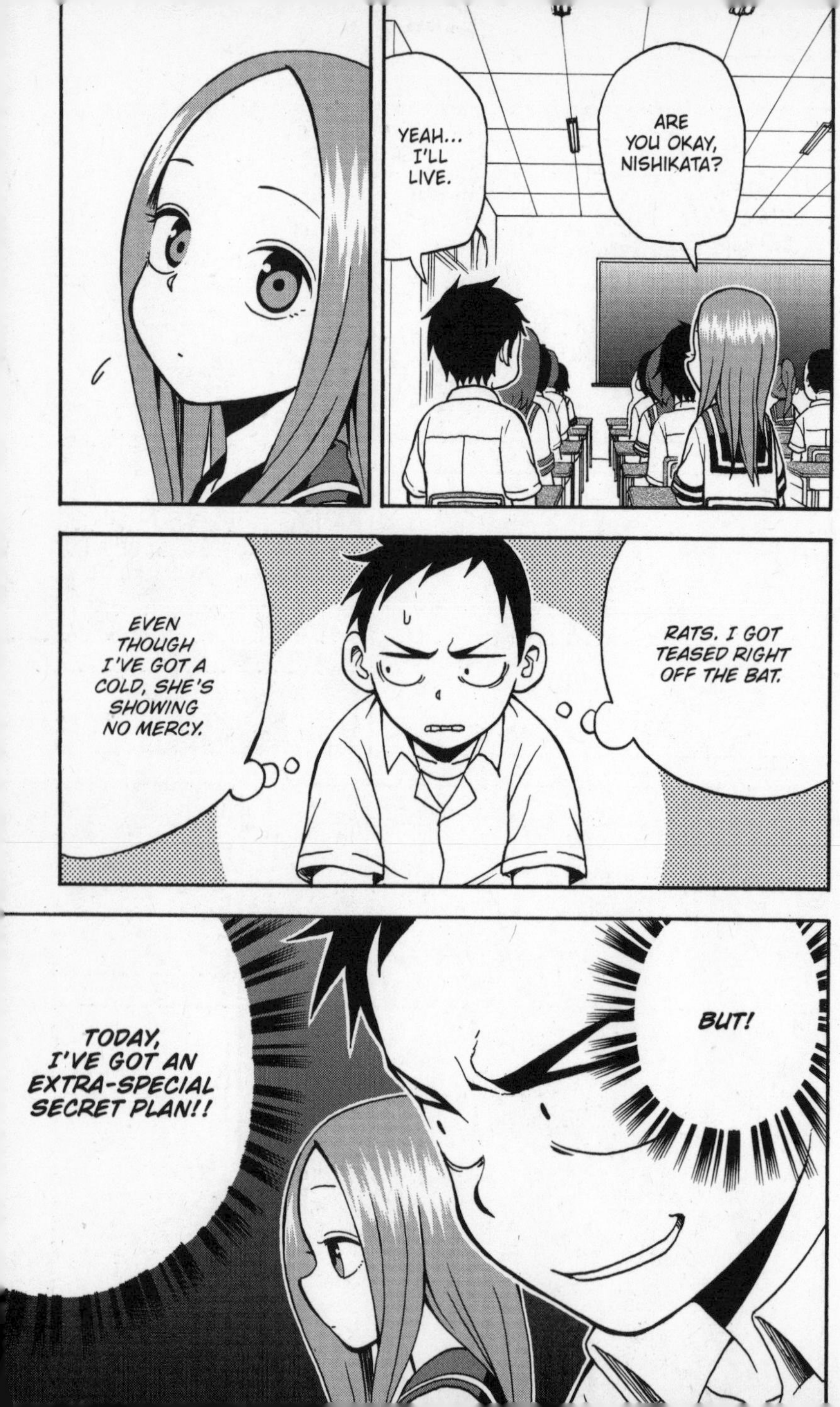
ARE YOU OKAY, NISHIKATA?
YEAH... I'LL LIVE.
RATS. I GOT TEASED RIGHT OFF THE BAT.
EVEN THOUGH I'VE GOT A COLD, SHE'S SHOWING NO MERCY.
BUT!
TODAY, I'VE GOT AN EXTRA-SPECIAL SECRET PLAN!!

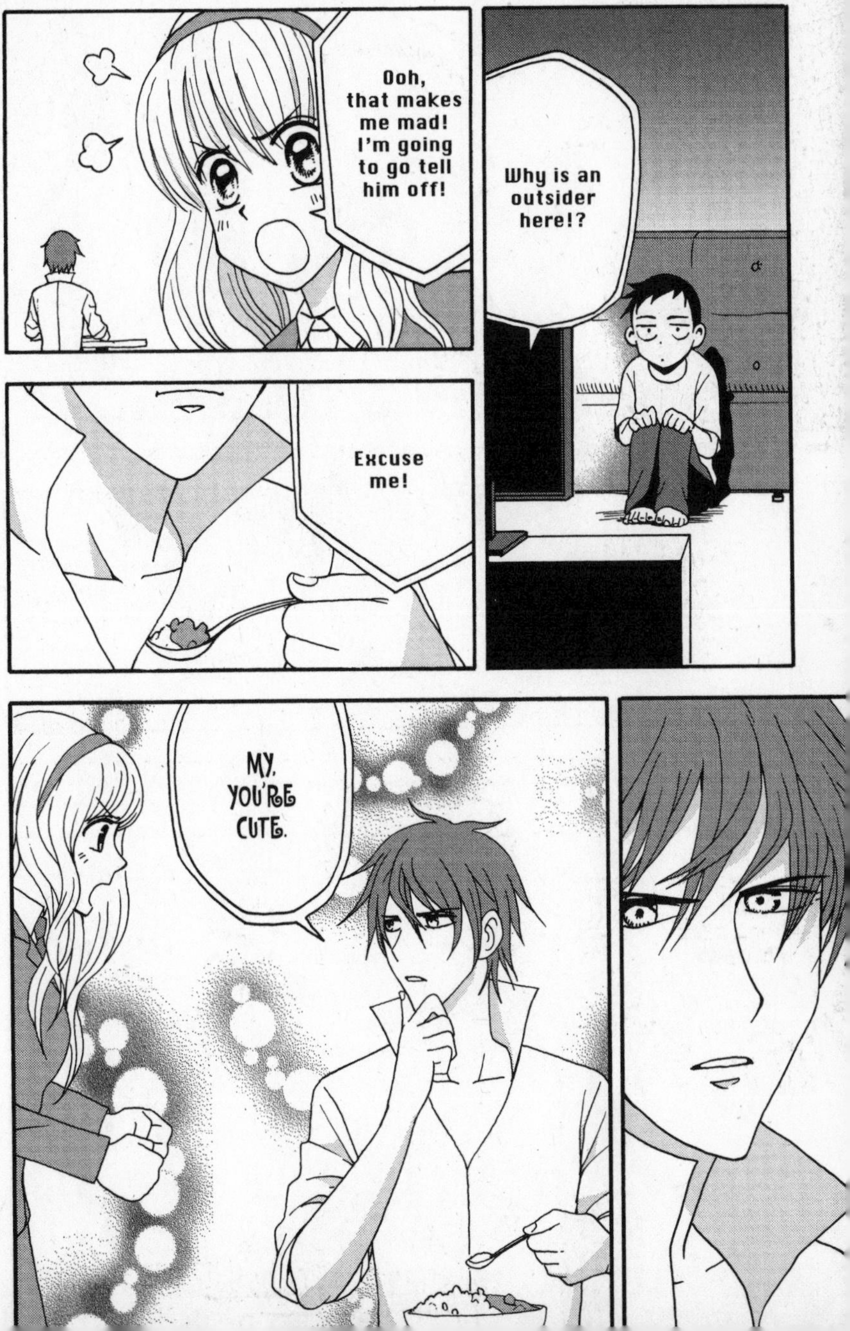
Why is an outsider here!?
Ooh, that makes me mad! I'm going to go tell him off!
Excuse me!
MY. YOU'RE CUTE.

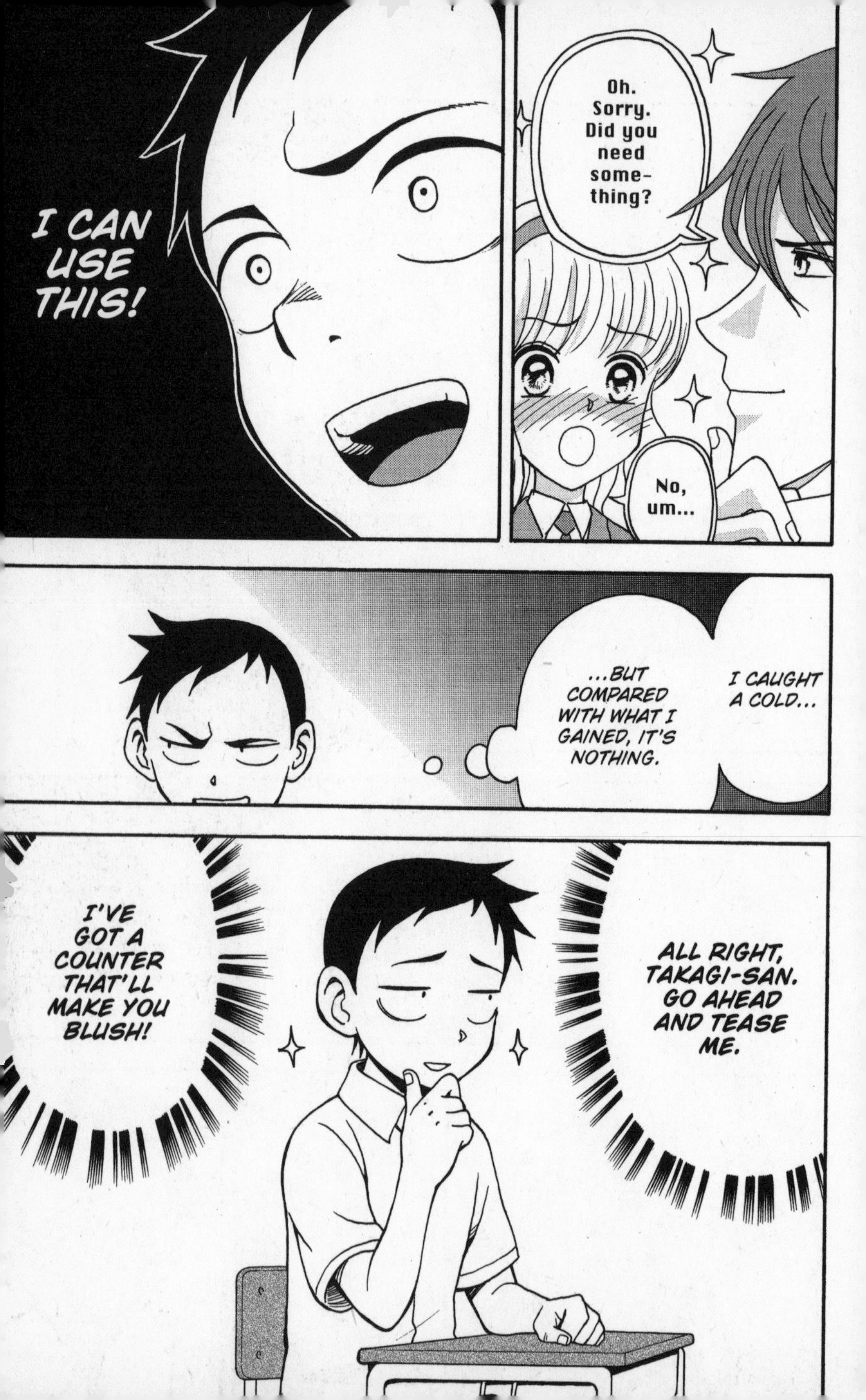
Oh. Sorry. Did you need some-thing?
No, um...
I CAN USE THIS!
I CAUGHT A COLD...
...BUT COMPARED WITH WHAT I GAINED, IT'S NOTHING.
ALL RIGHT, TAKAGI-SAN. GO AHEAD AND TEASE ME.
I'VE GOT A COUNTER THAT'LL MAKE YOU BLUSH!

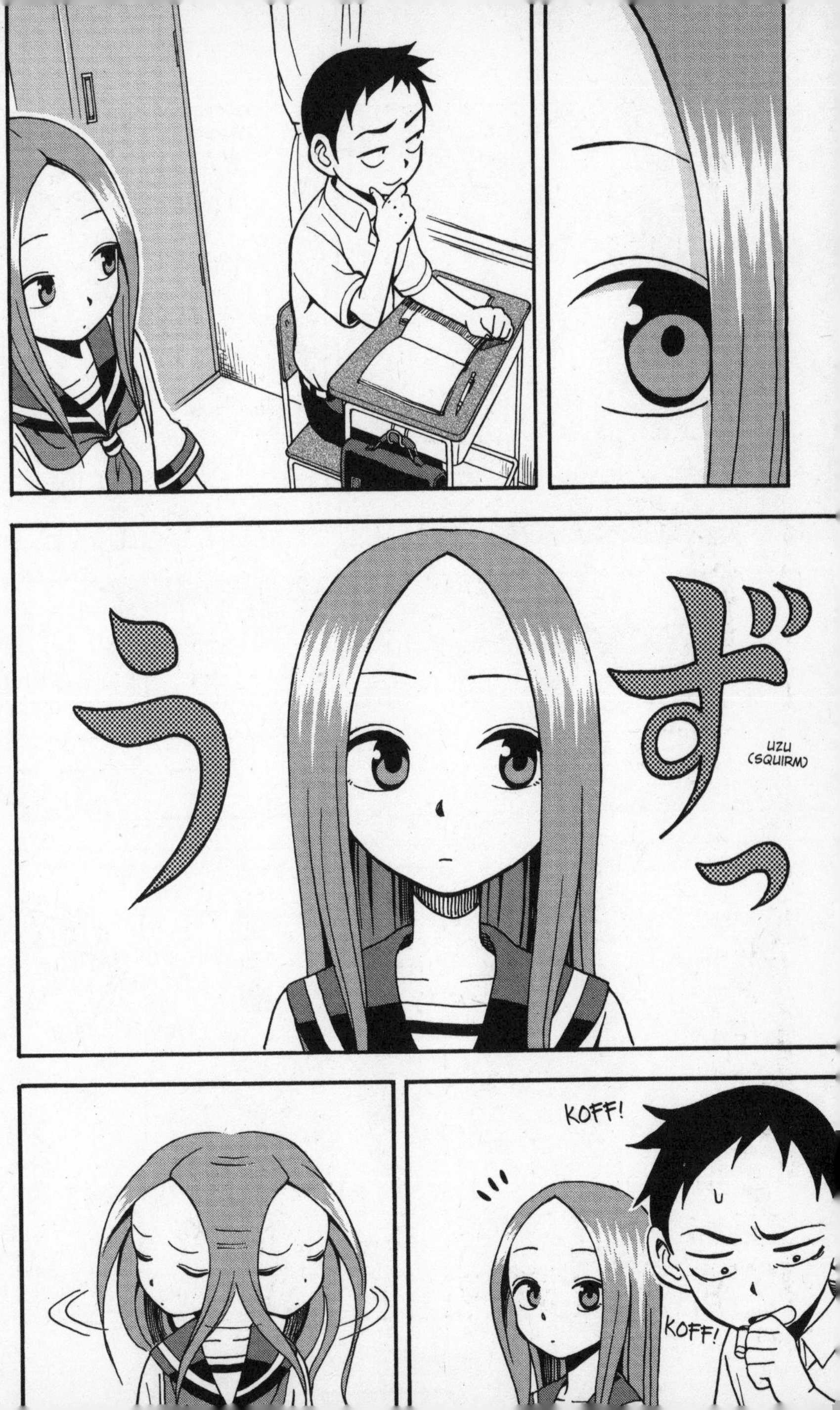
うずっ
UZU (SQUIRM)
KOFF!
KOFF!

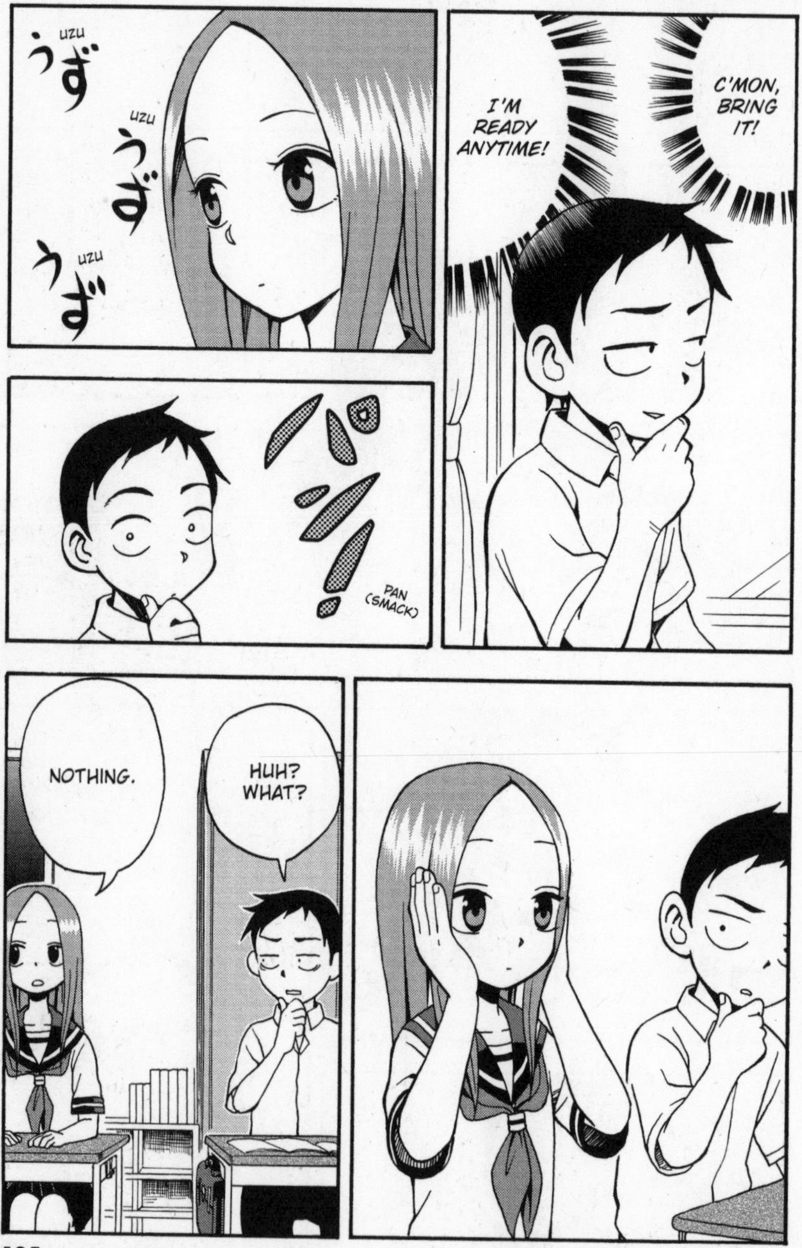
C'MON, BRING IT!
I'M READY ANYTIME!
うず
uzu
うず
uzu
うず
uzu
パン!
PAN (SMACK)
HUH? WHAT?
NOTHING.

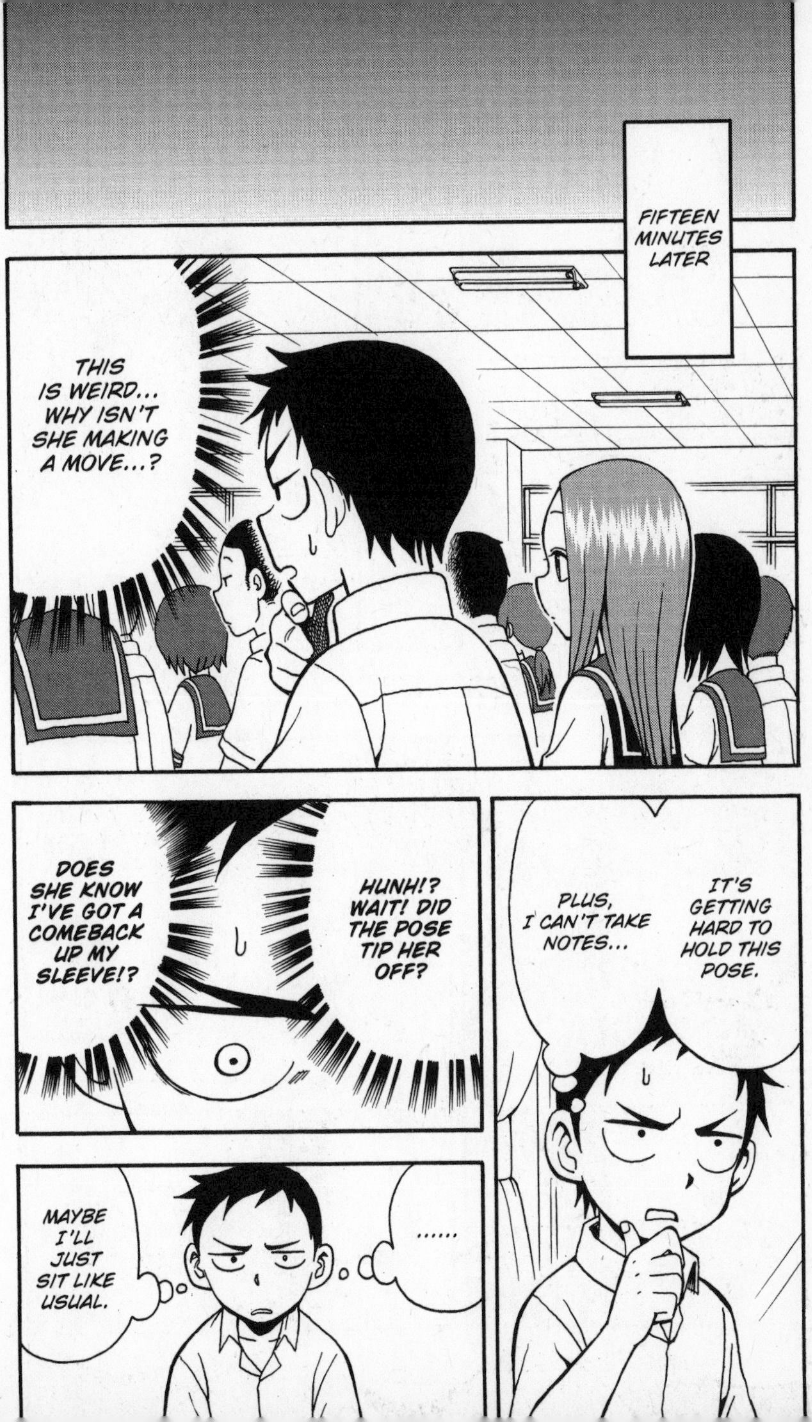
FIFTEEN MINUTES LATER
THIS IS WEIRD... WHY ISN'T SHE MAKING A MOVE...?
IT'S GETTING HARD TO HOLD THIS POSE.
PLUS, I CAN'T TAKE NOTES...
HUNH!? WAIT! DID THE POSE TIP HER OFF?
DOES SHE KNOW I'VE GOT A COMEBACK UP MY SLEEVE!?
......
MAYBE I'LL JUST SIT LIKE USUAL.

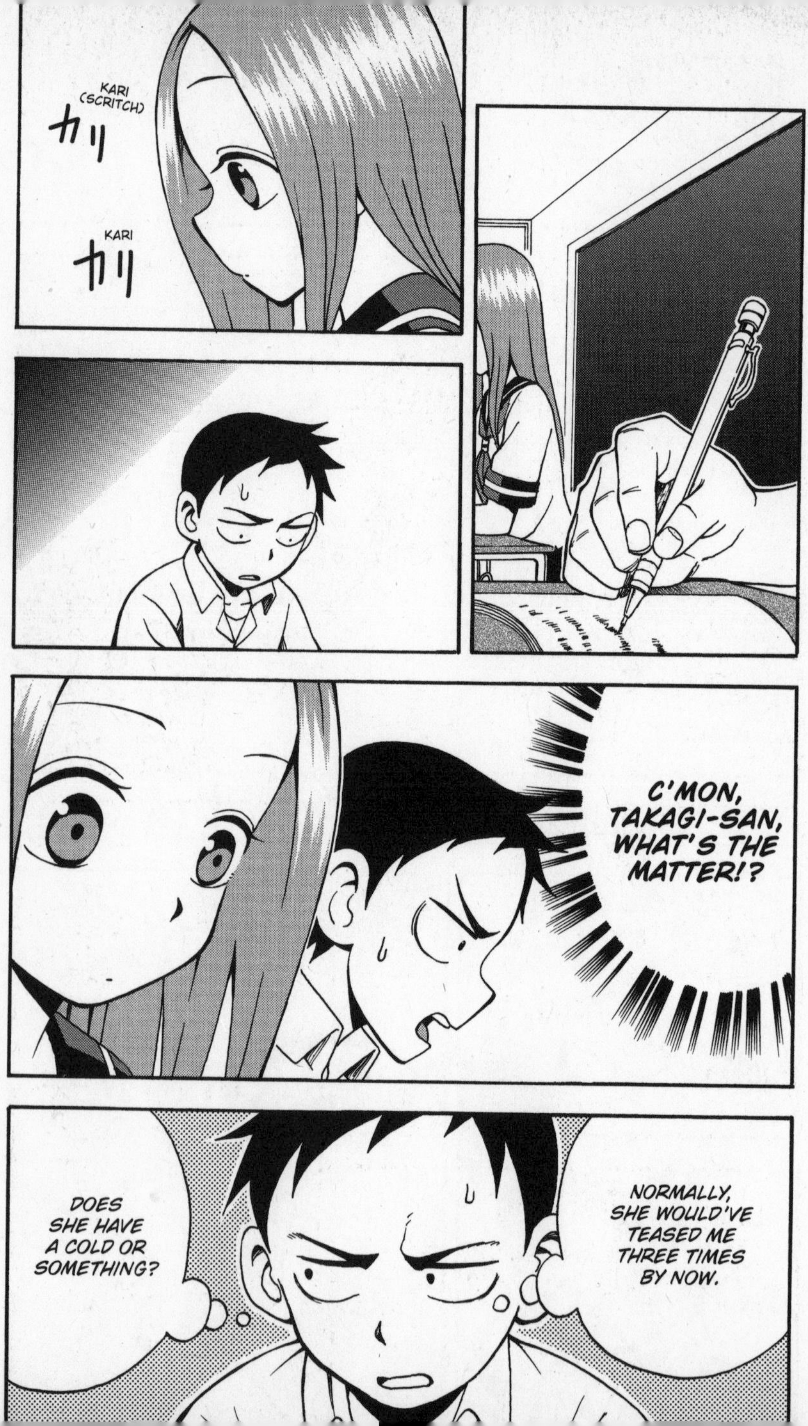

カリ
KARI (SCRITCH)
カリ
KARI
C'MON, TAKAGI-SAN, WHAT'S THE MATTER!?
NORMALLY, SHE WOULD'VE TEASED ME THREE TIMES BY NOW.
DOES SHE HAVE A COLD OR SOMETHING?

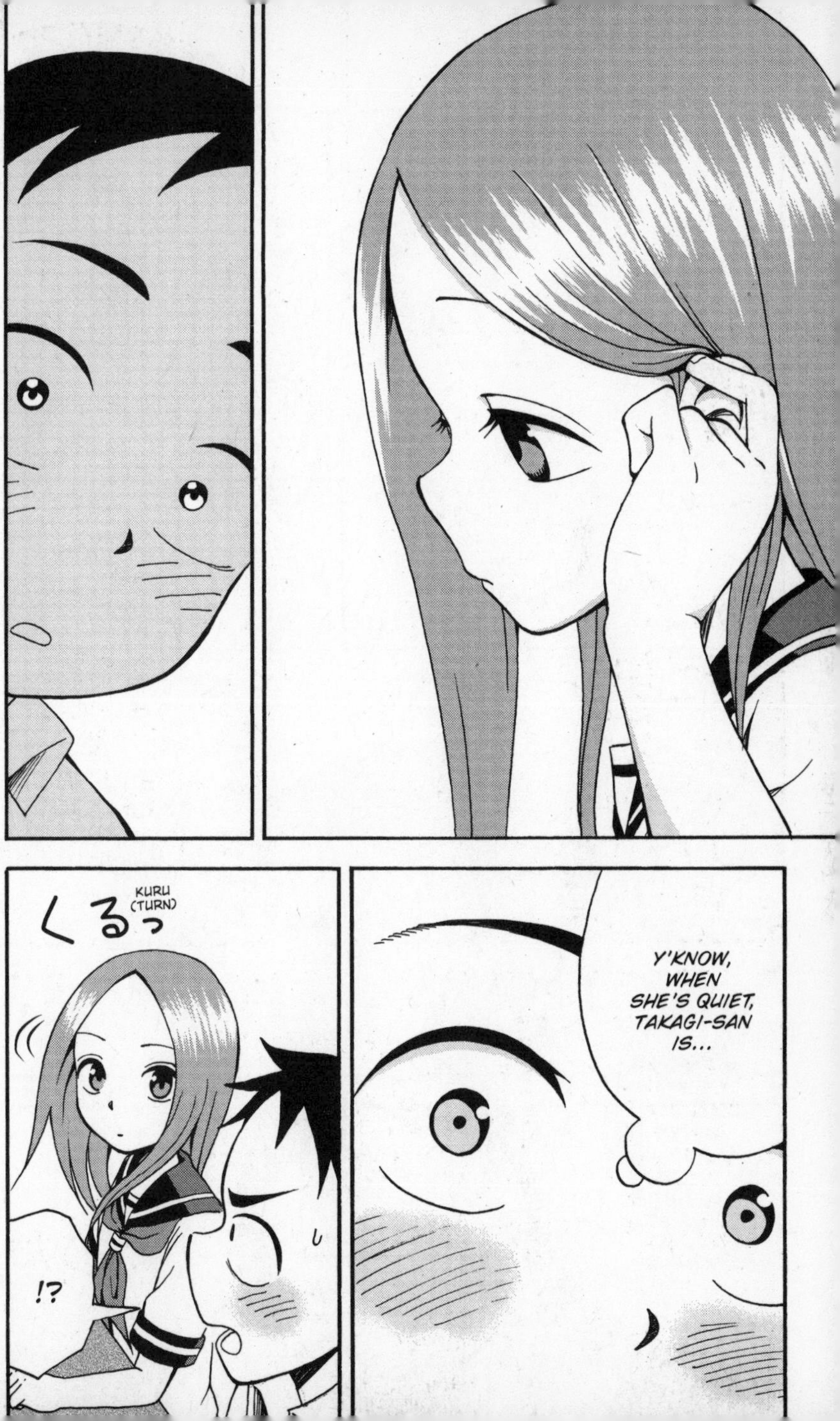
Y'KNOW, WHEN SHE'S QUIET, TAKAGI-SAN IS...
くるっ
KURU (TURN)
!?

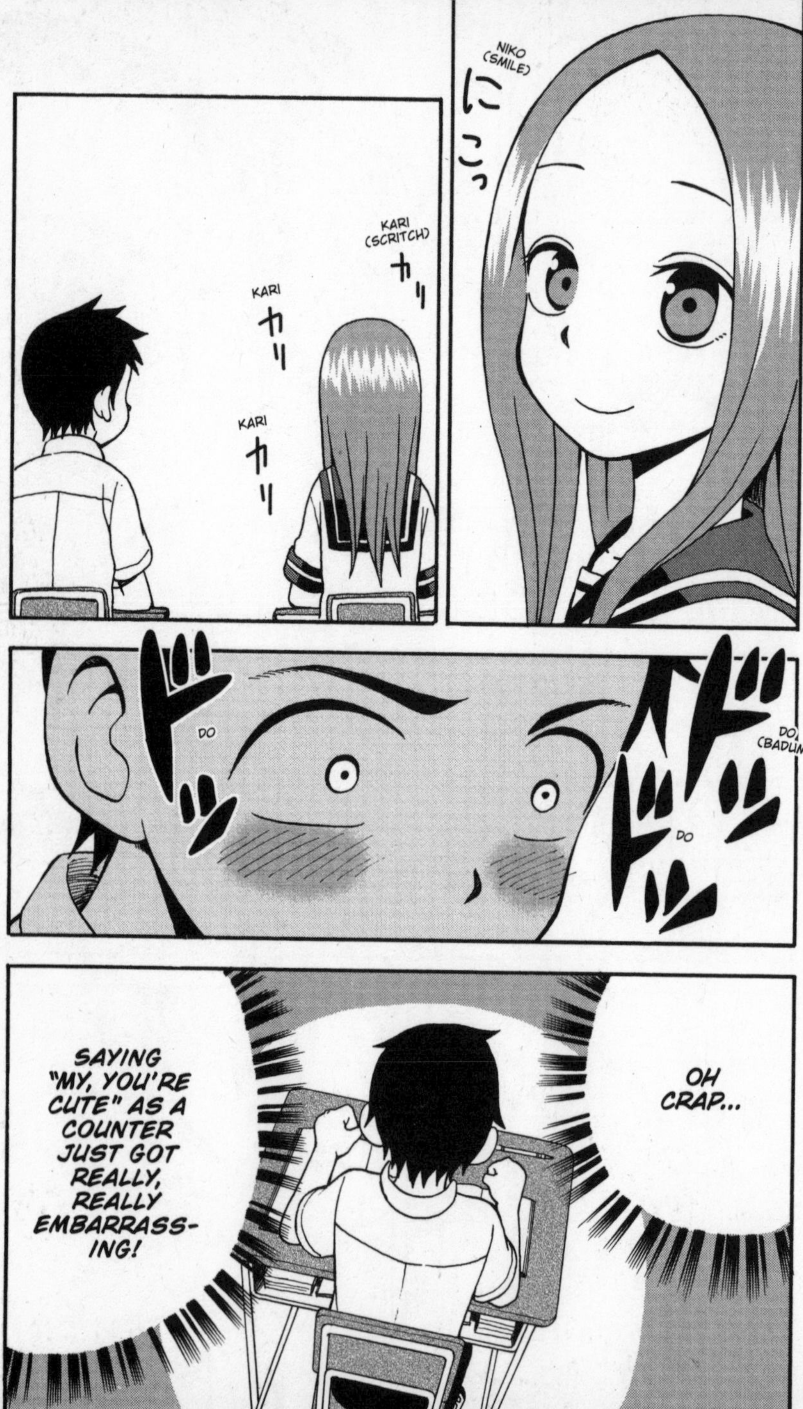
にこっ
NIKO (SMILE)
カリ
KARI (SCRITCH)
カリ
KARI
カリ
KARI
ドッ
DO (BADUM)
ドッ
DO
ドッ
DO
OH CRAP...
SAYING "MY, YOU'RE CUTE" AS A COUNTER JUST GOT REALLY, REALLY EMBARRASS-ING!

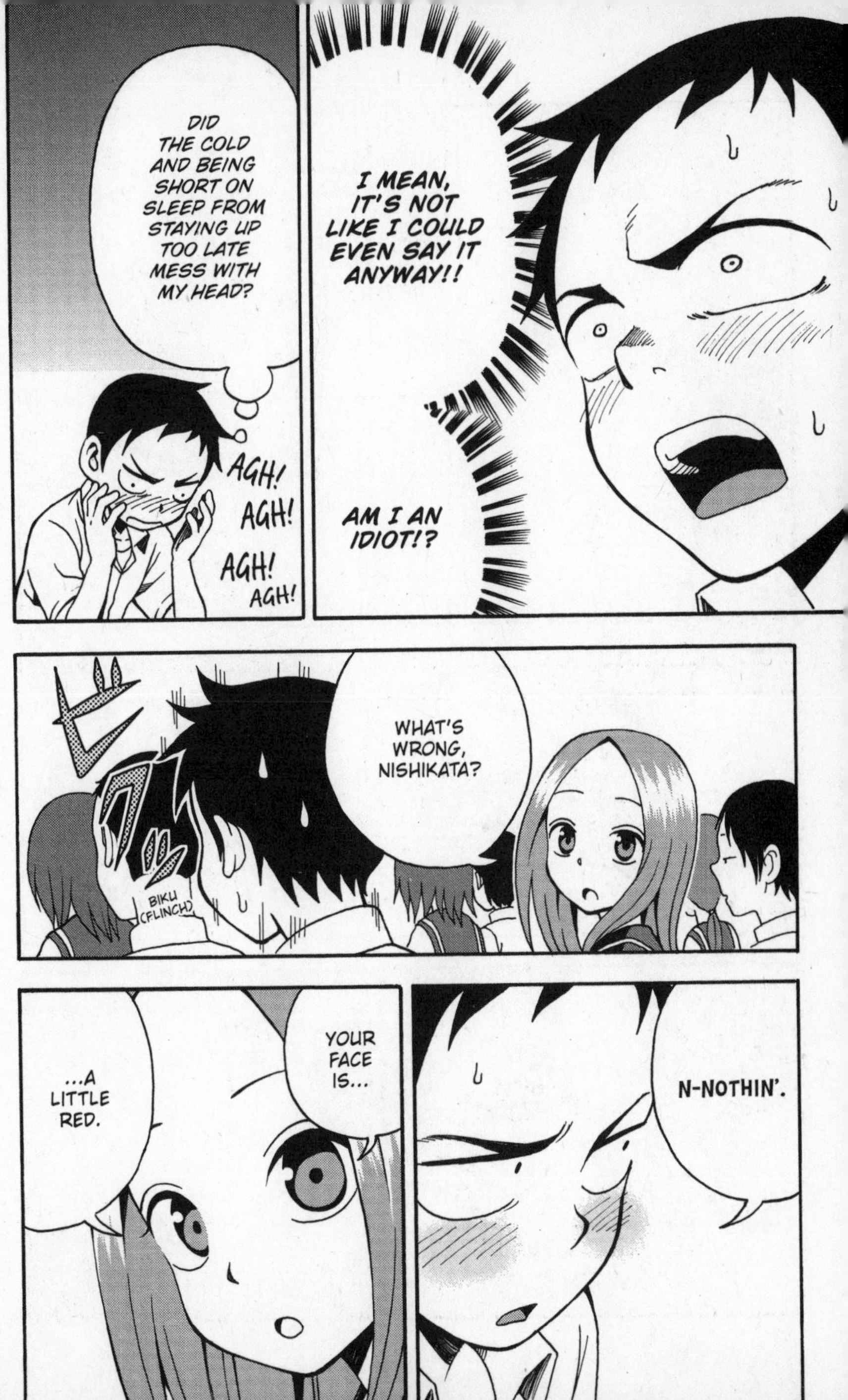
I MEAN, IT'S NOT LIKE I COULD EVEN SAY IT ANYWAY!!
AM I AN IDIOT!?
DID THE COLD AND BEING SHORT ON SLEEP FROM STAYING UP TOO LATE MESS WITH MY HEAD?
AGH! AGH! AGH! AGH!
WHAT'S WRONG, NISHIKATA?
BIKU (FLINCH)
N-NOTHIN'.
YOUR FACE IS...
...A LITTLE RED.

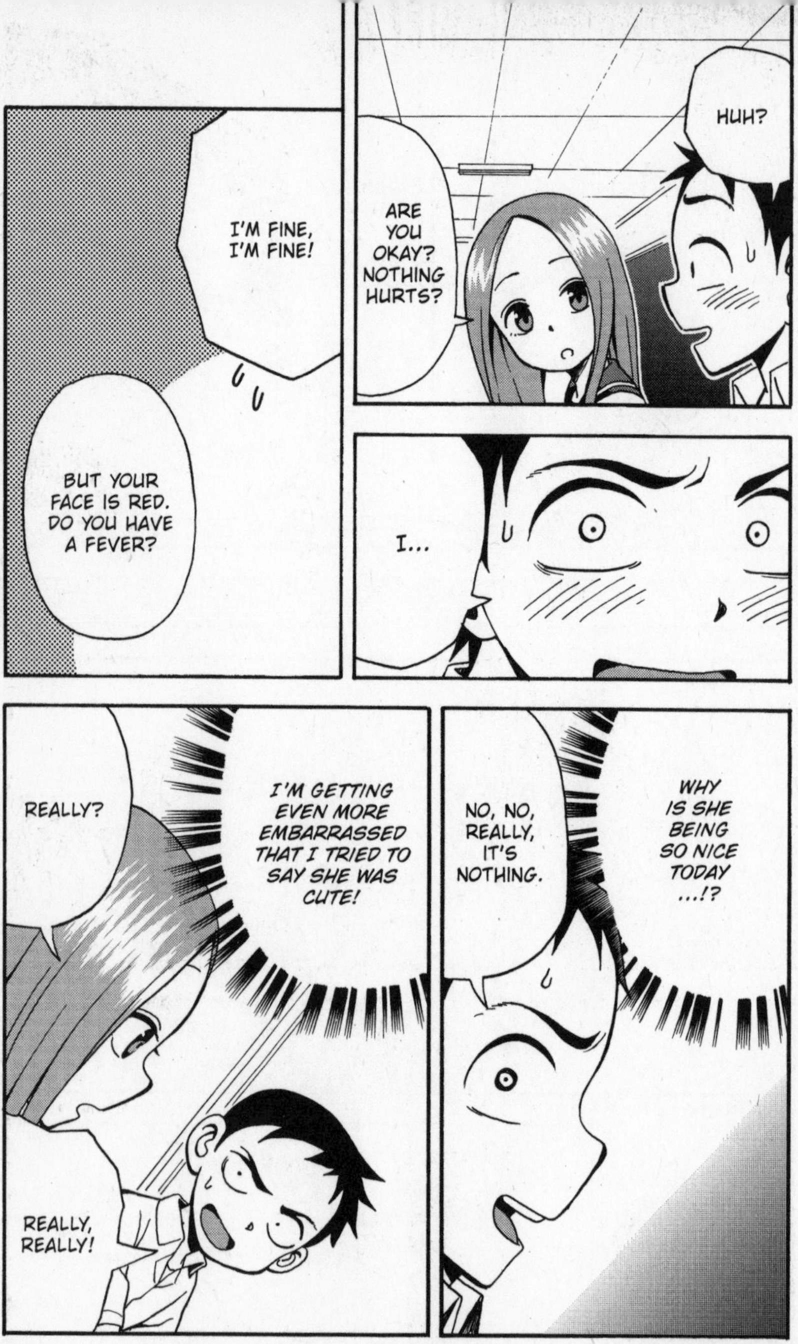
HUH?
ARE YOU OKAY? NOTHING HURTS?
I...
I'M FINE, I'M FINE!
BUT YOUR FACE IS RED. DO YOU HAVE A FEVER?
WHY IS SHE BEING SO NICE TODAY ...!?
NO, NO, REALLY, IT'S NOTHING.
I'M GETTING EVEN MORE EMBARRASSED THAT I TRIED TO SAY SHE WAS CUTE!
REALLY?
REALLY, REALLY!

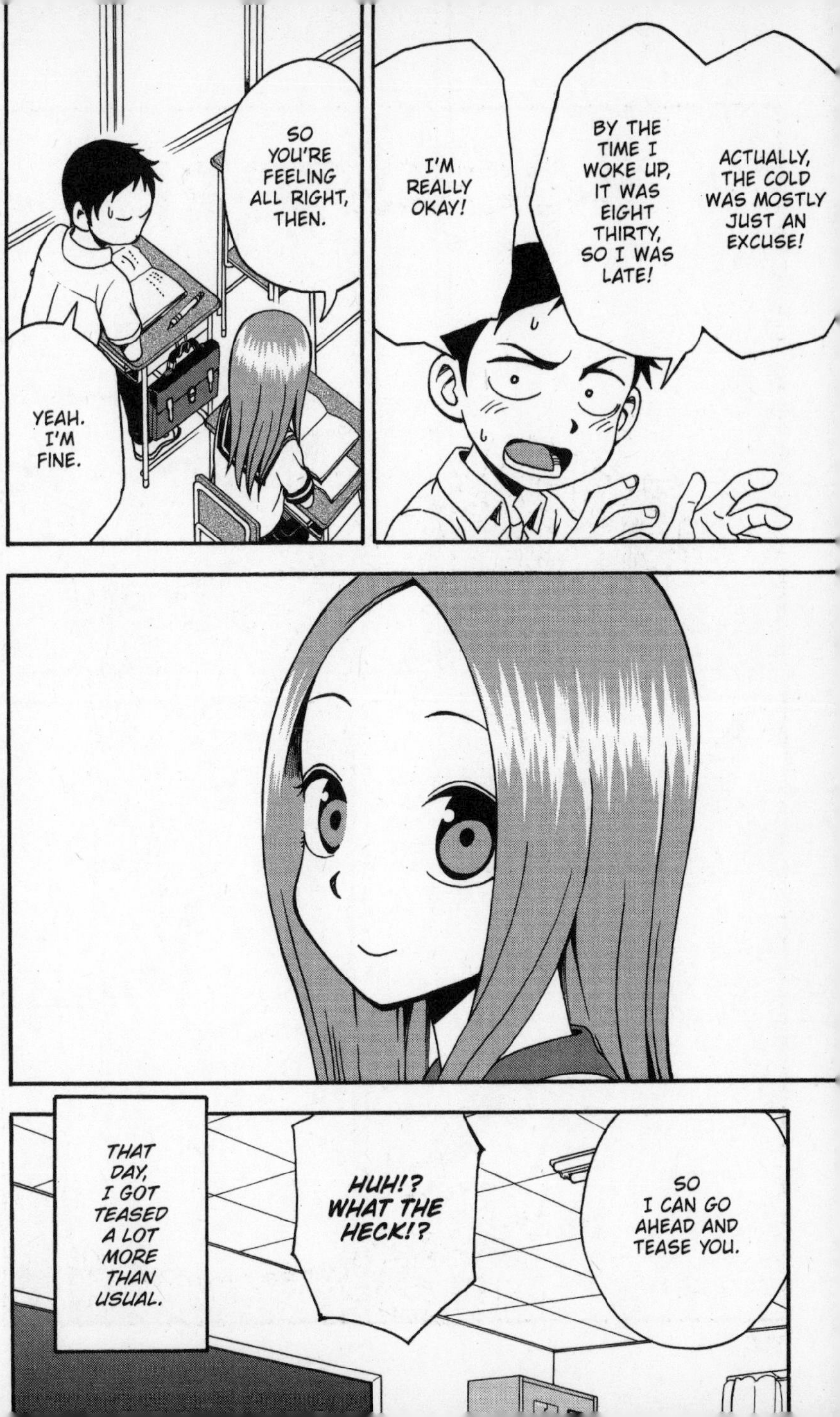
ACTUALLY, THE COLD WAS MOSTLY JUST AN EXCUSE!
BY THE TIME I WOKE UP, IT WAS EIGHT THIRTY, SO I WAS LATE!
I'M REALLY OKAY!
SO YOU'RE FEELING ALL RIGHT, THEN.
YEAH. I'M FINE.
SO I CAN GO AHEAD AND TEASE YOU.
HUH!? WHAT THE HECK!?
THAT DAY, I GOT TEASED A LOT MORE THAN USUAL.

BOOKSTORE

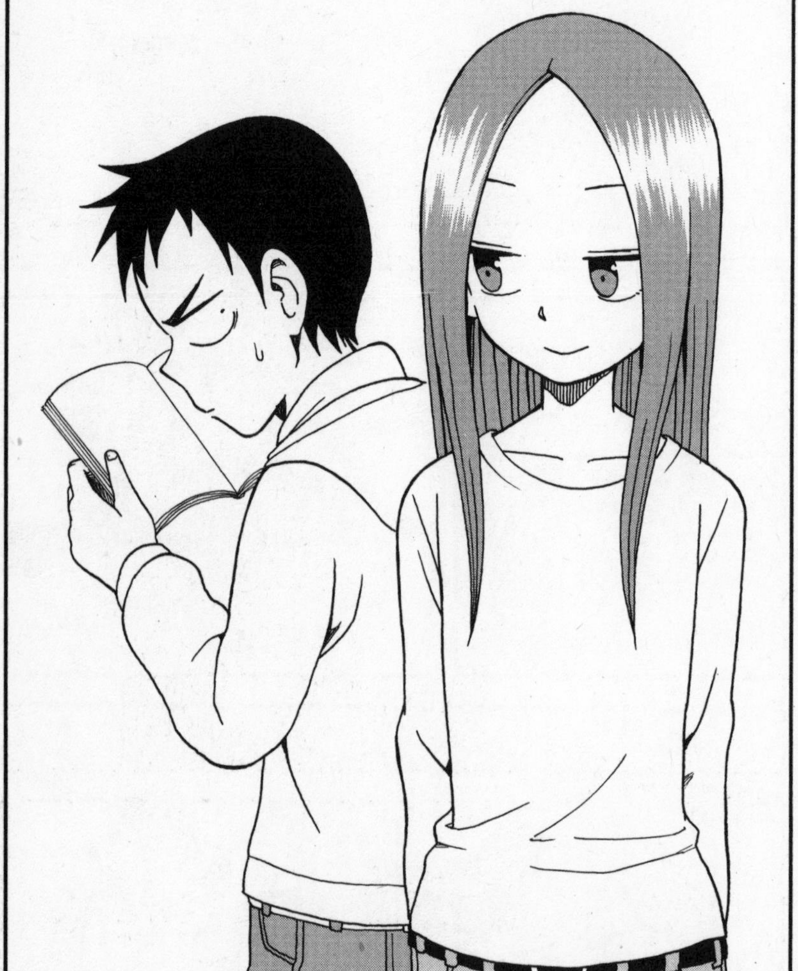

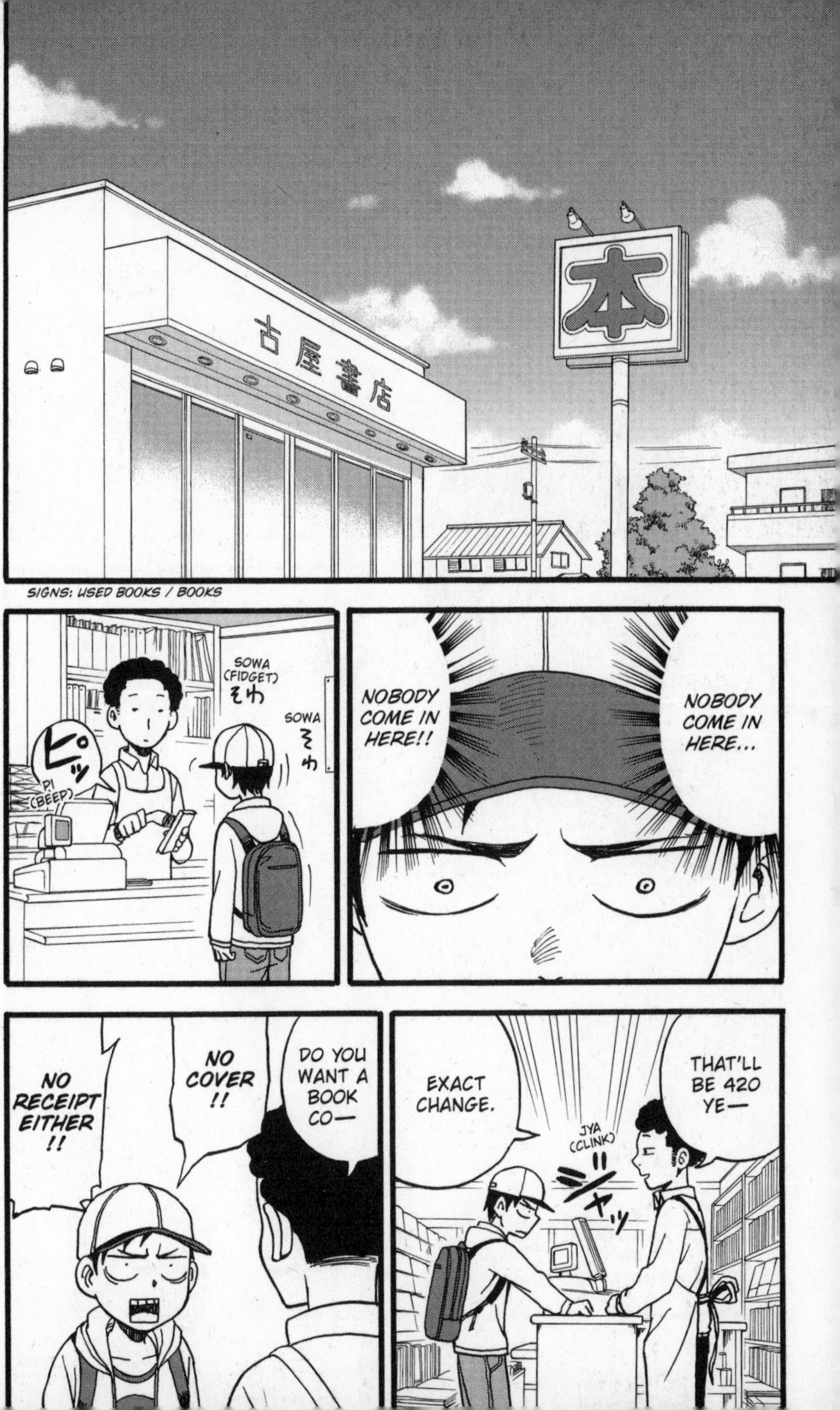
古屋書店
本
NOBODY COME IN HERE...
NOBODY COME IN HERE!!
SOWA (FIDGET) そわ
SOWA そわ
PI (BEEP) ピッ
THAT'LL BE 420 YE—
JYA (CLINK) ジャッ
EXACT CHANGE.
DO YOU WANT A BOOK CO—
NO COVER !!
NO RECEIPT EITHER !!
SIGNS: USED BOOKS / BOOKS

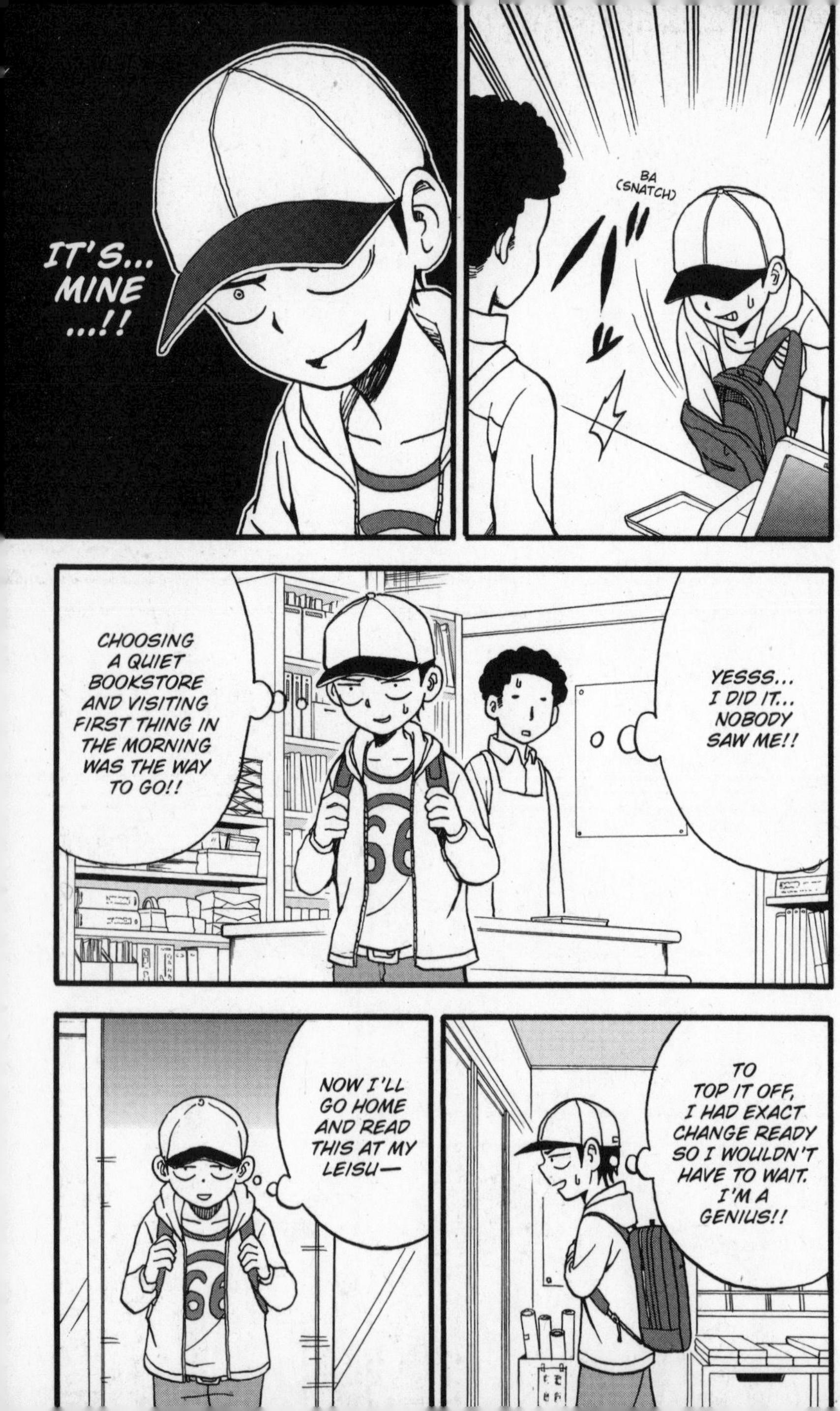
BA (SNATCH)
IT'S... MINE ...!!
YESSS... I DID IT... NOBODY SAW ME!!
CHOOSING A QUIET BOOKSTORE AND VISITING FIRST THING IN THE MORNING WAS THE WAY TO GO!!
TO TOP IT OFF, I HAD EXACT CHANGE READY SO I WOULDN'T HAVE TO WAIT. I'M A GENIUS!!
NOW I'LL GO HOME AND READ THIS AT MY LEISU—

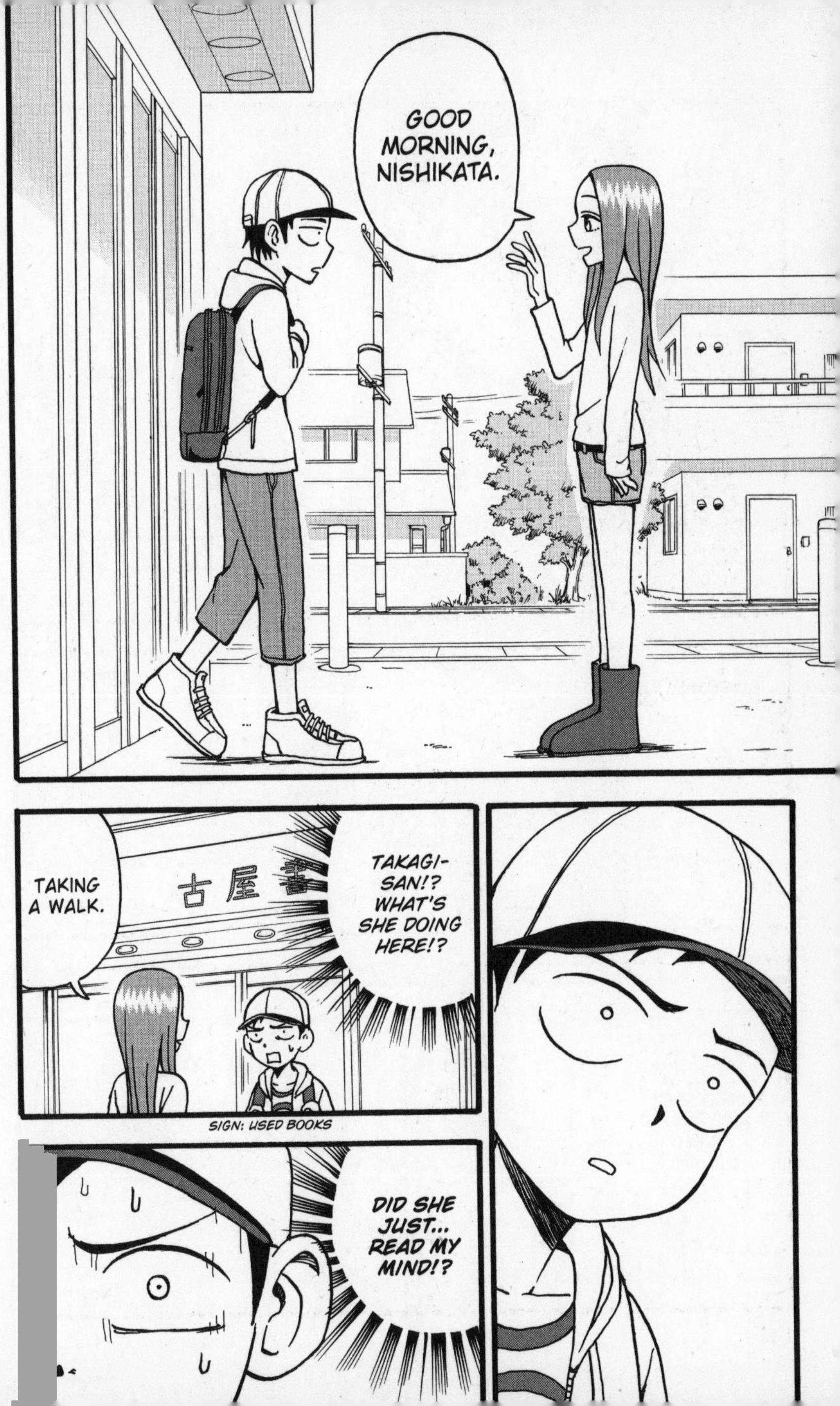
GOOD MORNING, NISHIKATA.
TAKAGI-SAN!? WHAT'S SHE DOING HERE!?
古屋書
TAKING A WALK.
SIGN: USED BOOKS
DID SHE JUST... READ MY MIND!?

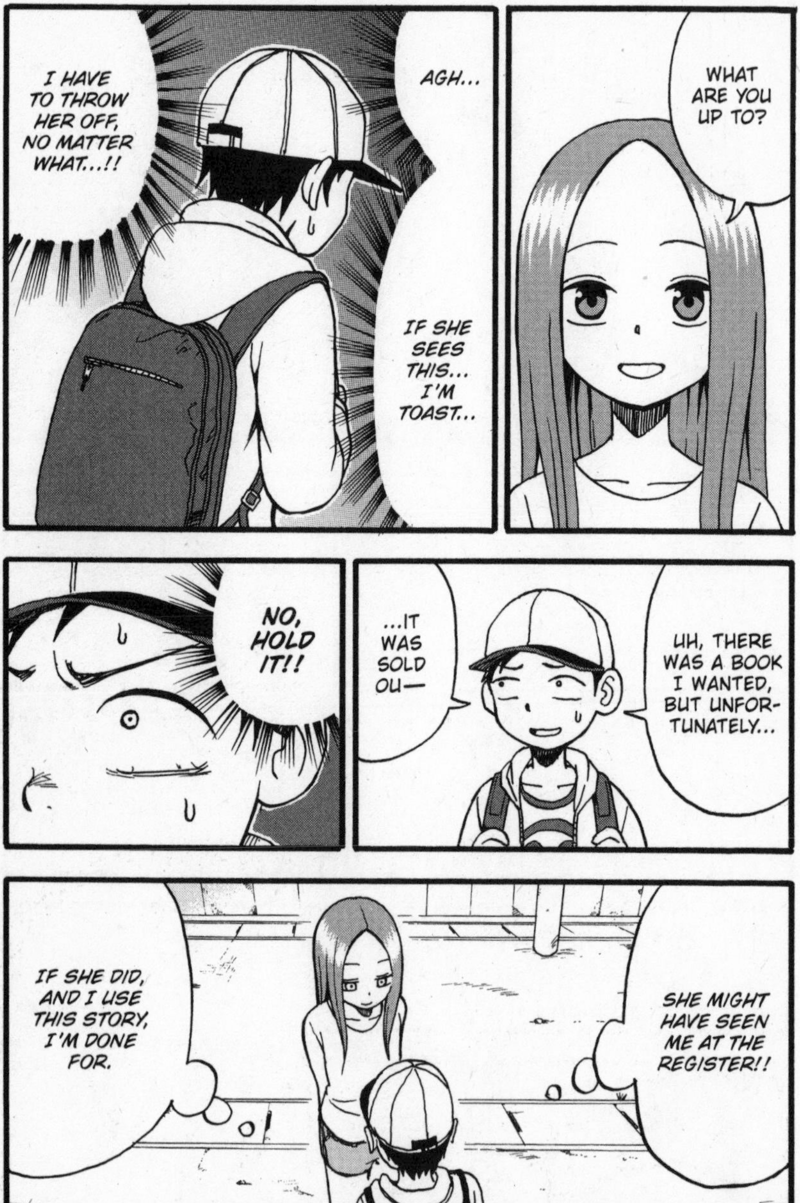
WHAT ARE YOU UP TO?
AGH...
IF SHE SEES THIS... I'M TOAST...
I HAVE TO THROW HER OFF, NO MATTER WHAT...!!
UH, THERE WAS A BOOK I WANTED, BUT UNFORTUNATELY...
...IT WAS SOLD OU—
NO, HOLD IT!!
SHE MIGHT HAVE SEEN ME AT THE REGISTER!!
IF SHE DID, AND I USE THIS STORY, I'M DONE FOR.

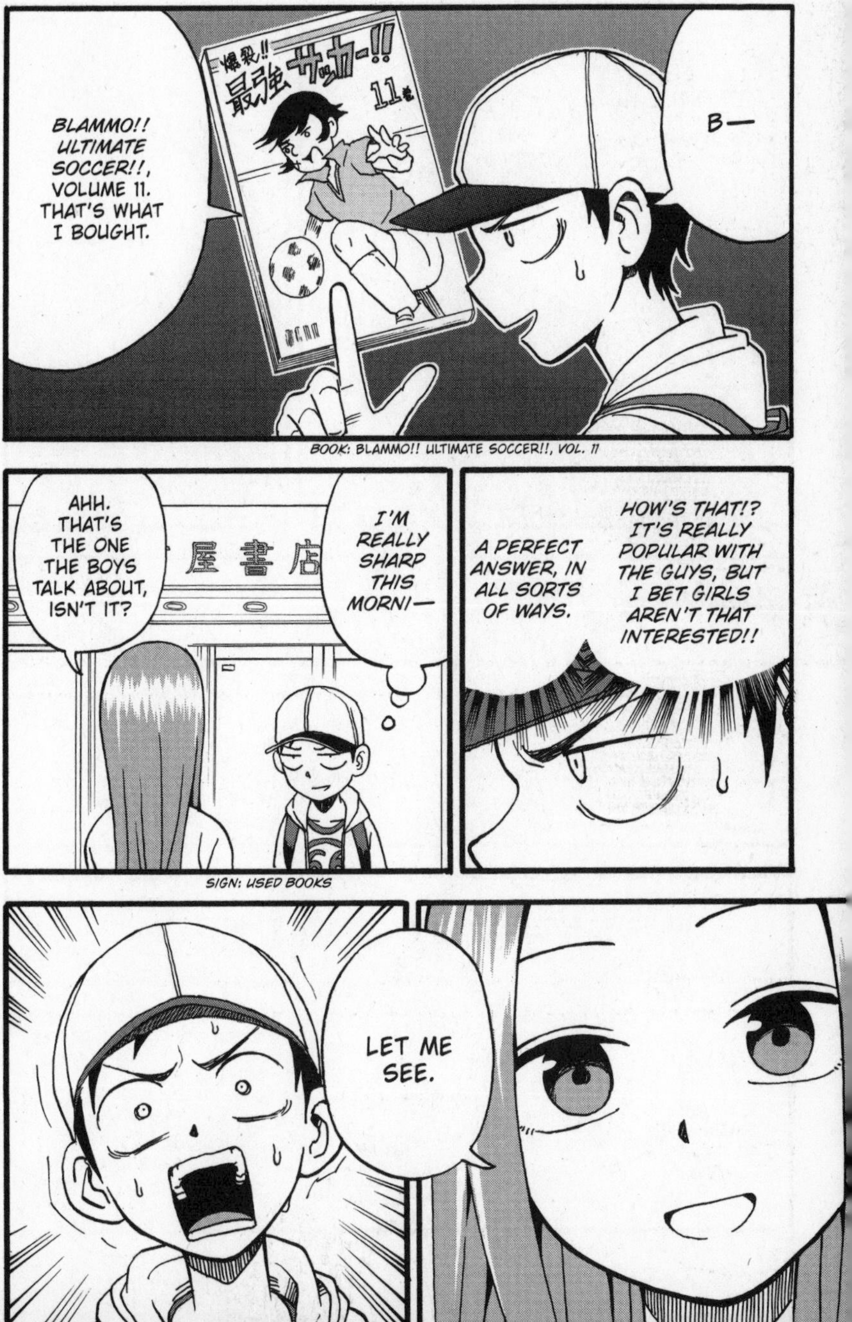
B—
爆殺!!
最強サッカー!!
11巻
BLAMMO!! ULTIMATE SOCCER!!, VOLUME 11. THAT'S WHAT I BOUGHT.
BOOK: BLAMMO!! ULTIMATE SOCCER!!, VOL. 11
HOW'S THAT!? IT'S REALLY POPULAR WITH THE GUYS, BUT I BET GIRLS AREN'T THAT INTERESTED!!
A PERFECT ANSWER, IN ALL SORTS OF WAYS.
I'M REALLY SHARP THIS MORNI—
屋書店
AHH. THAT'S THE ONE THE BOYS TALK ABOUT, ISN'T IT?
SIGN: USED BOOKS
LET ME SEE.

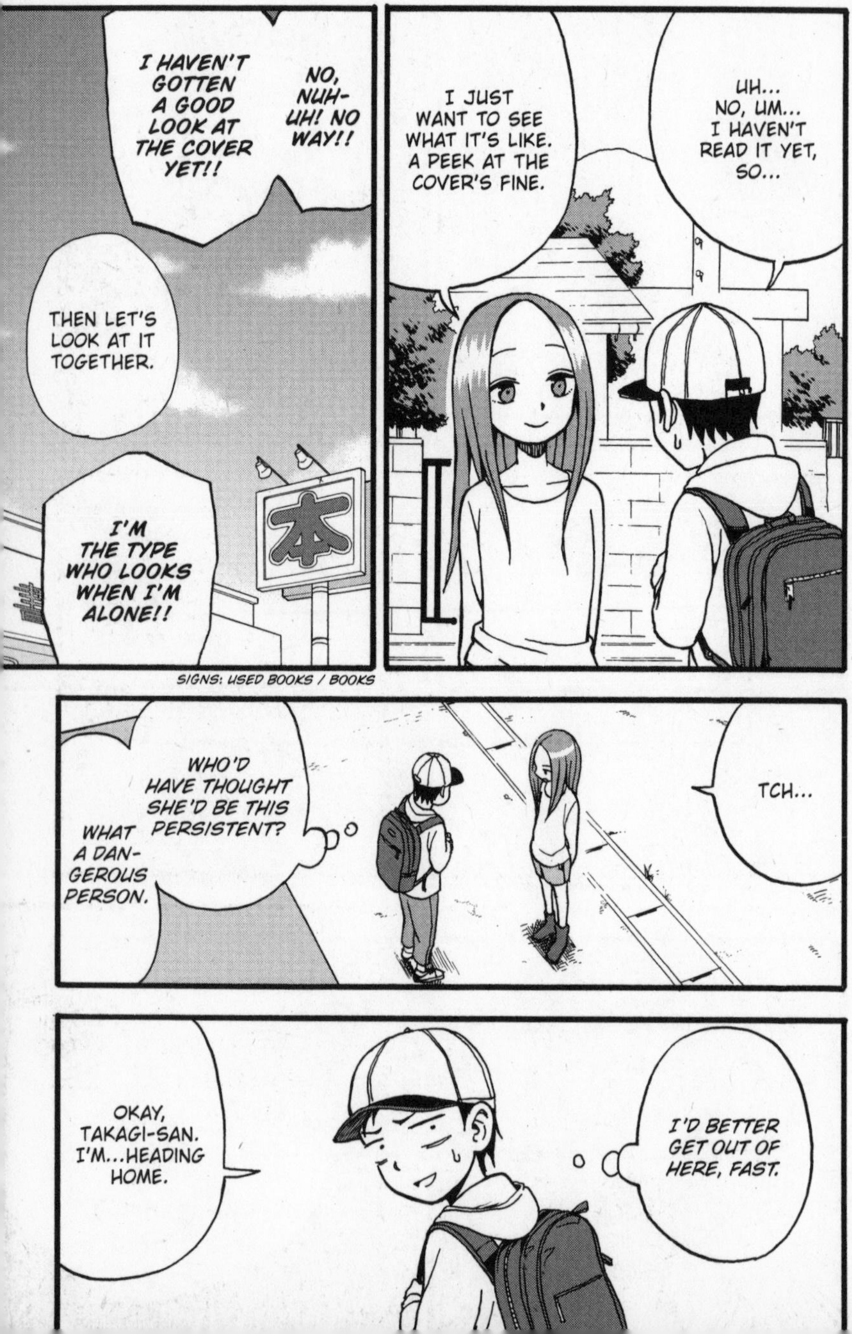
UH... NO, UM... I HAVEN'T READ IT YET, SO...
I JUST WANT TO SEE WHAT IT'S LIKE. A PEEK AT THE COVER'S FINE.
NO, NUH-UH! NO WAY!!
I HAVEN'T GOTTEN A GOOD LOOK AT THE COVER YET!!
THEN LET'S LOOK AT IT TOGETHER.
I'M THE TYPE WHO LOOKS WHEN I'M ALONE!!
SIGNS: USED BOOKS / BOOKS
TCH...
WHO'D HAVE THOUGHT SHE'D BE THIS PERSISTENT?
WHAT A DAN-GEROUS PERSON.
I'D BETTER GET OUT OF HERE, FAST.
OKAY, TAKAGI-SAN. I'M...HEADING HOME.

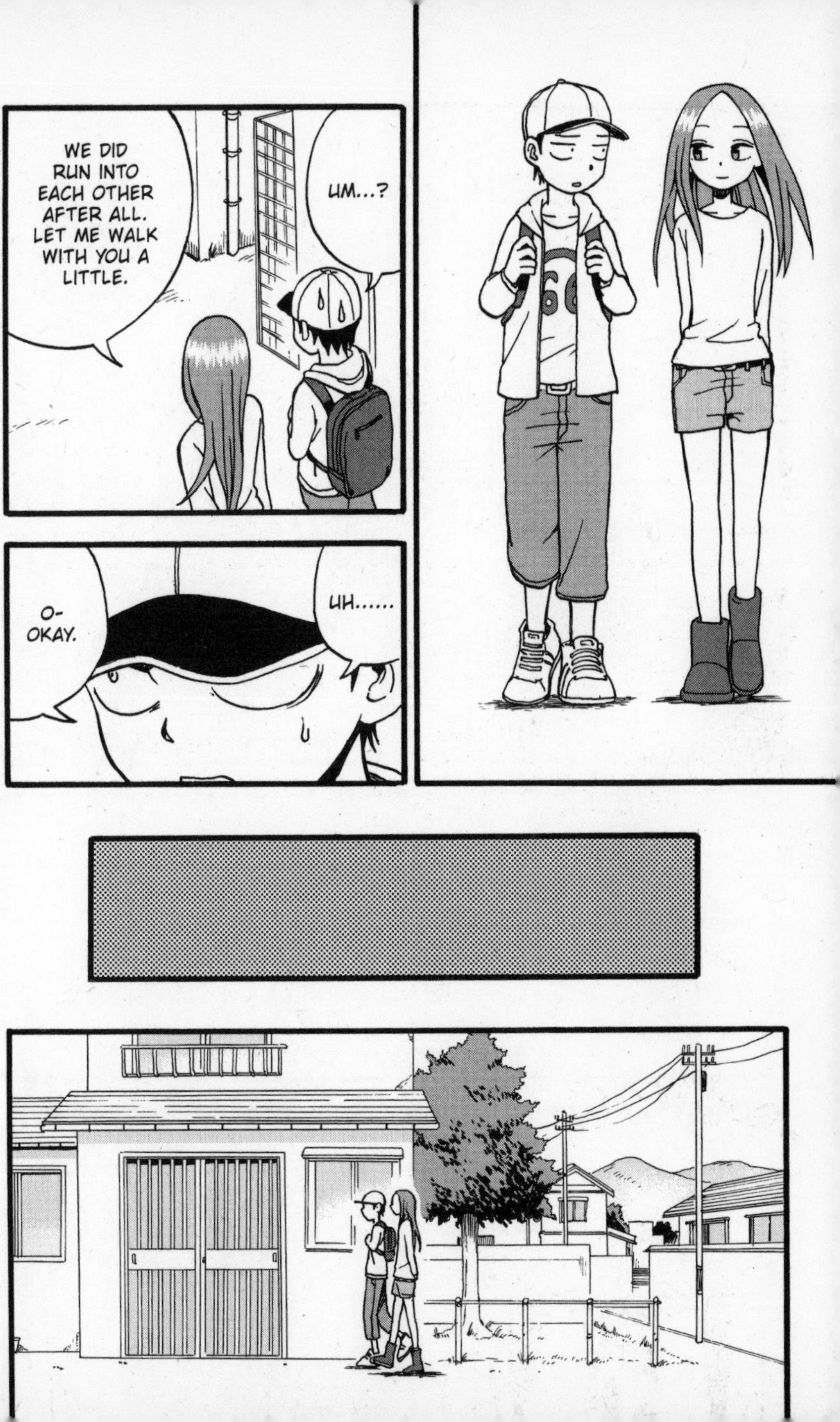
UM...?
WE DID RUN INTO EACH OTHER AFTER ALL. LET ME WALK WITH YOU A LITTLE.
UH......
O-OKAY.

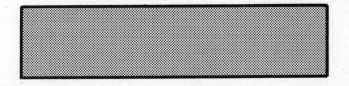

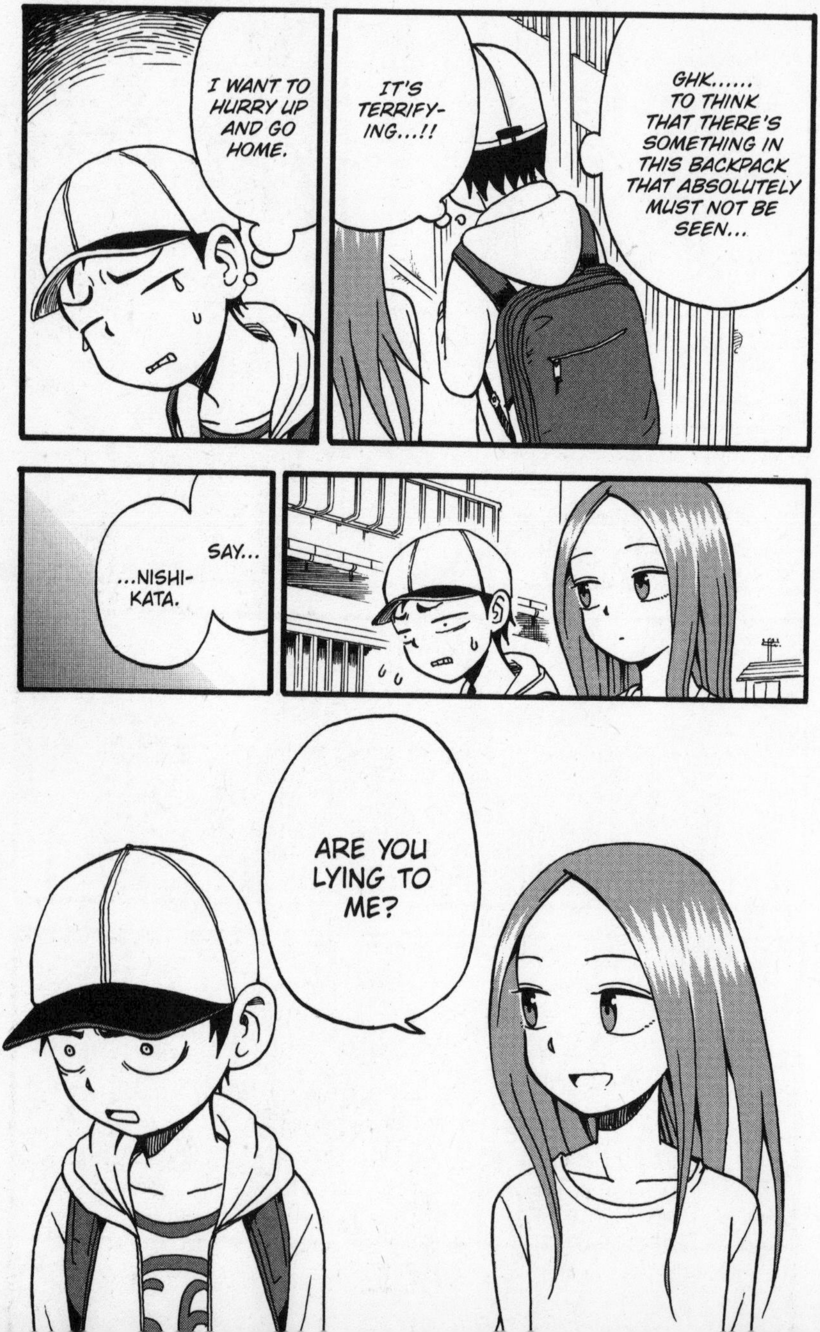
GHK...... TO THINK THAT THERE'S SOMETHING IN THIS BACKPACK THAT ABSOLUTELY MUST NOT BE SEEN...
IT'S TERRIFYING...!!
I WANT TO HURRY UP AND GO HOME.
SAY... ...NISHIKATA.
ARE YOU LYING TO ME?

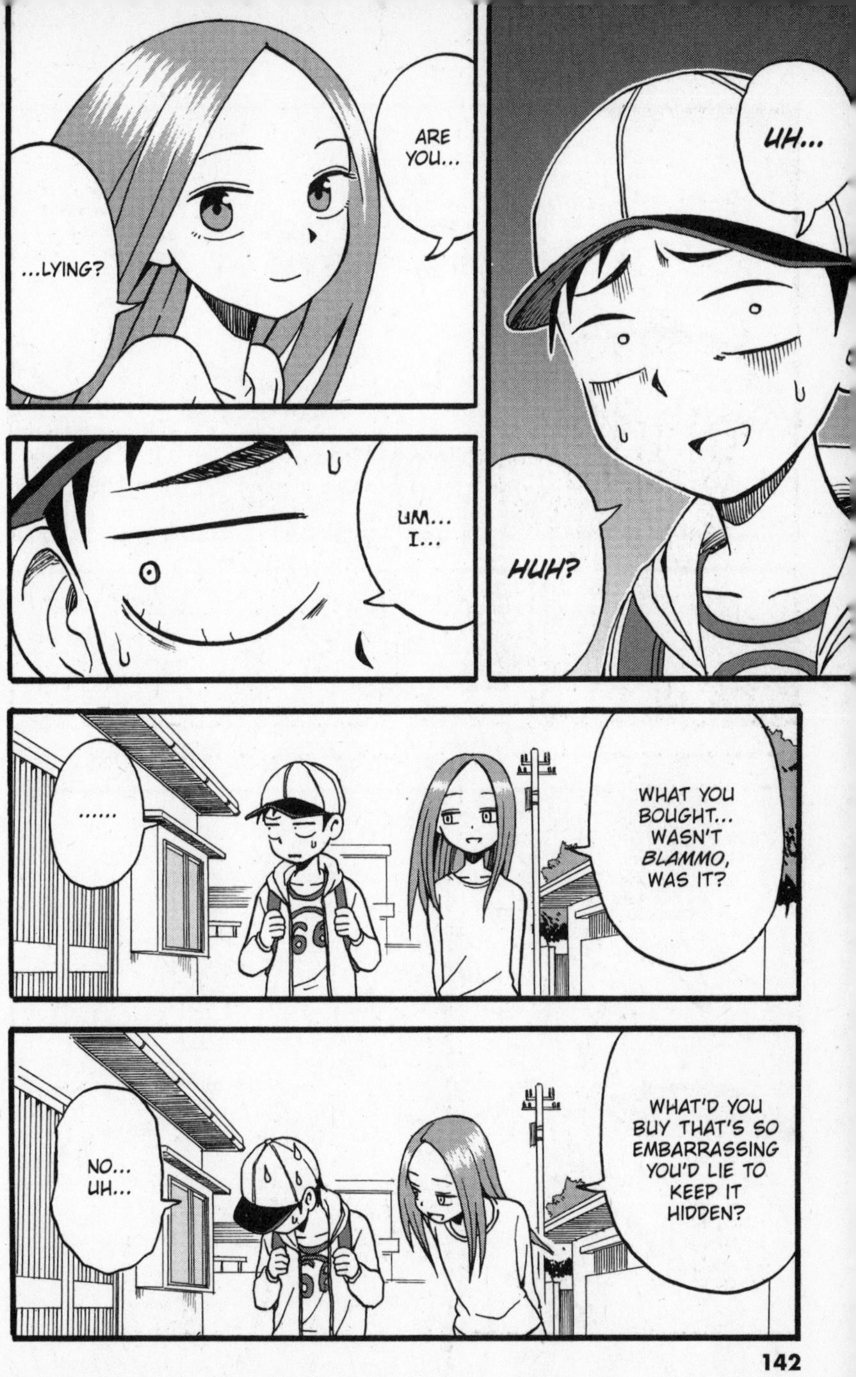
UH...
HUH?
ARE YOU...
...LYING?
UM... I...
WHAT YOU BOUGHT... WASN'T *BLAMMO*, WAS IT?
......
WHAT'D YOU BUY THAT'S SO EMBARRASSING YOU'D LIE TO KEEP IT HIDDEN?
NO... UH...

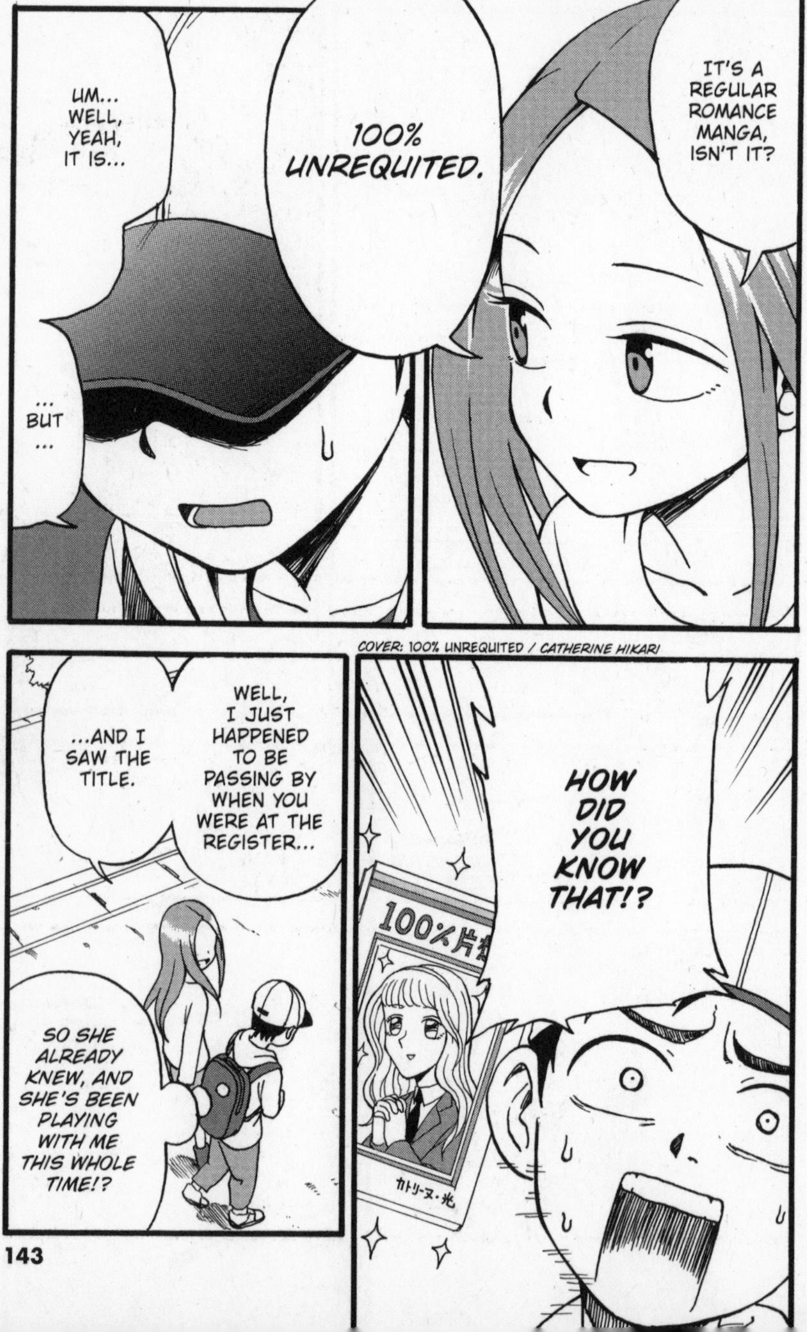
IT'S A REGULAR ROMANCE MANGA, ISN'T IT?
100% UNREQUITED.
UM... WELL, YEAH, IT IS...
...BUT...
COVER: 100% UNREQUITED / CATHERINE HIKARI
HOW DID YOU KNOW THAT!?
100%片
カトリーヌ・光
WELL, I JUST HAPPENED TO BE PASSING BY WHEN YOU WERE AT THE REGISTER...
...AND I SAW THE TITLE.
SO SHE ALREADY KNEW, AND SHE'S BEEN PLAYING WITH ME THIS WHOLE TIME!?

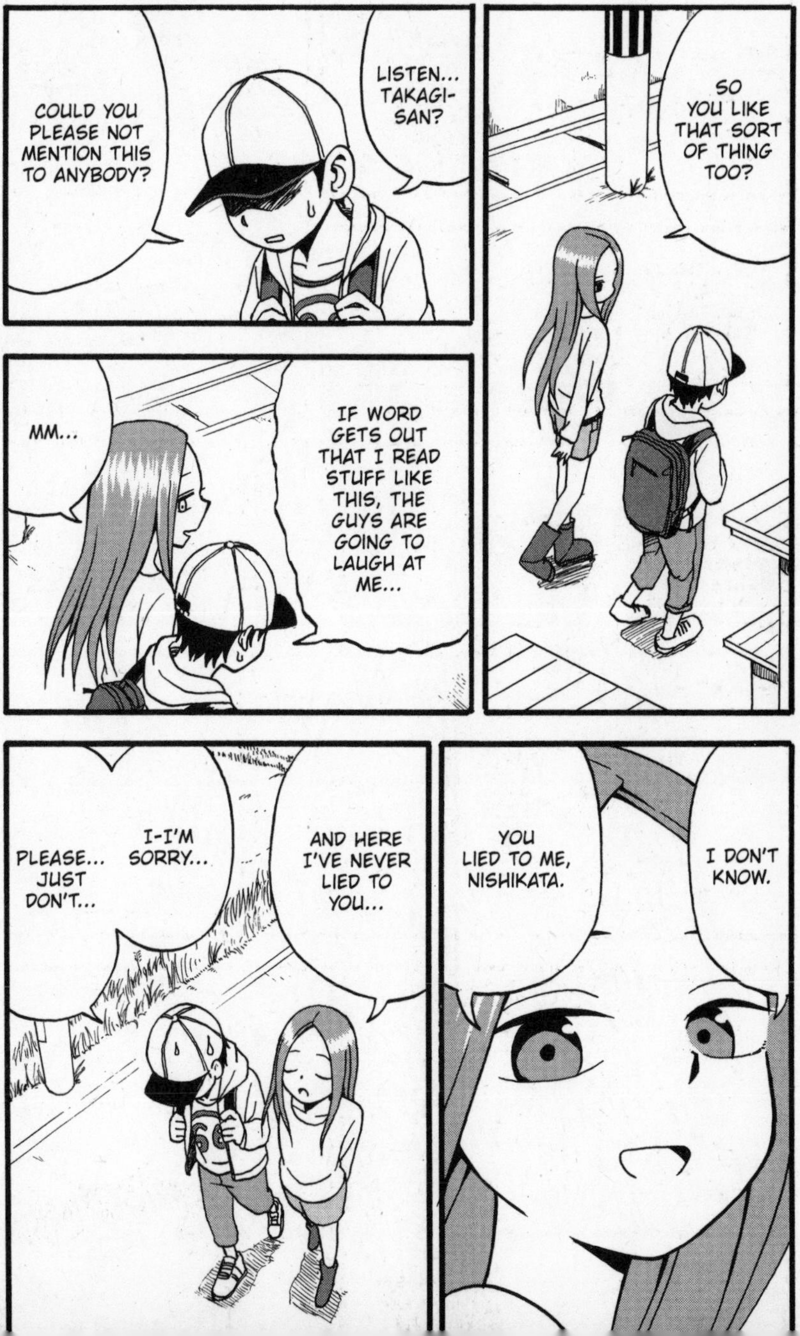
SO YOU LIKE THAT SORT OF THING TOO?
LISTEN... TAKAGI-SAN?
COULD YOU PLEASE NOT MENTION THIS TO ANYBODY?
IF WORD GETS OUT THAT I READ STUFF LIKE THIS, THE GUYS ARE GOING TO LAUGH AT ME...
MM...
I DON'T KNOW.
YOU LIED TO ME, NISHIKATA.
AND HERE I'VE NEVER LIED TO YOU...
I-I'M SORRY...
PLEASE... JUST DON'T...

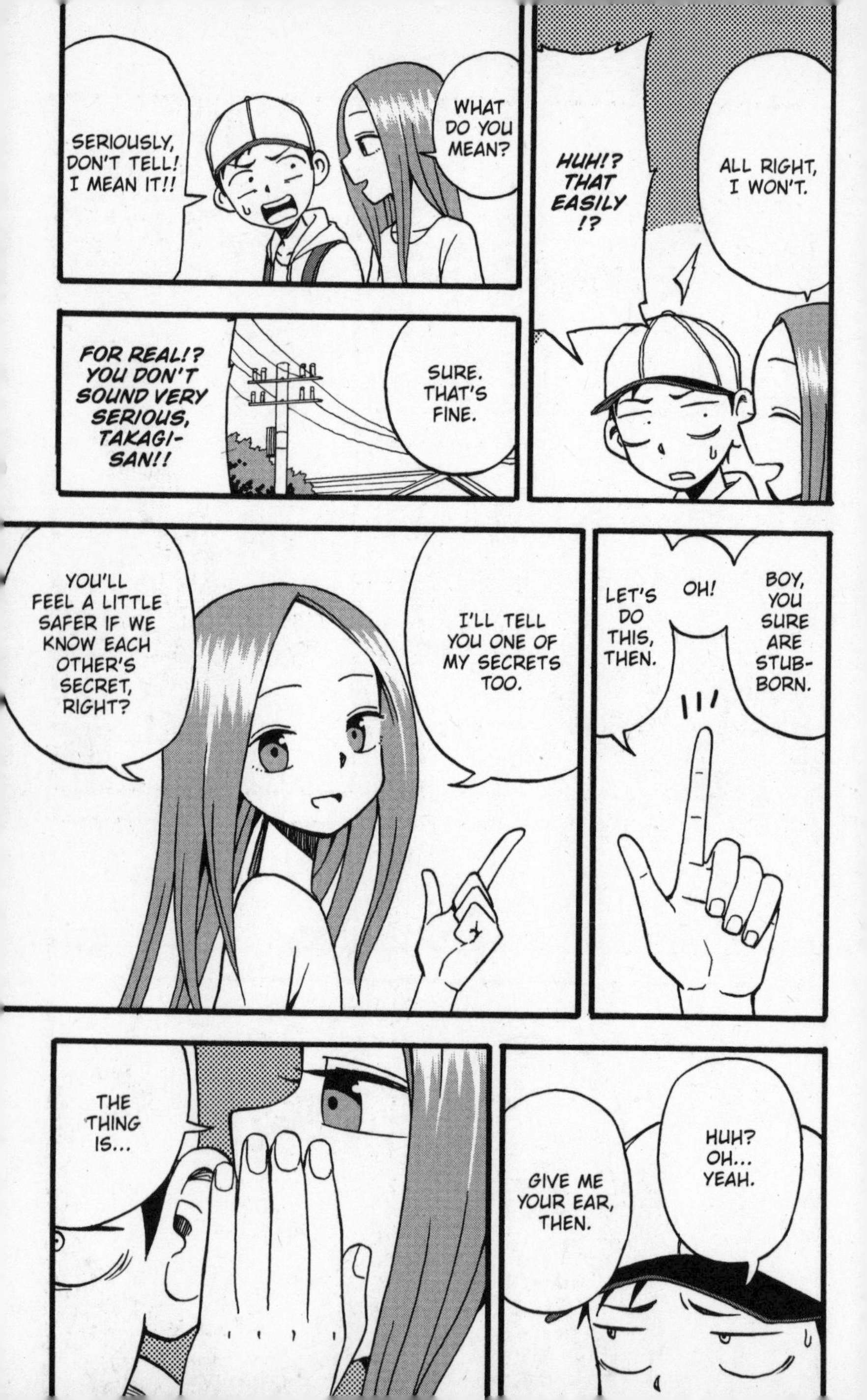
ALL RIGHT, I WON'T.
HUH!? THAT EASILY!?
WHAT DO YOU MEAN?
SERIOUSLY, DON'T TELL! I MEAN IT!!
SURE. THAT'S FINE.
FOR REAL!? YOU DON'T SOUND VERY SERIOUS, TAKAGI-SAN!!
BOY, YOU SURE ARE STUB-BORN.
OH!
LET'S DO THIS, THEN.
I'LL TELL YOU ONE OF MY SECRETS TOO.
YOU'LL FEEL A LITTLE SAFER IF WE KNOW EACH OTHER'S SECRET, RIGHT?
HUH? OH... YEAH.
GIVE ME YOUR EAR, THEN.
THE THING IS...

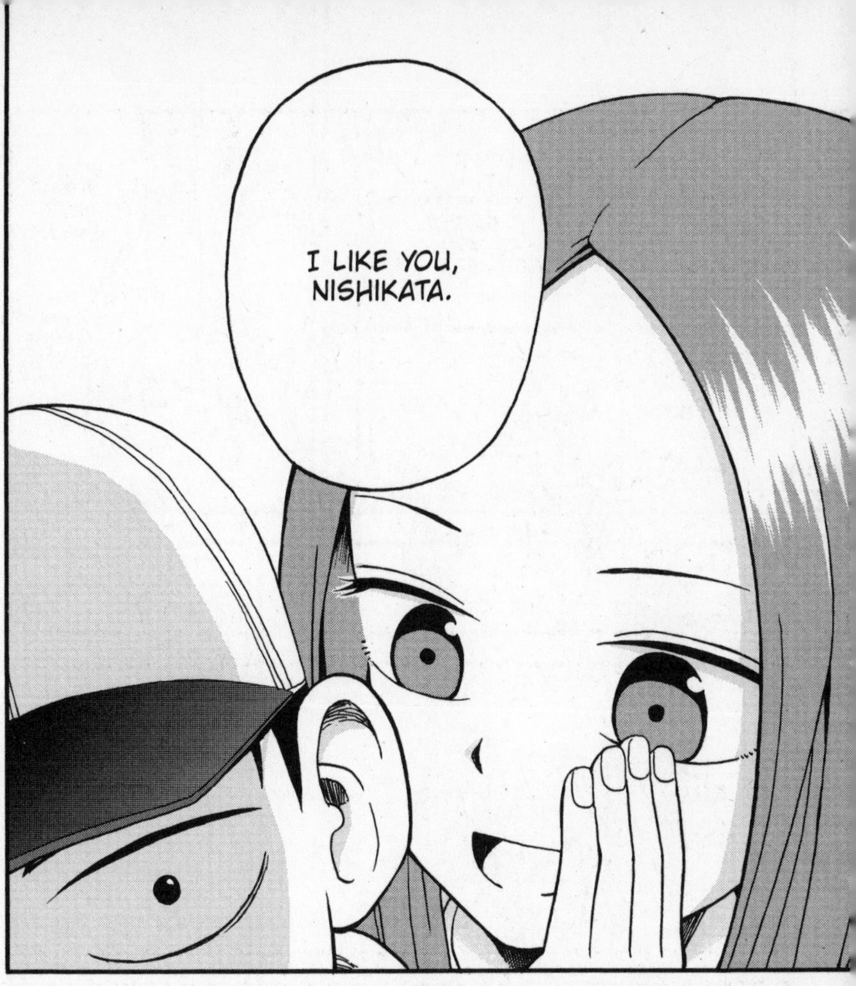
I LIKE YOU, NISHIKATA.
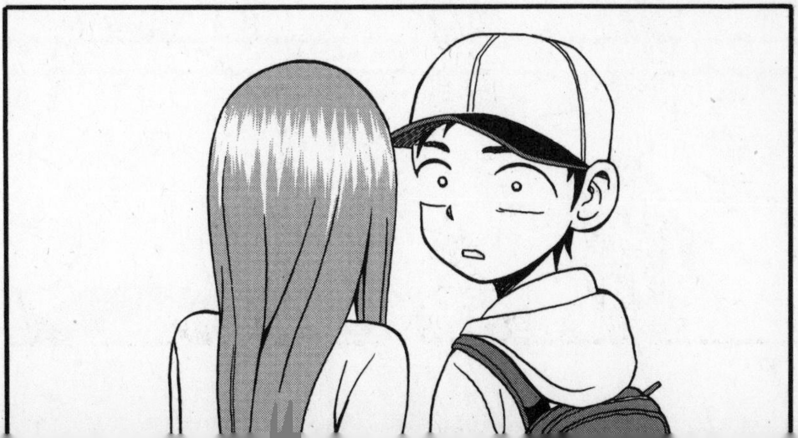

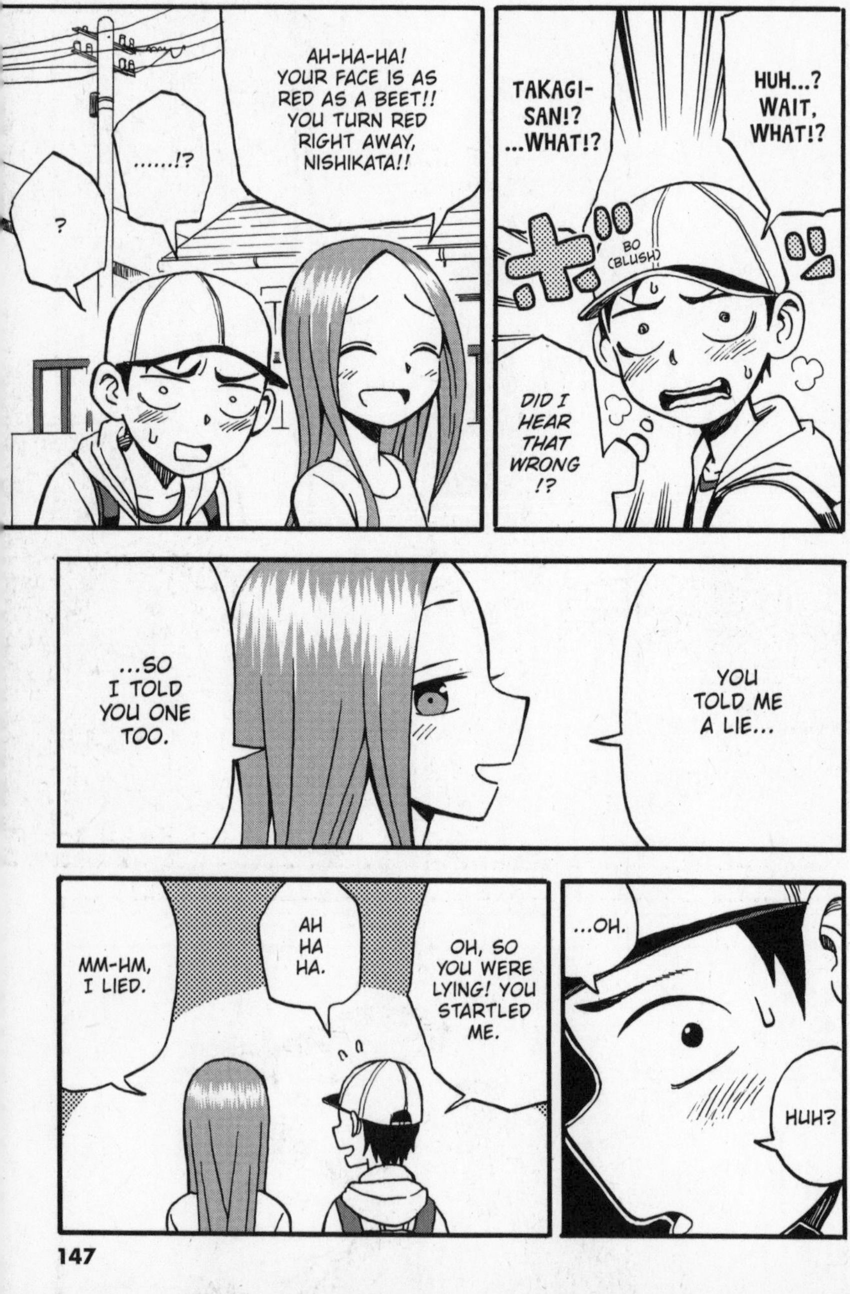
HUH...? WAIT, WHAT!?
TAKAGI-SAN!? ...WHAT!?
BO (BLUSH)
DID I HEAR THAT WRONG!?
AH-HA-HA! YOUR FACE IS AS RED AS A BEET!! YOU TURN RED RIGHT AWAY, NISHIKATA!!
.......!?
?
YOU TOLD ME A LIE...
...SO I TOLD YOU ONE TOO.
...OH.
HUH?
OH, SO YOU WERE LYING! YOU STARTLED ME.
AH HA HA.
MM-HM, I LIED.

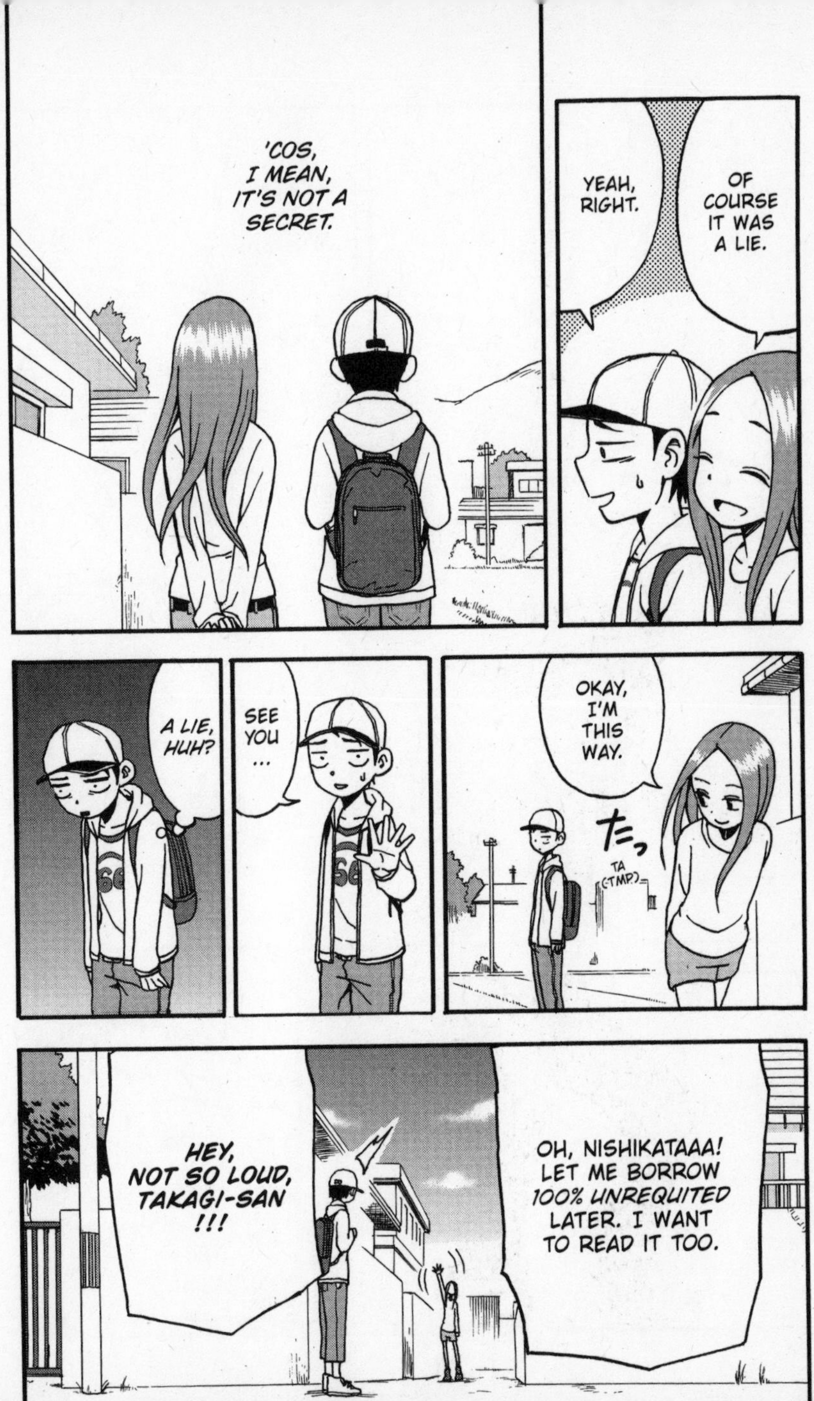
OF COURSE IT WAS A LIE.
YEAH, RIGHT.
'COS, I MEAN, IT'S NOT A SECRET.
OKAY, I'M THIS WAY.
TA (TMP)
SEE YOU ...
A LIE, HUH?
OH, NISHIKATAAA! LET ME BORROW 100% UNREQUITED LATER. I WANT TO READ IT TOO.
HEY, NOT SO LOUD, TAKAGI-SAN !!!

TEASING MASTER TAKAGI-SAN 1 / THE END

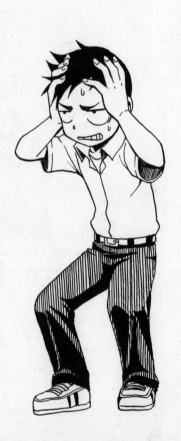

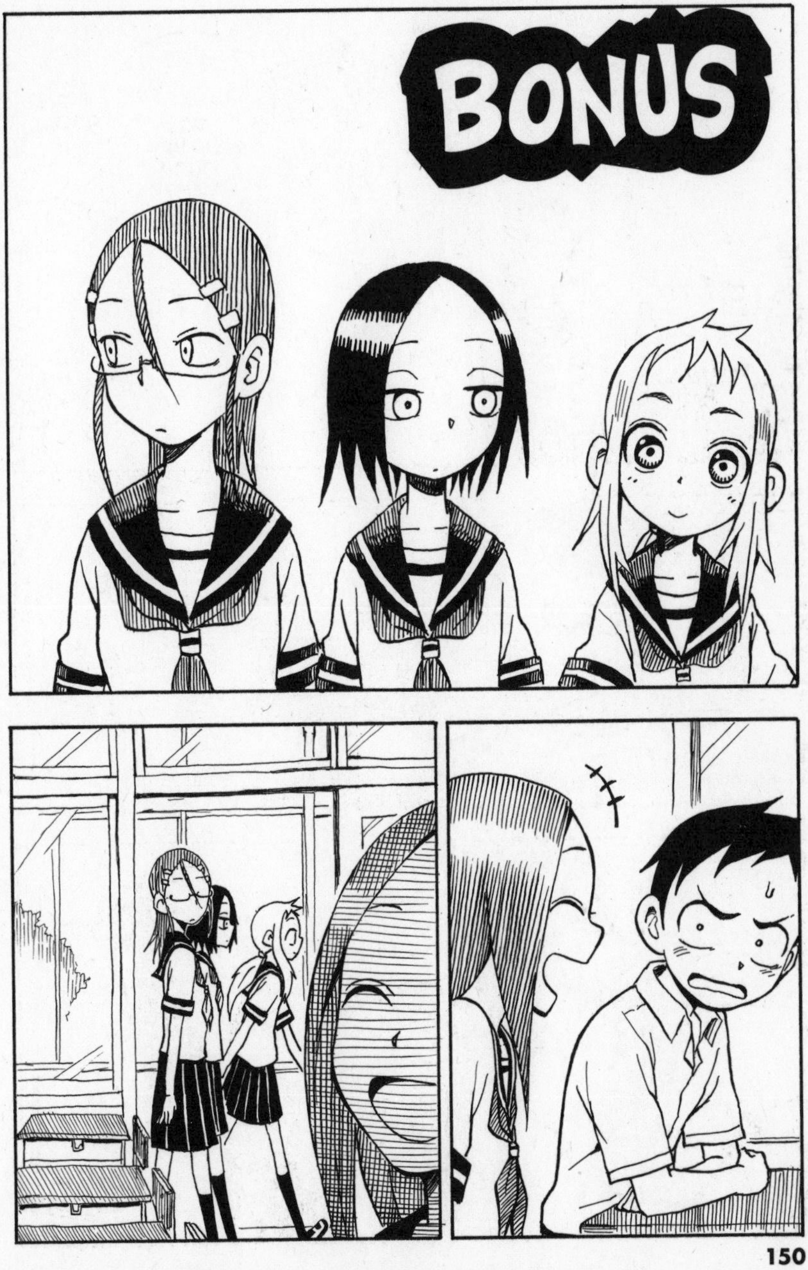
BONUS

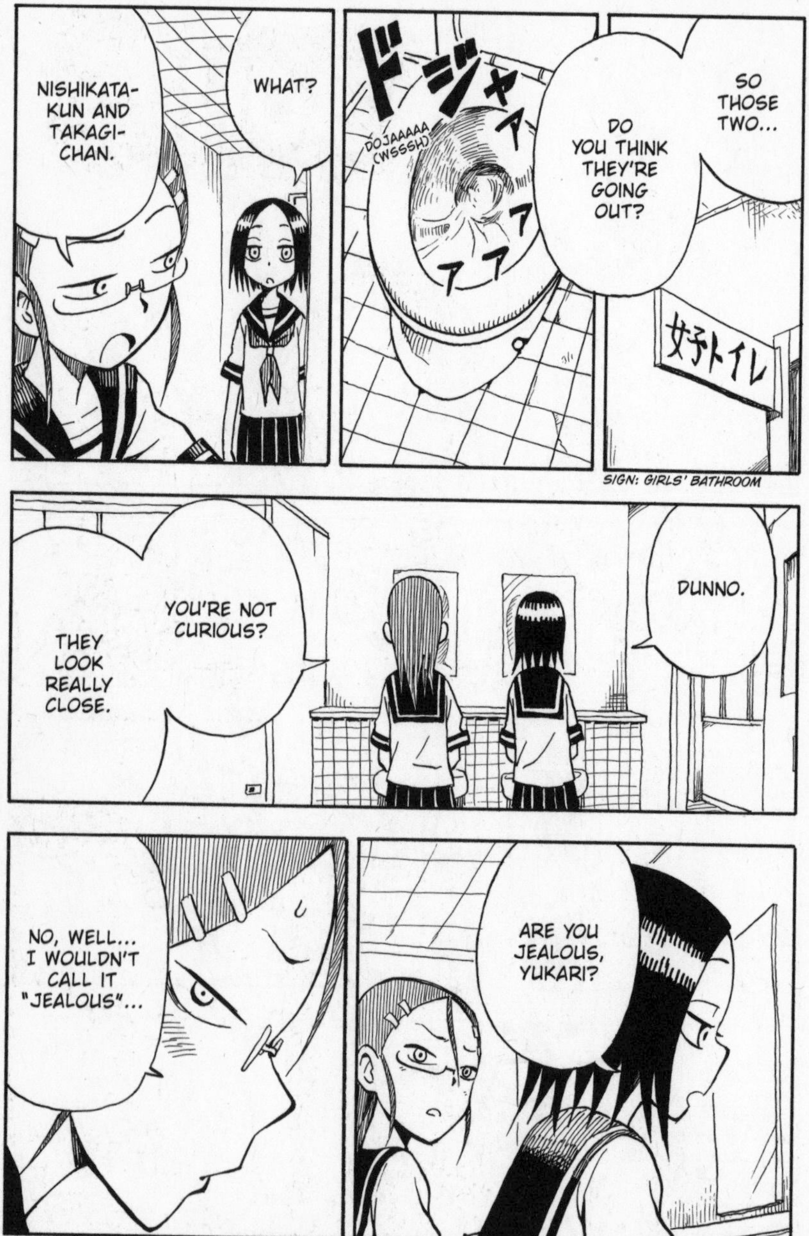
SO THOSE TWO...
DO YOU THINK THEY'RE GOING OUT?
女子トイレ
SIGN: GIRLS' BATHROOM
ドジャアアア
DOJAAAAA (WSSSH)
NISHIKATA-KUN AND TAKAGI-CHAN.
WHAT?
DUNNO.
YOU'RE NOT CURIOUS?
THEY LOOK REALLY CLOSE.
ARE YOU JEALOUS, YUKARI?
NO, WELL... I WOULDN'T CALL IT "JEALOUS"...

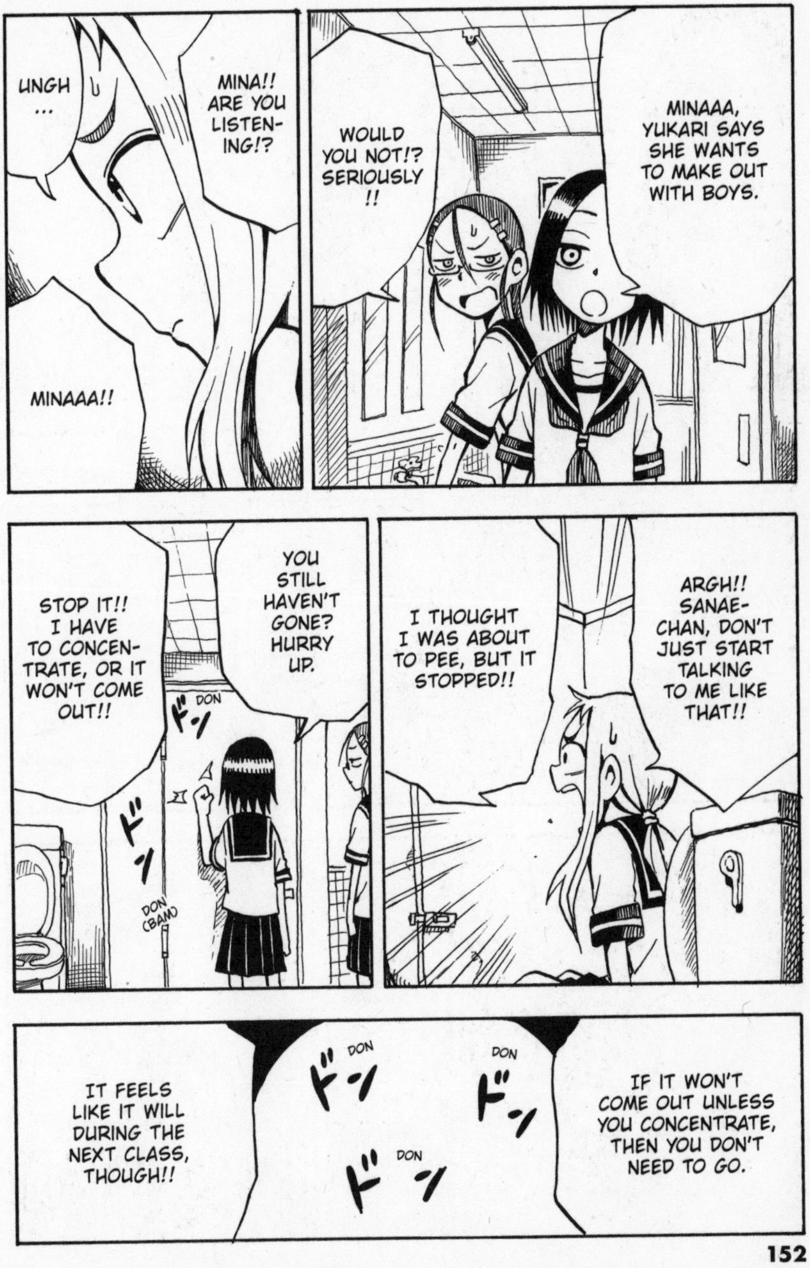
MINAAA, YUKARI SAYS SHE WANTS TO MAKE OUT WITH BOYS.
WOULD YOU NOT!? SERIOUSLY!!
MINA!! ARE YOU LISTENING!?
UNGH...
MINAAA!!
ARGH!! SANAE-CHAN, DON'T JUST START TALKING TO ME LIKE THAT!!
I THOUGHT I WAS ABOUT TO PEE, BUT IT STOPPED!!
YOU STILL HAVEN'T GONE? HURRY UP.
ドッ DON
STOP IT!! I HAVE TO CONCENTRATE, OR IT WON'T COME OUT!!
ドッ DON (BAM)
IF IT WON'T COME OUT UNLESS YOU CONCENTRATE, THEN YOU DON'T NEED TO GO.
ドッ DON
ドッ DON
ドッ DON
IT FEELS LIKE IT WILL DURING THE NEXT CLASS, THOUGH!!

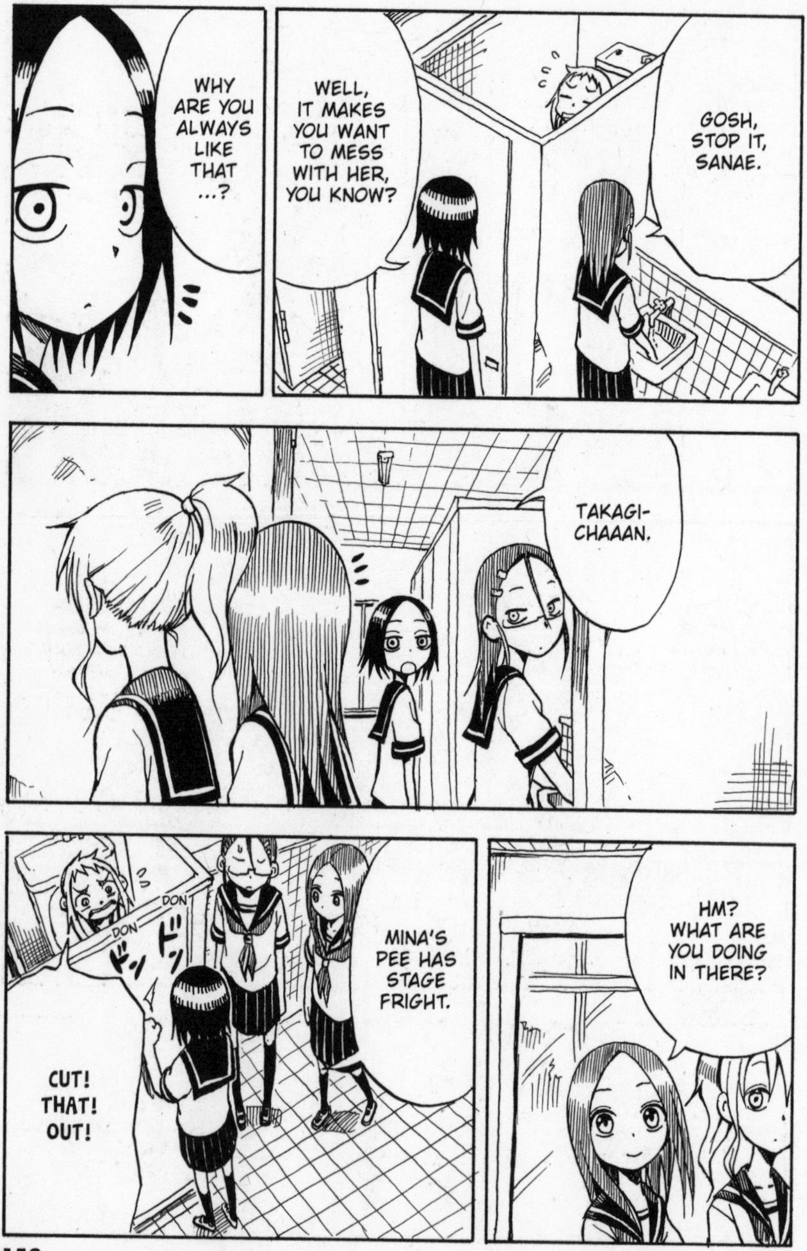
GOSH, STOP IT, SANAE.
WELL, IT MAKES YOU WANT TO MESS WITH HER, YOU KNOW?
WHY ARE YOU ALWAYS LIKE THAT ...?
TAKAGI-CHAAAN.
HM? WHAT ARE YOU DOING IN THERE?
MINA'S PEE HAS STAGE FRIGHT.
DON
ドッ
DON
ドッ
CUT! THAT! OUT!

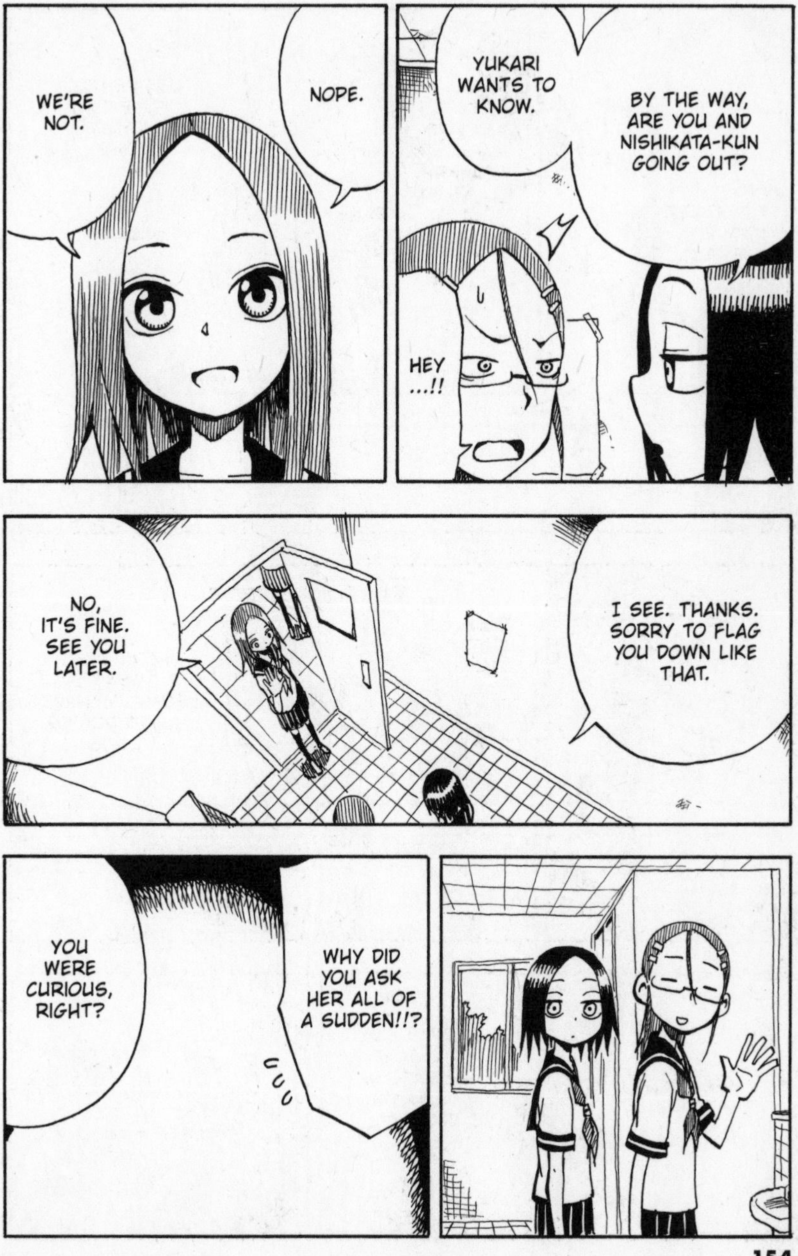
BY THE WAY, ARE YOU AND NISHIKATA-KUN GOING OUT?
YUKARI WANTS TO KNOW.
HEY ...!!
NOPE.
WE'RE NOT.
I SEE. THANKS. SORRY TO FLAG YOU DOWN LIKE THAT.
NO, IT'S FINE. SEE YOU LATER.
WHY DID YOU ASK HER ALL OF A SUDDEN!!?
YOU WERE CURIOUS, RIGHT?

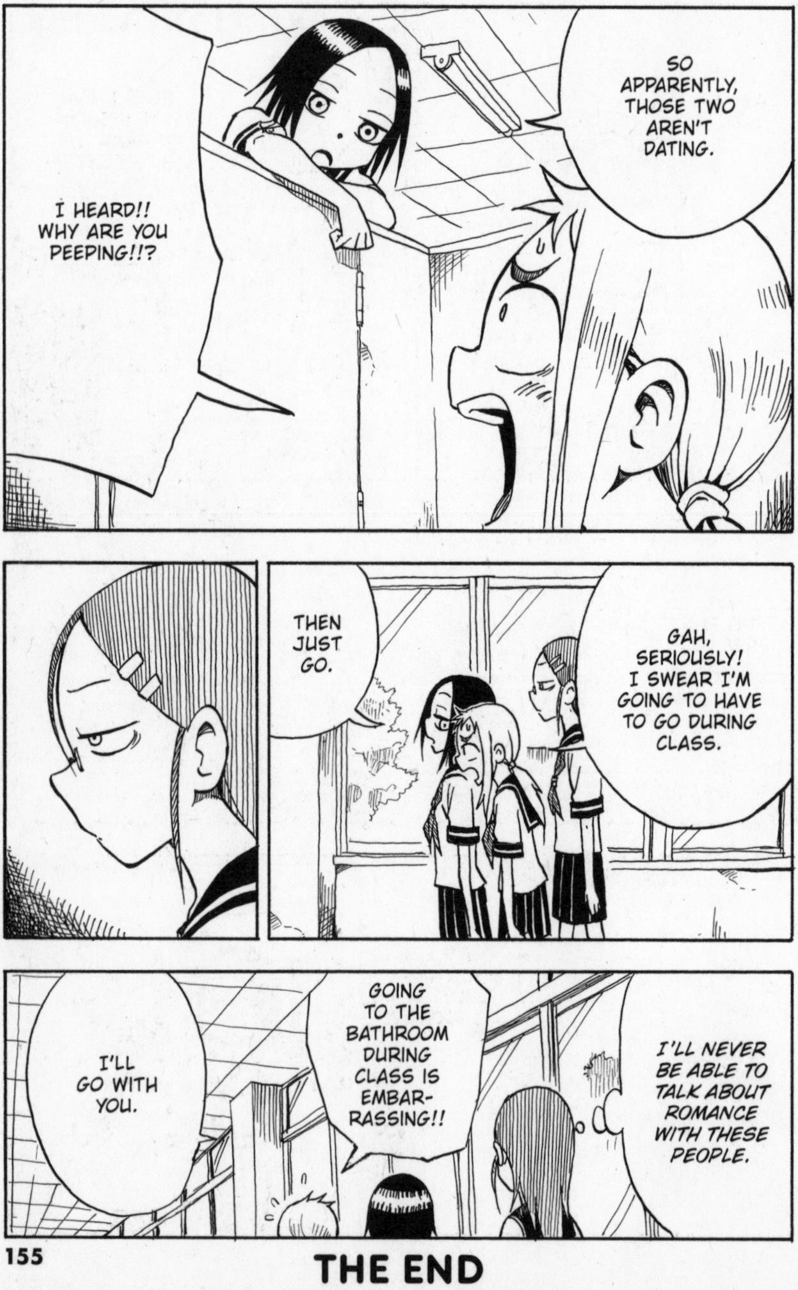
SO APPARENTLY, THOSE TWO AREN'T DATING.
I HEARD!! WHY ARE YOU PEEPING!!?
GAH, SERIOUSLY! I SWEAR I'M GOING TO HAVE TO GO DURING CLASS.
THEN JUST GO.
I'LL NEVER BE ABLE TO TALK ABOUT ROMANCE WITH THESE PEOPLE.
GOING TO THE BATHROOM DURING CLASS IS EMBAR-RASSING!!
I'LL GO WITH YOU.

THE END

Translation Notes

COMMON HONORIFICS

no honorific: Indicates familiarity or closeness; if used without permission or reason, addressing someone in this manner would constitute an insult.

-san: The Japanese equivalent of Mr./Mrs./Miss. If a situation calls for politeness, this is the fail-safe honorific.

-kun: Used most often when referring to boys, this indicates affection or familiarity. Occasionally used by older men among their peers, but it may also be used by anyone referring to a person of lower standing.

-chan: An affectionate honorific indicating familiarity used mostly in reference to girls; also used in reference to cute persons or animals of either gender.

-senpai: A suffix used to address upperclassmen or more experienced coworkers.

-sensei: A respectful term for teachers, artists, or high-level professionals.

Page 50
Takagi-san's playing an actual game. Kids sing a rhyme: "Daruma-san, Daruma-san, let's have a staring contest. If you laugh, you lose. Ah-pu-pu." (The Daruma-san bit tends to be left off.) On the second pu, players either make the weirdest face they can or try to stay perfectly expressionless. The one who laughs first loses.

Page 101
What Takagi-san is drawing is known as an ai-ai gasa, or "shared umbrella." It's a very common doodle in Japan, and it's used to show that the named couple is in a relationship (although it's usually written by someone else in order to tease said couple, and it can also be drawn as a private doodle by people who wish they were in a relationship with the other named party). The ambiguity may explain Nishikata's reaction.

Author's Note

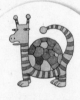

THANK YOU FOR
PICKING UP THIS BOOK.
I HOPE YOU HAVE FUN
READING IT.

Teasing Master
Takagi-san

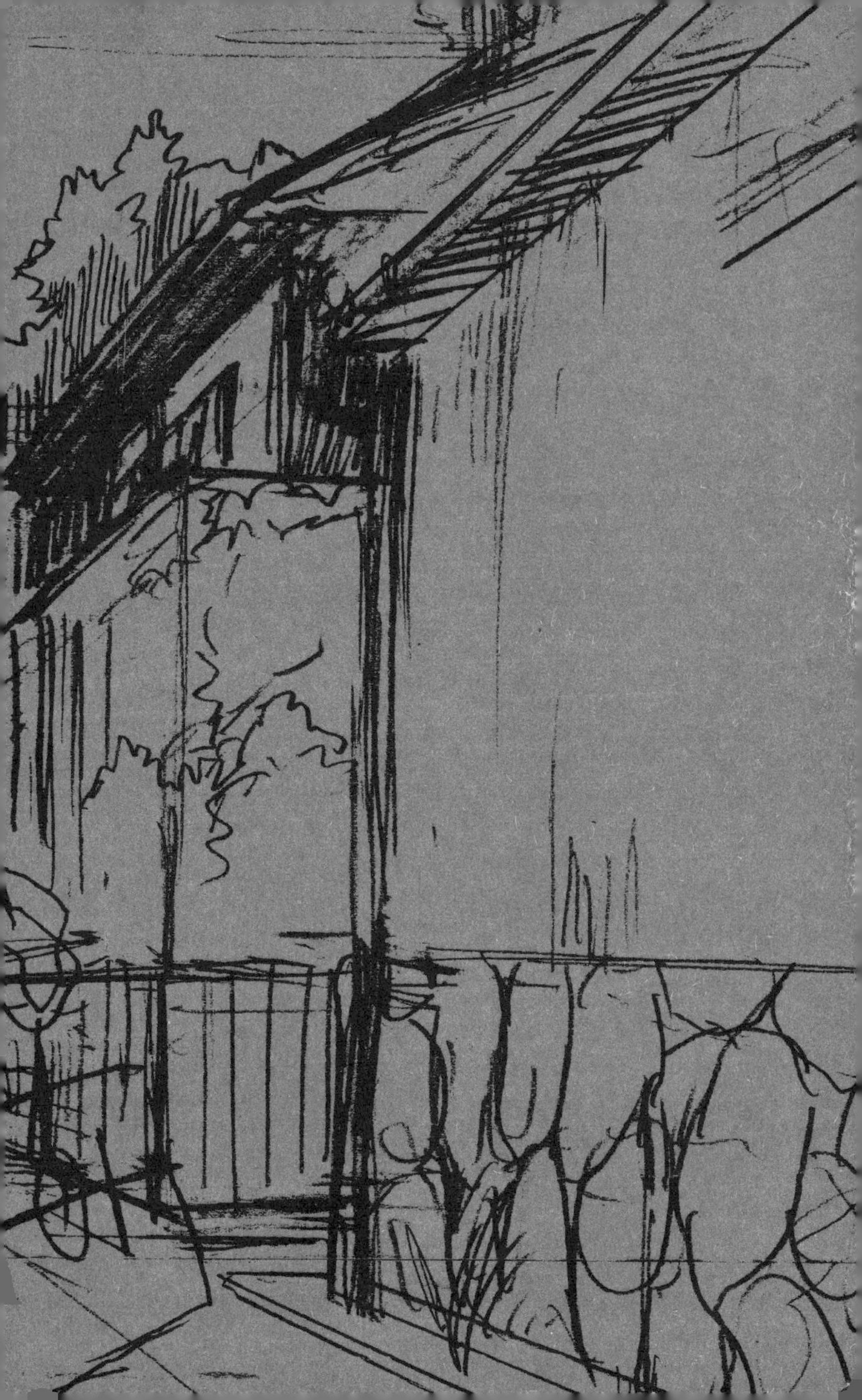

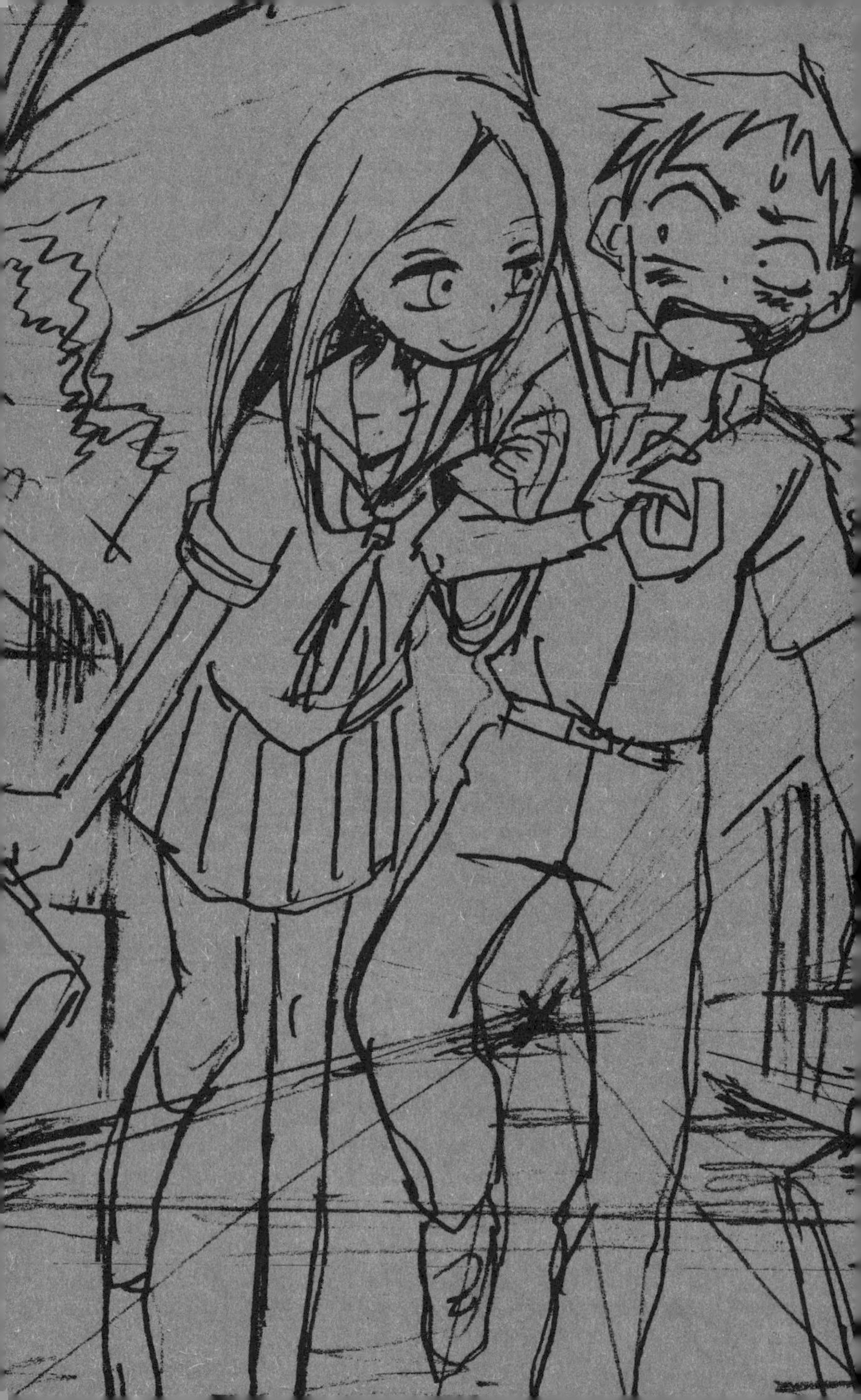

Teasing Master Takagi-san

1

Soichiro Yamamoto

TRANSLATION: Taylor Engel ♦ LETTERING: Takeshi Kamura

KARAKAI JOZU NO TAKAGI-SAN Vol. 1
by Soichiro YAMAMOTO
© 2014 Soichiro YAMAMOTO
All rights reserved.
Original Japanese edition published by SHOGAKUKAN.
English translation rights in the United States of America, Canada, the United Kingdom, Ireland, Australia and New Zealand arranged with SHOGAKUKAN
through Tuttle-Mori Agency, Inc.

English translation © 2018 by Yen Press, LLC

Yen Press
1290 Avenue of the Americas
New York, NY 10104

Visit us at yenpress.com

facebook.com/yenpress
twitter.com/yenpress

yenpress.tumblr.com
instagram.com/yenpress

First Yen Press Edition: July 2018

Yen Press is an imprint of Yen Press, LLC.
The Yen Press name and logo are trademarks of Yen Press, LLC.

The publisher is not responsible for websites (or their content) that are not owned by the publisher.

Library of Congress Control Number: 2018939489

ISBN: 978-1-9753-5330-8

10 9 8 7 6 5 4 3 2 1

WOR

Printed in the United States of America